"Hart is an expert at seamless storytelling."
Ft. Lauderdale Sun-Sentinel

"In the first eight pages, Hart introduces seven suspects, some of whom will become victims. There's no escape then; a reader is hooked. The book that follows is plotted and written just as efficiently. Hart's writing is a masterful example of the mystery writer's profession . . . We can only hope that she and Annie keep at their jobs."
Sunday Oklahoman

"With sharp and imaginative writing, plus a well-stocked cast of colorful characters, Hart spins a hard-to-put-down tale."
Orlando Sentinel

"It's always a delight to find a new book by Carolyn Hart."
Chattanooga Times

"The Darling duo is as winning as ever."
Baltimore Sun

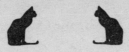

Books by Carolyn Hart

Henrie O

DEAD MAN'S ISLAND
SCANDAL IN FAIR HAVEN
DEATH IN LOVERS' LANE
DEATH IN PARADISE
DEATH ON THE RIVER WALK
RESORT TO MURDER
SET SAIL FOR MURDER

Death on Demand

DEATH ON DEMAND
DESIGN FOR MURDER
SOMETHING WICKED
HONEYMOON WITH MURDER
A LITTLE CLASS ON MURDER
DEADLY VALENTINE
THE CHRISTIE CAPER
SOUTHERN GHOST
MINT JULEP MURDER
YANKEE DOODLE DEAD
WHITE ELEPHANT DEAD
SUGARPLUM DEAD
APRIL FOOL DEAD
ENGAGED TO DIE
MURDER WALKS THE PLANK
DEATH OF THE PARTY
DEAD DAYS OF SUMMER
DEATH WALKED IN

MURDER WALKS THE PLANK

A DEATH ON DEMAND MYSTERY

CAROLYN HART

AVON BOOKS
An Imprint of HarperCollinsPublishers

This is a work of fiction. Names, characters, places, and incidents are products of the author's imagination or are used fictitiously and are not to be construed as real. Any resemblance to actual events, locales, organizations, or persons, living or dead, is entirely coincidental.

AVON BOOKS
An Imprint of HarperCollins*Publishers*
10 East 53rd Street
New York, New York 10022-5299

Copyright © 2004 by Carolyn Hart
Excerpt from *Death of the Party* copyright © 2005 by Carolyn Hart
ISBN: 0-06-000475-4
www.avonmystery.com

5550 8567 04/15

First Avon Books paperback printing: March 2005
First William Morrow hardcover printing: March 2004

Avon Trademark Reg. U.S. Pat. Off. and in Other Countries, Marca Registrada, Hecho en U.S.A.
HarperCollins ® is a trademark of HarperCollins Publishers Inc.

Printed in the U.S.A.

10 9 8 7 6 5 4 3

*To Carol Burr, with affection
and admiration*

MURDER WALKS THE PLANK

✌ *One* ✌

As THE FERRY PULLED away from the dock, a silver-haired man climbed out of his recently waxed red Mustang convertible and made his way slowly to the railing. He was natty in a blue-and-white striped silk blazer, pink linen shirt, and white sea island cotton slacks. He'd always dressed with a dramatic flair. Most men wouldn't dare. He'd always been willing to dare.

Bob Smith rested his arms on the white railing. Smiling, he looked across green water speckled with whitecaps at a dark smudge in the east, an island basking beneath the early morning sun. The warm moist air was rich with the heady scent of salt water. Gulls squalled overhead. He was aware of an eagerness that he'd not felt in years, an impatience for moments to pass so something wonderful might happen. He wanted to reach the island with an intensity and urgency that delighted him. And to think Meg had lived there for many years and he'd never known until he happened across her picture in that fancy magazine about rich folks' houses. He'd picked up the heavy slick magazine that day at the doctor's office, something to look at while he waited. Maybe he'd known even then that the news would not be good. But when

1

he walked out of the doctor's office, it seemed like an omen that he'd found out he was dying and discovered Meg's whereabouts on the same day. An omen.

The ferry rocked a little beneath his feet. He caught the railing, enjoyed the movement. He had always liked to be on the go. The minute he found out where Meg lived, he made up his mind to see her. He didn't give a damn if it was wise or foolish. Maybe he was past caring. She'd loved him once. All he wanted to do was say good-bye.

No, it was time to be honest, honest the way Meg had always been. He didn't give a damn about saying good-bye. That wasn't what he wanted. He wanted to see her, glory in her loveliness, hear her laughter. He'd never forgotten her.

Had she forgotten him?

Pamela Potts was tempted to call and say she couldn't come. It wasn't that she didn't like Mrs. Heath. Oh yes, of course, Meg. Mrs. Heath insisted that Pamela call her Meg. Pamela didn't feel comfortable using her first name. After all, Mrs. Heath—Meg—was famous. Oh well, perhaps not famous, but certainly anyone who read *People* magazine knew her name, a cover girl model who'd been linked to so many leading men, even those much younger than she. She was still a beauty though she must be near sixty, dark hair with only the faintest hint of silver, huge dark eyes, chiseled features classic as any Grecian sculpture. Even when she rested, thin and pensive, on a chaise longue, her presence dominated the room. When she laughed, well, there was something wicked about her laughter. It made Pamela think . . . Pamela felt her cheeks flame. Really, Mrs. Heath— Meg—shouldn't tell anyone about some things. And she knew she embarrassed Pamela. Last time she'd thrown back her head, her long black hair swinging, and gurgled with pleasure. Catching her breath, she'd patted Pamela's hand. "Sweetie, you are simply too good. That's why I can tell you everything. Oh, it's been a grand life, Pamela."

A grand life . . .

Pamela pushed away the quick thought that no one would ever term her own life grand. She'd stayed home with her invalid mother for many years. She hadn't finished college, so there weren't many jobs open to her. She didn't have the skills demanded in the computerized world. She'd managed to stay afloat because the house—a little two-bedroom frame—was paid for and she had inherited several CDs from her mother. She was very careful about money. She had to be because there was barely enough for food and taxes and medical expenses. It was frightening the way interest rates had dropped. There was less and less money and not a dime for extras. But that was all right. She volunteered all over the island and she was active at church, helping out when there was illness or death. She visited Mrs. Heath—Meg—on behalf of the church.

Everyone knew they could count on Pamela. So, she'd go to the Heath house this morning. Perhaps she could direct Mrs. Heath's thoughts more to the eternal.

Wayne Reed buzzed his secretary. He looked like what he was, a successful lawyer in a maroon and gray office. Despite his boyish good looks, he was turning forty this year. He was proud of his office, the heavy velvet drapes, the Persian rug, the cherry wood desk. "No calls. I'm out of the office." Nice to be protected. If only it were that easy to handle other problems. There was Stuart, who was close to being out of control. Maybe he should let him go live with Lori, but dammit, she'd walked out, left them both. Now she wanted Stuart to come and join her. Well, wanting wasn't getting. Maybe it was time she learned that. At least she wasn't asking for money. Money. He'd made a killing in that property deal. Clever, damn clever. The money he'd made had saved him from bankruptcy, built a fine house. Lori hadn't cared enough about the house—or him—to stay.

The phone rang. He glanced at the Caller ID and picked up the line despite his instructions to his secretary. He never ignored a call from Meg Heath. Too bad she was in poor health. However, she'd rallied this summer and he'd been to her house for several grand events. She loved to entertain, giving extravagant parties in her extravagant house. Even though she was now thin to the point of emaciation, her dark eyes feverish, her beauty and laughter still held men in thrall. Even he, twenty years her junior, had been swept away by her charm. She'd enjoyed him, then dropped him. But as she'd told him when she declined to meet him for a rendezvous, "You're a damn fine lawyer, Wayne. Let's leave it at that." Her charm—and the money—were such that he hadn't minded. He'd handled the settling of her husband's estate and she'd kept him as her lawyer. She was a dream client. When she died, he would handle her estate. He'd miss her.

As he answered the phone, he wondered why she'd called. Whatever it was, he would be happy to oblige.

Claudette Taylor stared at her reflection in the mirror and saw an old woman. But her blue eyes were still bright, her skin—she'd taken pride in her complexion—softly white. She smoothed back a strand of faded hair.

Once she'd had flaming curls, now they were ginger. In addition to intelligence and competence, valuable assets for an executive secretary, she'd had a quiet charm and a wholesome attractiveness when she was young. That charm and appeal hadn't been enough to compete with Meg's effervescence and beauty. Just for a while, Claudette had hoped that Duff might turn to her after June died. There had been a deepening of their relationship. He depended upon Claudette. He appreciated her. She had always been there for him. Then he met Meg, fascinating, elusive, lovely Meg. No one could compete with Meg, certainly not she.

Claudette thought of her employer with the old familiar mixture of bitterness and sorrow. She reached out, touched the shiny silver frame that contained Duff's picture, holding to the memory of his boisterous laughter, the deep resonance of his voice, the vividness of his dark brown eyes. *Oh, Duff, she never loved you the way I would have. Never, never, never.*

A bell rang softly. Meg wanted her.

Claudette walked toward the door. So odd to realize that vibrant, unquenchable Meg was nearing death. The house would be sold, of course. Neither of the children would wish to keep it. The house was too big, too dramatic, an appropriate setting only for someone like Meg. And there was no one else like Meg.

Claudette's lips twisted. Jealousy warred with admiration. She would never forgive Meg for taking Duff, but Meg was generous and fair. There wouldn't be any money worries when Meg died. Meg had told her often enough that she would be well taken care of.

Jenna Brown Carmody gave a swift appraisal to her image in the gilt-framed mirror. The summer blossoms

on her sheath—bright overblown roses against tan—
were a perfect foil for her sleek dark hair. She looked
quite perfect, as always, slender, cool, elegant. She
noted the confident swing of her arms, the slight smile
on her haughty face. She didn't see—would never
see—that her lips were too thin and her face too hard.

She stopped, looked up the metal staircase suspended in space. Her gaze was not admiring. Too
showy. And that article in the magazine was simply too
nouveau riche for words. But Meg would hoot with
laughter if she said anything to her. Meg didn't give a
damn what anyone thought about her or her life. That
had always been true. Trust her mother to have a strikingly different house, the glass-walled rooms on each
level open to view. Meg always laughed and said she
enjoyed living in a glass house and no one ever appreciated a place in the sun as much as she. Jenna didn't
smile at the memory. She should go upstairs and visit
her ailing mother. Her eyes narrowed. Sometimes she
wondered just how sick Meg was. She'd always called
her mother Meg. That's what everyone called Margaret
Crane Brown Sherman Heath. If Meg was as weak as
the doctor said, why was she insisting that they all go
on this absurd harbor cruise? Of course, Meg refused
to give in to illness, just as she'd spent her life refusing
to conform to convention.

Jenna's features sharpened. For an instant, she looked
foxlike. With an effort she loosened the tight muscles.
Marie had massaged her face at the last appointment,
murmured that tensed muscles creased her lovely skin.
Lovely skin. Yes, she'd always had lovely skin, though
men had never flocked around her as they had around
Meg.

Head high, Jenna started up the steps. It was too bad

that she had so little fondness for her mother. Meg Crane had garnered headlines for a quarter century in the tabloids that breathlessly recounted the antics of the jet set. Meg had parlayed a model's beauty and an adventuress's charm into an unending series of visits to the homes of the very wealthy. Jenna felt that she'd spent a lifetime living down her mother's notoriety. At least Meg had the good sense finally—after two marriages to impecunious fellow adventurers—to marry well. Her last husband, Duff Heath, was fabulously wealthy, a coal, zinc, and copper titan when those minerals mattered.

A genuine smile touched Jenna's thin lips. Dear Duff. So kind and generous. Jenna had only a hazy memory of Arthur Brown, her father. Her affection was centered on her late stepfather, who had shared her enthusiasms for art museums and charity balls. She owed everything to Duff.

Jason Brown ignored the blink of the answering machine. It would be a woman. One of them. His grin was as insouciant as the flick of a croupier's wrist. He paused. It might be news about that polo pony. But the message could wait until tomorrow. Most things could wait.

He crossed to the wet bar, opened the small fridge, pulled out a bottle of Bass. He flicked off the cap, drank down cold ale. He strolled to the couch, dropped onto the soft, comfortable cushions. He picked up the television remote, punched the channels looking for a soccer game. All was right with his world, a world of comfort, indulgence, and ease. He leaned back, content as a cosseted show cat.

Maybe he should listen to the messages. There were

several. He reached out a long arm, pushed the button. At the third message, Jason frowned, sat up straight, the beer forgotten, his smile gone.

Rachel Van Meer rode past Painted Lady Lane. She stayed on the bike path, pedaled furiously, her curly dark hair flying. She curved around a huge, sweet-smelling—just like bananas—pittosporum bush, then braked so quickly her back wheel slewed. She straddled the bike, hands tight on the grips. This was dumb. She should never have come here, miles from where she lived. What if Cole saw her? That would be sooo awful. But she had to see the house, the house where Pudge was spending so much time. She'd found out the address, searched it out on the island map.

She turned the bike around, hesitated when she reached the street, then swung into Painted Lady Lane. She kept to the far side of the dusty dirt road, ready to plunge into the woods if anyone—like Cole—came into view. Her face settled into a sneer. What would Pudge think if he knew that skinny Cole Crandall was one of the gang of nobodies who hung around Stuart Reed? Pudge wouldn't think much of Stuart.

The curving road was empty of traffic. There were only occasional houses. A few were well kept with freshly painted wood. Most were shabby, and there was an abandoned farmhouse that looked spooky even in the middle of a hot August day. The Crandall house sat by itself at the end of the road. Once it had been a bright blue. Now paint hung in peels. Some balusters were missing from the front porch. How tacky.

Surely Pudge would come to his senses, stop chasing after Cole's mother. He couldn't possibly enjoy coming to this ratty old place. She turned her bike, rode away, glad she didn't have to live there.

Annie Darling beamed at the poster prominently displayed in the front window of Death on Demand. "Max, isn't it terrific?"

His blue eyes amused, her tall blond husband studied the bright colors. Murder Ahoy! was splashed in crimson letters across the towering prow of a ship that resembled the *QEII*. A series of glistening silver daggers bulleted the announcements:

JOIN MYSTERY LOVERS ABOARD
THE ISLAND PACKET
Sunday, August 25, 7 p.m. to Midnight
Mystery Cruise with Food, Fun, and Prizes

Mystery Play • *Come-as-Your-Favorite-Sleuth*
Costume Contest • *Treasure Hunt*

Main Harbor
Hosted by Death on Demand Mystery Bookstore
New Books Available
Benefit for the Island Literacy Council
Tickets: Adults $75, Seniors $50, 12 and under $15

Annie folded her arms, awaiting praise. That stair-step effect—was she an artiste or not? She noted the tiny wiggle at the edges of Max's lips. So okay, to-night's cruise would be on an island excursion boat that bore not the faintest resemblance to the sleek black hull on the poster. "Creative license," she said firmly. "But hey, it will be cooler on the water"—she pushed back a tendril of damp hair; the afternoon high was in the midnineties and the humidity level made her favorite sea island of Broward's Rock, South Carolina, competitive with Calcutta on the discomfort index— "than on land."

"Creative license," he murmured.

She grinned. "Anyway, we're going to have a blast. We'll make a bundle for the literacy council and sell a lot of books to boot. Now"—she was suddenly intent— "have you checked with Ben to make sure he's got enough food for fifty?" She tried to do the math in her head: fifty-four tickets sold, twenty-five adult, nineteen seniors, ten children's. Okay, twenty-five at seventy-five, five times five, carry the two, five times two . . . Maybe she should get her calculator.

Max nodded. "Everything's set." Ben Parotti, owner of Parotti's Bar & Grill as well as the ferry, assorted island real estate, and the double-deck excursion boat, was an accomplished caterer. Annie had shaved five bucks off Ben's price per person by insisting firmly that the outing was as much an advertisement for the bar and grill as for her bookstore. Ben had, however, insisted on fish and chips, coleslaw, and beans for the menu, and Max estimated that Ben would still make a sizable profit. "In keeping with the family motif, sodas and iced tea are the drinks of choice."

Annie clapped her hands together. "Spiffing." She'd been reading Carola Dunn's delightful Daisy Dalrymple series and the slang of the twenties delighted her. She'd bet Daisy would love an orange crush. "Okay, Max, I still need to talk to Henny"—Henny Brawley was Annie's best customer, an island bon vivant, and an accomplished amateur actress—"about the mystery play." She clapped a hand to her head. "Did you pick up the copies of the Treasure Map?" Max had run a dozen errands for her yesterday. His business never opened on Saturday. Annie had the vagrant thought that Max's business—Confidential Commissions— might be open on weekdays but he spent more time reading about golf and tennis and practicing his putting on the indoor green she'd given him than solving problems for people, despite the fetching ad that appeared daily in the *Gazette* Personals column:

Troubled, Puzzled, Curious
Contact Confidential Commissions
321-HELP

Right this minute she was grateful for his laid-back and always cheerful approach to life. She needed all the help she could get.

"They're in the trunk of my car." His tone was relaxed.

"Why don't you bring them in? We'll add them to the boxes of books. And I'll check to see if the new Faye Kellerman title has arrived." She tried to keep her voice relaxed, but she was beginning to feel stressed. So much to do, so little time . . .

"Will do." He gave her a reassuring pat. Reassuring and lingering.

Annie's smile was agreeable, but absentminded. She reached for the doorknob, still talking at top speed, and scarcely heard Max's good-humored assent. She looked past the poster at the window display, paused just long enough to consider whether it should be changed.

Instead of new releases, the window held collectibles that caught at the essence of past days as memorably as long-ago photographs by Arthur Telfer, Charles J. Belden, or Chansonetta Emmons. The scuffed and faded books lay faceup, mystery treasures all: *The Scarlet Pimpernel* by Baroness Emma Orczy, *The Mystery of Dr. Fu-Manchu* by Sax Rohmer, *The Thirty-Nine Steps* by John Buchan, *Suicide Excepted* by Cyril Hare, and *Ming Yellow* by John P. Marquand. Oh hey, she loved all of these books. Let them enjoy another moment in the sun. The baroness's famous book had been published in 1905. Would a book published in 2005, say by Janet Evanovich or Elizabeth George, grace a bookstore window in 2105? She didn't give a thought to doomsayers who insisted that readers in the twenty-second century would use electronic gadgets that placed the books of the world a finger-punch away.

She rushed inside, flung a hurried hello to her clerk, Ingrid Webb, at the cash desk. Ingrid gave a distracted smile as she cradled the phone on her shoulder and peered at the computer screen. Death on Demand opened at one on Sundays during the summer. After Labor Day, Annie cut back to Tuesdays through Saturdays.

As she moved swiftly to the central corridor, Annie was filled with pride at the wonderful amenities of her bookstore: Edgar, the stuffed raven, peered down from a pedestal; the children's enclave featured all the Boxcar books and, of course, had a special section for Harry Potter; hundreds of brightly jacketed titles filled the bookshelves, everything from *Above Suspicion* by Helen MacInnes to *Zero at the Bone* by Mary Willis Walker; ferns and coffee tables flanked sofas and easy chairs. Bookmarks were stacked all around the store to discourage readers from bending pages to mark a place.

Annie skidded to a stop near the coffee bar at the back of the store. A sleek black cat lifted her head, regarding Annie with cool detachment.

Annie bent, kissed the top of her head. "Yes, Agatha. It's me. Your beloved owner."

Agatha yawned daintily.

Annie cautiously curved a hand under Agatha's midriff. "You are supposed to take your leisure, my queen, on your throne." Annie transported Agatha to an emerald silk cushion tucked next to the fireplace. "The Health Department frowns on cat encampment atop the coffee bar."

Agatha rose, padded four feet, and flowed through the air. She resettled herself on the wooden counter. Her green eyes slitted.

"*Okay*." Annie had no illusions about who was in charge. What a cat wanted, a cat got. Particularly this cat. Annie snaked a hand behind Agatha to give her a quick pat. She wasn't surprised when Agatha's head twisted faster than a speeding bullet and sharp fangs missed Annie's wrist by a millimeter. Annie eased behind the counter, tucked her purse on a lower shelf, all the while keeping a wary eye on her adored feline. She automatically reached beneath the counter for dry cat food and shook a mound in a clean plastic bowl. She hesitated, then placed it next to Agatha on the coffee bar. Surely there were no health inspectors skulking nearby.

She replaced the cat food and stood undecided. Should she see about the boxes of books yet to be delivered to the excursion boat or call Henny—Annie craned her head, Ingrid was still on the phone—to see if everything was in readiness for the mystery play or check her list? Where was her list? She bent, rustled through her purse. Oh, of course, she'd left the list in the storeroom.

In a moment, she was back at the coffee bar, list in hand. She scanned the sheet. Almost everything was done. Now she must relax and hope everything turned out for the best. The vague thought was as near as she wanted to come to acknowledging the elephant presently inhabiting her emotional landscape. Would Pudge . . .

No. She wasn't going to go there. If her father brought his new lady friend on the cruise tonight, that would be time enough to worry about his intentions. As for Rachel, her teenage stepsister had promised good behavior. Oh dear. Love and marriage might go together like a horse and carriage, but what havoc a late union could wreak on a family, especially a modern-day, complicated family such as Annie's.

At least she and Max had only been married to each other. She frowned. That sounded funny. Actually, she and Max had only been married once. She shook her head. To each other. Surely that covered it. Anyway, they weren't the norm. Not in their family. Laurel, Max's mother, had been married five times. As for relationships . . . Annie firmly redirected her thoughts. Just because Laurel attracted males from eight to eighty was no reason for her daughter-in-law to make assumptions. As for Pudge, he and Annie's mom had divorced when she was a little girl, and Pudge had at one time been married to Rachel's mother. And that's how Annie and Rachel were connected, but since Rachel's mom had been killed, the only family Rachel had was her stepfather, Pudge, and her new stepsister, Annie, and a faraway aunt in Hawaii. Now Rachel, with all the turbulent passion of a teenager, was ab-

solutely frothing about Pudge and Sylvia. Annie
clenched her fists, admonished herself emphatically,
"Stop it."

Ingrid peered down the central aisle. She covered
the receiver of the phone. "I would if I could."

Annie was shocked to realize she'd spoken aloud.
She lifted her hands, waggled them at Ingrid to indicate a misunderstanding. Annie knew she needed to get
a grip. Once past the cruise, she could deal with the
family vortex. Maybe. But her immediate responsibility was tonight's cruise. Okay, Max had the Treasure
Maps, and he'd help her move the boxes of books into
the panel truck she'd borrowed from Ben. Oh yeah,
how about card tables and folding chairs? They'd set
up sales booths on both decks. Had Ingrid been to the
bank yesterday, gotten enough cash for change?

She glanced again toward the front of the store. Ingrid was still on the phone. Looking on the bright side,
Annie imagined that a mystery-starved customer was
ordering at least ten books.

Ingrid leaned on her elbow on the counter, tapped a
pencil impatiently.

So, not a big order. Annie reached into her purse,
fished out her cell phone, punched a familiar number.
She got Henny's answering machine. "Henny, Annie.
Will you check with your cast and ask everyone to be
on board in their costumes by six-thirty?" Annie
frowned. "Golly, do you think it's a fair mystery?
Maybe we should make a change? It's not too late. We
could make Periwinkle the thief." As a special entertainment for the cruise, Annie had created the playlet
Heist about the theft of a necklace of matched emeralds from a Lowcountry plantation. Henny served as
the narrator, relating the circumstances and outlining

the motives. Each character made a short speech de-
scribing his or her presumed location at the time of the
theft. Cruise attendees were invited to drop a ballot
with their choice of the thief into a fishbowl. They
were, of course, asked to sign the ballot and give an
address and telephone number so the winner might be
notified. (And Death on Demand's mailing list
plumped up fatter than a Christmas goose in an Agatha
Christie short story.) "Let me know what you think."
She was ready to click off, then, flooded with magna-
nimity, she added, "Henny, what can I do to thank
you?" Even as the words were out, Annie realized what
she'd done. Henny loved mysteries. Henny collected
mysteries. She had her heart set on the signed VF first
edition copy of Sue Grafton's *A Is for Alibi*. No, she
couldn't give Henny carte blanche in the store. "I
know. Pick out five new mysteries"—the modifier was
ever so slightly emphasized—"on the house. Be my
guest." She clicked off the cell phone and gave a
whoosh of relief. Saved by quick thinking. And five
was a generous number. After all, Henny was no
stranger to free mysteries. She held the all-time record
for solving the mystery painting contest. Every month
Annie hung five watercolors. Each represented a mystery. The first person to identify the paintings by author
and title received a new book and free coffee for a
month. Annie glanced at the watercolors.

In the first painting, an attractive young woman
with a rounded face, honey brown hair, and blue eyes
was alone in a narrow, windowless room. A single
bulb dangled from the high ceiling, illuminating
whitewashed walls and a stone flagged floor. She
stood near photographic equipment ranged on a long
counter. She held up a newly developed photograph

and stared at it with puzzled eyes. It showed a bleak winter scene, a hole broken in a frozen pond, water dark against the ice. A series of irregular gashes surrounded the hole.

In the second painting, a dark-haired, broad-shouldered man was dressed as a pirate in a big floppy silk shirt and blue pantaloons. A red velvet sash served as a belt. An odd note was black Wellingtons in lieu of leather boots. He stood in a dark crypt, wet from rainwater, a Colt in his right hand. Far ahead in the darkness, a candle glimmered.

In the third painting, a disheveled woman in an opulent hotel room wore a crumpled, spotted, mended, blindingly pink fringed dress, kid boots with two-inch heels, peach stockings, and an electric blue plush cloche with an uneven brim. Three broken feathers on the hat dangled near her shoulder. Two strands of glass beads drooped down to her garters. Shoe polish added a grayish cast to her neck. Powder destroyed the sleekness of her cap of black hair. Thick rouge blared from her cheeks. She held a thick black cloak, a gun, cigarettes, and lighter. Her gray-green eyes glowed with excitement.

In the fourth painting, an athletic-looking man in a Palm Beach suit sat behind a white rolltop desk in a long room that served as a parlor and dining room. A bookcase held baseball guides and a collection of works by Mark Twain. He held a horsehide baseball the color of dark amber, rubbing with his thumb the red stitches on the covering. Painted red letters informed: Cin'ti BB Club July 2, '69.

In the fifth painting, a robed woman with long hair loose on her shoulders sat propped against two pillows on the rumpled sheets of a hotel room bed. A barefoot young man in shirt and pants, his hair mussed, leaned forward from the chair next to the bed and watched intently. She had just unwrapped a hand towel to reveal a vivid blue jewel about the size of four or five 50-cent pieces glued together.

Annie was pleased with the selections. Not only did she enjoy books set in this period, Henny hadn't figured them out yet and the month was almost over!

Coffee and books. There was no better combination. She stepped behind the coffee bar and reached for a mug. Each mug was decorated in red script with the name of a famous mystery. She chose *Mystery on the Queen Mary* by Bruce Graeme. She poured the steaming coffee, raised it in a salute. Graeme's book was one of the finest shipboard mysteries ever written and was inspired by his passage on the first sailing of the *Queen Mary*. Not, of course, that she was equating tonight's outing on the *Island Packet* excursion boat with Graeme's novel. The only mystery would be her entertainment about stolen jewels. But a good time would be had by—

"I swear." Ingrid stalked down the central aisle. "Annie, you owe me big time."

Annie reached for another mug, held out *Why Me?* by Donald Westlake. "A voice mail system from hell? Punch one for Perdition, two for Outer Hades, three for Beelzebub, four for Charon, five for the River Styx—"

"Okay, it wasn't that bad." Ingrid managed a small smile. "But for all three of them to call in a row." She flipped up her fingers one by one, "Henny, Laurel, Pamela. I wrote down Henny's message." She delved into a pocket of her peasant skirt, pulled out a white pad, read without expression, "She met him on a street called straight." Ingrid turned up her hands. "That's all.

Not another word. Hung up." Ingrid smoothed back a frizzled curl. "Do you know that one?" Her glance at Annie was anxious.

Annie was glad she wouldn't be letting down the side. Ingrid resented Henny's efforts to confront Annie with a mystery reference she couldn't identify. Occasionally Henny triumphed (another source of free books), but usually Annie was up to the task.

"She's supposed to be concentrating on tonight." Annie's tone was stern. She retrieved her cell phone, called Henny. Once again she spoke to the answering machine. "She met him on a street called Straight." Annie automatically supplied the capitalization. "That's the opening line in Mary Stewart's *The Gabriel Hounds*." A pause. "Okay, Henny, here's one for you. Thirty-one novels with Inspector McKee. But what is this author's other claim to mystery fame?" Annie added cheerily, "I'm sure you will tell me tonight." She clicked off the cell phone, glanced at Ingrid. "Helen Reilly, who was also the mother of Ursula Curtiss and Mary McMullen." Not until the present-day successes of Mary Higgins Clark's daughter, Carol Higgins Clark, and former daughter-in-law Mary Jane Clark, had there been such a successful family mystery triumvirate.

"And Laurel called?" Annie made a distinct effort to remove any trace of concern from her voice, although her mother-in-law's proclivity for the unexpected—in fact, the outrageous—kept Annie and Max always on the alert. Laurel, of course, would be on the cruise tonight. But surely . . . Unease quivered within.

Ingrid added two heaping teaspoons of brown sugar to her coffee, stirred vigorously. "I suppose she's all right." Her voice was conversational.

"I suppose," Annie agreed, waiting.

"She gave that whoop of laughter, you know, the one that sounds like Hepburn besting Tracy, and told me to tell you she was quite relieved there would be no alcohol served on the mystery cruise." Ingrid gulped the coffee. "She pointed out that tigers so loathe the odor of alcohol they are quite likely to make mincemeat out of anyone with whisky on their breath."

If there was an appropriate response, it escaped Annie. She stared at Ingrid.

Ingrid stared back. "You don't suppose . . ."

Annie's eyes widened. "No." Not even Laurel would bring a tiger on a mystery cruise. "Of course not. I'm sure she had a reason." Reason . . . Oh, of course. Annie felt the tight muscles of her throat ease. It's not that she really thought Laurel might show up with a tiger. Still, relief buoyed her voice. "It's her creativity thing."

Ingrid waited.

"You know, she's encouraging all of us to"—Annie concentrated, tried to recall Laurel's precise words— " 'unleash the child within, break the shackles that bind our minds, burst forth like a Yellowstone geyser, astonishing, unforgettable, magnificent.' "

"So what's a tiger's antipathy to whisky got to do with . . ." Ingrid frowned. "Oh. She murmured something about the understanding required to deal with the young, and violent aversions—"

Annie nodded. Laurel was using creativity to equate Rachel's hostility to Sylvia Crandall with a tiger's revulsion at the scent of whisky. But all the creativity in the world wouldn't enable Annie to banish Sylvia Crandall from Pudge's life as easily as she'd decreed no booze on the boat.

"—and the patience to be forbearing. Anyway, she said to tell you she'd be there with bells on." Ingrid's eyes were puzzled. "Then she exclaimed—and it definitely was an exclamation—that bells, even as a figure of speech, lacked flair. That we should think ribbons."

Annie thought ribbons. The picture it evoked of her elegant, soignée mother-in-law in swirling silk trailing a rainbow hue of ribbons made her smile. And maybe, give Laurel her due, that was the point.

"Anyway"—Ingrid was dismissive—"I'd just got rid of Laurel when Pamela called."

Annie always reminded herself firmly that Pamela Potts meant well. Pamela could be counted on. Pamela was serious, literal, and a fount of good works. Annie sighed. "What did Pamela want?"

"Pamela wanted to talk to you." Ingrid was long-suffering. "I told her you were up to here"—she lifted her hands to her throat—"with last-minute stuff for the cruise tonight. Pamela bleated that she would certainly be glad to do everything she could to help and she was sorry she hadn't been able to take part in any of the planning sessions but she'd been very involved—and she told me in excruciating detail just who she'd seen and what she'd done this week beginning with Altar Guild last Sunday and bringing me up to a few minutes ago when she'd delivered a casserole out to the Haney place for—"

Annie flung up her hands, palms forward. "Cease. Desist."

Ingrid gulped the coffee. "Okay, but you realize I listened to the bitter end. I can tell you about the midwife who delivered the Haney twins and what Mr. Haney said—before he fainted—and what Mrs. Haney said. And the utter amazement Pamela felt

upon the warmth with which Meg Heath always welcomed her. Anyway, the upshot is that Pamela is
deliriously grateful for your thoughtfulness in providing her with a free ticket for the cruise. She said she
could not express her excitement when she found the
envelope you'd left in the mailbox. Of course, since it
was Sunday she would not have thought to check the
mailbox, since mail—"

Annie snapped, "Ingrid, I know mail isn't delivered
on Sundays."

Ingrid's tone was obdurate. "What Pamela told me,
I am telling you. Anyway, she would not have had the
forethought to check her mail box, since—"

Annie joined in the chorus. "—there are no mail de-
liveries on Sundays, but—"

Ingrid nodded approvingly. "—you—meaning you,
Annie—were so clever to poke the envelope out of the
mailbox and so she found it. However, she understood
it was a federal offense for anyone other than a post-
person to place material in a designated mail recepta-
cle. However, she knew you were most likely in a rush,
and after all it was Sunday, and mail—"

In unison. "—is not delivered on Sundays—"

"—so it was probably not a serious offense. And
though she felt that she was totally undeserving as her
many duties had prevented her from being of any assistance to you in preparing for this grand fund-raising
event for the literacy council"—Ingrid stopped for
breath—"she accepted thankfully as she'd wanted to
go so badly but she couldn't afford a ticket though she
understood why the prices were so high, after all a benefit couldn't raise money any other way, but this was
one of her favorite organizations and if there was any
way she could repay you, she would certainly do so."

"Free ticket?" Annie's tone was blank. "But, Ingrid, I didn't."

"Didn't what?" Ingrid finished her coffee, leaned over the counter to rinse out the mug.

"I didn't send her a free ticket. That's so odd." Annie shook her head. "Oh well"—she made a mental note to be sure and tell Pamela to look elsewhere for her bene-factor—"it doesn't really matter."

The front door opened. Max called out, "Yo ho ho and a bottle of rum. Excuse me, Pepsi." He held up a brownish sheet of paper, styled to look like old parchment. "Treasure Maps at the ready."

Annie swung up the central aisle, hand outstretched, the puzzle of Pamela's free ticket receding in her mind. Probably on one of Pamela's many rounds of good works, she'd mentioned the cruise—which was admit-tedly expensive—and revealed her yearning to go. Somebody had done a nice thing, sending Pamela a free ticket.

Water slapped against pilings, the cheerful cadence punctuated by dull thumps as the *Island Packet* bumped against the tires that buffered the pier. The evening sun streaked the darkening water with bronze. Laughing gulls swooped near, their distinctive cackle almost a match for the frenzied blare of conversation aboard the boat. Passengers crowded the rails, many in costume.

Annie cradled a heavy megaphone. From her van-tage point behind the pilothouse, she looked down at the lower deck. Big bunches of helium balloons, red and gold and orange, bobbed from their tethers at the aft railing. She breathed in the scent of seawater and diesel fumes and gloried in the carnival atmosphere.

She spotted two Hercule Poirots (precise mustaches with carefully waxed points and shiny patent leather shoes were a dead giveaway), one Father Brown with the distinctive round black hat, several white-haired Miss Marples clutching knitting reticules, and—Annie was amazed—a bewigged and begowned barrister with an uncanny resemblance to portly Charles Laughton, who played Sir Wilfred Robarts, K.C., in the film version of Agatha Christie's immortal *Witness for the Prosecution.*

Pamela Potts was outfitted in a prim nurse's uniform and carrying a small black bag. Perched on one shoulder was a figurine of a small yellow canary. Annie nodded approval. Mary Roberts Rinehart's nurse sleuth, Hilda Adams, of course. Annie was impressed. Pamela must have visited with Laurel about creativity. The canary bobbing on her shoulder—sewn there? taped?— was certainly an imaginative stretch for Pamela. Her cheeks pink with excitement, Pamela waved.

Annie waved in return.

Pamela shouted, "Thank you so much, Annie. I'm having a wonderful time."

Annie's mouth opened and closed. This was not the moment to get into a discussion about Pamela's free ticket. As soon as the boat got under way, Annie would find Pamela and explain.

Annie lifted the megaphone, then lowered it. More than a dozen people were still on the dock, waiting to board. She leaned over the rail for a better look and her eyes widened in surprise. Meg Heath, of all people. She was in a wheelchair and thin as a stick figure but waving and smiling. Her son pushed the wheelchair up the slope of the gangway. A sullen frown marred his good looks. His glum expression was mirrored on his sister's discontented face. Claudette Taylor, Meg's secretary, carried Meg's purse. Claudette, too, looked grumpy. Annie felt like shouting down a reminder that this was a party, but that would sound surly and she was too excited and happy to waste even a minute worrying about ill-tempered voyagers. They'd bought tickets, all to the benefit of the literacy council, and if they didn't want to have fun, that was their problem. In any event, Annie would make a special point of finding Meg and saying hello. Meg knew how to have a good time. Right this minute she was calling out an animated hello to Henny. Meg hadn't been to the store for a long time, but her secretary often dropped in to pick up the latest Books on Tape. Meg liked her mysteries sassy and bold: Hiaasen, Evanovich, Friedman, and Strohmeyer.

Annie lost sight of Meg and her group. Everyone else she saw looked happy. She permitted herself to relax and enjoy the festive scene. Standing near the stern, the center of an admiring crowd of men (so what else was new), was her oh-so-creative mother-in-law. Only Laurel could look fetching in a long steel-gray gown. She carried a Ouija board and a flatiron-shaped board piece. Laurel was undeniably Dorothy L. Sayers's inimitable Miss Climpson in *Strong Poison.* However, the judges would surely deduct from Laurel's score for her white blond hair, which, though drawn back, bore little resemblance to Miss Climpson's steel-gray spinster's bun.

In any event, the roaming judges committee, made up of Edith Cummings, a sharp-tongued research librarian; Emma Clyde, creator of the Marigold Rembrandt mysteries; and Vince Ellis, editor and publisher of the *Island Gazette,* would be challenged to narrow the best costumes to a final five.

She and Max, of course, were disqualified to compete—after all, she would be handing out the prizes—but Annie was pleased at their costumes, he in a plaid shirt and brown knickers, a smiling Joe Hardy. She felt as stylish as Nancy Drew in a long-sleeved blue dress and patterned silk scarf straight from the original cover of *The Secret of the Old Clock*. Annie couldn't, of course, turn her gray eyes to blue, but her curly blond hair, while not titian, might qualify as bobbed and peeked becomingly from beneath a blue cloche. Annie had never been too clear on precisely what constituted bobbed hair. She confused it with marcelled. However, she felt as one with fabled Nancy, independent, curious, and ready for adventure. Now if she had a sporty blue roadster and chums like Bess and George . . . Of course, she had Henny and Laurel. . . .

Annie's smile slipped away as she spotted her father. She'd expected him to show up in costume, perhaps wearing a tweed jacket and cap, pipe in hand, a stalwart Richard Hannay, John Buchan's quintessential British man of derring-do. Ever since Pudge had arrived on the island, finding her after many years of separation, he'd enthusiastically participated in all the store events. His rounded face, gray eyes, and sandy hair flecked with gray were so familiar to her now. She knew her own face was a feminine version of his and took pleasure in that knowledge. Yesterday she'd almost rung him up, suggested he come as Fenton Hardy, but she'd smiled and decided to wait and see which sleuth he chose to represent. She tried not to admit how disappointed she was that he'd not bothered with a costume. His navy blazer, crisp chinos, and polished cordovan loafers were perfect for an evening out, but he might have been anywhere.

It was obvious, even from a distance, that his thoughts were far from the evening's entertainment. He gazed at his companion, his good-humored face nakedly vulnerable, eyes both hopeful and anxious. One hand touched her sleeve, the other brushed at his sandy mustache, a gesture he often made when under stress.

Sylvia Crandall was, as always, elegantly dressed. Tonight's green linen pantsuit emphasized her midnight dark eyes and willowy grace and made a bright foil for sleek brown hair glossy as polished mahogany. Sylvia would have been strikingly attractive except for the frown that twisted her heart-shaped face. She jerked away from Pudge, walked fast, head down, toward the stern.

Annie glowered. What was her problem? People having fun? Was she too sophisticated to engage in selfless tribute to a literary tradition? Did she think it gauche to dress up in costumes and play mystery games?

Pudge hurried after her, his expression bewildered and uncertain. He bent to look in her averted face, pointing at the gangway. Sylvia clutched at the gold beads of her necklace, shook her head.

As certainly as though she'd stood beside them, Annie knew Pudge had asked Sylvia if she wanted to leave. He was willing to abandon the mystery cruise if Sylvia wished. Annie felt a hot prick of tears. She blinked them away. Wait a minute. What was going on here? Up until this very moment she'd managed to stay cool about Sylvia. After all, if her father fell in love, she should be happy for him. Of course she should. And would. She wanted Pudge to be happy. That admirable thought, however, was followed by hot dismay at the prospect of Pudge giving his heart to arrogant, remote, self-absorbed Sylvia Crandall. Moreover, their relationship was threatening Rachel's hard-won equilibrium.

Annie leaned over the railing for a better view. Yes, there was Rachel, crouched in the shadow of a lifeboat, still and quiet, a picture of forlorn misery. Annie felt a hurt deep inside. She'd grown accustomed to her stepsister's smile, her eagerness, the lively warmth in her brown eyes. Instead Rachel once again looked like the too-thin, distraught girl who had burst into Death on Demand to plead Pudge's case after Annie had turned him away, too resentful to forgive the years of separation. Dark eyes brooding, angular face stiff beneath her mop of dark curls, Rachel watched Pudge and Sylvia.

Annie's mouth opened. Closed. If she called out, it would not only be Rachel who turned to look up. Rachel would feel humiliated before Sylvia. That would exacerbate her fierce resentment. Passionate, emotional Rachel had been through so much turmoil already, her mother's murder and the shock of crime that had touched her school. She'd survived with courage, but her wounds still ached. Rachel adored Pudge and Annie and Max and Death on Demand, Annie wasn't certain in which order. Rachel had been excited about tonight's cruise. If she hung back in the shadows, glaring at Pudge and Sylvia, Rachel's evening would be ruined. But maybe she would be distracted when the action began.

Annie lifted the megaphone. "Mystery lovers!" Annie hadn't intended to shout, but her voice boomed, startling her and everyone aboard. She rushed to take advantage of the abrupt silence and upturned faces. "Welcome to our first annual—" This wasn't in the script but why not? Obviously, tonight was a great success. People were still streaming aboard. Ingrid stood at the gangway, welcoming the last of the arrivals. Annie smiled at her longtime clerk and had no doubt that Ingrid's hat, which resembled a man's black bowler with a feminine feather, prim gray suit, and cotton blouse with a lacy collar represented Stuart Palmer's sleuth, former schoolteacher Hildegarde Withers. "—mystery cruise. The buffet is in the main lounge on the lower level. Dinner will be served until eight-thirty. Sodas and iced tea—sweetened and unsweetened—are available. Our interactive mystery—*Heist*—will be presented at thirty-minute intervals on the forward deck. The narrator is Detective Inspector Maguffin, aka island actress and mystery expert Henny Brawley. Inspector Maguffin will sketch the history of a daring jewel theft from a fabled Lowcountry plantation. Questions may be posed to the suspects. Write your solution to the mystery along with your name, address, and telephone number on a verdict card. The cards are available from the bookstalls set up at the stern on each deck. There is a limit of one verdict card per person." It wasn't that she had a dour view of human nature. She was simply a realist. If she didn't have a rule, at least one crafty player would submit a card with each suspect's name. "Also available at the bookstalls"—would this subliminal reminder encourage book buying?—"are Treasure Maps. The first five sleuths to find the hidden treasure chests will receive a free book of their choice from one of the bookstalls. And now"—she saw the gangway being pulled back—"welcome to Murder Ahoy!" She raised a hand to signal departure. A cheer rose on the night air as the *Island Packet* pulled away from the dock, its whistle shrilling.

Annie clicked off the megaphone. She swung about, ready to hurry to the main deck. She needed to talk to Rachel, though she hadn't an inkling what to say. And she'd find Pamela and . . .

Three figures blocked her way.

∻ *Two* ∻

RACHEL STOOD IN THE SHADOW of the lifeboat as the *Island Packet* moved slowly out of the harbor. It was sickening to see Pudge grovel in front of that woman. Rachel deliberately avoided looking at Sylvia, not wanting to recognize the distress that made the attractive woman look old beyond her years. She concentrated on Pudge. Last week when they'd talked about the mystery cruise, he'd promised to meet her at the stage to watch Annie's play, saying he'd bet six chocolate sundaes against a root beer float that he'd turn in a verdict card before she did. She'd grinned, knowing he would let her turn her card in first and take her to the soda fountain six times to pay off the bet. Despite the thick heat of the August night, she felt cold. He wouldn't meet her now. She knew it without any doubt. He'd forgotten all about his promise.

Sylvia turned, took a step toward the bow, calling out, "Cole, we're over here."

Rachel edged farther back into the shadow. The hard ridge of the lifeboat poked into her back. She glared at the figure moving in a reluctant shamble toward Pudge and Sylvia.

Cole Crandall wasn't much taller than Rachel. He

looked unfinished, all elbows and knees, in a floppy pink shirt, baggy black shorts, and high-top black sneakers. He might have been nice-looking if he didn't have such a morose expression. The thought was grudging, because she loathed him and his mother, and his face was just like his mom's, heart-shaped with dark eyebrows like streaks of coal, mournful dark eyes, and a pointed chin.

Sylvia looked hopefully at her son. "We're so glad you decided to come after all."

Rachel twined a strand of hair on one finger, pulled it to her lips. So Sylvia and Pudge had asked Cole to come with them. Resentment burned deep inside. Pudge hadn't asked her. Cole obviously had blown them off, yet here he was on the cruise.

"Yeah." His answer was clipped.

Sylvia managed a lopsided, uncertain smile. Her gaze was pleading. "Cole, Pudge thought it would be fun if we all went together to watch the mystery play—"

Rachel felt as if her heart were twisting inside her. They were asking Cole to go with them.

Cole didn't look toward Pudge. It was as though Pudge didn't exist and there was simply space next to his mother, not a stocky middle-aged man with anxious eyes.

"I'm with some guys. I only came because Stuart's dad had some extra tickets and wanted a bunch of us to use them. Anyway, they're waiting for me." He turned away, his gaze once again avoiding Pudge, and hurried toward the bow.

The invisible man looked after him.

Rachel wanted to shout to Pudge that he shouldn't care so much. Cole wasn't worth caring about. He was a jerk. A nobody. Pudge took a step toward the bow, then

Sylvia caught at his sleeve. Pudge would go after Cole, but he wouldn't remember his promise to her.

Rachel wormed to the other side of the lifeboat, fled toward the stairs.

Annie took a step back. She wasn't facing the Three Furies, but she had a definite sense of unfinished business about to be dumped in her lap.

"Annie!" Emma Clyde, the imposing island mystery author, gestured imperiously. "We need you on the bow." The ocean breeze billowed her black-and-silver caftan. Tonight Emma's springy curls were as silver as mercury. Her nails were silver also. Magenta lip gloss was the only touch of color. And, of course, the glacier blue of eyes that could quell any talk show host.

"Annie." Mrs. Ben clamped reddened hands to her white apron. "You got to come down to the galley. Five of those treasure hunters are poking around by my stove and I can't heat up beans with the galley full of squatters."

"Annie"—Mavis Cameron, wife of the island's acting police chief, was apologetic—"there may be a problem at the bow. Billy sent me." Mavis looked young and pretty in a candy-striped dress.

Annie prioritized. Billy Cameron was not an alarmist. She held up a hand to Emma and Mrs. Ben, turned to Mavis. "What's wrong?"

Mavis pointed forward. "There's a rowdy bunch of guys right at the front railing. High school boys. A lot of pushing and shoving. Billy thought he smelled beer. Anyway, he said if it's all right with you, he'll ask the boys to help him patrol the boat, tell them there's been word of a pickpocket and he'd like for them to take up posts around the boat and keep their eyes peeled."

Annie had provided free tickets for Billy and Mavis. The salary of an acting police chief didn't run to seventy-five-dollar tickets. Bless Billy for taking a busman's holiday. And for the wit and guile to channel rambunctious teenagers. "That's a great idea, Mavis. Please tell Billy I appreciate it."

Mavis's smile was warm. "He's glad to help. He was afraid things might get out of hand and somebody could get pushed overboard. Besides, he's not in a hurry to arrest Stuart Reed. Though," she added quickly, "he certainly will if he has to."

"That Reed boy"—Mrs. Ben was diverted—"needs a comeuppance. He and a bunch of his friends were throwing food and stuff on a Friday night a couple of weeks ago—and that's our biggest night of the week—and it made a big mess, and a can of pop broke the window of the jukebox. When Ben called his papa about it, Mr. Reed said he'd pay for any damage, and Ben said that wasn't the point, that Mr. Reed needed to settle that boy down, and Mr. Reed said boys would be boys and Ben said maybe so but he didn't want any of those boys to show a face inside Parotti's ever again. Mr. Reed got mad and hung up. If Stuart Reed's on board he better watch himself, or Ben will put him off on a sandbar and let his papa figure out how to get him back."

"In the meantime"—Emma was brusque—"Jolene"—she nodded her silver curls at Mrs. Ben—"has a galley to tend and Henny's short an actress for the play. She got a call on her cell from the gal who's supposed to be Periwinkle. She's at the emergency room with her husband, who was doing wheelies on his motorcycle and broke his wrist."

Annie caught Mavis as she was turning away. "After

you talk to Billy, could you give Henny some help? It's easy. Everything's in the script."

Mavis agreed, Emma departed to rejoin the costume committee, and Annie followed Jolene Parotti down the steps to the galley.

The recalcitrant five, fortune hunters all, were crammed in front of the stove. Annie greeted the mayor, the high school principal, a vacationer wearing an Ohio University T-shirt, a member of the Altar Guild, and a potter.

"Annie!" Five voices called out with loud complaints. ". . . says right here, five steps north, six steps south . . . supposed to be a little chest with cards"—the mayor waggled two cards—". . . not fair to keep us out. The others will be getting ahead. . . ."

Annie reached for the mayor's Treasure Map. There was a tug-of-war. "I'll give it back," she said gently.

His plump fingers reluctantly released the sheet, his pouter pigeon face puffed with impatience.

Annie held up the map, pointed to the first instruction. "Remember, the searches all begin at the Treasure Chest painted on the deck by the pilothouse." Annie was perhaps inordinately proud of the Treasure Map. The directions for each hidden chest contained the number of steps from the pilothouse and an enigmatic clue.

The mutiny in the galley pertained to chest number four. Annie read, "Five steps down—"

The potter clawed at his black beard. "Yeah, yeah. If you follow the steps, you end up in the corridor, and here's the galley, and if it has something to do with food—"

The vacationing buckeye rattled his sheet. "Let's cut to the chase. Right here"—a stubby forefinger tapped instruction number four—"it says: Hint—A carnival delight to some, but this one makes no crumbs."

Five sets of eyes glared at Annie.

If they cared that much . . . She said airily, "One of my favorite foods at the carnival is funnel cake, but on a boat . . ." She drew back against the bulkhead as the five stormed past her, thudding into the corridor and heading for the bow and the funnel.

Mrs. Ben shook her head. "I declare. What some folks will do to win a prize that probably don't amount to a hill of beans. If you don't mind my saying so. Now"—she moved toward the stove—"to *my* beans."

"They smell wonderful." Annie sniffed brown sugar and molasses and realized she was starving. She turned and hurried toward the stairs. She needed to check on the buffet, and find Rachel, and say hello to everybody.

Annie poked her head into the main saloon. Ben Parotti, natty in a Jack Nicklaus green blazer, lifted a hand in greeting. Ben had reminded Annie of a scruffy gnome until he met and married Miss Jolene and exchanged his long underwear tops and baggy coveralls for the latest in menswear from Belk's. His café had always been the island's premier eating spot, and as far as Annie was concerned Ben's fried oyster sandwich couldn't be bested. Tonight he was a genial host as well as boat owner and caterer.

"Eaten yet, Annie?" His gravelly voice exuded cheer. "The hush puppies are barking."

She grinned. "Pretty soon, Ben. Just making sure everything's going all right." The buffet line was moving quickly. She wrinkled her nose. Hmm. Hot fried fish, what a great smell. But work came first. . . .

On the lower deck, she stopped near the bookstall. Duane Webb, Ingrid's husband, was swamped. She hurried upstairs to find Ingrid equally busy on the upper deck. Annie was nearing the finish of her circuit when she saw a thin figure all alone at a side rail.

Annie stopped beside Rachel. "Hey, come with me and let's see how the play's doing."

Her young stepsister hunched her shoulders. In the moonlight her thin face was hard and still as alabaster. She yanked at the neck of her oversize striped T-shirt, shook her head violently.

Annie slipped an arm around rigid shoulders. She didn't know what to say. Was it better to say nothing or—

"Annie"—Rachel's voice was choked—"look!" A wavering finger pointed down to the deck below.

It took a moment for Annie's eyes to distinguish the couple embracing near the stern. Sylvia Crandall stood with her head pressed against Pudge's shoulder. Annie knew this was not passion. This was pain. Her father awkwardly patted Sylvia's back, a gesture of consolation.

Rachel shoved her hands into the pockets of her baggy shorts. "I'd push Cole right into the water if I could." She jerked to face Annie. "You should have seen the way he treated Pudge. He wouldn't speak to him. He wouldn't even look at him. He turned his back on Pudge to talk to his mom and then he slouched away."

Annie was puzzled. "Cole?"

"Cole Crandall." Her tone dripped disgust. "He's in my class. Thinks he's so special. Just like his mom."

Annie made a guess. "Is he a friend of Stuart Reed?"

Rachel's eyes widened.

Annie tweaked a dark curl. "No black magic. I'm fresh out of chicken entrails, but some guys were being rowdy downstairs, and Billy's enlisted their help to be on the lookout for a pickpocket."

"Those guys get to help Billy?" Rachel's voice was shrill. "Honestly, that's not fair. They already think they're special. Stuart Reed's rich and good-looking and he never lets anybody forget it. He has all these guys who follow him around and do whatever he says. I can't believe Billy would pick them to help him! And Pudge is all soppy about Sylvia and wants to be a buddy to Cole. Well, if Pudge wants to hang out with Cole he can forget me. But then"—her voice wavered—"I guess he already has. Oh, I hate everybody." She pulled away from Annie and rushed toward the steps.

Annie stared after her. Lordy.

Max Darling balanced two paper plates above his head as he worked his way around the customers massed at the book booth on the upper deck. Ingrid briskly made change and handed a purchase to a customer, then shouted, "Twenty-three." Maybe Annie should teach marketing at the community college on the mainland. Max had nodded politely when she told him she'd ordered dispensers with numbered slips for the book booths, which would be manned by Ingrid on the upper deck and her husband, Duane, on the lower. Annie had explained earnestly, "The boat isn't big enough for long lines. This way everyone pulls off a number, and Ingrid or Duane call each number in turn. Mystery readers like for everything to be orderly. And fair. They are very big on fair." Darned if she wasn't right. The crowd was good-humored, festive, and buying books at a rate that astonished him. Father Patton, the associate rector, was encumbered with two stuffed book bags, his face wreathed in a triumphant smile. He was a special fan of James Lee Burke.

Max found Annie on the platform near the pilothouse. She was silhouetted in the moonlight, graceful as a bronze of Diana. He stopped to admire her, a frequent and favorite pursuit. The wind ruffled her blond hair, tugged at her blouse. Enthusiastic, happy, serious, hardworking, levelheaded Annie, who lighted up his life. And later tonight . . . His grin was big enough to encompass Alaska.

She lifted her arms, held her hands high above her head to clap vigorously. "Huzzah!"

Max joined her, looked over the railing at the audience crowding near the raised platform near the bow. Henny Brawley swept off her hat, took a bow. Always fond of emulating favorite detectives, tonight she sported a brown fedora and rumpled, stained tan trench coat. Max suspected Lieutenant Columbo had served as her inspiration. She was beaming though flushed, which was understandable as the coat was a bit much for an August night though perfect for her role as Inspector Maguffin.

Annie pointed down to the forward deck, whispered, "She just described the setting, the old plantation house with wraparound porches surrounded by live oaks, a lagoon with an eight-foot alligator, a terraced garden with azaleas in full bloom, a raccoon who comes every evening to listen to Mozart, Wanda's room with the evening sun shining on the heart pine floor and the emerald necklace on the dresser." Annie heaved a happy sigh. She knew the play by heart. "Now she's going to introduce the characters at the time of the theft, according to their later testimony." Annie took a plate filled with crisp fried fish, Ben's homemade sweet potato chips, tangy coleslaw, baked beans, and those barking hush puppies. "Huzzah to you, too. I'm starving." They balanced their plates on the wooden railing, just wide enough to serve as a table.

On the forward deck, Henny introduced the players, one by one:

"Wanda Wintersmith, mistress of Mudhen Manor." A plump matron draped in a huge pink towel crossed the stage, blowing soap bubbles, her bare wet feet slapping on the wood. "I always take the most luxurious bath before a grand evening event."

"Walter Wintersmith, Wanda's errant husband." A balding actor in a tuxedo carried a pair of dress shoes. He brandished a swab dripping with black sole dressing. "As far as I'm concerned, a shoe isn't fully polished until the rims are done."

"Periwinkle Patton, Wanda's niece." Mavis Cameron held out a whisk broom and dustpan. "Oh dear, I don't know if I can get all this bath powder swept up. It's such a mess."

"Augustus Abernathy, Wanda's nephew." Augustus carried a hoe. He swiped at his face with a red bandana. "I know it's almost time for the party but I want to finish mulching the roses."

"Heather Hayworthy, an aspiring actress whom Walter—ah—admires." The voluptuous blonde flounced across the stage, sequins scattering from a tear in her fancy dress. "Oh, this is just too much. My dress is ruined and I don't have another for the party tonight!"

"Moose Mountebank, who believes he would make a fine squire of Mudhen Manor." The handsome actor reached down to swipe at his shoes, held up muddy fingers, his face chagrined. "Wanda despises people who arrive late. And here I am, out of gas and the road's a swamp from all the rain yesterday."

Henny's clear voice announced, "Detectives may

now pose their questions." Annie took another bite of delectable fish. A frown suddenly creased her face. "Have you seen Rachel?"

Max dipped his fish in tartar sauce. "She's sitting with a bunch of girls in the main saloon and studiously ignoring Pudge and Sylvia at the next table. Pudge looked tired."

Annie munched the crisp, delicious fish. Okay, when they got home tonight, it was time for her and Rachel to have a talk. But Rachel's unhappiness was the only blight on an otherwise perfect—

A voice rose in a shrill scream.

Annie's breath caught in her chest. She knew at once that something dreadful had happened. That cry had been freighted with horror. Harsh shouts rose in a discordant, frightening jumble. Another scream sliced through the night. She and Max ran to the starboard railing in time to see a geyser of water plume above the dark surface.

"Man overboard."

The stentorian yell shocked the crowd to silence for an instant. A hoarse call followed. "Stop the engines. Man overboard."

The boat shuddered to a stop. Running feet sounded, calls, shouts, cries.

". . . fell from there . . ."

". . . saw her on the way down . . ."

". . . what happened . . ."

". . . can they get her in time?"

". . . throw down life preservers. Yeah, over there . . ."

Ben Parotti's gravelly but authoritative voice barked over the PA system. "Remain where you are until further notice. Passenger sighted off starboard bow. Rescue efforts are under way."

A clanking creak signaled a winch lowering a rowboat.

Annie leaned over the railing as a limp figure bobbed to the surface. There was no life, no movement, no struggle.

A searchlight swung up, down, wavered, settled on hair streaming in the water and a floating arm. The arm moved with the surge of the water. A spot of yellow marked one shoulder. Two life preservers wobbled nearby.

Yellow . . . Annie grabbed Max's arm. "Oh God, it's Pamela." Pamela had been so clever, attaching the figure of a canary to one shoulder. "She doesn't know how to swim. Oh Max, she's going down—"

The body, weighted by sodden clothing, was slipping beneath the dark surface.

Max kicked off his loafers, climbed onto the railing. For an instant he was poised against the night sky and then he arched into space, down, down, down.

Annie clapped her hands to the railing, the sea-damp wood slick beneath her fingers. Max's dive seemed to take forever, though she knew he was plummeting faster and faster toward the surface. He knifed into black water that plumed in a high white ruffle. Rough voices shouted instructions, commands.

Annie struggled to breathe. If anybody could save Pamela, Max could. He was a champion diver, a superb swimmer. She tried not to think about the night sea and sharks and a heavy weight pulling him deeper and deeper. She stared at the unbroken surface of the ocean, opaque as the dark sky. How far down had Pamela gone? How could he find her? Oh, Max, come up, come up.

Abruptly, the water frothed. Max shot into view, one

arm in a tight lifeguard grip around Pamela. He treaded water, breathing deeply. Pamela's head lolled back and forth.

Annie's cheer melded into a triumphant roar from the onlookers.

A lifeboat smacked into the water. Two crew members wielded the oars, synchronizing the rise and fall as they pulled through the water.

Annie's heart steadied into a slower rhythm. Max was fine. He could tread water as long as necessary. But Pamela was clearly injured. Annie hung over the railing when the boat wallowed next to Max and his inert burden. It seemed to take so long, the careful easing of Pamela's limp body up and into the lifeboat, then Max clambering in the back. By the time the lifeboat was alongside the hull, a swing with a stretcher dangled near the water. Max held the swing steady as the crewmen gently strapped her onto the stretcher. Then there was a slow and careful ascent as Pamela was hauled aboard.

In a moment more, a sopping Max was beside her and she clung to him, not caring that he was wet, caring only that he was there, safe in the tight circle of her arms.

"I'm okay, honey." He was impatient. He gave her a squeeze, stepped back, looked toward the clump of people gathered around the stretcher. "Pamela's unconscious. Or . . ." The sentence trailed off.

Annie stood on tiptoe, craning to see. The boat engine rumbled as the *Island Packet* began a slow turn in the water. Max, still straining for breath, looked over the massed heads. "Billy's doing CPR. That means she's still alive."

Annie hoped that was true. She would try to believe that was true.

"He's stopped." Max's voice was grim. He folded his arms, frowned.

Annie wanted to shout and cry and push back time. Pamela must have been so proud of her costume. She obviously was having a wonderful time tonight. How could cautious, careful, prudent Pamela have tumbled overboard? Dear Pamela, serious, kind, good, well-meaning, and literal. What rhyme or reason was there? But accidents happen to everyone. Oh damn, damn, damn. Pamela had been so excited to be on the cruise, so grateful to Annie. But it wasn't Annie who'd sent her a ticket. Annie had forgotten all about finding Pamela, explaining the mix-up. Now it was forever too late. Poor Pamela, so grateful for kindness. How tragic that her exciting evening had ended like this. And how heartbreaking for her to lie there with no one near who cared for her. Sometimes people came around if they just kept working on them. . . .

Annie tried to push through the crowd.

Max caught her arm. "Annie, they need room. We shouldn't try to get closer."

Her throat ached as she pushed out the words. "He mustn't stop." Tears brimmed. "If he'll just keep on—"

The word swept through the onlookers like sea oats rustling in the wind. "She's breathing . . . breathing . . . breathing. . . ."

Annie lifted the megaphone. "I have wonderful news. Police Chief Billy Cameron successfully performed CPR on Pamela Potts, who was rescued"—Annie's glance at Max was proud, but his quick head shake precluded mention—"after falling overboard. Pamela is breathing well but remains unconscious." Surely Pamela would be all right. Surely she would. . . . "We are returning to the harbor where an ambulance will take her to the hospital. I know everyone joins with me in wishing Pamela a speedy recovery. Please feel free to continue with the mystery events as we return to shore. As a special thank-you for your understanding our shortened outing, I'd like to invite everyone to attend a free watermelon feast next Saturday afternoon on the boardwalk in front of Death on Demand. We will announce the winner of our jewel theft mystery. And Pamela Potts will be our special guest of honor." Please God.

Annie clicked off the megaphone and turned. "Max, let's go see." She headed for the steps down to the saloon where they had taken Pamela.

He stood in the door frame, blocking the way. "Sorry. Off-limits." He was young, muscular, cocky, and good-looking, with smooth olive skin, greenish eyes, and dark hair. His yellow polo shirt was a tight fit, his khakis fashionably baggy.

Annie peered around him. A teenage boy was stationed at every entrance. Billy had utilized his newly acquired cadre for more serious work than the search for a nonexistent pickpocket. Aft, a scarecrow-thin six-footer in a red and white rugby shirt stood with a jutting jaw and folded arms. Port, a sharp-featured, bony boy nervously paced. Starboard—Annie knew at once—was Sylvia Crandall's son, a tangle of brown curls framing a heart-shaped face. His brown eyes had the nervous look of a spooked horse.

In the center of the saloon, people clustered near a table. Billy Cameron, big and imposing, glanced at his wristwatch. It was odd to see Billy in a Hawaiian print shirt and blue jeans. She was accustomed to his khaki uniform. Ben Parotti had shed his green blazer. He stood with thumbs hooked onto orange braces, his gnome face glowering. Mavis Cameron bent over the table, her light brown hair falling forward, screening her face. Father Patton had a thoughtful, considering look on his face. His arms were folded across his chest.

Annie called out, "Billy. Hey, Billy!"

Billy turned. "Annie." His voice was tired. "That's okay, Stuart. Let them in."

The teenager stepped back to let Annie and Max enter, firmly closed the door after them.

Annie hurried across the floor, Max close behind. The boat was running hard and she had to concentrate to keep her balance. As they reached the group, Ben said gruffly, "Going as fast as we can. We dock in about ten minutes."

Annie felt a moment of surprise when she looked at the table and saw Emma Clyde seated next to Pamela, holding one hand in a firm grip. Emma glanced up. "Pulse is steady, Annie." Long ago Emma had been a nurse. And Emma could always be counted upon to take charge, whatever the situation.

Annie felt shaken when she looked at the limp form. She'd known that Pamela was unconscious, but to see her like this was shocking. Pamela was wrapped in a dark gray blanket. There was not a vestige of color in her skin. The slack muscles made her almost unrecognizable. Her face was as still as marble. The hair plastered against her head was darkened by the seawater. If she was breathing, it wasn't apparent. But Emma said her pulse was steady.

Annie noted the odd little lump beneath the blanket on Pamela's left shoulder and blinked back tears. She knew Pamela well enough to be sure that she'd been very proud of her costume and was eager to tell everyone about Miss Pinkerton's beloved canary, Dickie. Annie reached out, gripped Max's arm.

"She's breathing." Emma was reassuring. "Apparently she hit her head when she fell. They'll run tests. When the swelling goes down, she'll very likely regain consciousness."

Ben Parotti glared at the still figure. "Don't make no sense to me. She must've been where she had no business to be to fall from the upper deck. If she was behind the railing, there's no way she could take a tumble, not unless she climbed up and over and jumped."

"No." Annie was emphatic. Some things were possible. Some weren't. Pamela Potts was not a candidate for suicide. If ever anyone accepted seriously the charge to finish the course, it would be Pamela.

Ben lowered his head like a terrier ready to snap. "Then, missy, you tell me how it happened."

Max used a handful of paper napkins to wipe his face. He gave a couple of swipes at his head. His wet hair stood on end. Water dripped from his slacks. "Wait a minute, Ben. Didn't anybody see her fall?" He looked at Billy.

Billy frowned. "Nobody's come forward yet to say they saw her go over."

"We heard someone scream." Annie looked toward the windows of the saloon. Night pressed against the glass. The outside deck was invisible. Of course Pamela hadn't fallen from this level.

Billy kneaded the side of his neck. "By the time I got up there, a bunch of people were hanging over the rail, pointing to her bobbing in the water. Nobody admitted seeing her fall—or jump."

"She didn't jump." Annie's retort was swift and decisive.

"We'll have to see what an investigation reveals." Billy's answer was rather formal.

Max flapped the damp napkins at her. His blue eyes held a warning.

Annie understood. Damn. Why had she been so sharp? It wouldn't help matters to embarrass Billy. Billy was the hero of the night, along with Max. She spread her hand in apology. "I'm sorry. I didn't mean to be rude. But I know Pamela. She'd never, ever do anything like that." How could she make Billy understand that Pamela never met a rule she hadn't embraced? "She'd rather die than cause a public scene."

Mavis cleared her throat. "Maybe she felt sick. Or faint. Maybe she started to fall and she slipped between the railings."

Billy squinted his eyes in thought. "A chest-high wooden rail runs from stanchion to stanchion and knee-high metal rails. I don't see how anyone could fall accidentally."

Ben scratched at his bristly jaw. "Looked to me like she must of come off that portion of the deck by the upper lifeboat—and that's behind a chain. Ain't nobody got no cause to climb over that chain."

"Look"—Annie shoved a hand through her hair—"why don't we check it out? Ask people who were near that spot?"

"I expect someone would already have spoken up if she'd been seen. And Ben knows his boat. If he's right, she must have jumped." Billy spoke with authority, a man who'd covered a lot of accident scenes. "You say she wasn't the kind for a big scene. Likely she waited until the deck was empty and then she got over the rail. But we can try." His tone was equable. He flung up a meaty hand, gestured. "Hey, Cole, come over for a minute."

Cole Crandall stiffened. He looked like a truant summoned to the principal's office, wild-eyed and nervous. "Yeah?"

Billy waved his hand again. "You were closest to the spot where she went over."

Cole Crandall moved slowly across the saloon. He stopped a few feet away from Billy. "Yeah?" He hunched his thin shoulders, jammed his hands deep in the pockets of baggy black shorts. He averted his face from the table and its still burden.

"Okay, son." Billy was reassuring. "Tell us what you saw."

Cole licked his lips. "I didn't see *her*." He emphasized the pronoun, but he wouldn't look at the table. His face wrinkled in a puzzled frown. "Most people had gone in to get food. There wasn't anything going on where I was. I was between those two lifeboats. I kept walking up and down the deck, but there wasn't anybody out there. Anyway, it was real hot and I decided to go get a Pepsi. I must have been inside when she went overboard. I'd just stepped back on the deck when everybody started yelling." He rubbed his cheek with his knuckles. "I looked and she was in the air." He ducked his head toward the floor.

Annie had a sudden, hideous picture: Pamela head down, plummeting toward the water. Annie reached out a hand. "How did she fall?" Her words came fast. "Was it a jump? Like somebody leaping from a diving board? You know, hands up in the air, feet first toward the water? Or was it a real dive? Was she screaming?"

The teenager took a step back, shaking his head. "She was turning over and her arms and legs kind of flopped. She wasn't making any noise. There were screams, but they were coming"—he waved his hand—"from the front of the boat."

Annie swung toward Billy. "That means she was already unconscious." Annie struggled for understanding. If Pamela didn't jump—and she didn't—and if Pamela didn't fall—and why should she?—and if Pamela was unconscious when she went over the rail, then Pamela was pushed.

But Billy's face was placid. "Looks like she bumped her head as she went down." His eyes squeezed in thought. "Yeah. Say she took a leap and her feet went out from under her so her head came down on the rail. That knocked her out and she fell like a dummy." His nod at Cole was approving. "Anyway, you didn't see anybody near the spot where she went over. Right?"

Cole rocked back and forth on his sneakered feet. "You mean, somebody could have caught her?"

Before Billy could answer, Annie clapped her hands together. "Caught her? If there was anybody close to her, they pushed her!"

Cole took another step back. One eyelid jerked in a tic. "Why would anybody do that?" His voice shook.

The question hung in the air.

Annie looked at their startled faces. Max's gaze was puzzled. Emma yanked on a silver curl as if an answer might pop forth. Ben was an incredulous gnome. Mavis pressed one hand to her lips. Billy frowned, his good humor gone.

Annie lifted her chin, looked at each in turn. "I don't know why. But nothing else makes sense. If Pamela was unconscious when she went over the railing, how did she get over the railing?"

"Oh, Annie." Billy heaved a sigh. "Come on. You

got too many mysteries in your head. For starters, maybe she was conscious when she went over and then banged her head. If it was an accident, maybe she felt seasick—"

Annie wanted to point out that the Sound was mirror smooth.

"—or maybe somebody spilled something on the deck and she slipped and got knocked out, and the way she went down, she flopped through the rails. Accidents can be weird. We may never know what happened. Or maybe she'll wake up and tell us. But people"—his look at Annie was patient—"do the damndest things. Maybe she was down in the dumps and didn't tell anybody. Maybe that's why she came tonight, thinking she'd jump off and no one would even notice."

Annie clenched her hands into fists. To suggest that Pamela came on board with the idea—Annie stood still, her thoughts whirling. "Wait a minute. Wait a *minute*. Billy, that's not why she came." Annie spread out the words as if she were dropping diamonds on a velvet cloth, each one distinct and separate, hard and shiny and inescapable. "She . . . came . . . because . . . she . . . got . . . a . . . free . . . ticket."

Emma's piercing blue eyes narrowed. Max glanced toward the still form on the table. Ben fingered his bristly chin, pursed his mouth. Mavis nodded, murmured, "Just like us." Billy shrugged, unimpressed.

The excursion boat's whistle shrieked.

Ben clapped his hands together. "Coming in. I'll go see to the gangway—"

Billy was abruptly official. "I'll hold back the crowd till we get her off."

Annie reached out, caught his sleeve. "Billy, don't

you see?" Her words tumbled faster and faster. "Pamela didn't plan on coming. There's no way she could have planned to be here tonight. She got a free ticket"—Annie tried hard to remember Ingrid's report of her telephone conversation—"and she just got it today. She thought it was from me, but it wasn't. That means somebody wanted Pamela to be on board tonight." Annie could almost accept Billy's insistence that somehow in a freak accident Pamela had fallen overboard and was unconscious because she banged her head as she fell. Yes, but that didn't explain the free ticket. And if Pamela was enticed onto the boat and came close to dying, might yet die, the possibility of an accident seemed remote. Annie discounted it absolutely. "Somebody deliberately—"

Billy shook off her hand. "—did a good deed. Just like you, Annie, giving tickets to me and Mavis. Sure she thought the ticket came from you. Anybody would think that."

He was moving toward the port doorway.

Annie was on his heels. "Billy, before you go down to do crowd control, tell me one thing."

"Sure." He was patient, even though he obviously thought her deductions out of line. "What?"

She met his gaze, held it. "If somebody pushed Pamela over, that person is still on board. Right?"

"Yeah, yeah, yeah." He grinned. "In the event we got a maniac running around, he's still on board, because we didn't hear another splash. Now I got to get outside—"

The boat was slowing, wallowing a little as it neared the dock.

"While you're holding everybody back to give the medics a chance to move Pamela, wouldn't it make sense to have all of us fan out"—her hand sweep included Max and Emma and Mavis and Ben—"and get the names of everybody on board?" She saw him consider it, took heart. After all, why not? Quickly, she added, "That way we can ask if anybody saw anything. Maybe we can find an eyewitness. I'll bet Ben would appreciate a list of possible witnesses. In case of liability."

"Liability?" Ben sounded like a frog with a golf ball in his throat. "Now wait a damn minute. People go where they ain't supposed to go, there's no blame can be—"

Max clapped Ben on the shoulder. "Looks like Annie's got a good idea. That would be your best bet, Ben, in the event a lawsuit ever gets filed."

Ben's eyes were wild. "Yeah, let's get the names." He started for the door, called over his shoulder, "I'll round up paper and pens. Everybody meet me up by the gangway."

Billy clapped his hands together. "Sure. Get the names. Who knows? Like you said, we may find an eyewitness, settle everything."

Eyewitness.

Annie turned, strode toward Cole Crandall, who had returned to his post on the starboard side of the saloon.

He looked at her warily, hands still deep in his pockets.

"Listen, Cole, it's important to know everything that happened on the deck where you were. If you think of anything"—Annie plunged a hand into her pocket, pulled out a card—"be sure and call me. Okay?"

"Yeah, well, sure. But I didn't see anything." He moved from one foot to the other.

The boat shuddered to a stop.

She waited until a sticky hand took the card, jammed it into a pocket. He mumbled, "I never did see her come up there."

Annie whirled and hurried to Max. "Come on, let's get started."

Emma called out, "You have enough without me." Her gruff voice was determined.

Annie looked back in surprise.

Emma nodded toward the still figure on the table. "I'll stay with Pamela." She picked up her purse from the floor, opened it, pulled out car keys. "You can bring my car to the hospital. I'll go in the ambulance with Pamela." Emma tossed the keys to Annie. "I won't leave her."

Annie carried fear with her as she climbed the steps to the second deck, fear for Pamela, fear and a burning anger. Pamela was good and decent and kind, sustaining as oatmeal and just about as exciting. She never caused harm. She tried to do good. Somebody had lured her aboard a boat bound for fun, intending that Pamela would never return. As Annie took down names, she saw Max and Mavis and Ben moving alongside the lines waiting patiently to disembark, slowly filling up their sheets. Names and names and more names.

One belonged to Pamela's would-be murderer.

☙ *Three* ❧

THE AMBULANCE SIREN faded as its flashing red lights disappeared behind a stand of pines.

An offshore breeze, pungent with the scent of salt water and creosote, ruffled Annie's hair, lifted seabirds on rising currents. The dock echoed with the footsteps of disembarked passengers walking toward the parking lot. Headlights stabbed into the darkness as the long line of cars began a slow exit.

The excursion boat had a feeling of emptiness, the slap of water against the hull the only sound except for the cackle of gulls. On the upper deck, Annie moved her hand back and forth, the sharp white beam from the borrowed flashlight exposing the scuffed deck, dropped candy wrappers, and crumpled cups.

Ben Parotti glowered at the refuse. "People is pigs." He held a twin of Annie's big flashlight. "Okay"—his tone was demanding—"here we are. I don't see nothin' that isn't what it should be. The chains are up, the rails in place."

Annie swung her light toward the tarp-covered lifeboat beyond a chain. "Billy should be up here. Taking pictures. Looking for fingerprints. Figuring out what happened."

Max leaned against the railing, hands in his pockets. "Annie . . ."

She jerked toward him, hearing a world of comment in the sound of her name: caution, concern, and—most disturbing—patience. His gaze was kind, his dark blue eyes filled with understanding. And resistance.

"Max"—her voice was strained—"surely you don't believe Pamela jumped." Before he could answer, she pointed at the lifeboat. "That kid—Cole Crandall—was up here on pickpocket patrol for Billy, but Cole said he didn't see Pamela. Yet this is the spot where she must have gone overboard for him to turn around and spot her in midair. Where was she right before she fell?"

Max frowned at the projection of deck that curved over the water and was roped off by a chain. His gaze was measuring. "She must have climbed over the chain—or ducked under it—and squeezed past the lifeboat. She could have crouched behind the lifeboat and he wouldn't have seen her. If she did, that means she was trying not to be noticed. If she hid behind the lifeboat, she meant to jump. Why else would she go out there?"

Ben's grizzled head nodded emphatically. "Clear as clear. Annie—"

She bridled at Ben's patronizing tone, gave him glare for glare.

"—you got murder on the brain. The poor lady decided to jump. Some people can't get out on dark water at night without feeling lonesome and blue." His raspy voice was mournful. "You know she ain't got nobody at home. Her ma went and died last year, and maybe she got tired of always being an outsider—"

Annie bit her lip, a sudden vision of Pamela walking alone into church, smiling, nodding, but yes, she was always alone, doing good works but coming and going by herself. Annie stopped the beam of light on the small sign that dangled from the chain:

OFF-LIMITS

The bright red letters glistened against a white background.

"No." Annie spoke with certainty. "Pamela wouldn't go past the chain. Look at that sign! It means 'Don't go there.' Pamela followed the rules. All the rules. All the time. She would not go past that chain."

Max's glance was still kindly. "Okay, let's say she didn't jump. You say there's no way she would commit suicide. Maybe it was an accident. Maybe her hat blew off. Maybe she was trying to catch it."

When Pamela lay unmoving on the table, wrapped in the blanket, her wet head was bare. The hat might have come loose as she fell or when she went into the water. No matter. Annie was adamant. "She wouldn't go past the chain. Not for her hat. Not for her purse." As Annie spoke, she moved to the chain, swung her leg over it. She ignored the calls from behind her

"Careful now, missy." Ben's shoes clumped on the deck.

"Annie, watch out!" Max's tone was sharp.

—and pointed the sharp white beam at the painted surface. Ben and Max were right to warn her. The metal was damp and slippery as a slick skillet from the night air and sea mist. She leaned against the lifeboat, edged forward. Okay, the critical point was that Pamela wouldn't step over the chain. The men, including Max, dismissed Annie's claim that she knew what Pamela would and wouldn't do. Fine. But Annie knew she was right. The sun came up in the east, Max loved her, and Pamela Potts followed the rules. So if Pamela didn't step over the chain, how did she get out on this ledge?

Annie pictured Pamela being held at gunpoint, smooth countenance wrinkled in puzzlement, wide blue eyes questioning, pleasant voice perplexed: "Excuse me, please, that gun is pointed toward me. I believe it is improper to carry a firearm aboard a public conveyance. If you will be so kind . . ."

The whole prospect was absurd. That's why no one—with the possible exception of Emma Clyde, and Emma might have chosen to remain with Pamela simply because she was unconscious, not because Emma feared for Pamela's safety—was willing to believe Annie's insistence that murder had been attempted. Who would try to kill Pamela Potts? It was as ridiculous as imagining a plot against Raggedy Ann.

Annie pushed away that thought and focused on the lifeboat and the curve of metal overhanging the sea.

If Pamela had fallen on the other side of the lashed boat, she would not have been visible to Cole Crandall. Therefore she tumbled over right here, within inches of where Annie stood. Cole said there had been no one about and then he heard screams and he turned toward the bow. But Pamela wasn't screaming. Pamela was already unconscious.

Annie glanced toward the deck that ran between the railing and the housing for the upper saloon. The windows were now dark. When the boat was in the Sound, the cabin was lighted, but those inside would not be able to see out into the night.

There were occasional lights strung along the deck, but this portion was shadowy.

Someone—including Pamela—could have stepped out through the doorway as Cole sauntered aft.

Annie eased back to the chain, slipped beneath it. She walked to the cabin door. "Max"—she waved toward the stern—"pretend you are Cole. Go toward the stern. Take your time."

Max did as she asked. At a slow amble, he moved into the darkness.

Annie was quick. She darted from the doorway and ducked under the chain. There was even time to pause and watch Max's slow progress. Definitely there was time enough for someone to come out of the cabin and hurry across the corridor. Max was just now turning to look toward her.

But every time she came back to her bedrock conviction: Pamela followed the rules, all the rules, from a prohibition to remain behind a chain to the church's admonition to finish the course. Pamela wouldn't step over the chain, and most emphatically Pamela would never commit suicide. Pamela would have abhorred being a public spectacle, bringing the boat to a shuddering stop, becoming the subject of a dramatic rescue effort.

So, if there was time for Pamela to cross the deck, there was time for someone else to do so. But where was Pamela when this person crossed? Surely there wasn't enough time for an altercation. What could have happened?

The puzzle pieces slotted in her mind. Pamela didn't scream. The scream came from an onlooker who spotted Pamela in the air. She tumbled, arms and legs lax, because she was unconscious.

Annie moved out to the lifeboat, once again ignoring the cautioning calls. She ran the flashlight along the rim of the boat. A piece of the covering tarp sagged. It was loose. She tugged and the canvas yielded in her hand. She pulled it back, swung the flashlight over the interior of the wooden boat. The boat was old, the wood discolored. She squinted, bent nearer, held the beam steady. Careful not to touch anything, she craned to look between the seats, studied every inch of the flooring.

A scrap of black plastic was snagged on the bottom.

Annie felt a surge of triumph. "Come here, Ben. I need you to be a witness."

He approached slowly, his eyes suspicious. He stepped over the chain, held to the side of the boat, looked inside.

Annie pointed the light straight at her discovery. "Do you see that piece of plastic? It looks like it came from a big black trash bag."

"Maybe." His shrug was casual, disinterested. "Yeah, that's what it looks like."

"How did it get there?" She kept her tone reasonable, simply an inquiry.

Ben scratched his bristly cheek. "Maybe it blew there. Maybe it was stuck on a crewman's shoe the last time somebody checked the boat." He tilted his head. "Didn't you find the cover loose?"

"Yes." Annie knew why. There hadn't been time to fasten the tarp.

Ben tapped his flashlight on the boat. "A loose cover means that plastic could of got there a bunch of ways. The wind. Or maybe it was a crow. They carry things and put them the damndest places. One time on the *Miss Jolene,* I kept seeing a crow duck under a port lifeboat. I took a look and found a stash of shiny beads. That little scrap of plastic don't mean a thing. Thing is, you're trying to make something out of nothing."

Annie carefully replaced the tarp, her face grim.

Ben dismissed the importance of the snagged plastic. One glance at Max told her his attitude was the same. Billy would agree with them. Not with her.

Yet she knew what had happened as clearly as though she'd stood and watched. The murderer came aboard with a plastic trash bag folded as small as possible, tucked in a back pocket or a purse. At some point, the tarp on the lifeboat was loosened, the plastic bag spread between the seats, Pamela was knocked out, dragged to the lifeboat, and tumbled inside it. Later, when the coast was clear, the deck empty except for Cole Crandall walking aft, the murderer darted from the saloon, stepped over the chain, lifted Pamela from the lifeboat, and dumped her over the edge. Her attacker grabbed the trash bag, pulled the tarp over the boat, and ducked around the far side of the lifeboat to hurry along the deck to the stairs. By this time everyone's attention was focused on Pamela's fall. The bag was quickly folded and put in a pocket or purse.

Annie felt certain she knew what had happened. No one would believe her. No one, not Max or Ben or Billy. But the murderer knew that Pamela had survived and was now at the hospital.

Who was looking out for Pamela right this minute?

The taillights of the Maserati glowed.

Annie pulled even with the car, fumbled to find the window controls, lowered the pane on the passenger side of Emma's Rolls-Royce.

Max's window was down, too. "Annie, I'll meet you at the hospital."

She shook her head. "There's no need. You're still wet. Go home and take a hot shower. If I leave the hospital, Emma can bring me."

In the glow from the dash, his face was concerned. "*If* you leave?"

"Pamela's in danger. If somebody pushed her off the boat—and I know that's what happened—the objective was to kill her. Well, everybody on that boat knows she's going to be in the hospital." She wasn't angry, but she was determined. "I'll stay the night if there's no one who will be with her."

It took him a moment to answer. But he wasn't grudging when he spoke. "I understand. I don't believe she's in danger, but you could be right. Call me when you know what you'll be doing."

"I will. Give Dorothy L. a hug." Their plump white cat adored Max and most likely would never notice Annie's absence.

Max's car pulled ahead. Once on Sand Dollar Road in a long line of cars, Annie drummed her fingers impatiently on the steering wheel. She wished Max agreed with her conviction that Pamela was in danger. However, she understood his attitude and Billy's as well. They didn't really know Pamela. They saw her as a single woman who might have succumbed to depression. But she was grateful that Max understood her decision to go to the hospital to protect her friend. She saw his taillights receding as she turned right, taking the road to the hospital.

Traffic thinned and the big Rolls zoomed forward. Annie wondered if the captain of the *QEII* felt nearly as empowered. What a car, the engine a low throaty purr, the massive body rolling noiseless and unstoppable. No wonder Emma had such presence. Of course, Emma would see it the other way about, supremely confident that the magnificent driving machine merely reflected her persona.

At any other time, Annie would have been thrilled to drive the Rolls. She'd once bested Emma in a contest, winning the right to drive the Rolls as a prize, but at the last minute Emma had held tight to the keys.

Annie turned the car smoothly into the hospital parking lot, the occasional golden pool of light from the lampposts emphasizing the black shadows of the hedges, throwing long streaks of darkness from the tall pines. She wished the jaunt in the car was the reason for her outing, not the frightening prospect of a helpless Pamela at risk from an unknown attacker. The thought seemed absurd. Who would attack Pamela? Why Pamela?

She parked at the far end of the lot, leaving a free space on either side. Far be it from her to leave Emma's Rolls vulnerable to scratches. Walking fast, she headed for the emergency room, carrying with her, an odd accompaniment on a journey into fear, the ripe banana smell of a huge pittosporum bush. When she stepped inside, the sweet scent was overwhelmed by hospital odors, medicines and food and disinfectants and sickness.

Emma Clyde lounged, sandaled feet crossed, on a green vinyl sofa right next to the automatic door that led to the cubicles for emergency room patients. She held a cell phone pressed to one ear.

As Annie's shoes clicked on the faux marble floor, Emma looked up, lifted a stubby hand in greeting. Her silver nails matched the silver streaks in her georgette caftan. "We'll change shifts at two A.M. . . . No word yet. . . . I'll let you know." She clicked off the phone, patted the cushion next to her.

Annie didn't sit down. She laced her fingers together and stared at the closed door. "How is she?"

"So far as I know, there's been no change." Emma was reassuring. "The outlook is positive. She was breathing very well en route. Dr. Burford's with her now."

Annie flung out her hands, talked fast. "What if there's another entrance to the ER?" Annie thought there was. Maybe she ought to scout out the hospital right now, find out. "Somebody tried to kill her and now she's unconscious. We need a guard. The doctor will be in and out. If she's all by herself, she's helpless—"

Emma reached out, grabbed Annie's hand, pulled her down to the sofa. "Take a deep breath. I didn't forget what you said in the saloon. You think she was pushed." She raised an eyebrow. "Maybe she was. Maybe she wasn't. I'm not taking any chances." One silver-tipped finger pointed down the hall, empty except for a custodian pushing a mop. "There's one other entrance to the cubicles. You go through those swinging doors"—she pointed at doors to the left of the ER reception counter— "and go down a hall—the one that leads to the hospital proper—then turn right into a short hall. There's an unmarked door across from the women's rest room. It's for doctors and staff. I called Henny, told her everything. She came immediately and she's on duty there."

"Henny?" Annie began to relax. Henny was much more than simply an actress and a mystery devotee, she was capable and savvy, had been a World War II pilot, a teacher, and, after her retirement, a two-time Peace Corps volunteer. Henny could be counted on.

Emma held up her cell phone. "We've got it worked out. Henny's been on the phone to the members of the Altar Guild. They'll be here in relays. Two will be on duty through the night when she's moved to a room. Now, Annie, I want to know all about Pamela's cruise ticket."

Annie related what she knew, which, of course, wasn't much.

Emma tugged on a silver ringlet, pursed her crimson lips. "So, from what Ingrid told you, your impression is that Pamela had no doubt you'd sent the ticket. Pamela is very literal. There must have been a clear link to you."

"Exactly. Besides . . ." Annie reiterated Pamela's reverence for order. "So she didn't jump. She wouldn't do that. And in the lifeboat . . ." As Annie described the loose tarp and the scrap of plastic bag, she realized she had a rapt audience. Emma's sapphire blue eyes glowed. She reminded Annie of Agatha poised to leap, every muscle supple, dangerous to any creature unwise enough to make a sudden movement in her presence, a huntress sure to capture her prey.

"Very good, Annie." Emma's raspy voice exuded admiration. "All that from a scrap of plastic bag. Oh, that's very good. I'll have to use it someday, the torn piece of trash bag snagged in a lifeboat providing the only telltale trace of premeditated murder." She clapped her broad hands together, a huge diamond flashing. "Yet the scrap isn't definitive proof of a crime. Had there been a strand of Pamela's hair in the lifeboat, that would require the police to rethink their position. Instead, all we have is the remnant of a trash bag. . . . Sheer brilliance. Nothing to excite the police, only our canny investigator. Therefore Marigold—"

Annie gritted her teeth. That rapt attention was nothing more than Emma being a writer. The way Emma spoke the name of her septuagenarian sleuth— her voice brimming with blatant arrogance—drove Annie berserk. Annie wanted to shout, "She's a maddening character, and Emma, SHE ISN'T REAL." But

Annie knew without doubt that she'd rather come snout to snout with the alligator in the lagoon behind her house than confront the Grande Dame of the American Mystery.

Emma flicked Annie an amused glance, her square face almost crinkling into a smile.

Annie had a horrid sense Emma was reading her mind with the same ease with which she plotted her whodunits.

Emma folded her arms across her imposing chest. "—must pursue the investigation without assistance. The resolution, of course, demonstrates once again the ineptitude of Detective Inspector Hector Houlihan." Her canny blue eyes narrowed. "Marigold would perceive at once that Pamela was pushed. Just as you did." A decisive nod. The springy silver curls quivered.

Annie exploded. "Emma, I don't give a damn—" She jolted to a stop. Her eyes widened. "You believe me?"

"Of course." Emma's gaze was abstracted. "But I understand why no one else does. Have you ever considered a less likely candidate for attempted murder than Pamela Potts? Yet we can be assured that Pamela was the intended victim because of the ticket. Pamela was not a person to jump to conclusions. Or"—a raspy chuckle—"from a boat. Therefore she had reason to believe the ticket was provided by you. If that was a lie, it was deliberate, and the purpose was to hide the identity of the provider. When the result of Pamela's presence on the cruise was her near death, it is reasonable to assume—as you have and as Marigold would—that the generous gesture was a mask for murder. All right"— her tone was decisive—"Pamela's death is planned. Why?" Emma's eyes glowed. "Oh yes, I like it. Instead of the victim everyone loves to hate, we have a victim no one could possibly wish to kill. What are the classic motives?" She ticked them off, those silver nails flashing. "Passion. Pride. Greed. Hatred. Revenge. Fear. All presuppose an intensity of life that has entirely escaped dear Pamela. She has never had a love affair—"

Annie wanted to hold up a hand, stop the remorseless flow of words. But she was spellbound.

"—and a quarrel that caused enough offense to result in a plan for murder would surely have been public knowledge. Therefore we can dismiss pride as a motive. That leads us to greed." She shook her head. "Pamela has no money. We can, of course, check and see if she has a life insurance policy and, if so, the name of the beneficiary. But life insurance costs money. Pamela had no extra. Hatred? Who could hate inoffensive, boring Pamela? Revenge? Pamela's life is an open book. So"— her voice was as near a purr as Annie had ever heard in a human—"that brings us to fear. Why would anyone fear Pamela? Because—"

Annie leaned forward, scarcely daring to hope. But Emma sounded so certain, so confident.

The writer's eyes glittered with triumph. "—Pamela knows something."

Annie sagged back against the sofa. The plastic squeaked. What a disappointment. "Emma"—Annie tried not to sound pettish, knew she'd failed—"Pamela would immediately call Billy if she saw something illegal going on."

"Ah," Emma crowed with certainty and delight, "but she doesn't know that she knows."

"Wait a minute." Annie held up both hands. "If she knows, but doesn't know she knows, why would anybody care? To be specific, if she doesn't know she knows, there's no reason to silence her."

"But"—Emma's lips curved in pleasure—"the murderer foresees that Pamela is certain to realize the importance of some piece of information. Therefore, he—or she—has no choice. Pamela must go. Now . . ." Emma pressed silver-tipped fingers to her temples.

Annie watched with the same fascination she would accord a butterfly emerging from a chrysalis.

Emma's hands fell away. Her broad forceful face looked triumphant. In a rapid-fire, raspy monotone, she announced, "We will discover Pamela's schedule for the past week and the upcoming week. We will find out who she saw this past week and who she would be seeing. We will cross-check those names against the list of passengers from tonight's cruise. We will ascertain what activity on Pamela's part triggered the murderer's perception that information in her possession was of deadly importance."

Once again Annie sagged wearily against the sofa. "Oh sure, Emma. That's easier said than done. Talk about looking for needles in a haystack! My God, Pamela's all over the island doing good. No, our best hope is that she'll come to and be able to tell us what happened."

Emma pulled a cellophane packet of jelly beans from her pocket, ripped it open, held it out to Annie.

Annie took a half dozen in her palm, welcomed the swift surge of sweetness from a papaya jelly bean, ate a red one—hmm, cherry—and munched on two grape.

Emma plumped a half dozen in her mouth, chewed. Her words were indistinct. "The ticket benefactor struck Pamela from behind. She didn't see anybody. She won't remember getting hit. She may not remember being on the cruise. Head wounds"—Emma swallowed the rest of the candy and her voice became authoritative—"often result in short-term memory loss. Marigold never expects to learn anything from the victim of a head wound. Forget about Pamela. It's up to us." Her bright blue eyes swung to Annie. "Do you have the list of passengers?"

Annie pointed at her purse. "I haven't had a chance to look it over—"

A faint rendition of "Beer Barrel Polka" erupted.

Emma reached into her oversize carryall, pulled out her cell phone. The stanza, louder, sounded again. She punched on the phone. "Yes." She sat bolt upright, her face intent.

Annie leaned forward, wished she could hear.

"Good work, Henny. You called nine-one-one? Good. Keep the door blocked." A decisive nod. "Hold the fort. I'll get help."

Emma clicked off the cell, pushed up from the sofa. She took one step toward the main desk, frowned. The waiting room had that late-night feel of abandonment. Computer screens glowed a ghostly green beyond the counter. A paperback book lay spread open near a telephone. Annie recognized Eileen Dreyer's latest hospital thriller. Emma's gaze raked the area. "The attendant's gone."

Annie took a deep breath, tried to stay calm. "What's wrong?" Surely nothing bad had happened. The hospital was quiet as a grave. Oh, why had that simile come to mind? Quiet as a millpond . . . quiet as high noon in the desert . . . quiet as a cat sleeping in the sun . . .

"Trouble. I'll make sure help's on the way." Emma punched nine-one-one, barked into the phone. "Hospital ER, Emma Clyde speaking. An unauthorized intruder is attempting to gain access to the back entrance of the ER. Come immediately." She clicked off the phone, started for the desk. "Yo!" Her shout bellowed.

Annie had no intention of waiting for help from an attendant who might be snagging a nap in a quiet corner or washing his hands in the john or outside for a smoke. She pelted across the waiting room. What was it Emma had said? Through the swinging doors and down the main hall, turn right.

"Annie, hold up—" The swinging door cut off Emma's call. Annie took a deep breath. With the doors closed behind her, there was not a vestige of light. Her chest tightened. That was wrong, all wrong. The lights stayed on all night in hospital hallways. She could see nothing. She moved until her hand touched the wall to her right, swept it up and down, found a bank of switches. She flicked them and abruptly the long hallway was illuminated. She moved fast. At the cross hallway, she started to make the turn and stopped. Once again she faced darkness. She was suddenly frightened. She stared into gloom that exuded menace. Was this a true perception or was her uneasiness triggered by her awareness that the back door to the ER was somewhere ahead?

She listened. There might have been a scuffing sound. There might not have been. She felt a presence. "Who's there?" Her voice was sharp. There was no answer. She knew she shouldn't walk into that darkness. She knew it with certainty. Okay, okay. Where were these light switches? She moved to her right, once again searched a wall. Nothing. She tiptoed, hands outstretched, to the opposite wall, ran her fingers over the plaster, found switches. She flicked them. The lights behind her in the main hall went out. Annie's heart thudded. Quickly she turned those lights back on, found a second wall plate. This time she was in luck. Fluorescent lights slowly flared overhead. The tightness eased in Annie's chest. The hallway lay empty and still. She saw no one. Closed doors. Silence. At the far end of the hall, a chair sat next to a shut door.

Henny had been on guard at the back entrance to the ER. She would have found a chair, carried it there. Where was Henny? Why was it so deathly quiet?

Running lightly, Annie reached the door, turned the knob, pushed. It didn't budge. "Henny!"

Henny spoke from the other side of the door. "Is the coast clear?"

Annie looked up and down the hall, the blessedly empty hall. There was no danger now. If someone had crept through darkness, heading for the ER and a helpless Pamela, that person was long gone. "No one's here. Just me."

There was a fumbling at the bottom of the door. In an instant, the panel opened. Henny, her dark eyes bright and alert, held up car keys. "I jammed them under the door." She stepped out into the hall, looked toward the exit. "Whoever it was must have gotten away." She took a deep breath, pushed back a lock of silvered dark hair.

"Pamela." Annie was breathless. She started to step past Henny into the ER.

Henny caught her arm. "Wait. We better stay here. Emma's at the front, so we know no one can get in that way. I called nine-one-one, and Emma said she'd get help."

"She called nine-one-one, too." Help should arrive very soon. Annie looked at Henny. "What happened?"

"I was sitting here"—Henny gestured at the metal straight chair. "I'd brought a book with me." A quick smile. "Of course. Anyway, I was pretty absorbed, but I heard something, a"—she frowned in remembrance—"rattling sound." She gestured toward the exit.

"I looked that way. Then the lights went off. I didn't wait a minute. I jumped for the door, got inside. But it didn't have a lock! I shoved my car keys under the door—"

The exit door opened. "Police. Hands up." The shout was brusque and commanding. Lou Pirelli, one of Billy Cameron's men, burst into the hall, gun in hand, moving fast. Lou's dark hair was tousled. He wasn't in uniform. He'd pulled on a Braves top, faded jeans, and sneakers. When he saw them, he came out of his crouch. He moved swiftly toward them. His eyes scanned the hallway, and the gun in his hand never wavered. He gave them a swift nod of recognition but didn't speak as he moved past Henny to enter the ER area.

Annie started to follow, but Henny grabbed her arm. "We'd better stay here, let him check on Pamela."

As they waited, Annie paced. Surely Pamela was all right. . . . It seemed a long time, but it was only a few minutes later that heavy steps sounded in the main hallway and Billy Cameron came around the corner. He was in uniform, but his khaki shirt was crookedly tucked. He shoved his gun into its holster, stopped, and looked questioningly at Annie and Henny. "What's going on?"

"Pamela?" Annie's voice was thin, frightened.

"No problem." He gave an impatient shake of his head. "Nobody's been near her except ER personnel."

Lou Pirelli strode through the unmarked door, joined them in the hall.

Billy turned toward him. "Find anything, Lou?"

Lou clicked on the safety, lifted his floppy Braves jersey to slide the gun into a holster. "Nothing out of the ordinary. No one found loitering. After I checked on the patient, I took a look-see in the parking lot. Nobody was around." His tone was matter-of-fact, but he shot Henny and Annie a wondering glance.

"So Pamela's all right." Annie felt giddy with relief. "I guess the murderer—"

Billy shoved his hat to the back of his head. "Annie, I know you mean well. But I keep telling you, there's no reason to suspect Pamela's fall was anything other than an accident."

Henny lifted her hand, jangled the keys she'd wedged beneath the door. "There was a definite attempt to gain access to the ER." She lifted her head and looked regal despite the hour, the dark pouches under her eyes, and her purple warm-ups. "I was on guard to protect Pamela Potts." Her glance at Billy was determined. "Look at what's happened, Billy. We all know Pamela went overboard. Eyewitnesses report she was apparently unconscious as she fell. She was on board only because she received a ticket that she understood to be from Annie Darling. Annie provided no such ticket. Moreover, no one who knows Pamela believes she attempted suicide. So we're afraid she's in danger. That's why Emma Clyde was watching the ER entrance and I was here." Henny gestured toward the metal chair next to the door. "Somebody—"

Billy interrupted. "Plenty of people decide to kill themselves—walk out into the water and don't come back or put their heads in an oven or swig a dozen Valium with a shot of whisky—and you know what? Half the time, everybody says they were happy as larks, not a care in the world. Those kind of suicides don't talk about it. They don't leave notes. They do it. As for that ticket, somebody did her a good turn—"

"—and left no trace." Henny's tone was silky. "I talked to Ingrid Webb tonight after Pamela was hurt.

Ingrid told me all about the ticket Pamela found in her mailbox. Ingrid said Annie didn't send a ticket. That sounded strange to me. Pamela is always precise. Pamela, in fact, doesn't have the imagination of a rabbit. If Pamela said the ticket came from Annie, she had reason to believe that was true. Why would anyone leave a ticket with a message indicating Annie had sent it? The only possible reason would be to hide the source of the ticket. I thought about Pamela and the ticket all the way home. When Emma called and asked me to come help out at the hospital, I put on my warmups and went by Pamela's house on my way here. We know Pamela found an envelope with a free ticket in her mailbox. There must have been some kind of message inside indicating that it came from Annie—"

"Not so fast." Billy held up both hands like a traffic cop at noon on Saturday facing a bunch of tourist cars. "There could have been an envelope with nothing in it but the ticket and Pamela just guessed it came from Annie. What's got you so riled up? Are you saying you went in her house and didn't find a message?"

Henny spoke with deliberation. "I not only found no message, I found no envelope."

Lou cocked his head. "How'd you get in?"

Henny's face was suddenly sad. "The key was under the welcome mat on her front porch. That's how I got in, and that"—her voice was confident—"is how her attacker got in to retrieve the envelope."

Billy clasped his hands behind his back, rocked back on his heels. "She threw the envelope away."

Henny's dark eyes glinted. "I checked the wastebasket. And the garbage." A brief smile. "Pamela has very tidy garbage. She'd discarded an empty box of shredded wheat. The other trash was neatly layered above

the cereal box. No envelopes. That tells us that someone removed the envelope and any accompanying
message. The only possible reason to do so was to hide
the fact that Pamela was decoyed aboard the *Island
Packet*."

Billy frowned. "You figure all that because you
don't find one measly envelope? Look, the ticket came
in the envelope and she put the whole thing in her
purse. Her purse is at the bottom of the Sound. Hey,
that's easy. Anyway, I'm not worried about tickets or
envelopes. How come—"

The door leading to the ER examining rooms swung
open. Brisk steps clipped toward them. Emma's caftan
swirled. Her imperious blue eyes raked the group.
"How come everybody's standing here? Haven't you
found anybody?"

Billy wasn't cowed. His tired face was stubborn.
"We've looked. There's no evidence anybody's been
around here that doesn't have a right to be here. The
hospital, after all"—his irony was heavy—"is open to
the public."

Annie chimed in. "But the innocent public doesn't
turn off the lights."

"Seems to me"—Billy looked at Henny—"you
should have seen who turned them off." He pointed toward the main hall. "I can see the light switches from
here."

Henny pulled a paperback book out of the jacket of
her warm-ups, held it out. "I was reading. . . ."

As Henny described the sounds she'd heard, Annie
moved toward the exit, scanning the floor. She was a
few feet from the doors when she crouched. "Hey," she
called back to the knot near the ER door, "there are
broken oyster shells here. I'll bet that's what Henny

heard. Somebody"—she stood, pointed toward the other end of the hall—"threw the shells. Henny looked this way. That gave them time to dart into the hall and turn off the lights."

Lou sauntered down to join her. He nudged a piece of shell with the toe of his Reebok. "Could have stuck to somebody's shoe. Maybe some kid had a bunch in his pocket, dropped them."

Billy was dismissive. "Oyster shells don't tell us anything."

Annie hesitated. She almost picked up the pieces, but retrieving bits of shell wouldn't prove a thing. Probably the intruder had thrown half shells, which were heavy enough to fly through the air a good distance. When they landed, they broke apart. She picked up one remnant and hurried back to the doorway where they'd gathered. She held it out to Henny.

"Clever. I expect that's exactly what I heard. I looked that way and the lights went off." She looked soberly at Billy. "I felt that I was in danger."

Billy glanced at the paperback, which had a lurid cover showing a man waving a gun, and gave a tired grin. He pointed at the book. "Like you said. You were reading. Somebody came along and brushed against the lights. That's all that happened. Whoever it was heard you scrambling around and got scared and hightailed it out of here."

Henny stared at him and her gaze didn't falter. "When that ex-con was gunning for Frank," Henny said, recalling a threat faced by former Police Chief Frank Saulter, "and you were on guard that night, how did you feel?"

Billy's eyes were suddenly thoughtful. He cleared his throat. "I hear you. Okay, the lights went out. What happened?"

"I opened the door and stepped inside. There wasn't a lock." Her voice was tense. "So I jammed my car keys under the door."

"You didn't see anyone." He rubbed his cheek. "Did you hear anything out in the hall?"

"No. I'd guess the intruder had on sneakers. But the doorknob definitely moved. That's when I called nine-one-one and Emma on my cell phone." Henny gave a small, grim smile. "I spotted the fire extinguisher. If the door had opened . . ."

Billy gave her an admiring nod. "Good thinking, Henny. So"—his eyes narrowed as he looked toward the exit door—"somebody could have come. Yeah. It could be. But I got to say it doesn't seem likely. Anyway, we can take some precautions." He gestured toward Lou. "Stay the rest of the night, and tomorrow we'll decide if Pamela needs continued protection."

Annie could have hugged him. Billy was convinced tonight's alarm didn't amount to anything and he thought their cry of murder most foul was ridiculous, but he took his duties seriously.

Emma took charge. "Billy, I appreciate your offer, but I don't think that's necessary. I've already spoken to Dr. Burford and he's made arrangements for Pamela's protection."

Lou looked relieved at not having to spend the night in a hospital reclining chair.

Billy slowly nodded. "All right. Well"—he smothered a sudden yawn—"we'll check out everything tomorrow."

Annie almost spoke up. There were so many entrances and exits to the hospital. If Lou stayed, it would be one more protection for Pamela. Billy and Lou were heading toward the exit, their broad backs receding down the hallway. Annie's mouth was open, she was leaning forward, when Emma's hand clamped on her wrist. She shot a startled look at the author and saw a quick, firm head shake.

When the door closed on Billy and Lou, Annie demanded, "Why not have Lou spend the night?"

Emma was brisk and confident. "I've got Pamela covered. What really matters is convincing Billy she was a victim. I think I've got a way. I explained everything to Dr. Burford. He knows Pamela." Her eyes glinted. "It's odd how the way of the ungodly, as Simon Templar termed predators, can be foiled through chance, though some of us might call it fate. Dr. Burford says it is extremely unlikely that Pamela jumped. He once referred her to a specialist"—she paused for emphasis—"who treated her for a terror of heights, one so severe that she can't drive in the mountains. Dr. Burford has arranged for an orderly to spend the night in her room. She's been moved out of the ER, but the room number will not be given out, not to anyone under any circumstances. Only Dr. Burford and I know where she is. Tomorrow he'll talk to Billy."

Annie began to feel reassured. Here was Emma at her most redoubtable with the situation comfortably in hand. And if Pamela was out of the ER . . . "Emma, how is she?"

Emma was slow in answering. "Her breathing is good. There's an egg-shaped contusion behind her right ear." She moved her shoulders uncomfortably. "Nasty-looking. Purplish. The CAT scan didn't reveal intracranial bleeding, although there is always that possibility. Moreover"—her gaze was somber—"there's no way to tell if she suffered any permanent damage from near drowning or from the blow. She may wake up in a few minutes or hours or days. Or"—she took a breath—"she may never wake up. The prognosis is guardedly good." Emma smoothed back a straggling silver curl. "Henny, if you'll give Annie a ride home, I'll make a final check on Pamela. And"—Emma's blue eyes glittered—"map a campaign."

∿ *Four* ∾

HENNY'S OLD DODGE jolted to a stop in the driveway. The front porch light glowed deep yellow. More light spilled from the ground floor windows. "Looks like Max waited up."

As she slid out of the Dodge, Annie smiled at the welcoming lights, beacons of caring. Eager as she was to hurry inside, she took time to thank her old friend. She held the door open. "You were wonderful, Henny. As always."

Henny made a shoo-away gesture. "I'm not doing anything more than you and Emma. See you tomorrow."

"Tomorrow." Annie lifted a hand in farewell, clicked the door shut. Her spirits lifted as she hurried up the front walk, but she took a quick glance at the second floor. The upper windows were dark. She felt instant relief, thankful that Rachel was probably asleep. Annie didn't want to talk about Pudge and Sylvia and Cole. She had no answers for the hard and difficult tangle of love and loss and wanting and wishing. Max was her rock. She wished their kind of love for all the world. But to try to explain to Rachel that no matter how much we love someone, we can never decide the future for them was beyond Annie's capability tonight. Or tomorrow, for that matter.

Annie opened the front door to a blaze of lights in the entryway, the breakfast nook, and the kitchen, the cheerful rattle of crockery, and the scrumptious aroma of fresh cinnamon rolls and hot chocolate.

Max appeared in the kitchen doorway, one mitted hand holding a muffin tin. His quick glance swept her. The tension eased from his face. "Pamela's okay."

"So far, so good." Annie beamed at him. Lights, food, and a barefoot Max in a T-shirt and glen plaid boxer shorts changed her mood. Her fatigue evaporated.

Max put down the muffin tin. She dropped her purse on the kitchen counter. They moved together and she held tight to him, savored warmth and comfort. He gave her a hard squeeze, then held her at arm's length, his eyes admiring. "You do better justice to Nancy than Nancy did."

For an instant Annie was blank, and then she reached up, swept off the navy cloche, glanced down at her old-fashioned blue dress. "I'd forgotten all about Nancy Drew. Oh, Max, what a long night." Her lighthearted happiness when they'd boarded the mystery cruise seemed a lifetime ago. It had almost been a lifetime for Pamela.

They settled at the kitchen table. Annie took a huge bite of the just-out-of-the-oven roll made with freshly grated nutmeg, brown sugar, apple juice, plump raisins, and chopped pecans. Heavenly!

Dorothy L., excited by the postmidnight revelry, jumped onto the table, eying Annie's plate.

Annie made a halfhearted attempt to push her off the table.

Dorothy L. evaded her hand and scampered to Max. She ducked her head against his arm, purred.

Max stroked thick white fur. "Sweet girl. Good cat." His tone was just this side of a coo.

Annie wrinkled her nose. "You indulge that beast." But fair was fair, and Max often made the point that Annie was a slave to Agatha despite the black cat's tendency to bite the hand that petted. Dorothy L., he was fond of stressing, never bit. Annie decided the cinnamon rolls and hot chocolate were too divine to permit fussing about Dorothy L.'s presence on the table. With the innate perception peculiar to cats, the feline strolled back toward Annie. Annie took another bite, licked exquisite icing from one finger, then reached out and patted Dorothy L. Just one big happy family gathered around (and on) the kitchen table.

Peace, it was wonderful.

"Oh, Max." She reached out and grabbed his hand and it didn't matter that both of them had sticky fingers from the buns. "I'm so glad to be home. What a night. Listen—"

Max refilled their mugs with hot chocolate, tumbled miniature marshmallows onto the foam. As Annie talked faster and faster, she rose, pushed back her chair, and began to pace. Max slouched, taking occasional gulps from his mug, listened intently. He didn't say a word, but his face was skeptical.

Annie paused in midharangue about Billy's failure to recognize the significance of the missing envelope. "You don't get it?"

Max rubbed his knuckles against his bristly chin. Without replying, he got up, retrieved Annie's purse from the counter. He brought the brightly patterned canvas bag to the table and carefully eased out the contents: billfold, checkbook, coin purse, car keys, cell phone, crumpled Baby Ruth wrapper, small packet of Kleenex, lipstick, compact, eye shadow, four stamped envelopes ready to mail, two bank deposit slips, a grocery list on a note card, Selma Eichler's new paperback, a pen, two pencils, a road map, a receipt from Belk's . . . He held up a wedding invitation still in its envelope. He didn't say a word.

Annie gripped the back of the kitchen chair. Expressions fleeted across her face: chagrin, amusement, acknowledgment, determination. "Doesn't mean a thing. I put the envelope in my purse so I'd have the address at the store when I bought the gift. And okay, I'd forgotten it was there, ditto the candy wrapper, ditto the map. Ditto whatever. Yeah, I get your point. Pamela could have put the envelope in her purse. And I guess her purse is in the Sound. But"—she flung out a hand—"I never sent her a ticket. And if she hadn't gotten a ticket, she wouldn't have been on the cruise, and if she hadn't been on the cruise—"

"—she wouldn't have fallen in the water." He stacked their dishes, carried them to the sink, glanced at her. "Or been pushed overboard," he amended. "Okay. But you have to admit that everything you've told me has a reasonable explanation. The ticket may have been a perfectly innocent gift. She may simply, as Billy suggested, have assumed you sent it. She may have slipped, hit her head, and fallen from the boat. Tonight at the hospital, someone may have accidentally turned off the lights. Henny may be mistaken that the knob turned."

"The oyster shells?" Annie pulled out the chair, plopped in it.

"Like Billy said, some kid brought in a pocketful and dropped them. You know they're everywhere." He picked up the dishcloth, turned on the water.

Annie lifted her voice. "What did Henny hear?" She reached for her mug, finished the cocoa.

There was an odd tingling sound. They both looked at the cool air register.

Max grinned. "Something in the air-conditioning. Or some odd machine behind a closed door made some beeps. Who knows?" He began to rinse their dishes. "A funny noise and the lights went out. Guaranteed to hot up the imagination."

Annie popped up, brought her mug, bent to open the dishwasher. She picked up the rinsed dishes, slotted them in place. "So you think I should blow off the whole thing?"

Max reached for the dishwasher soap, filled the container. He clicked the dishwasher shut, punched the button. The soft whirr began. He looked at her, a slow smile curving his lips. "I've been wrong before. And it won't hurt to nose around, especially if there's nothing to it. I'll do what I can to help."

She flung herself into his arms, happy, grateful, relieved. Yes, she would have gone on by herself. But it was nice to know she wasn't alone. "Okay, first thing tomorrow—"

"Tomorrow. Yeah." There was an odd tone to his voice. "Well, there's something else you need to see to. First thing."

Annie stepped back, looked up into sympathetic eyes.

"I hate to worry you tonight." He caught her hand. "When I got home, there were a bunch of messages on voice mail, mostly people checking on Pamela. I wrote down the names and erased those calls. Except for Laurel's. And"—his brows drew down—"Pudge's."

Annie massaged one temple, then pushed the play button.

"Annie, my dear." Laurel's husky voice was a delicate mixture of solemnity and encouragement. "Remember that it is darkest before the dawn—"

Annie raised an eyebrow. So what else was new?

"—but it is precisely at that moment when one must think most creatively. As Aesop so cogently advised: Beware lest you lose the substance by grasping at the shadow." A pause. "My dear, look beyond."

As the message ended, Annie contrasted the trite beginning with the challenging ending. Shadow . . . Dammit, what was this creativity thing? It was time and time past to ignore Laurel. Yet . . . Annie sighed. Why did she have a feeling that something of utmost importance had been said? She demanded of Laurel's son, "Look beyond what?"

Max laughed. "I assume that's a rhetorical question." He inclined his head toward the phone. "Here's Pudge."

As she listened, Annie glanced toward a half dozen snapshots in clear plastic frames scattered on the counter. There were similar clusters of snapshots everywhere in their house, in a bookcase in the family room, atop the piano in the living room, on a butler's table in the entryway, on windowsills in the bedrooms, on the desk in the upstairs office, old pictures and new, family members and friends. The snapshot she now studied was a favorite, her father at the bookstore holding a Death on Demand mug, his broad face alight with a carefree smile, Agatha draped comfortably on his shoulder. Trust Pudge to charm her mercurial cat, just as he charmed everyone he met. She never saw a picture of Pudge without smiling, cherishing always his look of hopeful expectation, a man who was sure that this day, this moment, this place was going to be wonderful and special. Lately that hopeful look had been absent, the lines at the corners of his eyes and mouth deeper.

". . . sorry about the trouble tonight." His pleasant tenor voice sounded tired, strained. "I hope Pamela's okay. But accidents happen and you mustn't feel responsible. Let me know if there's anything I can do to help." A pause.

The pause went on so long, Annie looked questioningly at the recorder.

"Uh . . ." There was a sense of uncertainty. Pudge cleared his throat. "Annie, I wonder if you will do me a favor. I mean, when you have time. If you could"—a deep breath, then the words pelted her—"talk to Rachel, ask her to be nice to Cole. That's Cole Crandall, Sylvia's son. Oh hell, I don't know if it's fair to ask you. Or Rachel. But she's such a great kid. She likes everybody. Anyway, Annie, if you can help, it would mean the world to me. I'm feeling kind of down about the whole thing. I—oh, well. Let me know." The connection ended.

Annie slowly returned the receiver to its holder. She picked up two clear plastic frames. One held the picture of her father, the other a snapshot of a dark-haired girl looking up at a laughing Pudge, her thin face adoring. Rachel had added so much happiness to their home. She'd decided to stay with Annie and Max when Pudge moved to Annie's tree house. But it was Rachel who took the most pleasure in helping decorate the tree house. And Rachel always marked off the days until his return when Pudge was off island on one of his adventurous journeys. Oh my, oh my.

After the dishes were done and they'd crept silently up the stairs, careful not to awaken Rachel, and Annie lay against the warm, familiar curve of Max's body, she listened to the even cadence of his breath as he slept. She yearned for sleep, but her mind was beset by worry, her muscles too weary to relax. Tomorrow, what would she do tomorrow?

Rachel thudded down the stairs, backpack flapping. She skidded into the breakfast room, stared at the clock with wide eyes. She looked thinner than ever in her oversized clothes. A lacy blouse cascaded over denim pants that dragged on the floor, hiding all but the tips of her sneakers. "Oh golly."

Outside, a horn blared.

"Oops, there's Lisa. Got to go." She leaned over the breakfast table, grabbed a cinnamon roll. "Mmm."

Annie thrust a paper napkin at her. "Rachel, you haven't had breakfast. Breakfast is an essential—"

Rachel waggled the roll as she raced toward the front door. A slam and a bang and she was gone.

"—beginning to the day." Annie waved the napkin at Dorothy L., whose front paws were on the table. "Don't be a pig. You've already eaten."

Max placed a bowl on the table. "Papaya." He bent down, nuzzled the back of her neck, gave Dorothy L. a pat.

Annie's favorite fruit. And favorite husband. "Thank you." He knew her thanks included more than food. She dished up slices of the succulent fruit. "So Rachel's outta here. That was deliberate."

"Missing breakfast?" Max sliced a microwave-warmed cinnamon roll.

"Yep." Annie welcomed the distinctive taste of papaya. "She didn't want to talk to us about last night. Or the cruise. Or Pudge and Sylvia. Max, I don't know what to do."

Max's smile was sunny. "It will come to you." He

lifted the newspaper. "Looks like Tiger's on the prowl again. If I could hit a ball that far . . ."

Annie finished the fruit, reached for her coffee. It was all very well for Max to be confident that Annie could smooth over Rachel's roiled emotions. Annie wasn't at all certain she could. First she must talk to Pudge, figure out what he really wanted.

Sylvia.

Annie blinked. Her subconscious had whipped out the answer just like that. Maybe that simplified—

The brisk knock at the back door came without warning.

Annie looked at the clock. Ten after seven. Who would—?

The door opened. Emma Clyde stepped inside, her heavy face bleak and drawn. Her orange caftan swirled. A triple loop carnelian necklace hung almost to her waist. Her dress was the color of a summer sunrise, the beads the richest red of dawn, but her face looked like night.

Annie felt a sudden emptiness. She struggled for breath. She pushed back her chair, stumbled to her feet, hoping, yet in her heart knowing . . .

Emma marched inside, sandals slapping on the parquet floor. "Wanted to tell you myself. Dr. Burford called me. Pamela died shortly after six this morning. Intracranial bleeding. Pressure on the brain stem. There wasn't a thing that could be done."

Dead. Pamela dead.

Pamela with her smooth blond hair and wide-spaced, serious blue eyes and maddening, kind, bone-literal mind. Gone. Never to call Annie for another casserole. ("Annie, I know I can count on you for two.") Never to raise her hand with an earnest question at Bible study. ("Did the fish come out of the bottom of the basket or was a piece taken and instantly replaced?") Never to pronounce the obvious as if it were an astonishing revelation. ("Dogs are nicer than a lot of people." A thoughtful pause. "Except for pit bulls.")

Annie clasped her hands together, realized Emma's brisk voice hadn't stopped. ". . . taken care of everything. I've spoken to Father Patton. He told me she wanted to be cremated. That's all arranged for. The memorial service will be next Saturday. That will allow time for her cousin to come. The cousin lives in Australia. I told him I'll contact her."

Max got out a cup and saucer and a plate. "You know how sorry we are." His blue eyes were dark with sadness and with concern for Annie and Emma. He knew how much they laughed—had laughed—about Pamela, but he understood how much they genuinely cared for her. "Hey Emma, you look beat. Have some breakfast."

Emma plunged her hands into the pockets of her caftan, stood like a monolith near the table. "No thanks, Max. I'd better get home, make the other calls. I need to let Henny know we won't need the Altar Guild at the hospital."

"Dead." Annie felt as if the word, hard and painful, were lodged in her chest. "Have you talked to Billy?"

She nodded. "There will be an inquest." Emma's blue eyes were thoughtful. "I told him about Pamela's fear of heights. So he's thinking it must have been a freak accident. He plans to ask the *Gazette* to carry a statement encouraging anyone who saw her go overboard to contact the police. Like he said, he wants to find out as much as he can. But he told me he's now leaning toward asking for a verdict of accidental death."

"Accidental?" Annie's voice rose in protest.

Emma nodded. "I think," she said slowly, "that's a good thing."

Annie reached out a shaking hand. "Somebody pushed Pamela. She didn't jump."

"Oh, it was murder. No doubt in my mind. But having Billy mount a murder investigation wouldn't lead anywhere. He would follow the usual procedures, look for enemies. Pamela"—her voice was soft—"didn't have enemies." Emma glanced at the coffeepot. "God, I'm tired. That coffee looks good." She stepped to the counter, chose a bright yellow mug, filled it with steaming Colombian.

Max pulled out a chair at the table.

Emma sank onto the rattan seat, her caftan billowing. She waved ring-laden fingers at Annie. "Smooth your fur, sweetie. Sheathe your claws. Billy will still be looking around, trying to find out more facts. But a verdict of accidental death will be to our advantage. You see, we—or to be more specific, you—can go where Billy never could. Inside homes. To the bedsides of the sick. To the church." She drank the coffee, nodded in approval. Emma knew coffee.

Max's frown was instantaneous. "I don't think I like this."

Emma and Annie ignored him. Emma was nodding. "Pamela heeded the prayer"—and she quoted softly—
" 'and do all such good works as thou has prepared for us to walk in. . . .' " Her face drooped with sadness.

Annie swiped away a hot sheen of tears.

Emma looked steadily at Annie. "You can follow in her footsteps."

Max folded his arms, frowned. "Let's be clear on what we're talking about here."

Emma looped the strands of the necklace over stubby fingers. She looked old, her blocky, corrugated face ridged as weathered granite. "I may be wrong, but I am afraid. I am afraid someone may be at risk, someone Pamela was helping. We need to hurry, find out everyone she was seeing, try to discover what Pamela learned or saw or did that led to her death. I have to believe that Pamela was on the periphery of something deadly."

Annie understood. Ignore the shadow. Seek the substance. Look beyond.

"So you want Annie to nose into something that led to murder." Max's voice was angry. "Without having any idea where the danger lies."

"That's the beauty of an official verdict of accidental death." Emma drank the rest of the coffee, stood. "No one will know Annie is investigating. She will simply be taking Pamela's place as an emissary from the church."

"Where Pammie?"

The sound of Pamela's high sweet voice shocked Annie into immobility. She stood in the small foyer of Pamela's house and held the key she'd lifted from beneath the front mat in such a tight grip that her fingers hurt.

"Where Pammie?" The voice, uncannily like Pamela's, came from the living room.

Stiffly, Annie walked forward and looked through the archway into the small living room. The shades were drawn as Pamela must have left them when she departed for the mystery cruise. The room was dim and shadowy. A spectacular parrot in a silver cage, shiny feathers crimson and green and blue, flapped his wings. "Where Pammie? Johnnie want a cracker." The bright beady eyes glittered.

Annie started breathing again, smiled as she crossed to the cage.

The parrot tilted his bright head. "Have a happy, happy day."

The tone was so similar to Pamela's voice that Annie scrambled to remember what Laurel had told her about parrots. As the result of a memorable Mother's Day adventure, Laurel had gained possession of an African gray with a salty tongue and a rollicking laugh. According to Laurel, parrots often mimicked the tone of an owner's voice.

Annie stopped in front of the cage, looked into intelligent, curious eyes. There was water, but no food. "I'll find something for you." As she hurried into the kitchen, a loud thump sounded, a flap in the back door popped up, and a terrier bounded inside, barking.

Annie whirled to face the excited dog. She had never met him, but Pamela had proudly told her about the painting an island artist had done of the terrier. "Whistler?" Annie held down a hand and the dog frisked to her. A small cold black nose explored her fingers. "Whistler, I'm sorry." She knelt and petted the dog, who quivered with eagerness. A rough tongue lapped her chin.

Quickly Annie found dog food and refilled the water bowl. In the refrigerator, she found neatly chopped fruits and vegetables in small plastic containers. She carried some carrots and broccoli into the living room, refreshed the water in the cage. The parrot studied her. "Where Pammie?" The parrot began to eat.

Annie swallowed. "I'm Annie. I'm a friend of Pammie's." Pammie. That's what the bird called his owner. And he had learned it from Pamela.

Annie looked around the small living room. Lace doilies protected the arms of the sofa and chairs. All the pieces were old, the upholstery worn. The braided rug was clean but faded. Framed prints, not paintings, hung on the walls. A rose china antique clock sat on the mantel. There was the shabby aura of gentility underlain by poverty.

It was the first time Annie had ever been in Pamela's house. "Some friend," she said aloud.

Whistler pattered into the living room, stood close.

The parrot cocked his head. "Have a happy, happy day."

Annie blinked back tears. She knew the bird had heard the phrase many times from Pamela, smiling, her sweet voice a caress. Oh golly, something had to be done about the bird and the dog. But, almost as though she heard Emma's raspy voice—"We need to hurry"— she reminded herself that she wasn't here to feed pets, necessary though that might be.

Annie whirled, headed back to the kitchen. Whistler came right behind her. His nose poked against her leg as she stood in front of a big wall calender. She made a thumbs-up when she saw the spaces for each day filled with Pamela's neat printing.

Annie pulled a notebook out of her purse. The kitchen seemed untenanted and still, the only sounds the whirr of the old refrigerator and the tick of the wall clock. She avoided looking at the neatly folded tea towels and the flowered apron draped over a white kitchen chair.

Pamela had marked her schedule on the calendar, the times of appointments and the names of persons visited. Annie tapped her pen on the pad. Whatever Pamela saw or knew, whatever it was that set death on her trail, the triggering event most likely had occurred within a day or two of the cruise. The envelope with the cruise ticket was tucked in her mailbox on Sunday. That had the air of a hurried decision. Or possibly the free ticket was left at the last minute to prevent Pamela from speaking to Annie about the gift. Annie checked the names listed in Pamela's neat printing on Friday and Saturday. However, to be on the safe side, she wrote down everyone listed for the past week.

There was at least one overlap between the names on the calendar and the cruise passengers: Meg Heath. Annie shook her head. Wheelchair-bound Meg Heath could not have been involved in the attack on Pamela. Meg, in fact, could never have reached the second deck.

Annie sat at the kitchen table. Last night she'd taken up the sheets listing the passengers, tucked them in her purse. They were still there, a little crumpled but intact. She quickly checked the names taken from Pamela's calendar against the passenger list. There was only one match: Meg Heath. To be sure, she read the names again. . . .

From the living room came the forlorn cry, "Where Pammie?"

Whistler turned, clicked across the floor.

Annie slowly folded the passenger list, put the sheets in her purse along with the notebook. She got up, frowned at the calender—she'd had such high hopes—then returned to the living room.

"Have a happy, happy day." The parrot hopped from one stand to another.

She looked into coal-black eyes. She had to do something about the bird. She bent to smooth Whistler's fur.

The rose clock on the mantel chimed the hour. Already eight o'clock. Emma had imbued her with a sense of urgency, of time fleeting, of someone somewhere in danger. Emma was confident that Pamela had discovered something dangerous in her regular rounds and that all Annie had to do was insinuate herself into the lives of those Pamela had served.

Annie yanked her cell phone from her purse, punched Emma's number.

"Hello, Annie." Emma had Caller ID, of course. "What did you find?" The calm assumption that much had been discovered further demoralized Annie.

"If Meg Heath's wheelchair had wings, I guess we'd have our murderer." Annie knew she sounded sour. "Emma, this is a bust. I've checked out everyone Pamela saw last week—she noted everything on her wall calendar—but the only name that matches the cruise list is Meg Heath. Daily visits to Meg Heath at nine A.M. were the only constant. She went lots of places that aren't tied to a particular person. Ten o'clock Communion on Wednesday, Bible study on Thursday. She was on Altar Guild duty last week. I could possibly round up all those names, but this means your idea of Pamela seeing something at somebody's house doesn't work out. Maybe we're totally off on the wrong foot." And maybe, Annie realized with a sweet sense of release, no one else was in danger.

"Meg Heath." Emma's tone was thoughtful. "I saw her last night. I was impressed that she came. Heart trouble. And very little vision left. You know she has macular degeneration—"

Annie hadn't known.

"—and she can't read anymore. But she was there. With her entourage." There was the faintest emphasis on the final noun.

Annie was exasperated. She understood the import. No one in Meg Heath's group would have any difficulty climbing to the upper deck. Obviously Emma intended to cling to her theory. Which, Annie decided, was as full of holes as a rusted bucket.

Oblivious to—or disdainful of—Annie's resistant silence, Emma plowed ahead. "You said Pamela's been visiting Meg every weekday at nine in the morning."

Annie was impressed by Emma's quick recall. But she had to protest. "This is building a house out of straw." Everybody knew it took only a quick puff from the wolf to knock down a flimsy structure. Annie felt very wolflike. "There's no reason to fasten on Meg Heath and her family any more than anyone else Pamela saw this last week."

Emma was obdurate. "Meg was on the cruise. Pamela was at her house every day last week. And there's money there. I always like money as a motive." Her voice was clinical. "Start—"

A piercing whistle erupted. Whistler barked, a series of high shrill yaps.

Startled, Annie looked up at the parrot.

"Where Pammie?" The voice was so like Pamela's that Annie took a step back.

"Annie?" For once, cool unflappable Emma sounded perturbed. "What was that?"

"Pamela's parrot. He's gorgeous"—the parrot ruffled his feathers—"but I don't know what to do with him. I can't leave him here. I could call Laurel . . ." But she felt hesitant. What would two strange parrots say to each other? Do to each other? Of course, they lived in cages. Still, the possibility of acrimony—if parrots were anything like cats—seemed all too likely. Sad as Annie felt for the bereft bird, she knew full well that not even a cage would offer protection from either Agatha or Dorothy L. "But she has Long John Silver and I doubt strange parrots mix well. Pamela has a dog, too. A little terrier."

"Oh." A thoughtful pause. "I'll swing by. Pick up the bird and the dog."

"You will?" The minute the words were out, Annie realized the relief in her voice was too apparent. Perhaps even insulting.

A low chuckle. "You don't see me as Lady Bountiful?"

"Not at all." Annie knew she was talking too fast, which always got her in trouble. "I mean, of course, yes. You—" Oh damn, Emma didn't go out of her way for others. She was brilliant, clever, incredibly productive, but her world revolved around her work. If she was in the middle of a book, everything else went on hold. "I'll do it," she would say, "when the book is done." Annie was almost sure she'd just started a new book. Annie's face creased. "Aren't you just starting a book?" As soon as she spoke, she clapped a hand to her mouth.

The parrot said, "Oh dear, oh dear, oh dear, what have I done?"

Annie glared at him.

The spectacular bird gave a raucous laugh. Whistler jumped and barked, another series of excited yaps.

"On page twenty-two." Emma was amused. "I know. The books always come first. Almost always. But Pamela . . . Did you know I was once the recipient of her goodness?" Emma's usually crusty voice was reflective, gentle. "I had eye surgery last winter. Pamela came every morning and read the paper to me. With great deliberation and a tactful consideration of which stories I wished to hear and in what order. Lord, she can"—a pause, then careful amendment—"could

be maddening. I expect that's one service she—"
Emma's words broke off.

Annie clung to the cell phone. She had a sense of
rapid thought and calculation on Emma's part.

"Annie, my God, we may have found it. Meg has
macular degeneration. She can't read. I'll bet anything she depended upon Pamela to read the newspaper, letters, whatever." Emma's words came as
fast as boulders crashing down a hillside, picking up
speed and power, battering any obstacle in the way.
"Look at it! Pamela was there Friday. I'll bet you a
case of Jose Cuervo, Pamela read the Thursday paper—"

Annie nodded. The *Island Gazette* was an afternoon
paper Monday through Friday. The Sunday morning
edition went to press Saturday evening.

"—to Meg. Pamela wasn't there Saturday but there's
no Saturday edition of the *Gazette*. That means this
morning"—Emma's voice was excited—"she would
catch up on both the Friday and Sunday issues."

Annie thought again about straw houses. "Emma,
do you honestly think there was something published
in the *Gazette* that is so dangerous to someone that
they murdered Pamela to keep her from reading it
aloud to Meg Heath?"

"Something like that." Her tone was assured.

Annie wanted to say, "Come *on*." She didn't.

The parrot emitted a rude sound. Whistler erupted
with frantic yelps. Annie flapped a hand at them. She
hoped Emma hadn't heard or she might reconsider her
generous offer to come by for them.

Emma had. "Tell that bird to get his beak on straight
or I won't come and get him. And he's obviously a bad
influence on the dog. As for you, Annie, trust me on this

one. It's a quarter after eight. Pamela would have arrived at Meg's at nine o'clock. Get over there now."

Annie spoke aloud to her inner adult. "You are a grown woman. If you decide to make a detour on your way to Meg Heath's house, more power to you." Still, she felt a quiver of unease—why was she such a ninny when it came to dealing with Emma Clyde?—as she swung the wheel of the Volvo and headed up the familiar lonely road that ended at a weathered gray wooden house on stilts with a magnificent view of the marsh and Sound.

For starters, it made sense to talk to Henny. She knew practically everybody on the island, and Annie was sure she'd have an opinion about Meg Heath and her family. There wasn't time to call Max and ask him to scour the Net before Annie waltzed up to Meg's front door, pretending to be something she wasn't. And, okay, she had to be honest with herself. She was in no hurry to reach the Heath house. Annie didn't have a particle of faith in Emma's fanciful linkage of Pamela, the *Gazette,* and Meg Heath. Talk about a stretch . . .

Early morning sunlight speared through the live oak branches, dappling the gray road with an intricate mosaic of dark and light. Spanish moss hung still and straight. It was already warm, the sultry, heavy heat of August, the air thick with moisture, an ever-present reminder of coming storms. This was tropical storm season at best, hurricane season at worst.

Annie came around a curve and was relieved to see Henny's old black Dodge. She needed Henny's input. Maybe Henny could help persuade Emma that the Heath house was a dead end. They should focus on the night of the cruise, contact passengers, try to find those who had seen Pamela, perhaps noticed her in conversation. It made sense to start with Cole Crandall. He'd been stationed on the very deck from which Pamela had been pushed.

Annie parked next to the Dodge.

The front door opened. Henny backed out onto the deck, her yellow-and-white striped shoulder purse banging against her side. She was pulling a wheeled black suitcase. A carry-on bag hung from her other shoulder.

Annie hurried up the wooden steps. "Henny, where are you going?"

Henny closed the front door, checked to be sure the lock caught, turned. She looked fresh and summery in a yellow cotton tunic and slacks and white sandals. She brushed back a lock of silvered dark hair. "Oh, Annie, I have to be gone for a few days. I just got off the phone with Emma. It's so awful about Pamela."

They came together in a swift embrace.

Henny patted Annie's shoulder as they stepped apart. Her dark eyes were sad. "I wish I could stay and help. I have a friend off island who's just out of the hospital and needs some care. I got the call this morning."

"I understand." Annie picked up the black suitcase, carried it down the steps.

"Thanks, Annie." Henny was right behind her, her car keys jingling. But there was an odd defensive tone in her voice.

Annie tried not to let her disappointment show. Obviously, Henny felt bad to be leaving. Annie managed a quick smile. "I'm glad I caught you before you left." She waited as Henny unlocked the Dodge trunk, then swung the suitcase inside. "Do you know Meg Heath?"

"Sure. We've worked on a lot of projects together.

But she's been sick for about a year." Henny gave her a sharp look. "Is that where Pamela's been helping out?"

"Yes. I'm on my way there." Annie wished she didn't have a nervous feeling she should be there right this minute. What difference could a quarter hour make? "Apparently she has macular degeneration—"

Henny was nodding.

"—and Emma has this crazy idea that there's something in the *Gazette* that somebody didn't want Meg to know about."

Henny's eyes glinted. She patted the side of her carry-on bag. "I've got Sunday's paper with me. I'll look it over carefully. As for Meg Heath, I like her. Wealthy widow. A bit different from most. She's had an adventurous life, lived in England for a long time, had a house in Majorca. She was a model when she was young. She's been married several times. As I heard it, she and one husband had an old yacht they refurbished and sailed around the Mediterranean for a year or so, taking passengers and cargo. But it was her last husband who had all the money. They came here when he retired, built a fabulous home. Right on the ocean. It's an amazing house. Meg was active in a lot of charities until she got sick. She's smart, funny, strong-willed. Last night she was having a grand time even though she looked like death warmed over, white as alabaster." Henny's dark eyes gleamed. "She loved the mystery play. She had lots of questions for the actors. Good questions." Henny slid behind the wheel, rolled down the window to look up at Annie. She frowned. "Speaking of questions, what have you got in mind, Annie?"

Annie smoothed hair blown every which way by the on-shore breeze. "I don't have anything in mind. Emma told me to go to the Heath house and worm my way in as a substitute for Pamela. I'll try to find out what she and Meg talked about on Friday and I'll offer to read the *Gazette* and see if anything gets a big reaction from Meg. And I need to find out about her, as Emma termed it, *entourage*."

"Oh." Henny's answer was quick. "I saw them. They didn't look like they were having a lot of fun. Her daughter, Jenna, had her usual I'm-too-good-for-all-the-peasants-around-me attitude. Meg finds her boring. Her son, Jason, is a good-looking playboy who doesn't have a clue that men are supposed to work." Henny's tone was dry. "Meg adores him. And of course, Meg's secretary, Claudette Taylor. She's rather retiring, but I don't think she misses anything. I got to know her on the spring festival committee. I don't know if it will come to it, but if you need to know what's going on in that house, talk to Claudette."

Dust puffed from the oyster shells crunching beneath the wheels. The old live oaks on either side of the road met overhead to create a dim and ghostly tunnel. Annie braked as a doe and her fawn bolted across the curving road and plunged into the shadowy maritime forest. She eased the car forward, came around a curve. Her eyes widened. The house was like nothing she'd ever seen before, masses of windows in a two-story white steel framework high on metal supports. The sand dunes and sea were clearly visible through the open spaces. The rooms—actually modular bays suspended in space—were open to view, the rattan and white furnishings as indigenous as sea oats, except for one corner where the blinds had yet to be opened to the day and the sun and sea.

The dread Annie had felt in coming vanished, replaced by anticipation. Annie admired Meg Heath, a customer with charm and verve and taste, but she didn't know her well. Any woman who shared sky and sea and sand on an equal plane with gulls and pelicans was worth knowing well. The innovative house was a sure indicator of imagination and insight.

Near the front entrance—a corkscrew stairway to the suspended first floor—a bronze arrow inscribed Parking pointed to a line of palms. Annie turned left, found a parking area large enough for a half dozen cars hidden behind a line of pine trees. A white Mercedes and a black Camry were the only cars there. Annie parked next to the Camry.

She hurried across the oyster shell drive to the stairway. She was reaching for the bell pull when the wail of a siren sounded, coming nearer and nearer, louder and louder.

Siren shrilling, red lights flashing, an ambulance swung into the drive and headed straight for her.

∿ *Five* ∿

THE AMBULANCE ROCKED to a stop next to the circular staircase. The med techs climbed out, moving fast, a sharp-featured, broad-shouldered woman and a pink-faced giant with a mop of frizzy purple hair drawn back in a puffy ponytail.

The woman strode quickly to Annie. She poked glasses higher on a beaked nose, stared with cold green eyes. "Which way?" The big young man carried a square black case. Silver rings on one ear glinted in the sunlight.

Before Annie could answer, footsteps clattered above them on the metal platform outside the front door. "Up here. Hurry." The call was sharp and anxious.

Annie lifted her gaze.

Claudette Taylor bent over the railing. Ginger hair streamed onto the shoulders of a blue-and-white-striped seersucker robe. She flapped a hand, urging speed.

The techs brushed past Annie, started up the curving staircase.

Annie hesitated only for a moment, then followed. When she reached the doorway, she watched the EMTs follow Claudette up an interior flight of stairs. Stepping

into the foyer, she felt disoriented by a rapid sweep of
impressions, much like the dizzying quick cuts of a
television commercial. She looked in amazement at
metal conjunctions that created glass-walled rooms that
seemed to float within the boundaries of the house.
Splashes of orange, vermillion, and jade from paintings
and ceramics emphasized the bone white of the furnishings. A frightened face peered out from a shiny
chrome-and-white kitchen. Yet the fairy-tale house was
overshadowed by the dominating sweep of ocean, visible from every vantage point.

Annie blinked, fastened her gaze on Claudette. Her
plump face dazed, the secretary stood near the open
doorway to the only room in the house where bamboo
shades hung straight and still, shutting out the morning
sun. One hand clung to the lapel of her dressing gown.
"I found her. . . ." Her voice trailed away. She glanced
down at her robe. "I hadn't dressed yet."

Annie climbed the broad metal steps. She reached
the next floor and looked past Claudette into a huge
area, a bedroom and beyond it a sitting room. The furnishings and appointments were dazzling white here
too, the chest, the wardrobe, the nightstand, even the
love seat, white as brilliant as a seashell in the sunlight,
spellbinding and dramatic. The bed, too, was white except for the crimson of Meg Heath's nightgown. In
death Meg Heath was quite lovely, her face smooth,
untroubled, youthful, her dark hair flared against the
silk pillowcase.

The broad-shouldered tech bending near the bed
slowly straightened. She turned. Her face impassive,
she gazed at Claudette. "She's been dead for some time.
You just found her?"

"Yes." The secretary's voice was faint.

The tech pulled a small notebook from her pocket, flipped it open, wrote. She glanced at her watch, wrote again, looked toward Claudette. "Name?" She jerked her head toward the bed.

"Meg. That is"—a quick glance toward the bed, then away—"Margaret Heath. I'm Claudette Taylor."

"Next of kin?" The question was swift.

Claudette clasped her hands together. "No. I was her secretary. She has a son and daughter. I'll have to call them."

The tech pointed the pencil toward the bed. "Has she"—a glance at the notebook—"has Ms. Heath been sick?"

"Yes. But we didn't expect—" Claudette broke off, took a deep breath. "Heart trouble. She's been failing for almost a year. But I never thought anything was wrong this morning. She often doesn't—didn't come down for breakfast. I thought"—the secretary pushed back a strand of ginger hair—"she might still be resting. She was up late last night. We all were." She gestured at her robe. "I overslept. But she seemed to be fine when we said goodnight. I can't believe she's gone." A deep, steadying breath. "Shall I call the doctor?"

The self-possessed tech was firm. "We'll contact the doctor. We can't move the body without the doctor's permission. Who was her physician?"

Claudette seemed relieved to have a specific task. "Dr. Morris. Kay Morris. I can get the number."

Annie played tennis with Kay Morris, who moved quickly, on court and off. She always hit the ball where her opponents weren't—hard. She talked fast, was impatient and imperious.

"I got that number." The tech whipped out a cell phone, punched numbers.

Claudette folded her arms tightly across her robe. Her eyes moved from the tech back to the bed. Her face was blank with shock, but her gaze was somber, almost cold.

Annie wondered at that measuring look. It certainly didn't indicate sorrow. There was a hardness, an implacability in that level stare. And perhaps a hint of dislike?

Claudette held to the tie of her robe, pleated it in nervous fingers. "I must call Jenna and Jason." Her voice was brusque. "I'll get a phone." She turned, saw Annie. "Annie?" She was startled.

Annie stepped forward. "I came to take Pamela's place. I knew Meg was expecting her. I don't know if you've heard, but Pamela died this morning." Annie heard the thinness in her voice. It was hard to say the words, would be hard for a long time. "She never regained consciousness after her fall."

In the background, the tech spoke loudly. "I need to talk to the doctor in person. We got a dead patient of hers and we got to know what to do."

Claudette Taylor's lips parted. "Pamela's dead? Oh, that's dreadful. Meg will—" She swallowed hard. "I don't know what I'm saying. Meg's gone. And Pamela, too. I can't believe it."

Annie reached out, took cold, trembling hands in a tight grasp. "I'm so sorry. What can I do to help?"

Claudette's look was grateful. "It would be a wonderful help if you'd stay here while I try to find Jenna and Jason. I don't think we should leave Meg."

Annie squeezed Claudette's hands, gently released them, took a step nearer the bedroom. "I'll be glad to stay. I'll do whatever I can."

The tech's deep voice was matter-of-fact. ". . . looks like natural causes . . ."

Annie didn't believe it for a minute. Not on the heels of Pamela's murder.

Claudette swung away, muttering to herself. "Jenna . . . and Jason . . . Father Patton." Her shoes clattered on the metal stair treads.

Annie stepped into Meg's room. She took her time, surveying the long room, a combination of bedroom, study, and living area. Nothing seemed out of order, the body in repose so similar to sleep. There was nothing to suggest that Meg Heath's death was anything other than natural. The big young tech stood with his arms folded, face incurious, the unopened case on the floor beside him. The other tech tucked the phone between cheek and shoulder, made notes on her pad. "Yes, ma'am. Congestive heart failure? Yes, ma'am. If you will sign the death certificate, we'll transport the body to the mortuary."

Annie lifted a hand in protest. The mortuary. That meant the funeral home. She took two quick steps, stopped in front of the startled EMT. "Wait." If the body went to the funeral home, was embalmed, any trace of crime might be forever lost.

The tech frowned.

Annie held out her hand for the phone. "I need to speak with Dr. Morris." Annie's thoughts raced. There had to be an autopsy. But if she spoke out, she was destroying Emma's plan of Annie working quietly in the background, merging into Pamela's world of service. Claudette Taylor hadn't questioned Annie's arrival. She would be glad of help this morning and most likely in the days to come. When death comes, there are so many calls to make, so much to be done, the funeral to arrange, friends to notify, food to order. The ordered ritual of mourning gives peace to the living and matters not at all to the dead. No one knew that Annie had come this morning in hopes that Meg Heath would help solve the mystery of Pamela's murder.

The tech held tight to the phone. "What's the deal? Who're you?"

Annie glanced down at Meg's quite beautiful face, lovely but distant, robbed of the ineffable essence of life. Annie made up her mind. "I have information about the deceased that the doctor needs to know." Annie stood no more than a foot from the bed and its peaceful burden.

The tech frowned, cleared her throat, shrugged. "Dr. Morris? Sorry. Some lady wants to talk to you." She relinquished the phone to Annie.

Annie took a deep breath, striving for calm. "Kay, Annie Darling here."

"Yes?" Kay was always crisp. "I've released the body. The family can make its arrangements." She didn't ask why or how Annie was on the line. In Kay's world there were those who served and those who ordered and there was no confusion in her mind about her own role.

Annie knew that Kay's mind was already disengaging from Meg Heath. Meg was over and done with and there were patients to see, hospital rounds to make.

"Kay, there has to be an autopsy." The minute the words were out, Annie felt startled resistance laced with anger on the other end of the line.

"Excuse me." Kay's tone was icy. "When did you start practicing medicine? Meg is a longtime patient. She suffered from congestive—"

Annie interrupted. "I know that. An autopsy has nothing to do with you or with her illness. Please hear me out. I will be contacting Dr. Burford"—Kay Morris knew full well that Dr. Burford was the medical examiner for the island—"to request an autopsy because there is a possibility that Meg was killed by the same person who murdered Pamela Potts. I don't know if you are aware that Pamela was pushed overboard from the *Island Packet* last night. Pamela died this morning." Annie knew Pamela's death was being treated as an accident. Billy Cameron would not be pleased when he learned of this conversation. "I'm asking you to talk to Dr. Burford." Emma said Dr. Burford agreed that Pamela had been pushed. Dr. Burford knew Pamela would never cross over the railing, stand on the outside portion of the deck high above the water.

"Is there evidence of trauma?" Kay demanded, her voice sharp.

Annie looked at the beautiful woman who might simply have been asleep she looked so natural. "There are no wounds. I'd think a narcotic or poison of some sort."

"Is that what you'd think?" The sarcasm was evident. "So you've shown up and without any basis for inserting yourself in this affair, you are pronouncing Meg's death to be murder. Nonsense."

"Pamela was pushed overboard last night. Meg Heath was on the cruise. Meg died in her sleep." Annie was stubborn and beginning to get angry. "All I'm asking you to do is talk to Dr. Burford. He knows the circumstances and he—"

"I have no intention of talking to him. You initiated this situation. You talk to him. And"—each word dropped like a stone—"you talk to the family." The connection ended.

Annie held on to the cell phone. Damn Kay. But there were ways of dealing with lack of cooperation. "Thank you, Kay." She spoke quite pleasantly into silence. "Very well. I'm glad you agree. I will instruct the ambulance crew to deliver the body to the hospital, attention Dr. Burford." She clicked off the cell phone, returned it to the waiting tech.

The tech slipped the phone into her pocket along with the notebook. "To the hospital. Attention Dr. Burford?"

Annie nodded. "Attention Dr. Burford."

As the techs moved toward the bed, Annie walked out of the bedroom. She stood on the landing by the steps. Her hands were sweaty as she punched the number of Confidential Commissions.

"Hi, Annie." Max sounded genial. "You at Pamela's?"

Pamela Potts's tidy house with the sweet-voiced parrot and wet-nosed Whistler seemed eons ago. By now Emma had probably been by and picked up the pets.

"I'm at Meg Heath's house. That's where Pamela's been coming the last few weeks. Max"—a deep breath, but her voice was steady—"Meg's dead, too. Here's what I've done. . . ."

He listened without interrupting. It gave her strength and courage to picture him in his office. Only Max with his savoir faire would be at ease behind the dramatic Renaissance desk that had once served as a refectory table in a monastery. His lean, muscular body ensconced in a supercomfortable red leather chair, blond hair gleaming in the light from his desk lamp, tanned hand making swift, cogent notes, he was Tommy Beresford to her Tuppence, imperturbable, debonair, and beloved.

As she finished, he said briskly, "Here are Dr. Burford's numbers, home, office, hospital, cell. I'll get busy on the rest. Let's meet at Parotti's for lunch. Twelve-thirty."

As the connection ended, the techs eased the gurney with its shrouded burden past her. Annie followed them, stopping at the top of the stairs. She looked past the crew. Claudette waited in the hallway. She turned, opened the front door.

Annie was startled by the secretary's transformation. In that brief time, Claudette had dressed. Her hair was drawn into a chignon. A single-strand pearl necklace graced her black linen dress. She looked somber but well in control of herself.

Tires squealed in the front drive.

Annie wondered who was arriving. Had Claudette been able to reach the son and daughter? In a moment, the ambulance would depart for the hospital. She felt as if she stood beneath a boulder poised to drop. She'd better find Dr. Burford before she did anything else. She decided to try his cell phone first.

The call was answered on the second ring. "Burford." He was always brusque. White-haired, bulldog-faced, stocky, he wore stained suits with frayed cuffs. He'd spent a lifetime fighting illness. His patients knew he was with them from the start to the end. He hated death. He especially hated wrongful death.

Annie talked fast. "Dr. Burford, Meg Heath is dead. Pamela Potts was coming to see her every morning, reading the paper to her. First Pamela is killed. Then Meg Heath dies in her sleep. What if she was murdered, too? I talked to her doctor—"

"I already got an earful." His voice was heavy. "I told Kay—"

Annie was startled. Kay had changed her mind, gotten in touch with Dr. Burford. Was Kay trying to forestall an autopsy?

"—it's better to be safe than sorry. She wasn't pleased. But when I pressed her, she admitted Meg's death was unexpected, though it was quite possible she died of heart failure. I got a list of Meg's medications. I'll see what I can find out. There are some quick tests. If that doesn't turn up anything, we'll send the body to Charleston for a full-scale autopsy. That would take time to get results."

The connection ended.

Annie didn't care. The first hurdle was past. But now she had to face the family of the dead woman. Certainly Kay Morris would make no secret of the fact that it was Annie who had demanded an autopsy.

At the front door, Claudette reached out to take the hands of slender, dark-haired Jenna Carmody, Meg's daughter. Jenna and Claudette drew back as the EMTs reached the foyer. Jenna clung to Claudette, watched the passage of the gurney with a shudder, her face pale, her eyes huge and dark. Jenna looked as if she'd thrown on whatever clothes were at hand, a fuchsia sweater stained with paint, black slacks with a snagged knee.

Claudette was somber. "Jenna, I'm dreadfully sorry. Come inside." She gently tugged, pulling Jenna inside, and shut the door but not before Annie saw the techs start the awkward descent down the twisting staircase.

Jenna stood with one hand pressed against the marble top of a hall table. She waited, face sharp and still, until the rumble of a motor signaled the departure of the ambulance. She shivered, looked at Claudette. "Mother . . ." She shook her head. "She was all right last night. What happened to her?"

Claudette was slow in answering. "She didn't wake up. It must have been her heart. We knew it was coming."

"I guess so." Jenna's voice was faint. "But"—she lifted her hands—"what do we do now?"

Claudette was abruptly the efficient secretary. "I'll call the funeral home, but I expect you and Jason will want to choose the casket and make the arrangements."

"Arrangements . . ." Jenna's voice was dull. "Yes. We'll have to do that. And talk to Father Patton."

"I left Jason a message." Claudette looked troubled. "I didn't tell him Meg was gone. I told him we had an emergency and he should come at once."

"Jason." His sister's voice was disapproving. "He never gets up this early. He probably has the ringer turned off. I'll go over there, get him up. He damn well can help." There was no hint of sisterly love. Or support. Or, for that matter, any hint of grief. Jenna's eyes were dry. She was pale. There was shock, but not the bone-deep grief that grapples with loss of love. She lifted a thin hand, massaged one temple. "Casket. What a hideous word. I can't imagine Meg . . ." She shuddered.

Annie scolded herself. People show grief differently. Jenna was coping in her own way. Annie came quietly down the steps.

"It's her own fault." Jenna hunched her shoulders and her face twisted in a scowl. "She got too excited. She was such a romantic fool."

Annie stopped midway down the stairs.

"That doesn't matter now." Claudette's tone was sharp. "Don't think about it." The secretary looked up. Her expression was abruptly guarded. "Annie, please join us. Do you know Jenna?"

"Yes, we've met." Annie hurried down the steps. "I'm sorry about your mother." Annie reached the foyer. She would have given a kingdom to be elsewhere. She'd set in motion actions that would affect the lives of everyone connected to Meg Heath. She looked at Meg's secretary and her daughter. They'd borne a great shock and now they must bear another. It was time and past to tell what she'd done. "I spoke to the island's medical examiner. . . ."

Max Darling looked across his mahogany desk at Annie's photograph. He loved the picture, Annie with her flyaway blond hair and steady gray eyes and laughing face. "I don't know, babe," he murmured. This time Annie might have kicked a stone that would generate a landslide. If the autopsy showed death by natural causes, Annie was in big trouble.

Max knew his Annie. She would never agree that Pamela's death was anything other than murder, no matter what the result of the autopsy on Meg Heath. Even if Meg's death resulted from heart failure, Annie believed that Pamela had been murdered and that her murder was linked to her visits with Meg. He lounged in the sensuous comfort of the leather chair, but his eyes never left the photograph. Annie was always impetuous, sometimes reckless, often bullheaded. But, his eyes narrowed, she was intuitive.

And he agreed that it was double damn strange for the parishioner most recently visited by Pamela to die before anyone could ask what transpired the last time she and Pamela were together. Sure, it could be coincidence. Everything that had happened was capable of an innocent explanation. But taken all together, the circumstances suggested sinister possibilities.

Max sat up straight, yanked the legal pad close, began to write:

Sequence of Events

1. Pamela Potts visited Meg Heath every weekday and very likely read the previous day's newspaper to her.

2. Pamela's calendar indicated she was at the Heath residence Friday morning.

3. Pamela found a free ticket to the mystery cruise in her mailbox on Sunday afternoon. Pamela believed the ticket to be a gift from Annie.

4. Pamela fell (was pushed?) from the boat at approximately 10:40 P.M. Sunday. Emma Clyde reported that Pamela died early Monday morning at the hospital as a result of her injuries.

5. Meg Heath's body was discovered by her secretary shortly after 9 A.M. Monday.

Max softly hummed Woody Guthrie's "This Land Is Your Land," which Annie would have recognized as a sign of rapid calculation. He started a new page:

Facts to Discover

1. What happened between Friday morning and Sunday afternoon to make Pamela's death necessary?

2. Was Meg Heath likely to confide in someone as prim and proper as Pamela Potts?

3. Meg Heath was a very rich woman. Who inherits?

The phone rang. Max glanced at Caller ID. He yanked up the phone. "Hi, Ma."

"Maxwell, dear"—his mother's throaty voice always made him smile—"I understand dear Annie is once again violently tilting at windmills. I do urge—"

He raised an eyebrow. Surely Laurel wasn't already aware of Meg Heath's death and Annie's intervention.

"—an emphasis upon creative synthesis. I am shocked by Meg's death and so grateful Annie was there to prevent a miscarriage of justice—"

Max mentally tipped a top hat to his mother. He had no idea how she knew, but obviously her sources were impeccable.

"—although Emma—"

Aha! as Jan Karon's Father Tim often exclaimed. All was now clear. Max doodled on his pad the blunt head of a shark with many teeth. A cell phone was pressed against the shark's head. A dotted line snaked through space to a cell phone draped with a stethoscope.

"—is quite regretful that there can now be no possibility of working in the background without the murderer's knowledge. Dear Annie, so forthright."

There was a silence while she—and presumably he—acknowledged dear Annie's unfortunate proclivity for forthrightness.

Max felt compelled to offer a defense. "Ma, she had to speak up. They were going to"—he paused, decided *cart* was not a graceful verb—"uh, take the body to the funeral home."

"It would have been possible"—a gentle chiding laugh—"for the dear girl to privately contact Dr. Burford. However, be that as it may, we all must deal with the present situation"—her husky voice fell an octave—"a murderer en garde. Possibly poised to strike out at a pursuer."

Max had a quick vision of a masked figure flailing a sword, a long, sharp, dangerous sword, at Annie. Not a pretty picture. He frowned.

"Maxwell"—the reassuring voice flowed over the line quick as balm applied to a burn—"we shall defend our Dear Child. Now, she will, of course, in her direct way seek facts." Laurel's tone dismissed facts as superfluous, unimportant, the small change of the petit bourgeois. "I urge creativity. If, as appears possible, dear Pamela and dear Meg were both victims, it seems clear the reason for the crime must have sprung from Meg's life. Pamela's placid existence was an open book. Meg's unfettered exuberance, however, affords scope for inquiry. Therefore it is of the essence to understand Meg Heath. That, my dear Maxwell, is our charge. As Demosthenes observed: Though a man escape every other danger, he can never wholly escape those who do not want such a person as he to exist." A reflective pause. Then the honey-smooth voice observed lightly, "And sometimes, ah well, a man can speak better to a man. I've heard that Meg once was very close to a charming fellow named Rodney St. Clair. A writer of sorts." Another pause suggested myriad possible pursuits enjoyed by Mr. St. Clair. "Quite attractive to women. I understand he lives in Majorca. I suggest you have a chat with him. Apparently he and Meg were boon companions at one time. Meantime I shall seek visions of Meg, with the verve of a naturalist observing butterflies. Oh, the glory of monarchs and zebras, sulphurs and queens. . . . Ta ta."

Max slowly replaced the receiver. He had that old familiar feeling often engendered by contact with his mother, as if he'd stepped into a spiderweb and was enmeshed in silken strands. But, with almost the inevitability of automatic writing, he added to his list:

4. Who was Meg Heath?

He swung about to face his computer, reached for the mouse, chose a search engine.

*   *   *

Annie heard her own voice, but the words sounded hollow even to her. ". . . so we're sure"—Annie was sure—"Pamela was murdered. For Meg to die before anyone could ask her what she and Pamela did on Friday makes her death highly suspicious."

Two hostile and angry women stared at her. Red stained Jenna's pale cheeks. Claudette's hand clung tightly to her pearl necklace.

Annie wasn't surprised that her accusations of murder—Pamela pushed overboard, Meg a victim of some kind of drug or poison—produced shock and resentment.

Jenna twirled a silver bracelet on one wrist. "Nobody said anything last night about Pamela being pushed overboard. And even if somebody did push Pamela, what would it have to do with Mother?"

Annie turned to Claudette. "Pamela came here every morning. Did she read the *Gazette* to Meg?"

Claudette slowly nodded. "Yes. What difference does that make?"

"Perhaps there was something in the Sunday paper that someone was determined to keep from Meg." Annie wished she had Emma Clyde here to explain her theory. It sounded so unlikely that she rushed ahead. "Or perhaps Meg had told Pamela something. . . ." She trailed off.

Jenna and Claudette looked at Annie with similar expressions. Their faces didn't hold contempt or dismissal, they held sudden knowledge.

Annie felt the same thrill a treasure hunter experiences when a lump beneath the sand is unearthed to reveal the dark gold of a Spanish doubloon. That instant of comprehension was hidden abruptly behind carefully bland expressions. But Annie knew what she'd seen.

"Something happened to Meg this weekend." Annie's voice was confident now. She knew she'd stumbled on the truth, a truth these women knew.

Silence held for an instant too long, then Jenna tossed her dark hair. "I'll tell you what happened. She went on that stupid mystery cruise and overdid. She got too excited."

Once again there was a ring of truth. Something had excited Meg, but Annie knew it wasn't the mystery cruise. Jenna looked at Claudette, a wordless glance that held a meaning Annie couldn't fathom.

"Yes, she got too excited." Jenna spoke loudly. "That's what happened. That's all that happened." She glared at Annie. "She died because she had a weak heart, and you're here trying to make it a mystery. That's your business, isn't it? But you aren't going to capitalize on Mother's death. I won't let it happen." For an instant, her face was warped by sheer misery. "Mother would hate it."

Annie didn't back down. She doubted she'd be able to convince Billy that these women knew something important about Meg's last weekend, but she was certain she was on the right track. "Pamela and your mother. Their deaths have to be linked."

"Meg had congestive heart failure." Claudette was peremptory.

"I know. But don't you both want to be certain that's why she died?" Annie looked from Claudette to Jenna.

Jenna's face was stony. "Of course that's why."

Claudette half turned to look up the stairs toward the room where Meg had lived and died. There was an odd, considering expression on her face.

Jenna's breath came in quick-drawn gasps. "I'll call the hospital. I'll stop this." She swung away, her shoes clattering against the metal, taking fast steps, heading up the stairs.

Claudette's voice was shaky but strong. "Jenna, wait."

Jenna stumbled to a stop, whirled to stare down at Claudette. "You don't believe her?" It was a plea for reassurance. She didn't glance toward Annie.

Claudette stretched out her hands. "Jenna, we have to find out. We have to be certain. If someone killed Meg and we didn't do anything about it, she'd be furious! You know how she hated to be cheated."

"But why would anyone—" Jenna broke off, and once again she and Claudette exchanged wordless glances. Jenna's voice was harsh. "She got too excited and her heart gave out." Jenna darted up the stairs, her shoes clacking on the metal steps.

Annie started after Jenna. If Jenna called Dr. Burford, Annie wanted to hear what was said. She heard Claudette coming up the stairs behind her.

Jenna hurried through the open bedroom door, then stopped, her eyes on the rumpled bed.

Claudette came past Annie, slipped her arm around Jenna's shoulders. "She looked like she was asleep." Her voice was soft.

Her face a mask of misery, Jenna clutched at her throat.

Annie's gaze once again swept the long room. This end was a bedchamber with a delicately feminine white bedstead. A low line of bookcases, the book jackets bright swaths, separated the bedroom from a magnificent living room. All the furniture in the living area was white with crimson and navy cushions. A woven white carpet covered the floor. Artwork included a huge brass gong, vivid Chinese ceramics, and glass sculptures of shells and crescents and spokes. Plump-cushioned sofas formed a semicircle facing the sea.

The sea was everywhere visible through floor-to-ceiling sheets of glass that served as walls. Blinds controlled by a switch were embedded between the panes. The blinds facing the sea were open. Two archways decorated with Moorish tiles led to balconies. Beyond glass doors were screen doors so the room could be open in fall and spring to prevailing breezes. The room bespoke luxury, taste, and a passion for freedom.

"Meg loved this room and the balconies." Claudette absently brushed a piece of lint from the back of a sofa. "It didn't matter that she was ill. Here she could see forever. Ships and birds, storms with the waves crashing. If she couldn't sleep, she watched the moonlight on the sea and opened the doors to the balcony to hear the surf."

Annie walked across the white woven rug, her steps making no sound. She stopped at the first arch, opened the door. The screen wasn't latched. Annie looked back across the room. "This door isn't locked. Or the screen either."

Claudette looked surprised. "Why lock them? It's the second story."

Annie pulled open the screen and stepped onto the balcony, bright with terra cotta planters of begonias and white wicker furniture with yellow cushions. At one end of the balcony there was an opening in the railing for a small elevator. Annie looked at it in surprise, then realized it had probably been added to the house after Meg became ill and was no longer able to climb the stairs to the house.

Annie walked to the railing, looked down. Metal fretwork, painted the signature white of the house, decorated the columns all the way to the ground.

Any fairly agile person could climb a column to the balcony.

One chair was close to the railing. A shawl lay across a footstool. A wineglass with a small residue sat atop a glass table next to the chair.

Annie stepped back into the long room, closed the door behind her, stood in front of it. "There's a wineglass on the table outside."

"Meg always drank a glass of sherry at bedtime. We were out late, of course, but I saw her light on after I went to bed. I'm sure she went out on the balcony to drink her sherry." Claudette's voice was bleak. "I'll get the glass—"

"No." Annie held up a hand. "Don't touch anything." Her eyes scanned the living area, stopped at a sideboard. A crystal decanter held richly russet wine. "Can we lock this room, keep everyone out?"

"We could." Claudette looked at the gleaming crystal and its dark contents.

Jenna, too, stared at the sherry. "That's dreadful." She spoke in a bare whisper. "You think someone poisoned Mother." She shuddered. "I've got to go to Jason. Tell him." She whirled, hurried from the room.

Annie looked once more toward the balcony and the single glass resting on the small wrought-iron table. "I'm going to call the police."

❦ *Six* ❧

"ANNIE"—MAVIS CAMERON was hurried but definite—
"Billy said to tell you he's busy."

Annie's hand tightened on the cell phone. Although
Mavis was an old friend, her job at the police station
made her the guard at the gate. Of course, Billy probably thought Annie was calling to voice her opposition
to a verdict of accidental death at the inquest.

"I'm not calling about Pamela." To herself she
amended silently, not exactly. Annie kept her voice
level, though she knew she was about to toss the equiv-
alent of a stick of dynamite. "I'm calling about Meg
Heath. She died last night and Dr. Burford has authorized an autopsy. I'm at her house. She drank a glass of
wine before she went to bed and I think the contents of
the decanter and the glass should be analyzed."

"Hold on." Mavis's voice was steady but excited.

There was silence on the line. Annie held and
braced for a confrontation.

A click. "Stay there. Billy's on his way."

The transatlantic connection crackled, but the sense
of time and space was bridged by the vigor of the
acidulous voice. "My dear boy, it's like asking me to

capsulize the sinking of the *Titanic*. Let me see." A musing tone. "The greatest ship ever launched met an iceberg and went down while the band played on. There you go. In a sentence. To sum up Meg Heath: beauty, elegance, fascination. Every man who ever met her was enchanted. Meg"—his sigh was regretful—"was the one woman I never forgot. I actually asked her to marry me." Remembered surprise lifted his voice. "And marriage was never my aim with women. No, dear boy, if an old man can give you a bit of advice: Love them. Leave them. Promise the world and have a ticket to Singapore in your pocket." His chuckle was rich and unaffected.

Max tilted back his chair, crossed his feet, and prepared to enjoy his visit with Rodney St. Clair, roué, world traveler, and long-ago friend (the word can encompass many meanings) of the late Meg Heath. "She turned you down?"

"Scruples." He tossed up the word like a juggler spotting an exotic interloper among his dancing objects. "And it was such a small matter. A lady wrote me some indiscreet letters. I was quite willing to return them, and I saw nothing wrong with accepting a bit of a gift from her. Actually it was a substantial sum, enough for Meg and me to enjoy a lengthy stay in Monte Carlo. We could have had such fun. As for the lady, she was exceedingly grateful that her husband was spared reading the missives. I thought Meg's response was rather unkind. Certainly it wasn't a matter of blackmail. Simply a quid pro quo. The fellow was most disgustingly rich, so nobody suffered. That's what I told Meg. In fact, I was rather proud of how I brought it off. But Meg said, 'Rodney, you are great fun but you have on blinders when it comes to right and wrong.' She made me give the money back. Funny. I wouldn't have done that for anyone but Meg." His pause was thoughtful. "Now you say someone may have eased Meg out the door. You know, you might look about to see if Meg pointed out the error of his ways to the wrong chap."

For the second time that morning Annie stood in the sun—hotter now, the moist air steamy—at the base of the corkscrew stairs and listened to an approaching siren. She wondered if Billy was coming hell-for-leather to arrest her. She hadn't even had a chance to explain. Her eyes widened. Not one siren, two.

Billy slammed out of his patrol car. The forensic van pulled up behind him, Lou Pirelli driving, Frank Saulter his passenger. Lou was stocky with curly dark hair and a pleasant face. He looked like a nice girl's big brother, which, in fact, he was. Lou was Billy's sole staff since the call-up of the reserve unit had taken not only the chief, Pete Garrett, but the force's second patrolman. Lou's passenger, Frank Saulter, was the retired chief with whom Billy had worked for many years before Pete's arrival. Frank was always willing to help out on a volunteer basis. Frank's face beneath an iron-gray crew cut was furrowed in tight lines, he struggled with dyspepsia, and he had a short fuse. He was one of Annie's oldest and best friends on the island.

"I don't understand." Claudette peered toward the car and van. "Why have so many come?"

Annie didn't understand either. It wouldn't take every lawman on the island, past and present, for Billy to tell Annie she was out of line.

Billy didn't have his pugnacious look. Annie

breathed a little easier. In fact, he looked serious, intent, and purposeful. He strode toward them, stopped a scant foot away, looked from Annie to Claudette. Lou and Frank came up on either side of him.

Annie made the introductions. ". . . Claudette was Meg's secretary. She found Meg this morning."

"And you came—" Billy gave her a sharp look. "We'll get into that later. How did you know she didn't die of natural causes?"

"She didn't?" Abruptly everything clicked into place, Billy's arrival, the forensic van. "You've talked to Dr. Burford." Billy wasn't here because of Annie's call. He was here because the results of the toxicology tests had caused Dr. Burford to contact the police. "What killed her, Billy?"

"A bunch of tranquilizers. Valium. Too many to be an accident." He looked toward the secretary. "What's her mood been lately?"

Claudette was slow in answering. "Meg was ill. She'd been ill for a long time. She had"—a cautious pause—"overdone this weekend. But her mood was quite good last night. Are you suggesting Meg might have taken something deliberately? Committed suicide? That"—again a thoughtful pause—"would not be likely."

Annie watched Claudette. She had a sense of struggle within. The secretary struck her as a precise, careful woman with a strong core of honesty. She wouldn't take the easy route of blaming Meg's death on suicide.

Billy hooked his thumbs into his belt. "No signs of depression, anything like that?"

Claudette lightly touched her pearl necklace. Her face was composed, her eyes shadowed. She chose her words carefully. "She had a serious heart condition.

She was often quite weak and tired, but she lived every day to the fullest." The tone was almost, but not quite, admiring. "She insisted on going on the mystery cruise and she had a wonderful time. Of course, she was terribly tired when we got home. You say it couldn't have been an accidental overdose. But she might have made a mistake. . . ."

Billy shook his head. "The doc said at least twenty tablets." Billy looked up the winding steps, noted the glass walls of the house standing on the metal pillars. Annie suspected that he made it a point never to be impressed by the mansions on the island. Billy was a cop who would do his best for the owner of a ramshackle cabin as well as the possessor of a show home. But he did take a long moment to survey the magnificent glass structure from one end to the other.

"All right, ma'am." He nodded at Claudette. "If you'll show me where Mrs. Heath's body was found . . ."

Claudette turned to go up the steps, her shoulders bowed. She moved as if every step took an effort.

Annie turned, too, though she wasn't surprised when Billy cleared his throat and moved in front of her. Now his face had its bulldog look. "How come you showed up here this morning?"

She didn't mind answering. "To take Pamela's place. She came every morning to read the *Gazette* to Mrs. Heath. I thought maybe someone killed Pamela to keep her from reading the Sunday paper to Mrs. Heath. But I guess that's out. Maybe there was something in the *Gazette* that would mean something to both of them. . . ." Her voice trailed off.

Billy looked skeptical, but he didn't immediately reject her suggestion.

Annie felt a crack in his resistance. She said smoothly, "Think about it, Billy. Pamela Potts was here on Friday, and she and Meg Heath are both dead now. There has to be a connection."

Billy's expression was neutral. "We'll find out. Now, were you here when Mrs. Heath's body was discovered?"

Annie felt cold despite the sun. "No. I'd just arrived when the ambulance came."

"Fine. You don't need to stay, Annie. I'll keep in mind the fact that Pamela Potts was coming here. But for now, I need to get upstairs." He jerked his head toward Claudette. "All right, Ms. Taylor, let's go."

Claudette started up the steps. Billy was right behind her, his burly shoulders throwing a blocky shadow onto the dusty ground. Lou and Frank followed, murmuring hello to Annie as they passed by.

Annie watched as the front door closed and knew she was on the outside looking in as far as the investigation into Meg's death was concerned. But at least Billy had listened, and now he knew that Pamela had been here on Friday. He was fair-minded and thoughtful. For the first time since Pamela's injury, Annie felt a glimmer of hope that the truth might be found.

Sunlight reflected from the many windows. Talk about living in a fishbowl . . . She watched the progress of the men as they followed Claudette to Meg's room. They stepped inside and were lost to her view since the blinds on the interior side of the room were still closed. Though she couldn't see them now, she knew a careful and thorough investigation would ensue. The glass from which Meg had drunk her sherry would be taken as evidence and the crystal decanter as well. Billy would do it right, and with Frank Saulter there to help, they wouldn't miss anything.

From her vantage point, Annie saw the entrance to the kitchen. A stocky woman with blond hair edged out into the hallway to peer toward the closed door to Meg's room.

Annie almost reached for her car keys. She had accomplished her purpose. Meg Heath's death was being investigated.

But what about Pamela? Would Billy focus on her death? Maybe. Maybe not. After all, Annie was on the spot. What harm would it do to ask a few questions? She brushed away any thought of Billy's reaction if he knew. She made up her mind and moved fast, her sandals clicking on the mosaic that added color and gaiety to the shadowy expanse beneath the elevated base of the house. On the beach side of the house, between the patio and the dunes, was a tiled pool shaped like a dolphin. Blue water sparkled in the sun. Bright umbrellas were furled above glass tables. Red cushions added color to white wooden patio furniture. Sea oats on the dunes rippled in the breeze. It was a lovely August day, crows cawing, gulls swooping, the surf booming.

Annie reached broad steps leading up to a balcony behind the kitchen. Hoping mightily that Billy was fully occupied in Meg's suite, she hurried up the steps and across the porch and rapped loudly on the back door.

The woman on the far side of the beautifully appointed kitchen turned and stared across its wide expanse. In keeping with the rest of the house, everything—walls, cabinets, counters, tiled floor—was a brilliant white. She looked at Annie through the glass. Slowly, her broad face wary and uncertain, the stocky woman moved toward the door.

Max checked the clock. A quarter after ten. He placed the legal pad with page after page of notes to the right of the keyboard. It was time to organize the material he'd gleaned from phone calls and the Web. He opened a new file and began to type:

Possible Homicide Victim: Meg Heath
Family members: Jenna Brown Carmody, daughter
                              Jason Brown, son
Staff: Claudette Taylor, secretary
          Imogene Riley, housekeeper

Meg Heath

Meg Heath was born Margaret (Meg) Crane, April 11, 1944, in Charleston, South Carolina. Her father, George, was an ensign killed in the Pacific. Her mother, Adele Harris Crane, taught drama in a private school in Charleston. Meg finished high school there. She received a drama scholarship to the University of Southern California, but dropped out of school to become a model. Her grace and beauty led to modeling assignments for top ad agencies. She was one of the most photographed models of the late sixties. She married Carey Brown, a pro golfer, in 1968. Brown was more successful at partying than at putting and he lost his place on the tour in 1972. Meg spent a great deal of time in Europe, especially after the Vietnam war escalated. She was opposed to the war and offered sanctuary to men fleeing the draft. This caused a rift with Carey and they divorced in 1973. Their children were Jenna, born in 1971, and Jason, born in 1972.

The children lived with their grandmother but visited
their father in the summers until his death in a car
wreck in 1980. Meg was then briefly married to Tony
Sherman. He had left the United States to escape the
draft and stayed at her home in Majorca. They married
August 12, 1974. He was lost at sea in a small yacht
that sank in a storm off the coast of Italy in September
1976. Meg's antiwar views led to the cancellation of
several jobs. During this period she flitted from house
party to house party in England and on the Riviera. It
was at a party in Monte Carlo that she met Duff Heath,
a wealthy widower. His first wife, June, had died of
cancer the previous spring. They had one son, Peter.
Peter and his father were estranged. Duff and Meg
married June 23, 1978. They had homes in Paris,
Chicago, and Palm Springs. Meg's mother began to
fail in the early 1990s and the Heaths built a home on
Broward's Rock in 1992 to be near Adele. Adele
Crane died January 6, 1993. Duff Heath died March
22, 1998. The estate passed to Meg. Meg remained on
the island with—

The phone rang. Max looked at Caller ID, flicked on
the speakerphone. "Hi, Ma."

"I've always made it a point not to gamble." Laurel's tone was pleasant but firm.

Since Max was well aware of his mother's dislike
for gambling of any sort, he didn't feel a particular response was necessary. He murmured, "Mmm," and
continued to type.

—her secretary. She was diagnosed with congestive
heart failure last winter and her condition had
slowly—

"But you know how I enjoy social occasions." The words glistened bright as quartz in sunlight.

Indeed he did. Marriages, funerals, baptisms, cocktail parties, political rallies, theater openings, art receptions, charitable dinners, tailgate feasts, dances, balls, and barbecues—Laurel attended them all with delight.

"So you will understand that it is the social milieu, not the search for El Dorado, that prompts my attendance at the Ladies Investment Club." A contented sigh. "I do not, of course, purchase stocks."

Max shot a rueful look at the speakerphone. He and thousands of other bear-bitten investors surely would have been better off had they followed the example of his eccentric parent. But hindsight . . .

"I rather think no one else in the club followed that course. In particular"—and now her voice was sober—"it might be of interest to note that Claudette Taylor was in the unfortunate position of being heavily into Enron. I believe, in fact, that her portfolio was seriously diminished. As Alexandre Dumas the Younger once explained: 'Business? It's quite simple. It's other people's money.' " Laurel gave him a moment to appreciate Alexandre Dumas the Younger. "I remember her distress at the club luncheon last month. I remember how Meg scandalized everyone when she told Claudette never to cry over lost money, it was as silly as crying over a man, and neither men nor money were worth a single tear. Meg tossed that mane of dark hair and gave a whoop of laughter. She said, 'Besides, you and the children will be rich when I keel over, and that's going to be sooner rather than later. Enron won't matter at all.' "

The connection ended.

Max finished the sentence:

—worsened and she was not expected to live more than six months.

Max looked at the last line. Six months. Surely Claudette—and Meg's daughter and son as well— could wait that long to get rich. Unless one of them had a desperate need for money right now, this moment, this Monday, surely Meg was not killed by an heir.

Max flipped to the second page of his pad, found the third question listed under Facts to Discover. After the query Who inherits? he scrawled: NA.

The phone rang. He checked Caller ID, raised an eyebrow, punched on the speaker, lifted the receiver.

"I'm here from the church. To see if I can help." Annie hoped her smile was ingratiating and that her guardian angel was not hovering in a cloud of disapproval. After all, her intentions were honorable if not her methods. "I'm Annie Darling."

"Imogene Riley." She spoke with the innate confidence of a woman who was good at her job and knew it. "I don't know what will be needed yet. I'm waiting to talk to Claudette." She glanced toward the hall. "But now the police have come. . . ." She looked soberly at Annie. "Do you know why they're here?"

Annie doubted that Billy Cameron would approve of the public announcement of a murder investigation. In fact, Billy had not yet agreed that a murder had occurred. He was here because Meg had died from an overdose of Valium. Such an overdose could, in theory, have occurred by accident or on purpose. If on purpose, the determination would have to be made between suicide and murder. Annie had no doubt which had occurred. But now was not the time to explain this to the cook. Housekeeper? Whichever, she might hold knowledge Annie wanted. And she might be much more willing to divulge information if she were uninformed as to the cause of her employer's death.

Annie purposefully avoided a direct answer. "There are lots of formalities when someone dies without a doctor in attendance."

"Oh." Once again there was a sidelong glance toward the hallway.

Was there also an easing of tension in Imogene's broad shoulders? Annie maintained a pleasant, vacuous expression. "I wondered what I can do to be helpful. The police asked Claudette to go with them to Mrs. Heath's room."

"Please come in." Imogene held the door open.

Annie stepped into the immaculate kitchen. Gladiolas in a tall vase added a cheerful note. "I know this is a shock, though I suppose Mrs. Heath wasn't feeling well this weekend."

The reply was quick and definite. "Oh no, ma'am. She was chipper as could be Friday." The calm voice held an echo of remembered liveliness. "Oh, I know she was worn out from her heart, but you'd never have thought it to see her, her eyes shiny as a new penny. And she was so excited about tonight. I was getting things ready for the table when I heard the siren. The first siren." She pointed at a stack of china on the counter.

"Tonight?" Annie looked at the counter, saw silver in orderly rows, crystal, and damask napkins.

Imogene's face was sad. "Mrs. Heath said it was going to be the start of the rest of her life. Course, she talked like that. Everything was always the most or the

best. But this dinner"—her voice was assured—
"meant a lot to her. She said to use the Cartier china.
Her very favorite." She moved heavily across the tile
floor, held up a dinner plate with a stylized big cat,
black with yellow spots. The inside of the plate was
circled with red and the outer rim had a gold band.
Imogene ran a finger around the outer rim, slowly put
down the plate. "Nobody had prettier tables than Mrs.
Heath. But now . . ." She sighed. "People will start
coming with food pretty soon. I'd better get out the big
coffeepot." She walked to a closet, opened it, and
stepped inside. She came out with a huge coffeemaker,
holding it with both hands.

Annie hurried to help. Together they set the coffeemaker on the counter. "Did you talk to Mrs. Heath
about the dinner?"

Imogene poured water into the pot. "Claudette told
me the plans Friday afternoon, but I talked to Mrs.
Heath Friday evening when I took supper up to her.
Claudette had already given me the menu—"

Annie kept a pleasant, inquiring look on her face,
but a dozen questions whirled in her mind. Claudette
hadn't said a word about a special dinner party. Was
that the reason she and Jenna had exchanged a long,
wary look when Annie asked if anything special had
happened this weekend?

"—and the wine list and told me which china. We
always use a damask cloth with that china and crystal.
But Mrs. Heath changed her mind about the dessert.
She wanted me to fix Black Bottom Parfait instead of
Bananas Foster."

Annie watched as Imogene measured precisely for
twenty-four cups. "Is that when she said it was to be a
special dinner?"

Imogene fastened the strainer into the pot, put the lid in place. Plugging in the coffeemaker, she switched it on. "She was as thrilled as a kid at Christmas."

Annie wished for the old-fashioned days of place cards. It would be very helpful to know whom Meg had invited to this very special dinner. "Was it going to be a large dinner party?"

"Claudette said to set the table for six." The cook frowned, glanced toward a cabinet. "I wonder if I should get out pottery cups or Styrofoam?"

Annie was decisive. "Styrofoam." Six guests had been expected tonight. Now the dinner party would never occur, the dinner party that Claudette hadn't mentioned, the party that had Meg as excited as a child.

"I guess I'll put the china up." Imogene moved toward the stack of plates.

Annie looked toward the huge refrigerator. Was it full of delicacies? "What were you planning to serve tonight?"

"Oh, it would have been a fine meal." It was a lament. "Even with grits on the table."

Annie loved grits. Grits plain, grits with butter, grits with sugar, grits with syrup, grits with cheese and garlic. But grits at a dinner party? "Grits?"

"Grits." Imogene planted her hands on her hips. "It wouldn't have come up except she was having grits for her supper Friday. I'd fixed her grit cakes with shrimp sauce and a spinach salad. That woman loved grits any way they could be fixed. She told me a long time ago how she'd hungered for grits when she was in England and she couldn't have them because nobody'd ever heard of grits. She clapped her hands together and said grits was honest food. She kept talking about grits being real and honest and then she laughed and said she wanted a big bowl of grits for the dinner Monday night. With lots of fresh butter. I told her grits had no place on that fancy table—" She saw Annie's look of surprise. "I always told Mrs. Heath what I thought. She liked for me to speak up. But when I said grits would stick out like a sore thumb—we were to have Shrimp Chinois and apple-apricot-rice soufflé and asparagus with mustard-butter sauce—she shook her head and said grits would be perfect. Well, she had her mind made up, and that woman never took no for an answer. Then she said the oddest thing." Imogene's brow furrowed. "She wasn't looking at me. She was on her chaise longue and her face was kind of white and tired but her eyes were bright as stars. You know"—Imogene's tone was confiding—"she always reminded me of someone grand like a duchess or a movie star. Her face was long and thin and the bones kind of sharp but she looked real special, the way I always thought Anastasia must have looked—"

Annie felt a flicker of surprise, then scolded herself. Why should she assume Imogene would never have heard of Anastasia?

"—even though people say she wasn't really one of the Russian princesses. If a woman has that air, people pay attention. They always paid attention to Mrs. Heath. She had that look on Friday, like she ought to be wearing pearls and coming down a golden staircase in a red dress even though she was just lying there in her dressing gown. She was pleased. She looked out toward the ocean and said, real low and soft, 'I've always been a romantic fool. But I'd like for it to end that way, the two of us together.' She threw back her head and gave that laugh of hers." Imogene looked at Annie. "Did you ever hear her laugh?"

Annie, too, heard laughter in her memory, rich and throaty, effervescent as bubbles in champagne. She smiled at the cook. "Yes."

"She was real happy." Imogene snapped the lid on the coffee cannister. "That's the way I'll always remember her."

"Hi, Emma." Max's tone was genial but wary. He would never admit to being intimidated by the island mystery author, but any man would approach a wild boar with caution and with deep respect for the damage that can be inflicted by razor-sharp tusks. He sketched a grizzle-faced boar in a caftan, black hooves poised above a computer keyboard.

"Caller ID is hell for detective fiction." The author's raspy voice was dour. "To make an anonymous phone call you have to find a damn pay phone. And cell phones are an absolute bitch. Everybody's got one. Used to be, the heroine could go to the cemetery at midnight—you know, she gets a note from her lover but of course it is really from the wicked uncle—and the reader's palms are sweaty as the villain creeps toward her, and when she sees him and hides beneath an overturned wheelbarrow, the reader knows her doom is sealed, but now all she has to do is switch on her cell phone and punch nine-one-one." A huff of outrage. "Makes it almost impossible to put a character in jeopardy."

Max curled the lips of the feral hog in disgust, rapidly added a cell phone smashed by a flying hoof. "Damn shame," he agreed.

"And when they can be useful, the damn things are always turned off or you hit a dead pocket and it won't work. I've been calling Annie but all I get is voice mail." Emma was clearly irritated. "I've left messages on her home phone, at the store, and on her cell. Now, here's what I want her to do—"

Max wrote swiftly. When the call ended, he looked at his notes, grinned. Shades of E. Phillips Oppenheim.

Annie circled the block. Where had all these cars come from? But she could look at the license plates and tell. Most of them were from Georgia and South Carolina, but every third or fourth came from Ohio. Her eyes widened at one all the way from British Columbia. There was a hardy traveler. A downside to living on a resort island in summer was the search for a parking spot in the little downtown. Annie glowered. It was a gorgeous sunny day. Why didn't they go to the beach? However, as a merchant she never faulted tourists for shopping. Maybe a bunch of them would end up at Death on Demand today, as she herself should as soon as possible. Ingrid was probably wondering where she was. But Ingrid always managed. She'd ask her husband, Duane, to help out if the crowds got too thick. Annie thought with pleasure of customers flocking into Death on Demand, sunburned tourists shoulder to shoulder all buying beach books, hopefully the beautiful and expensive hardcovers.

Her third swing around the block she found a spot a street away from the offices of the *Island Gazette*. She parked, fumbled for a couple of quarters for the meter. By the time she reached the newspaper office she was dripping with sweat. Just short of the front door, she stopped and stared intently into the window of the shoe store. Hmm, pretty yellow slingbacks . . . She cut her eyes toward the *Gazette* front window. All she wanted to do was bop in and buy last Friday's paper as well as the Sunday issue, find out if there was something in the newspaper that the murderer wanted to make certain both Pamela Potts and Meg Heath never saw. But once inside the *Gazette* offices, she'd be sure to see either Vince Ellis, the owner and publisher, or Marian Kenyon, star reporter and, more to the point, human antenna. Marian would demand the skinny on everything that had happened on the mystery cruise. Marian had very likely already picked up the drumbeat that Annie was certain Pamela was a murder victim. Annie was in no position to describe her morning. It wasn't her place to announce the death of Meg Heath, much less the fact that the police were investigating an overdose of Valium. Billy Cameron would understandably oppose such a revelation.

Annie turned, walked away from the *Gazette* door. She was hotter than beach sand by the time she reached Parotti's, the down-home restaurant and bait shop. She scanned the newspaper racks near the entrance, scrounged four quarters from the bottom of her purse, and bought a Sunday paper. There were no Friday issues left.

She breathed deeply when she stepped inside. She loved the fascinating mixture of odors: fish bait, sawdust, beer on tap, and good old all-American french fry grease. The din was familiar and cheerful: swing on the jukebox, the rumble of animated conversation, the slam and bang of pans from the kitchen. When she first came to the island, Parotti's was a fisherman's delight with the best in chicken necks, mullet, mackerel, and live shrimp or minnows for bait. The food was mostly fried. Since Ben Parotti's marriage to Miss Jolene, who had owned a tea shop, there'd been a civilizing influence and now quiche was available as well as fried clams, oysters, and shrimp.

Unlike winter, when the old wooden booths and scarred wooden tables were sparsely filled, Parotti's was jammed today, every spot at the bar taken and a long line of people sitting on a narrow wooden bench to the left of the entrance.

Natty in a green sport coat, cream-colored polo shirt, and white slacks, Ben strode toward her, menus in hand. Not, of course, that she ever needed a menu. His welcoming smile slid into a sad frown as he segued from café host to owner of the *Island Packet* excursion boat. "Heard the bad news about Pamela Potts. Damn shame. I got to say again"—and his tone was combative—"she sure hadn't no call to be on the other side of that chain. But whether she fell or got pushed, like you say, it's a crime she's gone."

Annie's eyes brimmed. She blinked, reached out, patted his arm. "Thanks, Ben."

"Nice lady." He folded his lips, shook his head in tribute. "Anyway"—he brightened—"got your table ready. Max gave me a call."

Annie tried to ignore the sullen glances from the waiting customers. A burly tourist called out, "Thought you didn't take reservations."

Ben was unruffled. His crusty voice was mellow for him. "This here's a reg'lar, mister." He led her to a table in full view of the front door and pulled out a chair for her. If looks could kill . . .

Annie slipped into the chair, glad to focus on the here and now. She whispered, "Ben, aren't you afraid you'll lose business?"

"In August?" His raspy chuckle sounded over Fats Domino's "Blueberry Hill." "They keep coming. Don't matter how long they have to wait. Course we got the best food on the island." He was a satisfied gnome who was master of all he surveyed. "So what'll it be? The usual?"

"Yes. But I'll wait and order when Max gets here." She put down her purse and opened the newspaper. She scanned the front page: lawsuits over building covenants, the latest political news, a report on the excavation of the *Monitor,* and, at the bottom of the page, a boxed inset in boldface type:

HOMICIDE VICTIM

Shortly before press time Saturday night, the unidentified body of a man estimated to be in his seventies was found shot to death near Ghost Crab Pond in the forest preserve. Police said he wore a blue-and-white-striped blazer, pink linen shirt, and white trousers. Anyone with information about him or the crime is urged to contact the police.

Another murder? Annie felt a tingle in her mind. A tingle. That's what happened in the mind of Frances and Richard Lockridge's madcap sleuth Pam North when she had a hunch. Annie had a hunch. She spread mental wings over it, protective as a mother hen. By golly, maybe Emma was right. Maybe Emma's imaginative certainty would prove to be justified. Because this was definitely an unusual story in the *Gazette,* the kind of story Pamela would have been certain to read to Meg Heath. Almost as if she'd been a part of their morning news hour, Annie imagined Meg's burbling laughter and imperious instruction, "Scandal, my dear. That's what I like to hear." So, yes, had Pamela been at Meg's this morning, there would have been— with several gasps of dismay by Pamela—a perusal of the most exciting news in the paper. Murder trumps lawsuits, politics, and the watery end of the first armored warship.

Annie felt a misgiving. What possible connection could there be between this elderly victim, Pamela Potts, and Meg Heath?

Annie grabbed her cell phone. Wait until she told Emma. It was too bad she hadn't gone into the newsroom. They would know a lot more now about the murder victim. She clicked on the cell. Two sharp peals signaled messages.

Annie called up the first message. Her mother-in-law's husky voice was reflective: "As I told dear Maxwell, I am rather in the guise of a scientist seeking to study an elusive butterfly. They are such elegant creatures, swooping silently through the air, lovely and graceful, and quite predictable once the observer determines the flower that attracts that particular species. I rather see Meg Heath as a zebra, hovering over a passion flower. Passion." The noun was rich with meaning. Annie had a vision of moonlit nights and lovers meeting. "Ah, what passion attracted Meg? Oh"—a trill of laughter—"men, of course." The implication was clear. What was life without men? "But there are other passions. I believe I've found a glimpse of Meg's heart. Before her health began to fail, she was very active in island social events. I've been calling friends, asking for reminiscences of Meg—"

Annie gave a short exasperated sigh. So much for her effort to keep a lid on public revelations of Meg's death until there was an official announcement from the authorities. But Annie wasn't responsible for Laurel, and Billy could speak to Max's mother if he didn't like her activities.

"—and I was told of a book review Meg presented

at a Ladies of the Leaf meeting, a biography of one of the theater's grande dames. In the course of an exciting and far-flung career, the actress had left her daughter for long periods with her mother. In the discussion that followed, there was a great deal of criticism of what would be described by some as abandonment. Meg championed the actress. At one point she lifted her head and faced them all, saying, 'Choices have to be made. My children grew up with my mother, yet I didn't have the excuse of plays or films. I had to be a wanderer.' My friend told me some of the women never felt quite the same about Meg after that. But Meg was willing to accept responsibility for her actions. I think she was always willing to admit to the truth in her life as she understood it. I suspect"—and Laurel's tone was tinged with sadness—"we all can wish we had her courage."

Annie wondered what long-ago memory troubled Laurel. It was easy for Annie to be sardonic about her mother-in-law's five marriages and her mesmerizing attractiveness to men, but Laurel's search for love, for connection, for belonging was evidence that beyond her bright smile, sunny disposition, and gaiety lay profound loneliness.

Laurel's brightness was never quenched for long. "So, Dear Child, I know you recall *The Three Musketeers*—"

Annie concentrated, trying hard to bridge the gulf between a declaration of truth at the Ladies of the Leaf book club and the tale of adventure by Alexandre Dumas.

"—and perhaps you recall the passage: 'D'Artagnan admired by what fragile and unknown threads the destinies of nations and the lives of men are sometimes suspended.' "

Fragile threads . . . Annie held tight to the cell phone. The phone was real. She felt the hard plastic case in her hand. Imaginary threads shimmered in her mind in shades ranging from palest gold to midnight black. They were imaginary, but perhaps the reality they suggested—the consequences of an individual's thoughts, beliefs, and actions on the outcome of fate—was as pertinent to a modern death as the long-ago machinations of a lover to affairs of state.

"If we can find the proper strand, all will be known." The connection ended.

The proper strand . . . Annie glanced again at the boldface box on the front page of the *Gazette*. But first . . . She punched for the second message:

"Annie, Emma." The raspy voice was gruff. "Cell phones are a pestilence, but why the hell don't you have yours on? Been trying to get in touch for hours. Well, for a while. In any event, Max said he was having lunch with you. Here are your instructions—"

Annie's eyes slitted. Did Emma think she was Leslie Ford's Colonel Primrose ordering Grace Latham about?

"Take the two P.M. ferry to the mainland. Drive south for three-point-four miles. Turn left on Slash Pine Road. Go to the end of the pier. You will be met. Password: Avenger." Click.

Annie was torn between irritation and fascination. Emma was undoubtedly the rudest person she'd ever known. But she was also canny, clever, and mad as hell about Pamela's murder. Okay, okay. Annie punched the Save button. She could follow orders, even though she hated to leave the island just when she was making some progress.

Was she making progress? What did she really know? She dropped the cell phone in her purse. As she grabbed her notebook, the front door opened and Max walked in, a smile on his face and a folder under his arm.

The smile was for her.

∻ *Seven* ∻

THE MOMENT EXPANDED beyond ordinary time, encompassing past, present, and future. It took only seconds for Max to walk to the table, his face alight with anticipation, but into that brief span Annie packed memory and emotion and thankfulness. Perhaps the sadness in Laurel's voice permeated Annie's mind like the memory of a fragrance, triggering a wash of emotion. The rumble of sound that was Parotti's in summer faded. It was as if Max moved in a circle of love, everything excluded but her. He came toward her as he had on the night when they'd first met, with easy confidence and charm and determination. What a difference that night had made. He'd taken her hand, held it, and she'd not been surprised. Perhaps she'd known in that first instant that they would always be linked, although she'd resisted his charm in the early days. In fact, she'd run away from New York, fled to the island to escape him. He'd followed with his unfailing good humor and—for her—total commitment.

They were so different. He came from a background of privilege. She'd known months when macaroni and cheese was all she could afford. Max elevated the pursuit of pleasure to an art form. Annie made To-Do lists with joy. He was a dilettante; she was a taskmaster. He coasted; she struggled.

Together they loved.

Annie pushed back her chair, rose. They'd met so many times for lunch at Parotti's, during sultry summers and sun-drenched autumns, misty winters and azalea-bright springs. She'd taken those luncheons for granted, absorbed with the urgencies of the moment, the lost book order, the upcoming author signing, the tennis match she'd won, her hopes for him to work harder, worry about his mother's startling enthusiasms. But at this moment, she knew what mattered: the two of them together, come what may, heart to heart, hand in hand. She moved into his arms, welcomed the containment of his embrace.

"Love you," she murmured.

"Always." His lips were warm against her ear.

The café sounds swirled around them, "Moonlight Serenade" on the jukebox, the clatter of dishes, the swell of voices, and in particular one high-pitched observation, "Honeymooners, of course."

Max laughed. "Sounds good to me." He gave her another squeeze. "Hey, let's go home."

Annie smiled, loving his response. The folder poked into her back. She reached over her shoulder, grabbed it. "Have you found out a lot?" Then she shook her head, blond hair flying, holding the folder unopened. "Max, have you seen the *Gazette*? I've got a wild idea. But it makes sense to me. Did you know Meg was murdered? That's not official, but she died of an overdose and Billy's there and—"

"No and yes. No time to read the newspaper, but I talked to Emma." He pulled out her chair.

Annie sat down, still clutching the folder. "Emma."

Even Annie was amazed at the layers of meaning she loaded into two syllables: outrage, resentment, respect, hostility, fear, and surrender.

Max threw back his head and roared, a peal of mirth that made those nearby smile. Except Annie.

She glared. Her voice was stiff. "If you think it's funny to be treated like a mouse cornered by Agatha, maybe you ought to jump into the tiger's cage at the Atlanta zoo."

Max reached across the table, patted her hand. "I know. Emma's tough. Obviously you got her message—"

Ben Parotti stopped at the table, waggled menus. "Glad to see you and the missus in good spirits." He glanced at Annie. "Fried flounder sandwich, heavy on the tartar sauce, coleslaw and fries with iced tea. Unsweetened." He gave her a thumbs-up. "Oyster season opens in a couple of weeks."

Annie was passionate about Ben's fried oyster sandwiches. Flounder was next best.

Ben looked at Max.

Max didn't need a menu either. "Fish chowder. Pile on the hot smoked sausage." He looked to see if there was a bottle of tabasco sauce on the table. "And a Bud Light."

As Ben turned away, Annie called out, "A double order of jalapeño corn muffins." Annie adored the treats, which were studded with kernels of sweet corn and thick with jalapeño slices. Her glower returned. "Yeah, I got Emma's message."

Max scooted his chair closer. "I'll come with you. A password and a pier at the end of Slash Pine Road. That's almost as good as a treasure map with X marks the spot."

There was no denying that Emma had flair. "Oh dammit, I'll go. She's probably found out something we need to know. But look at this—" Annie pushed the *Gazette* toward him, pointed at the boxed inset.

Ben brought Max's beer and Annie's tea and the basket with hot jalapeño corn muffins nestled in a red-checked napkin and two miniature crocks of fresh whipped butter. But he didn't move on after delivering the food. He kneaded one cheek with a rough hand. "Anything I can do about Pamela, you let me know. Like if you want to look over the boat again." He swung on his heel and marched away.

Max looked after him. "Happened on his watch. I know he's upset."

"It wasn't his fault." Her tone was firm. "Or Pamela's fault." Annie pointed again at the front page of the *Gazette*. "Look at the bulletin, Max."

Max scanned the paper, gazed inquiringly at Annie.

She picked up a warm muffin, poked a hole, and dropped in a glob of the soft butter. "I've got to go see what Emma's up to, but maybe you can find out more"—she spoke in an indistinct mumble over a mouthful of muffin—"about the dead guy. You can drop in at the *Gazette,* talk to Marian Kenyon."

His face puzzled, Max tapped the front page. "What's the connection?"

She was not quite defensive. "You know how Laurel encourages us to be creative. It may be a reach, but I didn't find anything else in the paper that anyone could possibly care about. Look at it—" She pointed at the *Gazette.* "What if"—was she on a creative tear, thanks to Laurel?—"this guy was somebody Meg knew? She was planning a special dinner for tonight. What if this guy was one of the guests?" Annie was determined to find out whom Meg had invited. Did Claudette know the guest list as well as the menu? "What if the minute Meg heard the description of the unidentified dead man, she'd know who it was? What if she talked about him to Pamela and maybe there was something . . ." She trailed off. It was easy in an Eric Ambler novel or an Alistair MacLean thriller. Somebody had the specifications of a new weapon or there was a cache of gold hidden by the Nazis. Right this minute, with "Begin the Beguine" throbbing in the background, tourists looking askance at the bait barrels, and Ben bringing a steaming bowl of chowder and a mountainous po' boy fried flounder sandwich to their table, she saw no way to take imaginary threads and bind an unknown homicide victim to the deaths of Meg Heath and Pamela Potts. "Oh, I don't know," she admitted. "But it seems strange that an unidentified corpse shows up the same weekend two women are murdered."

"Yeah." Max wasn't convinced. He sprinkled tabasco in his chowder. "But I'll be glad to talk to Marian, see what I can find out." He read the bulletin again. "It says he was shot. Wonder if they found a gun? At least he's definitely a murder victim."

The massive sandwich stopped midway to Annie's mouth. "Excuse me?"

Max poured more beer into his still frosty glass. "Come on, Annie, face it. Pamela could have fallen—"

"Fallen?" She put down the sandwich, a clear indication of her distress. "She wouldn't climb over the chain. I know she—"

He held up a hand. "Easy. Let's just discuss it." His lips twitched. "Have I ever told you that you look like a porcupine when you're mad? Anyway, Pamela could have fallen. Meg may have popped pills into her wine. But if this guy was shot, that's a different matter."

Annie took a big bite. She ate, then looked at him soberly. "Why are you so reluctant to think Pamela and Meg were victims, too?"

Max spooned up broth and okra and sausage. "Meg was dying. She wasn't expected to live another six months. What was so urgent that somebody had to kill her last night? And the idea that somebody shoved Pamela into the ocean to keep her from reading—" He looked past Annie toward the door. A broad smile lighted his face. He lifted his left hand and gestured. He put down his spoon, pushed back his chair.

Annie twisted to look. Max was rising, moving to greet her father and Sylvia Crandall. It was too late to stop him. Of course he was going to ask Pudge and Sylvia to join them. On any other day she would have been—well, maybe pleased was too strong a word, and darn it, why did she have this aversion to Sylvia?—but it would have been fine. Today she was appalled. She had a horrid sense of unease and urgency, though truth to tell, Emma had already thrown a wrench in her plans for the afternoon. Max might think Emma's brusque orders funny. Annie wasn't amused. Now there would be the distraction of dealing with Pudge and Sylvia as well as Annie's foray off island. She sat frozen in her seat.

Pudge looked toward Annie. Her father was at one and the same moment both familiar and strange: sandy hair a little askew from the wind, gray eyes seeking reassurance, genial face hopeful yet uncertain. He was Pudge but not the Pudge she'd come to know and love. He lacked his usual easy manner. Instead of strolling across the floor with an insouciant smile, shoulders in a relaxed slouch, this man planted his feet like a soldier crossing a bog. Sylvia Crandall, pale and tense, clung to his arm as if he were a rescuer leading her to safety. Sylvia's linen dress was worthy of Gauguin, red hibiscus flaring against a cream background, but the narrow face beneath the cap of sleek chestnut hair drooped in discontent. She gripped the handle of her crimson woven bag so tightly that her fingers looked cramped.

For an instant too long, Annie stared blankly toward the door.

Her father checked in midstride. His hand closed over Sylvia's and they came to a stop. Pudge looked toward Annie, his gray eyes met hers in mute appeal.

Annie knew Pudge had seen her stare, blank at best, unfriendly at worst. She scrambled to her feet, forced a smile, knew Pudge would know it was forced. She felt a thrill at that knowledge. She'd spent so many years without her father, it was amazing to realize that he was here now, coming toward her, love and trust in his gaze. Pudge knew. So surely he knew, too, that whatever held her back—she pushed away the thought of Sylvia—there was a bond that nothing could destroy. Thoughts and emotions swirled and she wished she could channel her mind, exclude all the untidy ragtag feelings threatening to tumble out in public, bumptious as spaniel puppies.

It was the firm handclasp between Pudge and Max that propelled her forward. It spoke of friendship and admiration and connection. She hurried to the threesome, gripped Pudge's other hand, and, surprising herself, reached out to take Sylvia's long, slender, cold hand in a welcoming grasp. "Come join us."

Max, oblivious to Annie's initial hesitation, shepherded them back to the table, pulled out a chair for

Sylvia, his voice warm and friendly. "Glad to see you. Annie and I are trying to figure out what happened yesterday to Pamela." He shot Annie a warning glance.

She understood. At this point, so far as the public knew, Pamela's death was an accident, and they wouldn't discuss Meg's death. But Pamela's fall had happened on Annie's cruise.

Pudge's face creased in concern. "I heard Pamela died this morning. Damn shame." But his voice was abstracted and his eyes kept darting toward Sylvia.

Sylvia still stood beside the chair Max had pulled out. The rigid line of her body was as clear as a shout that she didn't want to sit down.

Pudge gestured at the chair. "I'll order us something quick." He glanced at Ben, who stood nearby with menus. "Hey, Ben, two bowls of chowder. Iced tea. Unsweetened."

Ben nodded and backed away.

"You'll feel a lot better when we eat something." Pudge's tone was hearty. A quick flush stained Sylvia's pale cheeks. She dropped into the chair, sat like a stone.

As Annie slipped into her seat, she was struck anew by the validity of the Mars-Venus analogy of male-female relationships. Pudge wanted to think there was something he could do that would banish Sylvia's misery. A bowl of chowder to the rescue. Sylvia would have liked to shove all of them into a boat without oars and send it into the Atlantic. Max looked at the deaths of Pamela and Meg from the outside in, and Annie looked from the inside out, and both of them were sure they were right. And in Max's male view, here was good old Pudge, so of course they would eat together with no thought to the vibrations of latent hostility exuded by the two women whose faces were determinedly molded in pleasant masks. But Annie realized there was more than hostility in Sylvia's face. Annie looked into dark eyes stricken by unhappiness. Annie's gaze swiveled to her father. He watched Sylvia, his face heavy with pain.

Maybe it was time to toss pretense. And jealousy. As the word fluttered in her mind, dark as a brown bat skittering against the rose sky of evening, Annie felt a sense of relief. The release was as welcome as yanking a thorn from tender skin.

"Sylvia." Annie's voice was gentle. "What's wrong?"

Sylvia clasped her hands together, long, thin, elegant fingers bedecked with several old-fashioned rings, the nails a glistening pink, all of a piece with her highly bred beauty, the chiseled perfection of thin features, the glisten of softly brown hair. Tears spilled from anguished eyes, ran unchecked down sunken cheeks.

Ben's look was uneasy as he placed the big tumblers of iced tea in front of Pudge and Sylvia. He eased quietly toward the kitchen.

Annie stared across the table at Sylvia. She didn't see the haughty fashion plate she'd always found cool and unappealing. She saw a quite beautiful older woman struggling to regain her composure.

Pudge slammed his hand on the table. "Dammit, Sylvia, I'll go get him." He scooted back his chair.

"Oh no. You mustn't. That would never do. He would be even angrier. . . ." She bent forward, buried her face in her hands.

"Maybe . . ." Pudge turned to Annie. "Look, Rachel knows Cole. Maybe she can help us." He hiked his chair closer to the table, leaned on his elbows, and talked twice as fast as he usually did. "Sometimes one kid can talk to another. And with all Rachel's been through—"

Oh, Pudge, Annie thought, you don't understand. Rachel doesn't want to share you with Sylvia, and her resentment is as hot and wild as bubbling lava.

"—with losing her mom. Maybe she can talk to Cole. His dad's still alive, and he loves Cole and Cole gets to visit him. I won't try to take his dad's place. I wouldn't do that." Pudge's tone was forlorn.

Sylvia's hands dropped. She sniffed and opened her purse for tissues. She scrubbed at her cheeks, took a deep breath, wadded the tissues into a tight ball. "I'm sorry, Pudge." The face she turned toward him was a map of misery, deep lines bracketing her eyes and lips, the muscles sagging. "I shouldn't have met you for lunch. There's nothing any of you can do." She stared at Annie, her gaze empty of expression. "You don't like me—"

Annie lifted both hands in protest. "That's not true." Suddenly she knew that it wasn't true. How could she resent this haggard, hurt woman? "No. It's just"—she didn't look toward Pudge—"it's hard to share." She dredged out the painfully honest words.

"Share . . ." Sylvia's lips quivered. "That's what's wrong with Cole. That—and the divorce. He adores his dad. Oh—" She pushed back her chair so quickly it tumbled to the floor behind her, but she didn't appear to hear the noise, even though there was that peculiar instant of silence when something untoward occurs in a noisy crowded room. She thrust out a hand toward Pudge. "I'm sorry. Stay here. I've got to get back to work. Maybe Cole will call." Her eyes were sad but determined. "Maybe he'll come back. . . ." She turned and walked swiftly away, her shoes clattering on the wooden floor.

Max rose, quickly lifted the fallen chair, pushed it up to the table. He returned to his seat, almost spoke, shook his head.

Lips in a tight line, Pudge watched until Sylvia was through the door.

Ben was a few feet away, two bowls of steaming chowder on his expertly held tray. He ducked his head, placed a bowl before Pudge, retreated with the second serving.

Pudge slumped in his chair. He looked old. Defeated.

Annie was suddenly angry. Maybe she didn't like Sylvia after all. "That's rude." She glared toward the front door, but Sylvia was gone.

Pudge's defense was immediate. He sat up straight. "She's got to try and get Cole to come home. He walked out last night. He yelled at her that she didn't care about him, all she cared about was me." For an instant there was a glow in his eyes, then memory quenched the light. "It's a mess. Sylvia and Sam just got divorced a year ago and she hated to take Cole so far away from his dad—they lived in Chicago—but she wants to make it on her own. She gets child support but nothing more. That's the way she wants it." His voice was admiring.

"Anyway, Cole hates her seeing me and he hates school. This summer he hung out at the park with his skateboard. That's how he met Stuart Reed. He's Wayne Reed's son. Cole's at the Reed house now. He went over there last night and he says he's not coming back as long as Sylvia has anything to do with me. I talked to Wayne this morning. He advises Sylvia to play it cool. He thinks Cole will get homesick and the best thing is just to let him hang out over there for a while." Pudge made no effort to pick up his spoon.

"Trouble is"—Pudge looked around, lowered his voice despite the roar of conversation that ricocheted from the wooden rafters to the floor and back again—"Sylvia doesn't like Stuart. She thinks he's a bad influence. Cocky and insolent. Spoiled. Stuart's the only reason Cole was on the boat Sunday night. Wayne had a bunch of tickets—he's big on island civic stuff—and he told Stuart to round up some friends. Cole sure wouldn't have come with us. Oh hell." Pudge pushed the bowl of chowder out of the way. "I don't know what to do. I know you and Max"—his glance at Annie was confiding—"eat here a lot. I thought if Sylvia and I kind of ran into you, maybe we'd get together and you'd help us. Anyway, I decided to bring her here and see if we'd find you. Annie, if you'd talk to Rachel, maybe she could explain to Cole that I'm not such a bad guy." He looked at her eagerly.

Not such a bad guy . . . Annie felt the sting of tears. She blinked, managed a bright smile. "Testimonials by the dozen." But she had a vivid picture of Rachel scowling, lips drawn back like a hissing cat. "Uh, you know, it's a nice idea about Rachel, but I don't know if they know each other"—she saw the hope drain out of Pudge's face—"and kids can be really shy. You know, a girl and a guy." She knew she was babbling. She had to do something to encourage Pudge. She could never tell him how Rachel felt. But maybe there was a solution. "I'll talk to Cole. I've been planning on seeing him anyway."

Pudge looked at her in surprise. Max fished in his bowl for whiting, his expression skeptical.

Annie focused her attention on Pudge. Max could continue in his stubborn male fashion to think Pamela's fall was an accident. She knew better. "You see"—her voice was earnest, and this was true so it sounded well—"Cole was on the upper deck where Pamela went overboard." Her enthusiasm grew. She would do her best at some point in the conversation to urge Cole to give Pudge a chance, but what a heaven-sent opportunity to talk to the person who had been nearest Pamela when she went overboard. "I want to find out as much as I can about the circumstances. I feel I owe it to Pamela's family. I'll get in touch with Cole later today."

Pudge's rounded face re-formed from sadness to gratitude, his gray eyes glowing, his lips curving in a smile.

Annie tried not to look as stricken as she felt. It was terribly unlikely that she could make a difference in Pudge's effort to forge a relationship with Cole. Always prone to impulsive actions, she clapped her hands together. "And we'll invite Sylvia and Cole over to dinner Friday night. Max can grill hamburgers."

"Oh, that's great, Annie." Pudge looked upbeat, excited. "I'll tell Sylvia and Cole to bring their swimsuits." Some of the eagerness seeped from his face. "Yeah. If he comes home. But you'll make it happen, I know you will. Annie, you're the best." He was up and out of his chair, flinging his napkin on the table. He pulled out his wallet, dropped two twenties on the table. "That'll take care of lunch. And have some pineapple upside-down cake for dessert." Pudge knew what Annie loved. "I've got to let Sylvia know." Pudge grabbed Annie's hands for a quick squeeze. "She'll be so happy." He bent, kissed the top of Annie's head, whispered, "Thank you, honey." He strode away from the table, almost breaking into a run, ducking around waiting customers and out the door.

Annie avoided looking at Max. She picked up her sandwich, took a bite. It was as delicious as usual, but she needed more than succulent flounder to revive her spirits. There was a lengthy pause. Max spooned. She bit and chewed.

Max poured the last of his beer. "I suppose"—his tone was conversational—"that you have a plan. Some way to change Cole's attitude, bring him home, convince him that Pudge is a great guy?"

Annie determinedly ate.

"No? Problem is, I don't think the earth is going to open up and swallow either one of us." He sighed. "So between now and Friday night, we've got to come up with a miracle."

Sweat trickled down Annie's face. Her blouse stuck to her. All the car windows were down and the sea breeze swept over her, but that wasn't much comfort on an August afternoon. Usually she got out and leaned against the railing as the ferry chugged steadily across the Sound toward the mainland, watching the laughing gulls, welcoming the ever-fresh scent of the sea, clapping when dolphins made a graceful arc above the water. Today she wanted to learn as much as she could as fast as possible, all the while ignoring the potential for disaster when Sylvia, Pudge, and possibly Cole arrived at the Darling house Friday night. What was she going to say to Rachel? Maybe her subconscious would figure out a good approach. But for now . . .

She finished Max's dossier on Meg. The sentences were brief, but they evoked the picture of a flamboyant, independent—some might say self-centered—woman who went her own way. Meg most likely saw her decisions as honest. Annie wondered about Meg's mother, her children, the men she had loved and left or lost. What price had others paid for Meg to enjoy her freedom? Had she paid the ultimate price? And always, sorrowful as the distant cry of a mourning dove, there was the image of Pamela, serious, earnest, kind, and now dead because she tried to do good.

Annie's face was stern. No matter how long it took, whatever she had to do, Pamela's death wasn't going to be ignored. And Annie was afraid that Billy would separate her death from Meg's unless a direct link could be proven. Maybe there was some hint, some clue in Max's summary of these lives. She began to read:

Carey Brown

Carey Harwood Brown was born January 4, 1942, in Birmingham, Alabama, the youngest of five children. His father owned a car dealership. His mother was a renowned hostess. During the war years, the senior Browns were active with the local USO chapter and were part of a program that provided sandwiches and cigarettes to troops moving through by train. According to a longtime friend and fellow golfer, Carey was the darling of his family, indulged and adored. Carey was a natural athlete who possessed considerable charm and was a favorite of the press. Tall, dark-haired, with an ever-present smile, he had two passions in life, golf and, later, Meg Crane, whom he married in 1968. They were one of the most glamorous couples on the pro tour. He loved to party and drink. He never admitted that he had a problem with alcohol, but after he and Meg divorced in 1973 he drank more heavily. He missed two tournaments because he was drunk and ultimately was dismissed from the tour. He always pulled himself together when his children came in the summer, but every fall after they returned to their grandmother in Charleston for the school year he started drinking again. He was drunk when his car plowed into a bridge shortly after midnight on October 9, 1980.

There was a picture from a June 22, 1971, *Atlanta Constitution* sports page. The computer print had obviously been scanned from an old clipping, but even so there was vibrancy and energy in the replica of the yellowed newsprint. Brown cradled a silver trophy in one arm. His other curved around Meg's shoulders. Their faces were inches apart, caught in a moment of exuberant joy. He was sunburned, his dark hair damp from heat and exertion, a generous mouth stretched in a triumphant smile. Meg's spectacular beauty— the narrow, intelligent face, deep-set eyes, hollow cheeks—was evident despite windswept hair and too much sun. Two happy people captured forever in a sunlit moment before the shadows came.

Annie wondered what the memory of that day had meant to each of them. She turned to the next sheet:

Tony Sherman

There is some confusion about her second husband. An old friend of Meg's, Juliet Thomas, worked with her finding jobs and homes for those fleeing the Vietnam draft. Juliet thought Sherman was from California, but later someone told her he was from

Wisconsin. He had been a graduate student working on his doctorate in English literature at Kent State when the shootings occurred. When he was drafted, he fled through Canada and eventually reached Paris, then went to Majorca, where he met Meg. At that time Meg was passionately involved in the antiwar movement. Sherman was glad to avoid the draft, but he was more interested in studying Lord Byron than in the latest troop movements. He was sailing in the Gulf of La Spezia when his small boat went down in a storm.

There were no photographs with this sparse report. Possibly Meg had pictures in old scrapbooks of this husband to whom she had been so briefly married. Or possibly not. Was Meg the kind of woman to have keepsakes? Perhaps her daughter would know.

Jenna Brown Carmody / Jason Brown

Born March 3, 1971, in Stuart, Florida. Jenna periodically saw her mother and spent summers with her father until his death in 1980. Along with her younger brother, Jason, she lived most of the time with her grandmother in Charleston. The children were very young when Meg relocated to Europe. Jenna graduated from the University of South Carolina with a B.A. in English. She lived in Atlanta and worked in fashion merchandising for a large department store. In 1994 she married Hunter Carmody, a fashion photographer. They separated the next year and divorced in 1996. No children. When her stepfather's health began to fail, she moved to the island. That reunited the family, as her brother keeps an apartment here. Jason, born July 3, 1972, is a top-ranked amateur golfer but has never tried to become a professional. He attended the University of South Carolina but dropped out as a sophomore. A golf reporter once described him wryly in a roundup on up-and-coming amateurs: "Jason Brown doesn't struggle with Demon Rum as did his father, Carey, but this young man isn't one to opt for practice over play, especially if the playmate is young and nubile."

In the margin, Max had scrawled: First things first.

Annie laughed, then continued reading. Not much she didn't know. Neither Jenna nor Jason had to work. They were TFBs, thanks to the generosity of their stepfather. Her eyes lingered on the abbreviation. Trust Fund Baby. It was a way of life for the Brown children. And for her own husband. Max knew her Puritan ethic had always equated work with worth, but now she was wise enough—she hoped—to understand that there was more to any person than a job. Still, what was life without work? All right, all right. What was her life without work? She knew the answer to that one. Let others find their own answers. And Max was working hard for her—and for Pamela—right this minute.

Her eyes dropped again to the sheet and Max's conclusion:

Jenna works part-time at Hodder's Antiques, obviously more for pleasure than money. Sue Hodder was circumspect, but I don't think she likes her a lot. Sue says Jenna obviously resents her mother, talks about seeing her only occasionally when a child, but she was devoted to her stepfather, said he's the one who had her and Jason come live with them. Jason's a chip off the old block, always going off for a cruise on somebody's yacht, occasionally plays in tournaments and usually does well, lots of girlfriends, buckets of charm, and his mother thought he hung the moon. There's no indication either sibling is in debt or in urgent need of money. In fact, they both should have plenty of funds since Meg was almost profligately generous with them. Heath left his entire estate to his wife. So an inheritance from their mother doesn't seem a likely motive. Both Jenna and Jason were at the Heath house on Saturday and Sunday.

Annie wriggled against the hot leather car seat. No, money was not going to be the motive for Meg's murder. Unless . . .

Claudette Taylor

Claudette Taylor was Duff Heath's executive secretary for the last twenty years of his career. After his retirement, she remained in his employ and after his death became Meg's personal assistant. Claudette is sixty-four and well regarded in the Atlanta home office of the Heath empire. She is remembered as responsible, careful, thoughtful, and discreet. She grew up in Atlanta. She is single with no living family members. Her last sibling died two years ago. Claudette is active in her church (First Methodist), a past treasurer of the Friends of the Library and current chair of the used book fair, a member of the island Kiwanis Club and the Red Cross. She and Meg appeared to be on good terms. She had no living expenses as she resided at the Heath home. However, much of her permanent savings was in Enron stock so her net worth has declined sharply. Apparently she expected a substantial bequest from Meg.

Annie brushed back damp curls. She almost popped out of the car to go up to the second deck and the small snack bar. Ben Parotti, who owned the ferry as well as the *Island Packet* excursion boat and the restaurant and a Gas 'n Go, never overlooked a possibility for profit. Right this minute she was desperate for a tall frosty bottle of water. Her lips were dry and her tongue parched. She looked out across the water and the heat haze shimmering above the pea-green surface. She willed herself to stay put. It was only another half mile to shore, and she wanted to finish the dossiers before she set off to find the pier at the end of Slash Pine Road.

Imogene Riley

Imogene Holman Riley, fifty-two, is a native of Bluffton. She dropped out of high school when she married J. B. Riley. The marriage ended in divorce ten years ago. They have two children, Leroy and Terry. Leroy is a truck driver and lives in Atlanta with his wife and two children. Terry is a crewman on a charter yacht out of Hilton Head Island. Imogene has worked as a cook in private residences. She was hired by the Heaths shortly after they moved to Broward's Rock. She is renowned for her Lowcountry cooking and is active in her church. Her credit rating is good. She makes her car, house, and credit card payments on time. Whether she is among Meg Heath's beneficiaries isn't known.

Annie slowly closed the folder. Max's information, gleaned from credit reports and most likely a church friend or neighbor, was in keeping with the cook's stolid demeanor. But the matter-of-fact report gave no hint of a woman familiar with Anastasia. It was a lesson all good detectives should remember: Don't be misled by surface appearances.

Surface appearances . . .

Pamela Potts spent her days helping others. Could there be more to her bland existence than appeared on the surface?

Meg Heath clearly was a woman who had followed her own desires. By all accounts, devil take the hindmost was the leitmotiv of her life. Who was to have been the sixth guest at her table tonight?

Jenna Brown Carmody wasn't devastated by her mother's death and she resented any suggestion of foul play.

Jason Carmody had the reputation of a ne'er-do-well, but his mother adored him.

Claudette Taylor appeared to be a cheerful servitor to Meg Heath. She had been Meg's husband's personal secretary. Claudette had never married. She'd stayed with Meg after Duff Heath's death. Surely that argued fondness for the widow. Claudette didn't seem to be in debt, but she was among those whose savings went down with Enron. How important to her was an inheritance from Meg?

Imogene Riley was matter-of-fact and calm, showing little emotion about the death of her mistress. Yet in her last meeting with Meg, Imogene remembered her as looking really special, like a grand duchess or a movie star.

Surface appearances . . .

The hoarse whistle of the *Miss Jolene* signaled the approaching shore. Annie dropped the folder on the passenger seat. The ferry jolted up to the dock. As the ramp lowered, she turned on the motor. She stared grimly ahead as the cars slowly bumped off the ferry. Emma better have something good up the sleeve of her caftan. Slash Pine Road and a password!

✧ *Eight* ✧

THE NEWSROOM OF THE *Island Gazette* had an air of spent calm similar to that of a beach after a storm or a deserted stadium after a big game, lots of litter and nobody around. The huge gray wastebasket near the newsroom printer overflowed with crumpled computer paper. Styrofoam cups half filled with cold coffee, discarded candy wrappers, and wadded-up fast-food sacks cluttered newsroom desks. The monitors glowed an inviting green, but the desk chairs were unoccupied. The deadline for tomorrow's *Gazette* had come and gone, and the troops had withdrawn from the front line for R&R.

"Hi, Lisa." Max waved hello to the receptionist, a svelte blonde with a ready smile and a sharp gaze. "Marian around?"

Lisa pointed down a hallway near the printer. "Coffee room." She started to rise. "I'll get her."

Max opened the swinging gate that led past a counter into the newsroom. "That's okay. I know the way."

Lisa settled back in her chair. "Do you know an eight-letter word for an Australian eucalyptus tree?"

Max was crossing the newsroom. "Ironbark."

He heard a muffled whoop as he opened the door to the coffee room.

Star reporter Marian Kenyon sat cross-legged on the floor, eyes closed, back straight, arms folded. Marian's salt-and-pepper black hair stuck out in odd tangles, most likely disarranged by frantic hand swipes as she worked. An empty one-ounce sack of roasted peanuts was crumpled beside the can of Pepsi in front of her. One arm unfolded. The can was seized, lifted to vivid red lips. Marian combined chewing and drinking, returned the can to the floor. "Whatever it is"—she didn't open her eyes—"come back next week."

Max pulled out a straight chair from the table, turned it around to straddle. He folded his arms on the back, prepared to bargain. "Like they say in literate crime flicks, quid pro quo."

One dark eye opened, regarded him without warmth. "I haven't seen a literate crime film since *Chinatown*. As for you, it better be good. I'm down to my last quantum of energy. Saturday night we picked up the report of a man found shot to death. I got the bulletin written, then went out to the crime scene. Sunday night I came back on the last ferry from Savannah and got the scoop on Pamela's plunge from the *Island Packet*. I was the early bird at Billy Cameron's office this morning and nobody tells the press nada until my deadline is closer than a guillotine to a French aristocrat's neck. Then from the funeral home we get"—she turned up fingers one by one—"a well-known community do-gooder dying as the result of her fall from the excursion boat and the unexpected death of an island socialite who was once a world-class model. Then it turns out the murder victim in snazzy clothes has no ID. I had to get the facts and write the copy for all three stories by noon. Do you know how many inches I wrote between eleven twenty-five and noon? Do you care? I care. Seventy-two inches. In thirty-five minutes. It may be my personal best." She closed the eye, raised the Pepsi, drank, and chewed.

The eyelid fell, but Max noted that her face had lifted and turned toward him. Were the eyelids slitted? Whatever, Marian was alert and listening.

Max dangled his bait. "I might be a Deep Throat"— would the truth behind the elusive source used by Bob Woodward and Carl Bernstein ever be revealed?— "with some interesting stuff about Pamela and Meg." Emma Clyde would be appalled at leaking suspicion of murder to the press, but Max figured Annie's accusations would surely be known to the murderer, if murderer there was. If both deaths were accidental, no harm done.

Marian's dark eyes popped wide. "What'cha got?"

"Some questions you might want to ask Chief Cameron." His smile was pleasant. And innocent. "Guaranteed to raise hackles at the cop shop."

Marian finished off the Pepsi and peanuts, stiffly rose. She scooted a chair to face Max, perched on the edge, dark eyes bright and penetrating. "And you want what?"

"Everything you know about the unidentified man found shot to death near Ghost Crab Pond." Max fished a small notebook from his pocket.

"The cop shop questions?" She reached into a wastebasket, retrieved crumpled computer sheets, turned them to the blank side, and pulled a pen from her pocket.

Max wasn't surprised. Marian's fearsome reputation as a reporter who always got her story hadn't resulted from being an easy touch. She would judge the worth of his offering before sharing what she knew above and beyond the official statements. "Who gave Pamela Potts a free ticket to the mystery cruise and why? Pamela apparently fell from a ledge on the far side of a chained-off area by a lifeboat. Pamela was deathly afraid of heights, so how—"

Marian wrote fast, her face scrunched in concentration.

"—did she end up on that ledge? Why was a scrap from a garbage bag snagged in the bottom of the lifeboat where she went over? Pamela Potts visited Meg Heath Friday morning." He let a long pause provide emphasis. "She was scheduled to see Meg this morning." Another pause. "So"—he made the linkage clear—"this morning Pamela died and Meg Heath was found dead from an overdose of Valium. How was it administered? Why did Meg plan a celebratory dinner for tonight? Who were the guests to be? And finally"—his tone was pleasant—"the *Gazette* might inquire if the police plan to release a plea for anyone with information about Pamela or Meg's final days to contact them."

Marian's eyes glittered. "Billy Cameron didn't mention Pamela or Meg, and he sure as hell never suggested either was a homicide victim. I get it. Billy's probably opted for accident with Pamela, suicide with Meg." She shook her head, curls quivering. "Just like a guy. Any woman would know better." Her glance at Max was piercing. "I'll bet there was a Private or No Trespass or No Admittance sign on the chain by the ledge. Pamela was born to follow the rules. As for Meg Heath, giving up wasn't in her game plan. I'll start with Doc Burford, go from there." She wrote with a flourish, wadded the folded sheets into her pocket.

Max flipped open his notebook, waited, pen poised.

Marian's bright dark eyes scoured his face. "You want info on the dead stranger. How come?"

Max didn't point out that his motives weren't part of the bargain. Right this minute Marian held the cards. Besides, he didn't mind revealing Annie's reasoning. Marian knew Annie well enough not to be surprised. "Annie's convinced there has to be a link between Pamela getting shoved off the boat and Meg overdosing. Annie's theory is that maybe the two of them knew something about the dead man." It sounded weak as he explained. "Or maybe it would mean something special to them if they found out he'd been shot."

"So somebody kills them to keep them from finding out this guy was shot Saturday night?" Marian stretched her face in disbelief. "Sounds pretty damn drastic. But for what it's worth . . ." She briefly pressed the tips of her fingers against her temples, took a deep breath. "Got a tip there was a crime scene about eleven o'clock Saturday night. Enough for a bulletin in the Sunday paper. I buzzed out there. The mosquitos and chiggers were big enough to have served in Patton's Tank Corps." She pointed at a series of red welts on her wrists. "I was smart enough to wear long sleeves, but the damn things bit me right through the cloth. I'll probably get West Nile.

"Anyway"—a weary sigh—"a Boy Scout troop on a campout found the body." For an instant her gamine face lost its tough patina. "Poor guys. Bad stuff to see when you still think you're invincible." She scrabbled in the other pocket of her slacks, dragged out a sack of hard candies, popped a red ball in her mouth. She sucked, gave Max a level look. "Not good even when you know life's like walking across a bog. You can get sucked down without warning. Anyway"—she rolled the candy to a corner of one cheek—"they were almost finished when I got there. Doc Burford had left. Flood-lights were set up on the corners, body still in situ. Looked like he'd been shot and the force knocked him down. He was on his back, wedged between a saw palmetto and an old log. One hand clutched at his chest. Congealed blood on his fingers. I'd guess he died pretty quick. Doc Burford can probably tell you. Nifty clothes—if you ignored the blood. White-and-blue-striped blazer, pink linen shirt, white trousers. Pretty pricey stuff. Even white shoes. He'd been a good-looking guy. Silver hair now, probably blond when he was young. Trim little mustache. Kind of re-minded me of an older Jeff Kent." Her eyes warmed. Marian was a big-time baseball fan. "Slick."

Max raised an eyebrow. "Doesn't sound like the kind of guy to be wandering around a swamp."

The reporter nodded, her wiry curls bouncing. "You got that one right. Now get the rest of the picture. The body's lying next to this rough track. It's not a road, just a couple of sandy ruts. The track comes off Marsh Tacky Road and dead-ends at Ghost Crab Pond."

Max knew the area well. Ghost Crab Pond was part of King Snake Park, a pocket of wilderness that abutted the developed area around the golf course. It had been the site of the murder of a mysterious island resident several years ago.

"Okay. The body's on the ground next to the sandy lane." Marian leaned forward. "You remember that tor-rential downpour we had last Friday?"

Knowing Marian, Max assumed that the weather detail was not a non sequitur. "Washed out my golf game." He'd missed playing, but all had not been lost.

He remembered the passionate afternoon with Annie. As he'd later told her, a rainy day has its own charm.

"Buckets of rain. Tropical storm number whatever. Water still standing in the ruts. I took a good look at his shoes. Whiter than Casper in a spotlight." Her bright eyes locked with Max's.

Max got it. "He didn't walk there. You haven't mentioned a car."

"No car there. Just the body. But he must have come in a car. If he'd been on a bike or scooter there would have been mud splashes on those white pants." Marian brushed back a wiry curl, still looked unkempt as a sheepdog. "There are tire tread prints. You can see where a car backed and turned. Interesting thing is that no effort was made to obscure those prints. However"—she paused for emphasis—"there were a couple of places on the track near the body where the ground looked like it had been swept over with the fronds of a palm tree. Now why"—she propped her pointed chin on a fist—"would anybody clean up footprints and not worry about the car treads?"

Max sketched the outline of a car. "Because there is no link between the car and the murderer?"

"That's my take." Her tone was approving. "Either the car belonged to the victim or maybe it was a rental car."

"A tourist?" Max frowned. "What's a stranger doing out there?"

Marian punched a fist into a palm. "Following directions." Her voice was silky. "Let's say our dandy guy is on his way somewhere with a passenger. That passenger knows the island damn well. A stranger wouldn't have a clue that the road dead-ends at Ghost Crab Pond and is, as a matter of fact, damn remote and a perfect spot for homicide. I see it this way. The victim picks up somebody. We don't know who or why, but the passenger gives directions. Go this way. Turn here. The car fetches up at the dead end. The road runs east-west up to the pond. The body was on the south side of the tracks. That makes me think the victim was driving. He stopped the car, got out. Why? Maybe the passenger got out first, saying he'd check to see if they were going the right way. Maybe instead he—or she—came around the car, pulled a gun, ordered the driver out, shot him. Then the killer picked up a handy frond, dusted out all the footprints, got in the car, drove like hell."

Max tapped his pen on the pad. "No ID on the victim."

"According to police, there was no wallet, nothing in his pockets but some change. Of course, that suggests robbery was the motive." She pursed her lips. "His clothes were expensive."

Max looked skeptical. The island had its share of crime, but holdups resulting in murder weren't the norm. "It could have been a drug deal gone wrong"—that kind of crime occurred everywhere along the coast—"but I don't think a holdup is likely."

"Probably not. Anyway, I'm sure Billy's got his prints, sent them out. But . . ." Her shrug was eloquent. There might be a military record, perhaps even a police record. Matching up prints would take time and luck. "I'd say for sure he wasn't a local. I don't claim to know everybody on the island, but I know most of the gentry. I'm betting he was a tourist. If he was a tourist, hell, he could have come from anywhere. Billy sent out a bulletin with the description. Unless somebody turns in a missing persons report, he may always be the mystery man of Ghost Crab Pond."

Max shut his notebook. A tourist. The island was

crammed now with vacationing families. But somebody might have noticed a handsome older man in a
striped blazer and white trousers. Max pushed up from
the chair. "You say he looked like an older Jeff Kent?
That gives me an idea."

Slash Pine Road twisted and curled through the maritime forest, ending at a stand of cane. This was nature
in the raw, the woods as early explorers found it, wild
and overgrown, huge pines swaying in the breeze, dead
trees poking out of ferns and tangled bushes, live oak
limbs meeting overhead to create a dim tunnel swarming with flies, gnats, mosquitos, horseflies, and bum-
blebees. Annie peered through milky green light and
spotted a faint break in the cane, possibly a path. Reluctantly she stepped out of the car, flapped her hands
to dispel a cloud of no-see-ums. The hot air hummed
with the distinctive rasp of cicadas and chirp of crick-
ets. Pine straw blanketed the ground. There could be
snakes. In fact, snakes were a certainty, everything
from scarlet kings to cottonmouths. She edged slowly
forward, watching the ground, stepping slowly and
cautiously. It was only fifteen or twenty yards on the
path to the edge of the Sound, but she grudged every
step. What was Emma up to?

The mudflat stretched a hundred yards at low tide,
steaming beneath the hot summer sun. Annie steamed,
too, sweat beading her skin. She took a deep breath, sa-
voring the distinctive gassy smell. The stench appalled
tourists, who were sure a sewage main had broken.
Annie knew the odor for what it was, the richness of
decay and growth that made the marsh a haven for blue
crabs, shrimp, oysters, and wading birds. Fiddler crabs
scurried like commuters racing to the subway. A weath-

ered pier poked out to the water. As far as she could see, she was the only human creature for miles. A sailboat scudded far out in the Sound, its white sail puffed by the wind.

Annie looked behind her. The cane rippled in the breeze. She faced the water and bent forward, listening to the crackle of the fiddler crabs and the occasional squelch as air bubbles popped in the muck. There was no sound of anyone approaching by land or by sea. Frowning, she climbed the rickety steps to the pier. Occasional boards were missing on the narrow walkway. She skirted the hazards, hoping the ramshackle, obviously abandoned structure wouldn't collapse beneath her. She stopped at the far end near a ladder. The water here was deep enough for a boat to moor. She shaded her eyes and gazed out into the Sound. Should she stay on the pier? Despite the breeze, it was hotter than a griddle in a short-order kitchen. If she returned to the woods, the buzzing insects would swarm for blood. Hers.

Her cell phone jangled in her purse. Annie grabbed it, pulled it out. If Emma had further instructions, she was going to get an earful in response.

"Hello." She intended to sound crisp, but surly was nearer the mark.

"Dear Child." The appellation was affectionate. "I detect stress. Hostility. I see you now"—Laurel's husky voice was soothing—"perturbed, uncertain. Sweaty?"

Annie pushed back a tangle of damp hair. Okay, it was August, so why shouldn't she be sweaty? Laurel didn't have second sight. She didn't know Annie was marooned at the end of a pier in a marsh. Of course she didn't. "What can I do for you, Laurel?" Her lips felt dry. Her throat ached for water. Why hadn't she bought a bottle of water on the ferry?

A sweet laugh. "One for all and all for one. It is a fine motto not simply for the Musketeers but for all of us. I see my task as bolstering your efforts to discover the truth about the deaths of Pamela and Meg. We all knew our dear Pamela quite well, her intensity and devotion and serious nature. It is easy to see how Pamela, in the pursuit of duty, might have put herself in danger. Clearly, Pamela's most recent activities involved Meg Heath. I have"—and now she was brisk—"continued to explore Meg's relationships. I spoke at length with a nurse—-Eileen Moody—-who attended Duff Heath during his final illness. Eileen recounted to me an exchange that occurred a week before Duff died. He had been in and out of awareness. One afternoon, he awoke. Meg was sitting beside him. Duff looked up and said, 'We had a good run, didn't we?' Meg smiled. 'Very good.' He was quiet for a moment, then asked, 'Not the best?' She took his hand, held it with both of hers. 'A very good run. I wouldn't trade it for anything.' He got a funny look on his face, kind of a sad smile, then he murmured, 'Nothing except Tony.' She didn't say anything for a long time. Finally, she bent close. 'You are by far the finer man.' He closed his eyes, drifted to sleep. Eileen said Meg held his hand, stayed there, tears slipping down her cheeks."

Annie was no longer aware of the glare of the sun or the itch of insect bites. She was at the bedside of a dying man and a woman with tearstained cheeks.

"Actually"—there was a note of wonder in Laurel's voice—"I've always counted white lies a kindness. Although Mark Twain perhaps had a clearer moral view."

Annie was not a Twain scholar. "Which was?"

"Twain said, 'One of the most striking differences between a cat and a lie is that a cat has only nine lives.' But"—Laurel was thoughtful—"in the case of Meg and Duff, the effect was quite the opposite."

Annie wished for a sixteen-ounce cup of icy water. She pulled her sticky blouse away from her skin, tried to sort out the images of cats, white lies, and a tearful Meg holding Duff's lax hand. "What effect?"

"The reason Eileen Moody remembers that exchange so clearly is because there was no lie. Meg wouldn't tell Duff she loved him more than Tony. Not even as Duff was dying." The final words drifted soft as a sigh. The connection ended.

Annie dropped the cell phone back into her purse. She knew Laurel meant well, but nothing about Duff Heath, his life or his death, pertained to the murder of his widow.

Except money.

She could hear in her mind Emma's gruff pronouncement: I always like money as a motive. But that was simply Emma being a mystery writer. Meg's estate was willed to her children and her secretary. Meg hadn't had long to live. So far as Max had been able to discover, neither of Meg's children was in dire financial straits. Claudette's holdings had been much diminished, but she didn't appear to be in any urgent need. So the money didn't matter.

What did matter?

Annie closed her eyes. Pamela knew something or saw something. . . .

A faint thrum sounded.

Annie's eyes popped open. She stared out at the pea-green water. A motorboat surged around the point and headed toward the pier. A lanky man in a T-shirt and faded jeans slouched in the bucket seat, his face shaded by a straw hat. Years of sun reflected from salt water had reddened his fair skin to a permanent pink. The boat pulled up next to the ladder, idled. He threw out a line, tied it, stood with one freckled hand curled around a step. "You got the word?" His drawl was as slow as a possum's stroll.

Annie was not amused. Emma was obviously harking back to the days of old-time thrillers. Had she recently reread William Le Queux or F. Van Wyck Mason? Whatever, Annie knew she'd remain hot and chigger-bitten at the end of this isolated pier if she didn't play the game and offer up the password. Annie snapped, "Avenger."

He nodded, steadied the boat. "Come aboard."

Max held a colored pencil above the computer-generated color print of the Astros second baseman Jeff Kent. The smiling athlete wore a soft gray business suit. Max tinted the hair—

Marian fluffed her wiry curls. "More hair. Lots of it. Thick."

—and mustache silver. He added strokes, three, four, more until Marian nodded in satisfaction. Max selected another pencil, delicately shaded lines onto the smooth face, darkened soft pouches beneath the eyes.

"Oh hey, that's good." Marian pointed at the eyes. "Make 'em brown."

Max complied. A blue pencil alternated with white to achieve the striped blazer. He stopped twice to sharpen the white pencil before he finished transforming the trousers and shoes.

Marian's dark eyes squeezed in concentration. "I

got it. The part—" she tapped the thick mane of white hair—"was on the right side. See, I was looking down so it was my left. But he parted it on the right."

Max erased, adjusted, made the change, handed the altered print to Marian.

The reporter's expression was curious. Her usual sardonic gaze softened. "Yeah. Damn close. This is how he might have looked if I'd met him when he was alive. Death has a dampening effect, you know. But yeah, this is amazing." She peered up at Max. "What are you going to do with it?"

"Ask around." Max gestured with the pencil. "That blazer would attract attention."

Marian lifted her shoulders, let them fall. "Tourist season, Max."

He understood. All God's children, black, white, yellow, and brown, jammed the island in August. This annual flood of easy spenders delighted the shopkeepers and astonished the residents who fled the muggy island for Cape Cod or the Rockies. Vacationers' attire included everything from solar topees to thongs, but the victim when alive might have been attractive enough that most women would notice him. And it was women Max intended to ask.

The motorboat chugged up to a pier even rattier than the derelict structure that poked into the Sound at the end of Slash Pine Road. A sleek white motorboat was moored at the end. Annie squinted against the sun. The name was painted in crimson: *SLEUTH*. Emma Clyde had already arrived. "Why?" had to be the question of the hour. A cabin high on stilts sat in solitary splendor at the edge of the marsh. The densely vegetated island had an aura of isolation. Annie guessed this was one of the many small islands that were mostly uninhabited and used for hunting.

Her silent companion held the boat steady and gestured at the ladder. "Ms. Clyde'll take you back."

As Annie clambered up the ladder, the motor roared as he gave his boat full throttle to bounce out of the cove. Annie's footsteps echoed on the wooden pier. She walked fast despite the heat. When she reached shore, she followed a sandy path that curved around a grove of pines.

As she looked up at the weathered cabin, the screen door opened and Emma stepped out. Her ice-blue curls frizzed from the damp heat and her thin cotton caftan drooped against her, but she looked triumphant.

Annie climbed to the porch. She was too hot and tired to vent her irritation. "Water?" It was almost a croak.

"You bet. No electricity, but we have an icebox. Reminds me of being on safari. Come on in." She held open the door. "I'll get you some water in a minute. But first . . ."

Annie stepped into dimness. A familiar voice called out, "Have a happy day."

Annie's eyes jerked to the right. Pamela's parrot preened in a cage near a wall adorned with trophies of the hunt—the head of a massive buck, two mourning doves, a rabbit, quail, and three ducks. Annie found the display off-putting. She preferred her wildlife alive. Nails clicked on the wooden floor and Whistler pattered up to her, nuzzled one hand with a moist nose. Henny came forward smiling, hands outstretched. Despite the heat, Henny sparkled. She'd changed into a crisp white blouse, tan walking shorts, and tennis shoes. She looked sporty and comfortable. And happy.

Annie's eyes widened. "I thought you were going to stay with a sick friend."

Henny stepped out of the way, gestured toward the bed in the far corner of the one-room cabin. The spread was pulled back. Its folds stirred in a ripple of breeze from the battery-powered fan swiveling back and forth in front of an aluminum tub filled with ice.

Annie's eyes adjusted to the dimness. She saw bunched-up pillows, the white gauze of a bandage, lank blond hair, a wan face, puzzled blue eyes—

"Pamela!" Annie scarcely breathed. "Oh, Pamela." Annie hurried forward, glad tears blurring her vision. She dropped into the straight chair next to the bed, picked up a limp hand.

Henny was close behind. Her soft murmur pierced Annie's shock. ". . . just awakened a few minutes ago. I've brought her medicines up-to-date. She doesn't know about Meg Heath, and I haven't asked about last night."

Pamela blinked uncertainly. The hand in Annie's grasp suddenly tightened. Pamela's gaze moved from Annie to Henny to Emma. She stared past them at the rough interior of the cabin. "Where am I?" She struggled to sit up.

Emma bustled closer. "Henny, give me a hand." The two of them helped Pamela to sit up against the pillows. "Relax, Pamela. You're going to be fine. You got banged on the head. This is Dr. Burford's hunting cabin. He thought it would be a good place for you to recover." Emma spoke as if patients with head wounds routinely ended up in their doctors' hunting cabins.

Annie glared at Emma. "You could have told me."

Emma raised a cautionary finger to her lips. "Later."

Annie understood. This was no time to tell Pamela

she'd been declared dead with the connivance of the chief medical examiner and whisked away because her life might still be in danger.

Pamela yanked her hand free from Annie's, lifted it to gingerly touch the dressing on the back of her head. "Ouch. I don't understand."

Emma, Henny, and Annie looked at one another. Emma frowned, pursed her lips. Henny looked uncertain. Annie hesitated. For an instant, the only sound in the rustic room was the whistle from the parrot's cage.

Pamela twisted to look. "Rhett Butler?" Amazement mingled with delight.

The bird cocked his head. "Pammie better?"

The terrier bounded to the bed, stood on his back legs, yipped. He wriggled with eagerness, his high bark a celebration.

"Whistler." Pamela's voice was weak but the joy in her face made her look stronger, better. She reached out to stroke his wiry fur.

Emma tugged at his collar. "Sit."

Pamela started to shake her head, winced. "My head hurts. What happened to me?"

Annie scooted the chair forward. "You had a fall last night on the mystery cruise." Absently, Annie accepted an ice-cold bottle of water, already uncapped by Emma, and drank it down without taking her eyes off Pamela's pale, drawn face. "Can you tell us what happened?"

Pamela looked bewildered. "I don't know." She sounded frightened, bewildered.

Emma spoke gently. "Let's take it step by step. Why did you go on the cruise?"

A sweet smile curved pale lips. Pamela's blue eyes looked toward Annie. "Annie, that was so generous of you. I went out to lunch after church on Sunday. Jared Wheeler took me. I don't know if you know him. He moved to the island last fall and he is such a nice man. He bought the house next door to mine. It was such a lovely day. We went to the inn and it was the most wonderful brunch I've ever been to. The specialty was blue crab and scallop cakes. The array of vegetables was amazing. I wish I had the recipe for the candied yams. I think there might have been some prunes—"

Annie folded her fingers tightly together to keep from strangling Pamela. "Pamela, what about the cruise?"

"Oh yes. It was almost three when I got home from brunch. I saw at once that someone had left something in the letter box. Did you know—"

Annie remembered past exchanges with Pamela. Dear, serious, intense, literal Pamela could describe any event, large or small, in excruciating detail. Before Annie could attempt a diversion, Emma took charge.

"—that it's against the law for a letter box to be used for any purpose other than delivery of authorized mail. Yes, indeed." Emma was at her most commanding. "Pamela, we must conserve your strength. I'll ask questions, and you answer in as few words as possible. Now. You got home from brunch and found an envelope in the mailbox. What was in it?"

Pamela brightened. "A ticket to the cruise. And one of Annie's bookmarks—"

There were stacks of Death on Demand bookmarks available everywhere at the store.

"—and Annie had printed 'FOR YOU' in capital letters at the top." Another appreciative smile was beamed at Annie. "I thought it was so nice." Pamela smoothed back a strand of hair. "I looked for you on the boat, but you were so busy. It was a lovely cruise." The smile gradually dissolved. She lifted her hand to touch the bandage. "How did I get hurt?"

Emma's brusque voice was uncharacteristically gentle. "You tell us. What's the last thing you remember?"

Pamela clutched the sheet. "I was in the main saloon after dinner. I didn't do the Treasure Map." She looked embarrassed. "I don't like climbing up and down and going near the railing. I know it's silly"—Annie reached out, patted a tense hand—"but I don't have a good head for heights. I used the interior steps to go up and down from the main deck to the upper deck. But it was awfully hot in the saloon. I decided to step out on the deck for some air. I walked out"—her blue eyes were suddenly troubled—"and it was still hot but I smelled the water. Then my head hurt. That's all I remember." Her face was anxious. "What happened?"

Henny dipped a washcloth in the melting water from the ice, wrung it out, placed the cold cloth against Pamela's face. "You fell overboard."

"Off the ship?" Horror lifted Pamela's voice. "Into the water? Oh no."

Emma folded her arms. Her cold blue eyes narrowed. "Hit from behind. That's clear. She doesn't know a damn thing. Pamela, think." The raspy voice was compelling. "Right before the pain in your head, what did you hear? Smell? See? Feel?" Her stare at Pamela never wavered.

Annie watched in fascination, knowing this was an exhibition of how Marigold Rembrandt would handle a witness in an Emma Clyde novel.

"Oh." Pamela had the look of a bird mesmerized by a snake. "I was standing there, looking out at the lights on the water. That's when my head exploded. It was awful. Everything turned red and black."

"Billy will have to admit this couldn't have been an accident." Annie felt vindicated. "She never got close to the chain and the railing."

Emma kept her focus on Pamela. She leaned across the bed, her face inches from the pillow. "What else? Think hard."

Pamela tensed. "There was something. . . ." Her voice faded away. She strained, then closed her eyes. "I heard something. But I don't know what it was."

Emma smiled. "You're doing well, Pamela. You heard someone."

"Someone?" The big blue eyes opened.

Emma was brusque. "The person who hit you."

Pamela gasped. Her hands lifted to her throat.

Annie patted her shoulder. "Don't be frightened. We're going to figure out what happened."

"Somebody hit me? Why?" Now there were slow tears.

Henny refreshed the cold cloth, gently swiped Pamela's cheeks. "We're hoping you can remember something out of the way that happened to you in the last few days, some reason why you might be in danger."

Pamela stared at them in bewilderment. Clearly her return to consciousness wasn't going to provide a solution.

Emma broke the discouraged silence. She spoke to Annie and Henny. "There's nothing else for it. We have to tell her about Meg." She gestured at Annie. "You were there."

Annie described what she had discovered at the Heath house. She hated seeing the look of sadness and distress as Pamela listened. ". . . and it turns out she died from an overdose of Valium. Billy Cameron wondered if she might have done it herself."

Pamela tried to shake her head, winced in pain. But her voice was strong and determined. "No. Not Mrs. Heath."

Annie nodded. "That's what we think, too. Anyway, you came every morning to read the *Gazette* to her. In the Sunday paper there's a bulletin about an unidentified man shot to death near Ghost Crab Pond"— Annie felt a sinking disappointment; there was no change at all in Pamela's face—"and I wondered if that's why Meg was killed. To keep you from reading the paper to her."

Pamela sagged against the pillows. "I can't believe she's gone. I know she was sick, but she had so much energy. Not physical energy but psychic. Reading the newspaper to her was always challenging. She wanted to know everything that was odd and strange. Not the kind of stories I like to read to sick people."

Annie was nodding. Yes, Meg Heath would have teased and cajoled and ordered until she learned all the news that was barely fit to print. If she'd lived until this morning and Pamela had made her customary visit, Meg would have seized on the cryptic bulletin about the unidentified murder victim. But the news of that murder made no impression on Pamela. So Annie's hunch wasn't worth the flicker of the neuron that created it. Maybe the contents of the *Gazette* were irrelevant. But dammit, something must have happened on Friday morning! "Meg had planned a special dinner party for tonight. Did she mention that to you?"

Pamela lay limply against the pillows. Her eyelids fluttered.

Henny stepped to the bedside table, poured water into a glass. She leaned forward, held the glass to Pamela's lips. "Here. Drink a little."

Pamela took several sips, turned her head away.

Emma lifted Pamela's hand, fingers at her wrist. "Pulse fast. That's enough for now."

Annie knew it was time to leave. But she'd been so sure. . . . She bent forward, spoke fast. "Pamela, one more thing before you rest. What did you and Meg talk about Friday morning?"

Slowly Pamela's eyes opened. Her voice was drowsy. "I didn't spend any time with her Friday. I'd just got there when the doorbell rang. I answered it because no one else was there. A man wanted to see Meg. He said he was an old friend. He gave me a card to take up to her."

Emma and Henny stood frozen, watching Pamela. Annie scarcely breathed. She kept her voice casual. "What happened?"

Pamela yawned. "I took the card up. Meg was—" For an instant she seemed uncertain. "She seemed stunned. She stared at the card and said, 'I'll be damned. Or maybe *he* will.' Then she laughed and said, 'Tell him to come up. You can take a holiday, Pamela. He can read to me this morning, bring me up-to-date on everything.' She seemed to think that was very funny." Tears filled Pamela's eyes again. "It's so sad to remember."

"For God's sake"—Emma's impatience boiled over—"what happened?"

Pamela was startled. "Nothing. I went down and told him he could go up and showed him the way to Meg's suite and then I left. I went over to the church—"

"Pamela." Annie forced herself to remain calm

and patient. "What was on the card that you took up to Meg?"

Pamela's blue eyes were dumfounded. "On the card? How would I know?"

"You didn't read it?" The cry came almost in unison from Annie, Emma, and Henny.

Pamela looked from one to another. "It wasn't intended for me."

Annie reached over, patted a thin hand. "Of course you didn't read it. So you don't know his name or anything about him. Pamela, what did he look like?"

"He was very handsome." Her tone was bright. "The kind of man Meg would know, silver hair and beautifully dressed, a blue-and-white-striped blazer and pink shirt and white trousers. . . ."

As the careful, accurate description continued, Annie clapped her hands together. Someone had committed two murders to keep anyone from knowing this man had come to see Meg. Now all they had to do was find out who he was and why he had come.

❖ *Nine* ❖

GUESTS BUNCHED AT THE front desk of the Sea Side Inn. The clerks, one elderly and calm, the other a frazzled college girl, worked at a brisk pace. A baby wailed in the arms of a young mother leaning against a pillar next to a pile of luggage, a diaper bag, a stroller, and a folded playpen. A sour-faced man with a bald head and walrus mustache glanced irritably at his watch.

Max was in a hurry. He didn't have time to join a line. He moved toward the wide central stairway leading to the second floor and took the steps two at a time. Deep-cushioned chairs and sofas provided a cozy enclave outside the Magnolia Room. Max poked his head inside the restaurant. Afternoon tea was over and it hadn't opened yet for dinner. The swinging doors to the kitchen were propped wide. The chatter of soft voices mingled with the clatter of dishes. Max walked through the shadowy room to the brightly lit kitchen with its array of shelving and cabinets and counters, all sparkling clean.

A heavyset woman with a genial face paused from unloading a huge dishwasher. She held a tea glass in one hand. "We open at five."

"I know." He was polite, respectful. "I'm Max Darling. Freddie Whipple is a friend of mine." He didn't hesitate to use the owner's name. Annie was a good customer of the tearoom though her heart belonged to Parotti's. "May I speak to you for a moment?" He moved toward her, opening the folder he was carrying.

She placed the glass on a tray, studied him with bright, curious eyes. "Well . . ."

Max handed her the altered photograph. He spoke in a pleasant voice. "I'm trying to find this man. Have you seen him?"

She studied the picture. Slowly she shook her head. "I don't think so. Course, we get about a couple of hundred folks a day and there's new faces all the time." Her lips pursed. "But I think I would have remembered him."

Max opened the folder again. "I'll leave several copies with you and some of my cards. If you'd check with the wait staff, I'd appreciate it. If anyone recognizes him, ask them to call me. There's a fifty-dollar reward for any information that will help me find him."

Her fine brows drew together. "Would he mind?"

Max met her gaze. "No, ma'am. He won't mind. I can promise you that."

Max watched as she turned away, moving toward the other employees in the kitchen. He took his time walking through the dim dining area in case anyone hurried after him with information. No one did.

The inn had three stories. He started on the top floor, looking for cleaning staff. He found a maid with her cart at the far end of the second floor. She spoke very little English and shook her head at his questions, her eyes wide and frightened. On the first floor, he found a cart outside Room 124. He looked inside, waited until the maid finished vacuuming. When the rumble ceased, he knocked on the jamb.

She turned, looked at him with stolid courtesy.

"Excuse me, please." He held out the picture. "I'm looking for this man. There's a fifty-dollar reward."

She stared down at the printed sheet, her face impassive, then lifted her eyes. "Fifty dollars?"

Max reached for his billfold. He took out two twenties and a ten, held them in his hand. "Was he staying here?"

Slowly she nodded. "He asked for ice. I brought him a bucket. He gave me five dollars. Lots of folks give a dollar. Some folks don't give anything."

Max kept his tone casual. "What was the room number?"

She stared at the money, frowned. "Room"—her eyes squeezed in concentration—"108."

Annie clung to the seat rest as the sleek speedboat sliced through the water, foam spewing to either side. The shore hurtled nearer. Annie welcomed the cooling effect of the whipping wind, but the speed was enough to scare a luge team. She gasped as the boat slewed around a buoy, broke off relating her morning at the Heath house.

The wind puffed Emma's curls. She looked like a grizzled bulldog in a blue wig, her square face lifted into the wind. Without glancing away from the water, Emma barked, "Relax, Annie. I haven't sunk a boat since the Solomons."

Annie was in no mood for war stories though she'd never doubt Emma's heroics. At the moment, all she wanted was to set foot again on the rickety pier at the end of Slash Pine Road.

"So then?" Emma's brusque demand jerked Annie like a dog brought to heel.

Annie took a deep breath and picked up where she'd left off. "Anyway, I'd swear that Claudette and Jenna know about something that happened to Meg this weekend, something they don't want to talk about."

She fought the temptation to ask Emma to slow down. Knowing the redoubtable author as she did, the outcome would most likely be more speed, not less. Annie remained silent and hung on.

But the boat slowed as Emma glanced toward Annie, her blue eyes bright. "Sure they're hiding something. Meg's visitor. Therefore we need for you—"

Annie braced against the seat, this time not for safety but in anticipation of an unpalatable task. She felt she'd done all she could manage for one day.

"—to confront them." Emma's smile was wolfish.

"Maybe *you* should talk to them." Annie didn't go on to point out that Emma was a lot tougher proposition than Annie. No point in stating the obvious.

The boat picked up speed. "I would, but I've got to see Billy and explain what we've done."

A rollicking but muffled rendition of "Beer Barrel Polka" sounded over the thump of the bow on the water.

Emma pointed with her elbow toward her oversize canvas purse. "Grab the cell, will you?"

Annie loosed her hold, bounced in the seat, grabbed Emma's orange-striped carryall. She braced her feet and pulled out the cell phone. "Hello." Her shout came back at her, lost in the wind.

"Annie? Doc Burford. Emma handy?" As usual, his deep voice was brusque and impatient.

"Hi, Doc. We're on the Sound. In the *Sleuth*. Can I take a message?" She held tight to the cell. She had no intention of permitting Emma to be deflected from her piloting. They were only a hundred yards offshore now.

His laughter boomed. "Better hang on. And bring me up-to-date. How's my patient?"

"She's conscious." Once again Annie felt the incredible uplift she'd experienced when she realized Pamela was alive. Alive and safe. Or safe for the moment. "She doesn't know who hit her. All she remembers is her head hurting. I can't believe you connived with Emma and spirited her away."

He made a growling noise. "We got a second chance. Emma and I took advantage of it. Damn few times that happens." His dour tone recalled the murder victims he'd examined.

"There are going to be a lot of happy people when the word gets out that she's okay." Annie knew she'd never truly accorded Pamela her due. When Pamela was strong again, Annie intended to tell her just how much everyone cared. "Is she still officially dead?"

Doc Burford didn't answer for an instant. Finally, his voice slow and deliberate, he decreed, "No. I'll announce that there was some confusion when Miss Potts was moved to a rehabilitation institution in Savannah. Her prognosis is good. No visitors permitted. Friends may send cards and flowers in care of Annie Darling at Death on Demand. That okay with you?"

"Of course." But Annie's thoughts were racing. "Dr. Burford, you did the autopsy on the man who was found dead at Ghost Crab Pond, didn't you?"

"Right. No gun was found but I got out the bullet in good condition—"

Annie interrupted. "Friday morning he came to see Meg. Pamela saw him."

"You don't say?" He was excited. "That's important. We need to tell Billy. Hmm. He'll want to talk to Pamela."

Annie looked at Emma. "Dr. Burford says Billy will want to ask Pamela about Meg's visitor." Annie remembered Pamela's wan face and her drift into healing sleep. Pamela didn't need a session with the police. She turned back to the cell phone. "Dr. Burford, instead of Billy coming to the cabin, couldn't we tell him what she—"

Emma's elbow jabbed Annie's arm.

Annie broke off. "Just a second." She looked toward Emma.

Emma eased up on the throttle. The *Sleuth* nosed toward the dock. "Tell him I taped our conversation with Pamela. I'm on my way to the station now."

Annie found a shady spot on the starboard side of the ferry. She called Max, but his cell phone wasn't turned on. She left a brief and joyous message about her happy excursion to Doc Burford's hunting cabin and reunion with Pamela. "I'm going to drop by the store, then I'll be home. Love you." She clicked off the phone, leaned against the railing, and drank from her just-purchased bottle of icy water. Despite the afternoon temperature nudging into the nineties, the shade and the breeze and the water combined to cool her. For the first time since Pamela's rescue last night, she didn't feel anxious. Billy would see the connection among the attack on Pamela, Meg's death, and the murder of Meg's Friday morning visitor. What were the odds the murdered man was going to be a guest at the special dinner?

Annie wished she could see the police chief's face

when Emma played the tape with Pamela's description of Meg's visitor. Annie drank deeply, watched a flight of pelicans skimming above the waves. Who was the handsome stranger, and why had he come to the island?

Max held out a print of the altered photograph.

Sun glanced through the window, emphasizing the silver in Billy Cameron's thatch of blond hair and the lines of fatigue in his face. He looked at the image, lifted a startled gaze to Max. "Where did you get this?"

Max explained Marian Kenyon's observations and description. "She claims it's a spitting image—if the guy was alive."

Billy rattled the sheet, his face pleased. "This is good stuff. I'll send it out. We still don't have an ID on him."

Max settled back in the straight chair next to Billy's metal desk. "I've got a lead, Billy. . . ." Max concluded with the room number at the inn.

Billy picked up the phone, punched. "Chief Cameron here. I need information about a guest who was staying at the inn . . ." He looked toward Max.

Max didn't need to check his notes. The maid had remembered that five-dollar tip. "Friday night for sure."

"Friday night. Room 108." Billy turned on the speakerphone. He pulled a notepad nearer, waited with pen in hand.

"Room 108." The voice was young. "Friday night. Robert Smith. Home address: 1583 Peachtree Street, apartment 103, Atlanta. Mr. Smith was here for two nights, checked out by video"—there was a slight pause—"at two-oh-seven A.M. on Sunday. Left the charge on his Visa."

Max and Billy exchanged glances. The man lying

dead near Ghost Crab Pond on Saturday night certainly wasn't enjoying the convenience of video checkout early Sunday morning. Obviously the murderer had retrieved his victim's room key along with his wallet and all identifying contents. It was simple for the murderer to enter the side door of the inn using the electronic key card, hurry down a deserted hallway to the room. It wouldn't take long to toss the dead man's belongings into a suitcase, use the video checkout, and return to the victim's car.

Billy tapped his pen on the desktop. "Is the room currently occupied?"

"Oh yes, sir. We don't have any vacancies." A sigh. "I've got people in line—"

"Give me the credit card number. And connect me with Freddie Whipple." In a moment, the number scrawled on the pad, Billy had the hotel manager on the line.

"Freddie, we may have traced a homicide victim to the inn. We think he was staying in Room 108 Friday night. I want to check the room for fingerprints."

Max understood Billy's plan. Even though the room had been cleaned on Sunday and was currently occupied, there might be vagrant prints on the television remote, the television cabinet, the bedside table, the door panels. It was worth checking out. Even a partial match would identify the victim as Robert Smith, and the full powers of a police investigation could be focused on the visitor from Atlanta.

Robert Smith. Max glanced down at the print. Well-dressed, sporty. Probably called Bob. Or Bobby. There were several hundred thousand Bob Smiths across America. Who was this Bob Smith, and why had he come to the island?

Billy punched the intercom on his desk. "Mavis, round up Lou. We need to look for some prints over at the inn. A guest there this weekend may turn out to be the guy shot out at Ghost Crab Pond."

Max was at the door, lifting his hand in farewell. Now it was up to Billy and his staff to find out about Bob Smith. He said good-bye to Mavis at the front counter, stepped out into the asphalt-melting, Calcutta-humid heat of late afternoon. He cranked up the air-conditioning in his car. He felt like a sun-parched camel. Maybe gazpacho for dinner? A Caesar salad with grilled chicken? Of course, Annie would want lots of anchovies. In any event, a salad would be something cool. . . .

Cool. Bob Smith looked like a cool guy. Max turned one vent so the flow hit him directly in the face. As he started to pull away from the curb, his gaze stopped at the bright blue newspaper display case of the *Island Gazette*. Marian Kenyon would be furious if he didn't alert her. He pulled out his cell phone and turned it on. One message. His eyes widened in surprise as he listened to Annie's buoyant voice. Tot up a coup for Emma Clyde. He thought about Marian Kenyon's stark description of Saturday night at Ghost Crab Pond and knew that Pamela was lucky, lucky to have survived the fall from the *Island Packet* and lucky to have friends like Emma Clyde, Doc Burford, and Henny Brawley. Max wondered if they might be persuaded to give a blow-by-blow account of their success in spiriting Pamela off island. Marian could do a bang-up story. In any event, Marian would definitely want to know that the dead man had been seen at Meg's house and that he might be Robert Smith from Atlanta. Max punched in the number of the *Gazette*.

*   *   *

Annie banged through the front door of Death on Demand. She felt as if she were returning from a far journey. But wasn't she? This morning she'd grieved. Now she celebrated. There was no greater distance than that between heartbreak and happiness. "Ingrid?" Annie started down the central aisle.

Ingrid Webb hurried from the back of the store clutching a copy of Simon Hawke's *Much Ado About Murder*. Her eyes were red-rimmed and her face forlorn. She stopped, lifted a corner of her book apron to rub at her eyes. "It's so awful about Pamela."

Annie rushed forward to hug her. "Oh Ingrid, she's alive and going to get well. They moved her to a hospital in Savannah and somebody got it wrong."

By the time they'd exchanged glad hoorays and Annie, noting interested faces of several of the island's most gregarious women, had explained in a clear and carrying voice that Pamela had no idea who'd struck her on the mystery cruise and, further, didn't know a thing about the handsome mystery man who'd visited Meg Heath Friday morning, she and Ingrid were settled at the coffee bar with whipped cream–topped cappuccinos.

Ingrid pushed steel-rimmed glasses higher on her nose. "I don't quite see how that kind of mistake could be made, but"—she lifted thin shoulders in a shrug—"I read the other day about a basketball player who went into the hospital for an operation on a sore bone in his left foot and woke up minus that bone in his right foot."

Annie lifted her mug in a salute. "No harm done for Pamela." In fact, fatal harm had been avoided. The attack on the mystery cruise had been intended to elimi-

nate Pamela as a witness. The odd episode in the hallway near the back entrance to the ER clearly meant the
murderer was on the prowl. Pamela would have been
very vulnerable in the hospital. But for now, she was
safe, and Annie wanted to reclaim her normal life. Let
Billy deal with the deaths of Meg and her visitor.
"So"—Annie licked away a whipped-cream mustache—"how's everything gone today?"

Agatha padded toward Annie, green eyes glittering.

"I fed her a little while ago." Ingrid sniffed. "She
didn't eat a bite." Ingrid was unsympathetic to trying
different food when Agatha evinced disdain for a serving. Food, Ingrid insisted, was food.

Annie knew better than to resist. Agatha obviously
was in no mood to trifle with an absentee owner who
was putting in a late appearance without proper indi-
cations of remorse, abasement, and adoration. Annie
put down her mug and stepped behind the coffee bar to
pour a fresh—and different—dry cat food into
Agatha's bowl.

Agatha's tail whipped. She sheered toward Annie's
retreating arm, showed fangs, relented, and settled at
the bowl. She crunched the pellets, but her tail still
flicked.

Annie cautiously and circumspectly patted her sleek
black cat. "Why do I love you?" But she knew. Agatha
was elegant, unpredictable, fascinating, and occasionally affectionate.

Ingrid's tone was dry. She loved dogs. "Agatha
shredded the ferns in the cozy area. And I swear she
tried to topple the display of the Rita Mae Brown
books. And we had a busload of tourists from the
Church of the Servant in Chastain. They bought every
last one of Mignon Ballard's new angel mystery.

Duane got on the Web"—Ingrid's husband not only handled most of the duties as manager of the residential cabins where they lived, he was a whiz at finding obscure titles for bookstore customers—"and found those reprints by Rue Morgue Press of the ghost mysteries by Manning Coles."

Annie put down her mug, studied her clerk. Ingrid was not laconic, but she didn't chatter. And she hadn't answered Annie's question. "What's wrong?"

Ingrid downed the rest of her mug, reluctantly faced Annie. "You look awfully tired."

Annie didn't doubt Ingrid's appraisal. It had been a long day after a horrific night. But her relief at reaching the bookstore was quickly ebbing. "Tell me."

"I didn't want to bother you." Ingrid jammed her fingers in wiry iron-gray curls. "Duane says I could never pull off a crime, that I'm as transparent as a politician. But I've read so many mysteries I should be able to outwit anyone." She sighed. "It's no big deal, but you've had a lot of phone calls. I thought maybe they could wait until tomorrow." A frown bunched her eyebrows. "But one of them . . ." Just for an instant she looked embarrassed. "If I were a gothic heroine, I'd come all over faint and bleat something about being overwhelmed with a sense of impending doom." The tone was lighthearted. Her face was not. "Anyway," she rushed ahead, brisk and factual, "here's the list." She pulled a sheet of scratch paper from her pocket, handed it to Annie.

Ingrid's printing was small and precise:

Calls
Young man. 11:03 A.M. Didn't leave name. Abrupt, demanding. Called back at 1:20 P.M., 3:06 P.M., 4:38

P.M. Never left name. Caller ID identified caller as Jason Brown. Isn't that Meg Heath's son?

Wayne Reed. 4:05 P.M. Asked you to contact him at his office or home when convenient. Said he wished to speak to you in regard to Meg Heath. Sounded grim.

Whisperer.

Annie was not a gothic heroine, but her gaze jerked toward Ingrid. "Whisperer?"

"Came up Unknown Caller. Can't even guess as to sex. Could have been a man or a woman. The call came just a few minutes ago, a faint voice—like someone was hunkered over a phone and trying not to be heard—asking if you were here." Ingrid gripped her empty mug. "I had the strangest feeling. I know that's silly—"

"No, it's not." Annie wasn't ready to dismiss Ingrid's response. In fact, she felt a prickle of her own. Who was trying to get in touch with her and afraid to speak out loud? That's what it came down to, wasn't it? Someone was afraid. She looked into Ingrid's eyes and knew her sensible, everyday, practical clerk had found the call frightening.

Ingrid frowned. "I shouldn't have told you. There's not a thing you can do about it unless there's another call. I don't suppose you saw anyone today who might be trying to catch you?"

Annie flicked through her day like clicking the images in a stereoscope: the Heath house, Parotti's, the pier at Slash Pine Road, Doc Burford's hunting cabin, Emma's speedboat, the ferry. Slowly Annie shook her head. She looked down at Ingrid's neat printing:

Whisperer. 4:22 P.M. Asked if you were here. Static in the background. Cell phone? I said you weren't in and offered to take a message but the connection was broken before I finished.

Her face troubled, Annie folded the list, put it in her pocket.

"Another cappuccino?" Ingrid reached for Annie's mug.

"No." Not even her favorite drink, divinely inspired so far as Annie was concerned, would provide a lift now. She glanced at her watch. Almost five. "I'm going home. Will you close up this evening?"

"I was planning on it." Ingrid nodded in approval. "You look exhausted, Annie. Go home and relax." Ingrid was forceful. "Forget all this. Have dinner with Max and Rachel and—oh golly, I just remembered. There was one more call." Ingrid took both the mugs, stepped to the sink behind the counter. She turned on the water, squirted soap, began to wash. "Pudge rang up a little while ago. He didn't leave a message. Let's see"—she was casual, unconcerned—"he asked if you were here and then he muttered something about you promising to take care of something but you were probably busy and he didn't want to bother you, that he'd catch you tomorrow."

Annie forgot about the list of calls, even the whisperer. She wanted to go home. She wanted to put this day behind her, savor Pamela's return to life, leave the search for the murderer of Meg Heath and the natty stranger to Chief Billy Cameron. But—and she reached for the phone book to find an address—she couldn't go home yet. She had a promise to keep.

Rachel slammed the plate onto the breakfast room table. She didn't stamp her foot but the effect was the same. "Stuart is a world-class jerk! It's pathetic"—disdain dripped from her voice—"how Cole Crandall snuffles after him like a dog who's been kicked but comes back for more." She walked to the counter, grabbed silverware for the place settings.

Max diced tomatoes, pushed them next to the mound of cut green peppers and onions. He was no authority on teenage girls. He found Annie's volatile stepsister interesting, fun, endearing, but a little unnerving in her prickly demeanor, rather like a cat that purred one instant, bit the next. He had a sudden image of Agatha. Annie was always quick to explain away Agatha's unpredictability, saying, "All she needs is love." Max wished—he glanced toward the ceramic clock above the sink—that Annie would get home soon and divert Rachel from her diatribe against Cole Crandall.

The table set, Rachel plopped onto the step stool. She sat with her knees bunched near her chin, arms wrapped around skinny legs bare beneath chambray shorts. Glossy black curls framed her thin, angular face. Her scowl was scornful. "Don't you think that's stupid?"

Max temporized. "I'll bet Cole was embarrassed."

Rachel considered his suggestion. Some of the anger seeped from her face. "Yeah. Well, maybe." The moment of empathy evaporated faster than water sprinkled in a hot skillet. "He doesn't have the guts of an inchworm. Why didn't he tell Stuart to go jump in the Sound? It was *so* bad. Everybody's milling around after school—you know, sometimes we all hang out for a while in the parking lot. Stuart went on and on about Cole missing out on all the action when Pamela went overboard. Stuart acted like Cole was some kind of idiot that he didn't see a thing that happened. And what did Cole do?" Her tone was scathing. "He got this funny look on his face and muttered something like he wished he'd never gone on the cruise." Abruptly Rachel popped down from the step stool, her face as lugubrious as a tragedy mask. "Me, too. I wish I hadn't. There was Pudge and that awful woman hanging all over him."

Running steps clattered as Rachel raced out of the kitchen, thumped up the stairs. Dimly Max heard the slam of her bedroom door upstairs. He finished chopping the tomatoes, began to slice a crisp garden-fresh cucumber. Everything was going to be swell for the gazpacho, but dinner wasn't going to be a jolly meal unless Annie worked some magic with Rachel. Rachel . . . Max considered the invitation tendered by Annie to Pudge and Sylvia and Cole. How Annie hoped to persuade Rachel to welcome these guests was beyond his understanding. Once again he glanced at the clock. Almost six. Where was Annie?

Annie braked for a tawny red doe and her half-grown fawn, his spots almost gone. The dusty road curved and twisted toward the ocean through a thick stand of pines and live oaks crowded by ferns and shrubs. The wilderness to her left was part of the island nature preserve.

She drove slowly. How should she approach Cole Crandall? Oh sure, she could talk to him about the excursion boat, but that wasn't the point. The point, unfortunately, was for Annie to perform a miracle resulting in a congenial family gathering at the Darling household Friday evening. She pictured Cole, sullen, resentful, and defensive. How should she begin? *I'm Annie Darling and my father's Pudge Laurance, the guy who's hanging around your mom, and you don't like him but he's really swell.* That wouldn't do. *My stepsister's Rachel Van Meer and she thinks you're a real creep.* Scratch that. The car nosed around a huge live oak, and there was the Reed house. Quickly, quickly, she needed inspiration.

She pulled into the drive, looked up at one of the island's boutique mansions, a two-story modern stucco with an ocean view. In today's market, it had probably cost a half million. Annie marveled every weekend when she saw the real estate section of the Sunday paper. Prices of homes and condos had risen astronomically in recent years. What had sold for a hundred thousand ten years ago might now fetch nearly a million. She feared the building boom in the Southeast coastal regions was out of control. She studied the Reed house. It looked awfully new, which most likely meant Wayne Reed had paid a bundle. She hoped he could afford to lose his investment. If a Category 3 storm ever hit the island full force, the storm surge would undoubtedly wreck this house. Most of the island would be under four feet of water. Old homes built on high foundations and cabins secure on pilings would survive.

"Come on." She spoke aloud, knowing that her mind was skittering from the real estate bubble to hurricanes to avoid the intractable challenge she faced. All right. All she could do was her best. She had a good excuse to talk to Cole. She could tell him Pamela was going to recover. It would be interesting to ask if Cole had remembered seeing anyone on the deck before Pamela's fall. From there, she would segue to Pudge and dinner at the Darling house. Segue—a lovely word suggesting a smooth transition. Oh yeah, she would have to be a verbal gymnast to achieve this one. *Cole, you did such a good job keeping your eyes open on the second deck, and I saw your mother, and she was with my father—yes, Pudge Laurance is my father, didn't you know?—and we're going to grill hamburgers. . . .* Drat. Was Cole as hostile to Rachel as she was to him? Would it do any good to mention Rachel? Annie would have to feel her way, emotional antennas twirling like radar gone berserk.

She parked beneath a spreading live oak and left her car windows down. Closing up a car in this heat turned the interior into a sauna stoked with glee by an imp from hell. She kept to the shade as she walked up a crushed oyster shell path to the single bricked step leading to a narrow porch framed by twin pillars.

Flush on the ground, she thought to herself, *ripe for flooding.* Then, *Stop it, Annie, you don't care if this house washes out to the Gulf Stream. Think about Cole and what you are going to say to him. Pudge's heart is riding on your words.* That thought was such a burden, the hand lifted to grip the bronze knocker froze in place.

The door banged open.

Annie let her hand fall, took a step back. She recognized Wayne Reed from his campaign posters. He'd run for city council in the last election, losing to Henny Brawley. Annie, in fact, had worked hard for her old friend, passing out campaign brochures, holding a tea at the bookstore, going door-to-door to urge support. At the time, she'd thought Reed's efforts lackluster. Max's take had been that the lawyer was running more for name recognition than out of any real interest in the job.

Reed stood on the threshold, staring at Annie. He was tall and slender, his shoulders bony beneath his polo shirt. His khaki shorts sagged. His huaraches had a battered appearance as if they'd been immersed in salt water and left to dry in a hot sun. He looked like a man who'd just arrived home from the office, a trace of five o'clock shadow on his pointed chin, and changed into casual clothes. In the campaign posters there had been more of a youthful aura, his dark hair neatly combed.

He broke the silence. "Hello." The single brusque word held surprise and a question.

Annie understood his response. Obviously she'd not arrived on his doorstep by chance. The house was isolated, bounded by the forest reserve on one side, an undeveloped tract on the other, the ocean to the east. It didn't attract itinerant salespersons or distributors of handbills.

"Hello." Annie tried for a charming smile. "I'm Annie Darling—"

"Annie Darling!" It was an exclamation. There was immediate recognition and a flash of something—was it hostility or wariness or perhaps simply curiosity?—in his light green eyes. Then the moment was past and Annie was uncertain what, if anything, she had glimpsed.

He pulled open the door. "Come in. But you didn't need to come and see me." He looked uncomfortable, almost sheepish. "I wanted to talk to you about your calling up the medical examiner in regard to Meg's death. Her daughter asked me to speak with you. Jenna was upset, but as it turns out—I had a talk with the police chief—your insistence on an autopsy was warranted." His sudden frown was dark, intense. He looked angry, sad, and forlorn. "I can't believe Meg's dead." He took a deep breath. "So there's no complaint to be made. I should"—his look and smile were suddenly boyish and much more attractive—"have made sure of my facts before I called you. No harm done, I hope. But I'm sorry you came all the way out here for nothing."

Annie brushed back a tangle of thick curls. "Oh, I didn't come to see you."

If he'd been puzzled earlier, he now looked bewildered.

Annie wished she weren't always blurting out the truth. His phone call afforded a great opening to talk to him, possibly to learn more about Meg Heath and what had been happening in her life. But no, here she was, making it clear she wasn't in this out-of-the-way spot in regard to Meg Heath's death. Well, that was all right. Billy Cameron wouldn't thank her for sticking her nose into his investigation anyway.

"Mr. Reed, I'm looking for Cole Crandall." She darted a look beyond him into the spacious hallway with its pale gold ceramic floor and slender, twisting terra-cotta vases. With dramatic flowers—perhaps vivid and elegant stalks of bird of paradise or Heliconia—the passageway would have glowed with romance and style. Instead, the vases were empty, dust smeared the golden floor, and the mirror along one wall was streaked. Even as she spoke, Annie realized the house behind him had an air of emptiness with no sounds of occupancy, no voices or footsteps, music, or murmur of television. She pulled facts from her memory. Reed was divorced. She didn't recall the circumstances. Obviously his son, Stuart, was in his custody because the high school student was of an age where the choice to go or stay would be his. In any event, the lack of commotion probably meant that Stuart Reed wasn't there nor was his guest, Cole, if Annie's experience with

Rachel was any indicator. The house immediately began to buzz when she came home from school, with phone calls, giggling girls coming in and out, Ping-Pong, TV, and always music, usually the latest by BBMac and Rascall Flats. She considered Annie and Max's jazz favorites bo-ring.

"Cole?" He glanced behind him as if a visiting teenager might tumble from behind a curtain. "Yeah." His tone was vague. "He's been staying with Stuart but they aren't here. You know how it is"—a shrug. "They're probably at some pizza hangout."

Annie was no authority on dealing with teens. Rachel had only been living with them for a year and a half. But there were some rules. If Rachel didn't intend to come straight home from school, she called and left word where she would be. Maybe it was different for guys. Obviously it was different for Stuart Reed.

"Anyway"—Wayne's smile was disarming—"they'll roll in sometime. I can ask Cole to call you. Any message?" Reed jingled car keys in his pocket.

There was, of course, no way to give any inkling of the true reason for her visit. It would be hideously embarrassing to Cole for there to be any discussion of his mother and Pudge. Annie thought it likely Wayne Reed would be understanding, but it would be counterproductive to give Cole a reason to dislike her and by extension add to his grievances against Pudge. Realizing that her silence had stretched to an uncomfortable length, she bolted into speech. "Oh, it's not important. I wanted to talk to him about what he saw Sunday night on the *Island Packet*." She backed down the steps. "Don't worry about it. I'll get in touch with him. Sorry to have bothered you. . . ." And she was at her car and opening the door.

As she drove off, Annie slumped in the seat, hot, tired, and cross. She hadn't handled that very well. But at least she hadn't revealed the true reason for her effort to contact Cole. Let Wayne Reed make of her visit what he would.

Tomorrow, after all, was only Tuesday. Sometime before Friday she'd figure a way to talk to Cole Crandall. The car picked up speed. For now, she was going home.

Home. What a lovely, happy, good word.

She whistled "A Happy Wanderer" all the way to their gray curving road and only broke off in midtune when she saw the long pink Rolls-Royce parked in the drive.

∾ *Ten* ∾

EMMA'S GLARE GAVE her strong features a Mount Rushmore grandeur. A summery pink caftan with white polka dots in no way softened her appearance. It was rather like adorning one of the massive granite visages with a peppermint-striped bowtie. She stood in front of the mantel in their terrace room, grim, purposeful, and determined. She held a tumbler of iced tea in a good imitation of a death grip.

Annie took a deep swallow of Max's perfectly brewed iced tea, enhanced by a sprig of mint from their garden and slices of orange and lemon. It didn't cool her off. The more she thought about Emma's astonishing news, the madder—and hotter—she got. "I can't believe that's what Billy's decided! It doesn't make sense."

Max was quick to come to his old friend's defense. "Now, ladies, let's be fair—"

"Fair." The grumble came from deep in Emma's throat. "As far as I'm concerned, he's a sexist pig."

Annie plopped her glass on a coaster, popped up from the cheerful yellow sofa, began to pace. "That's exactly right. Now if we were talking men, he'd never insist on accident or suicide. Women, hey, they fall down, pop pills, whatever. According to Billy, Pamela somehow fell overboard, and since she doesn't remember what happened, well, what else do you expect with a head wound?"

Emma joined in. "And he insists Meg committed suicide even though she was planning a special dinner for tonight. Women do not plan dinner parties and then gulp down enough sedatives to choke a horse."

Max folded his arms. "Give Billy his due. His judgment has nothing to do with sex. He's looking at the facts, Emma, just like he told you. Nobody saw anything on the excursion boat to suggest that Pamela was attacked. Admittedly Pamela doesn't remember what happened. Billy says she's obviously too weak to be dissembling, so Annie was right and she didn't jump. But he thinks she had a touch of vertigo—you know how she hates heights—and stumbled forward, lost her balance, banged her head, and over she went. He's on even firmer ground with Meg's death. He says it has to be suicide since there was no trace of the drug in the sherry decanter and Dr. Burford says the dose was much too big to be accidental."

Max looked from Annie to Emma. He lifted his shoulders in a rueful shrug. "You've got to admit nothing in the evidence points to murder."

Emma glowered. "All right. Let's look at it. Here are the facts according to Billy: One—Meg's death resulted from ingesting an overdose of a sedative, specifically diazepam, aka Valium. Two—residue in the wineglass was drugged. Three—no trace of the sedative was found in the sherry decanter. Four—in her bathroom wastebasket, a prescription vial in her name for Valium was found empty. Five—her fingerprints overlay any foreign prints on the vial. Six—the assumption is that she—and only she—dissolved the tablets in her bedtime glass of sherry." Emma looked like Mount Rushmore on a glacial day in February. "I don't give a rat's ass about facts. She didn't do it."

"And Pamela was pushed." Annie drank thirstily. "If Billy refuses to see that the three crimes are linked, he'll never solve this case."

Max leaned back in the overstuffed chair, turned his hands palm up. "What difference does it make which crime he solves if there's only one perp?"

"Because"—Emma sounded as didactic as Sherlock Holmes—"motive matters. Billy's going to look in all the wrong places. His theory is that Smith's murder grew out of a carjacking or holdup. Maybe even a sour drug deal."

Annie fluffed her hair, wished she could do the same for her spirits. "How can he ignore the fact that Bob Smith came to see Meg Friday morning? Doesn't he think it's just a tiny bit curious that Smith is shot Saturday night, Pamela is pushed off the boat Sunday night, and Meg is dead Monday morning?"

Emma was sardonic. "Billy doesn't quite go so far as to claim it's all a coincidence, but his mind is working on the general theme that Smith was probably an old friend of Meg's and that Smith's arrival couldn't have been a very big deal because Meg kept right on with her regular schedule. Billy talked to Claudette Taylor and she said Meg had dinner at the club Friday evening with Wayne Reed, saw Jenna and Jason Saturday afternoon, went to the ten o'clock service Sunday morning and on the mystery cruise Sunday night. There's no suggestion she had any further contact with Smith. Billy's trying to trace Smith's activities on Saturday. Billy hopes someone will remember seeing him, but in August it's hard for anyone to stand out, even a dandy in white trousers and a striped blazer."

Annie plucked the slice of orange from her glass, chewed the pulp. "That's the trouble with writing off Meg as a suicide. Billy's not looking at the main suspects."

"What suspects?" Max looked blank.

"Like Emma said"—she was sure Emma had said it at some point—"money is a very good motive. Jason and Jenna are going to be very rich now and I'll bet Claudette's legacy is substantial."

Max slowly shook his head. "If there was no sedative in the sherry in the decanter, the sedative must have been put into the glass. I don't see how anyone except Meg could have done that."

Emma's blue eyes gleamed. "As Marigold said in *The Case of the Lumbering Lizard:* When the dragon of impossibility lifts his fire-breathing snout, beware the sting in the tail."

Annie did not look at Max. He did not look at her. They were both silent. Annie would not have admitted to a stricken silence. Indeed, she was once again fighting a compulsion to shout, "Marigold isn't real." Instead, she tried to frame a response. What could she say? Beware the sting in the tail. . . . What the heck did that mean? Was Marigold suggesting that appearances are deceptive? Annie was appalled to realize she was seriously considering the pronouncements of a fictional detective. Moreover, as far as Annie was concerned, Marigold Rembrandt, despite her legion of admirers, had all the charm of Emma on a bad day. Marigold reflected her creator's overweening confidence and she did it with just about as much grace as that lumbering lizard. . . . Sting in the tail . . . If you were looking at the burst of flame from the creature's head, you wouldn't watch the tail.

"Oh." Annie was as excited as a retriever splashing toward game. "Of course. That's what we're supposed to think. That's why there isn't any Valium in the decanter. The murderer emptied it out and put in fresh sherry. Therefore when the lab found residue of the drug only in the glass, everyone was supposed to assume Meg put it there."

Emma was nodding her approval. Max looked thoughtful.

"Exactly." Emma was utterly confident. "It's the only possibility. Someone ground up the pills and put them in the decanter. Meg drank the glass of sherry Sunday evening, and of course she never woke up."

"Wait a minute." Max held up a hand. "Are you suggesting someone entered her room late Sunday night and replaced the sherry in the decanter?"

"Précisément." Emma smiled with the regal condescension of a queen dealing with doltish ministers.

Annie gritted her teeth. Marigold's habit of replying in French was another irritant. "Yeah." Annie's all-American growl went right over Emma's silver coiffure. But Annie was too excited at their theory to harbor a grudge. "Of course that's what happened. And"—she leaned forward excitedly—"this morning Claudette found her body, and that means the door to Meg's suite was unlocked."

Max reached out to stroke Dorothy L. The plump white cat gazed at him with adoring blue eyes. "So I guess Billy needs to get out the handcuffs for Claudette. Isn't she the only one who was there Sunday night?"

Emma tapped stubby fingers in a quick tattoo on the

mantel. "Surely Meg's children have keys to the house. I don't think we can assume Claudette is guilty simply because she was the only one in the house last night."

Annie recalled the sunporch with its view of the sea. "This morning the door from the balcony into Meg's suite was unlocked. If you saw that house, you'd know that anyone could easily climb to the second floor up the iron grillwork of the supporting columns."

Max's expression was skeptical. "So somebody—this mythical murderer—poisoned the decanter sometime on Sunday—"

Annie broke in. "It was easy as pie. Smith was killed Saturday night, and everything must have been planned by then. Meg went to church Sunday morning and very likely Claudette went with her. That left the house empty. There are no neighbors. Anybody could climb one of those wrought-iron pillars, scoot inside, drug the sherry, and be out of there in five minutes. Or if it was one of the family, unlock the front door and hurry up the stairs. If Claudette's the murderer, she had all afternoon to drug the sherry."

Max continued unabashed. "—and returns that night, presuming Meg to be dead, and unlocks the front door or crawls up to the balcony or tiptoes in from the hallway with a fresh bottle of sherry, dumps out the contents of the decanter, rinses it, pours in fresh sherry, and departs, carrying the empty bottle. Sounds too complicated."

"Somebody *has* gone"—Annie's tone was grave—"to a lot of trouble, decoying Bob Smith out to Ghost Crab Pond, checking him out of the inn and removing all his belongings, delivering a free ticket to entice Pamela on the cruise. If we're right, if somehow the decanter was cleaned up, look how successful it was! Billy's sure that Meg committed suicide and he's not looking at anyone connected to Meg."

"But we will." Emma was as confident as Marigold Rembrandt at her most insufferable.

For once, Annie was in complete agreement.

Annie and Max climbed the stairs hand in hand. On the second floor, she stopped, looking toward Rachel's room and the line of light beneath her door.

Max squeezed her fingers. He understood without her saying a word. "Are you going to talk to her now?"

She hesitated. When would there be a better time? Despite the grim day, dinner had been fun, with cheerful descriptions of Rachel's day at school, an admiring discussion of Emma and Dr. Burford's stratagem to protect Pamela, and a serious discussion, although Max didn't contribute, of whether Ben Affleck was the handsomest star of all. Annie hadn't mentioned the plan to have Pudge, Sylvia, and Cole over on Friday night. She had grown up with the maxim that unpleasant topics are never discussed at the dinner table and she was afraid that no matter how she couched the invitation, Rachel would be upset. Annie remembered Rachel's cheerful goodnight. "Don't let the bedbugs bite," she'd caroled as she raced up the stairs. Rachel always moved fast when she was happy, and tonight she'd been her energetic, bubbly, laughing self.

Annie squared her shoulders, tapped on the door. "Rachel?"

Max gave an approving nod and strolled toward their room.

There was no answer.

Annie knocked again, eased the door open wide

enough to peek inside. Rachel, fresh from her bath in green shorty pajamas, reclined in the comfortable embrace of her purple beanbag chair, eyes closed, headphones covering her ears. One foot waggled in time to music that would most likely have sounded like clanging trash cans to the unschooled taste of Annie and Max. Max loved jazz and Annie adored show tunes. In fact, she had a secret admiration for John Philip Sousa. A good march pleased her almost as much as a mesmerizing mystery. There was nothing like a march to energize spirits.

Annie's face softened. How dear of Rachel to use headphones. Yes, in the afternoon their house boomed like a teenage haunt, but at night Rachel was sensitive to the presence of others.

Rachel's eyes popped open. She saw Annie, smiled, pulled off the headphones. The music blared, then she switched it off.

"Hi. May I come in?" Annie waited in the doorway.

Rachel spread her hand at a blue beanbag. "Sure. What's up?"

Annie dropped onto the supple vinyl and felt as if she were back in college. There had been lots of late-night talks about life and love and men and dreams. She curled her legs underneath her. "Rachel, have I told you lately that I love you?"

Rachel made a circle with her thumb and forefinger. "Me, too."

That's what love was. A circle. Without start or finish. A golden band of caring and goodness and respect.

"Pudge loves you." There was no doubt in Annie's voice.

Rachel twirled a glossy black curl around one finger. Her face lost its glow. She hunched her knees to her chin, stared at the floor. She didn't say a word.

"The thing about love is that the more you love, the more love you have to give." Annie knew this was true. She couldn't prove it in any tangible way, but the truth of the heart doesn't have to be proved. The truth of the heart can be seen in shining lives. "Pudge loves you and me and Max. He loved your mom and mine. But there's room in his heart—"

Rachel scrambled to her feet. "I guess I better get to bed." Her voice was muffled. She darted across the room, pulled the comforter down, slipped into the bed. "I have to get up early tomorrow. We're having a cappella practice before school."

The room no longer felt like a haven. Anger and disappointment and hurt feelings swirled around Annie like autumn leaves in a gusting wind. She pushed herself up from the beanbag. By the time she reached the door, Rachel was stretched out on her bed, tense as a statue, her back to the hall.

Annie stood with her hand on the knob. She didn't know any other way than to blurt out the hard fact. She could only hope the coming days would soften Rachel's heart. "Max and I invited Pudge and Sylvia for hamburgers Friday night. Pudge is hoping Cole will come."

Dark curls pressed against the pillow.

"Rachel, I was going to try and talk to Cole, ask him to come over. But he's so mad at his mom, he's staying at Stuart Reed's house. I went out there this afternoon, but Cole and Stuart weren't there. I was going to ask Cole if he saw anyone up on the deck just before Pamela went overboard, then try to ease into talking about Pudge." Annie twisted the knob, opened the door. "The problem is I don't know how to talk to Cole about Pudge and I thought maybe you . . ." She trailed off. "Well, I guess not. Goodnight, honey."

*   *   *

Annie loved air-conditioning. So it was August. So what? She snuggled a sheet beneath her chin, turned on her side, welcomed the warmth as she curled next to Max. "What if Rachel won't come?" Her voice was forlorn.

"She'll do what she has to do." Max smoothed out Annie's nightgown where it was bunched above her knee. His hand lingered on her thigh. "It may just be us and Pudge and Sylvia. But Rachel's a sweetheart. I'll bet she has second thoughts."

"I don't think so." Annie was discouraged. "She may decide to go visit that aunt who keeps inviting her to come and live with her in Hawaii." Annie flounced over and lay facing him, one hand clutching his arm. "Oh, Max, why does love have to be so impossible?"

His breath was warm against her cheek. "Not for us." His lips sought hers and Annie stopped worrying about Pudge and Rachel and the future.

The shrill wail of the telephone shredded the peace of the night, bringing Annie's head from the pillow, her hand to her throat. She stared at the luminous numbers on the digital clock: 3:29. As she watched, the numbers changed: 3:30. Good news does not come at three-thirty in the morning.

Max fumbled for the receiver. "H'lo." Concern roughened his sleep-thickened voice.

Annie rolled out of bed, turned on the light. She reached for her seersucker robe. The air-conditioning had made the room chilly. But the coldness inside had nothing to do with temperature. A call at this hour . . .

Max was sitting up, eyes blinking against the brightness. He looked like a tousled blond bear. "Yeah? Fire?

Hold on a minute." He covered the receiver. "Grab a phone. Marian Kenyon. A fire out at the Heath house."

Annie slipped into her scuffies, hurried to the hall and down the stairs to the kitchen, flicking lights as she went, pulling on her robe. She ran to the counter, punched the button for the speakerphone.

". . . thought one good turn deserved another." Marian's tone was sardonic. "Sorry to wake you but I figured you'd want to know. I've got an arrangement with a fire official that needn't be explored in detail. Any big burns and I get a buzz. The call came in about twenty minutes ago, and here I am, prowling around the outskirts of the action. Seems the Heaths built a fancy storage building behind some pines across from the main house. I guess the really rich have too much stuff to stash in closets like the rest of us. Anyway, it's burning like a Roman candle. Wow. Flames are shooting up twenty feet, maybe thirty. The fire unit has spotlights aimed at—as training manuals elegantly put it—the conflagration. Another siren—"

Marian's voice rasped against a background medley of sounds, the siren, a rushing roar, yells, thuds, thumps.

"—signals the arrival of our police chief. I'll let him confab with the fire chief, then I'll amble over and say hello. No doubt my presence will add a fillip to his evening. Actually, morning. Hmm, Billy does not look like a happy man. Hang on unless you prefer to slumber. . . ."

Annie paced by the counter. The speakerphone emitted a rushing, crackling sound, the slam of car doors, men's shouts.

Marian's clipped words evoked a powerful picture. "Dense smoke, swirling up in clouds blacker than the night sky. Can't see the stars now. Three hoses working. When the streams hit, the flames waver and there's a sizzle like water hitting a giant griddle, smoke coils. Another hose wets down the perimeter. Forest preserve's bone-dry from drought, but it looks like they're going to be able to keep the flames from firing the trees. It's quite a scene." Her voice was dispassionate. "The light from the fire is sulfurous. The yellow coats of the firemen glisten. Their sweaty faces are tomato red and carbon-streaked beneath their helmets. Another burst of flame engulfs the structure. Dammit, I've got to find out what it is. Not a garage. The firemen are backing away. Front wall collapses."

Marian's voice was drowned out by a rush, a roar, a rumble.

"Everything within appears crumpled, charred, twisted. A distinct odor of gasoline as well as the rather nasty stink of burning manufactured materials. Probably plastics. Oh yeah, I see the secretary, Claudette Taylor. She's huddling near the back of one of the trucks. She'll know what was in there. I'll keep the phone on. I've got a little tape recorder in my pocket."

Annie opened the refrigerator door, found the orange juice. She poured a big frothing glass, selected two peanut butter cookies from the cat cookie jar, settled at the kitchen table, all to the accompaniment of the odd distorted sounds from the speakerphone. She drank the glass half down, savored a big mouthful of cookie. She scooted her chair nearer as faraway voices spoke:

"Looks like a total loss." Even at a distance, Marian's deep tone was unmistakable. "Hello, Claudette. Marian Kenyon. The *Gazette*."

"Oh, please, do you know what happened?" Claudette Taylor's voice shook. "I called when I saw the flames, then I ran over here."

"Did you see anybody? Hear a car?" The questions came fast and hard from Marian.

"No. I didn't see anybody. Oh"—a cry—"look at that! Everything's burning. I know the fire trucks got here as fast as they could, but they're too late. Have they told you how it started?"

"They're a little busy right now for chitchat. I'd say it's probably arson." Marian tossed out the word like skipping a stone over water.

"Arson?" Claudette's voice rose in disbelief. "Oh my Lord. Why? It's just a storage shed. Well, not a shed. There was so much that had to be kept out of the house. Because of Meg." Her voice was angry. "Meg insisted the house be open with windows everywhere and space. No clutter, that's what she said. And"—there was an edge of bitterness—"Duff indulged her. They fixed the house just the way she wanted it, then they had to find a place for all their papers. This was built to hold everything she didn't want in the house, things from her mother's house, from Meg's years when she lived abroad. And Duff's papers. They're gone now, too."

"What monetary value would you place on the contents?" Marian's question was crisp.

"I doubt any of it was worth money. But Duff's papers were there. She didn't care about them." Claudette's voice shook. "She"—the emphasis on the pronoun was definite, sharp, angry—"never paid any attention to keepsakes, not even her own, much less Duff's. His daybooks, his files from the companies, his family papers, pictures of him as a boy. Gone. All gone." Her voice was deep with bitterness.

There was a pause, unidentifiable sounds, the tramp of feet.

Abruptly Marian's voice was loud and clear. "Got that on tape. When the last wall went down, she headed back toward the house. Lots of smoke, little bursts of flame, nothing big. Forest's safe. Fire Chief Gallagher's heading toward Billy Cameron. I'll see what I can get."

The speakerphone continued to produce chaotic sounds. Annie pictured Marian Kenyon, curly hair wild and unruly, gleaming dark eyes absorbing details, skirting hoses, tape recorder in one hand, cell phone in the other, making slow but determined progress toward Billy Cameron.

"Chief Cameron!" Marian's voice was again at a distance. Was the cell phone in one hand, the tape recorder in the other? "Is it arson?"

"Chief Gallagher says the back of the building was doused with gasoline, then torched. By the time the unit arrived, the fire was too intense to permit saving the structure." Billy cleared his throat. "No known fatalities. Apparently the building was used for storage."

"Who reported it? When?" As always, Marian sounded impatient.

"Nine-one-one from Ms. Taylor. Said she woke up, saw flames, called the fire department. Call was logged in at three-fourteen." He spoke in a measured voice.

Marian was dismissive. "I talked to her. She saw the flames. Said she didn't see anybody or hear a car."

Annie finished the orange juice and cookie. She was glad to be comfortable in her kitchen and far away from the crackle of flames, clouds of smoke, and rank smell of burned, wet wood. She'd often thought Marian Kenyon had a fun job. Maybe not.

"We'll interview Ms. Taylor." There was a sense of finality to his statement. "For now, that's all we've—"

Marian wasn't going to let her big fish wriggle off the hook without a battle. "Any connection to the Heath kill, Captain?"

"Rumors to the contrary, the death of Mrs. Heath is at this time considered to be either accidental or self-inflicted." He was brusque. "Out of deference to the family, the police department declines to characterize the nature of her demise. At this time there is no evidence that this instance of arson is in any way connected to Mrs. Heath's death." Billy's voice was growing less and less distinct. Annie pictured him turning away. "For further information regarding the arson investigation, you may contact my office or Chief Gallagher's office." The last was scarcely understandable.

Marian's sharp high call sounded like a hound yelping at a raccoon. "Any comment on the fact that Meg Heath was one of the last persons to see the Ghost Crab Pond murder victim?"

The only answer was the thud of footsteps, distant calls, a continuing dull roar.

Marian's disembodied chuckle was distinct. "Thanks for tuning in. If we have another episode, I'll alert you. Episodes . . . Like they were separate and distinct. I think not. Think I'll see if Vince wants to print a map of the island and put stars on all the places where there's been a so-called accident or murder or arson since Saturday night. I'll send a copy to Billy, add a little P.S.: Could be coincidence. Sure. And the house just happens to win in Vegas. But Billy's probably already drawn his own map. I'd lay odds that he'll be giving another look at everything that's happened. *Hasta la vista.*" The connection ended.

Annie was dishing up a bowl of butter brickle ice

cream when Max padded into the kitchen. She held up the scoop. "Want some?"

"Thanks, I'd rather have sorbet. I'll get it." He reached for the can of mixed nuts.

Annie slipped into her place, took a big spoonful of her favorite ice cream. So yes, it was a tad sweet. She glanced at the clock. At nine minutes before four o'clock in the morning, she needed a pick-me-up.

Max joined her, munching on nuts, carrying a dish with raspberry sorbet. "Marian's right. Billy will have his own map. He's never been big on coincidences."

Annie licked a clump of brickle from her spoon, waggled it. "Why would anybody burn down that storeroom?"

Max poured out more nuts. "That's simple. Somebody wanted to destroy something. Somebody *had* to destroy something." He gazed thoughtfully into the distance.

Annie propped her elbows on the table. She was suddenly unutterably tired, waves of fatigue rolling over her. She'd scarcely slept last night, worried about Pamela. And today—well, today would have tired anybody, including, she thought bitterly, Emma's indefatigable Marigold Rembrandt. Annie yawned. She pushed back her bowl, too tired to finish the ice cream, a fatigue level beyond her experience. "Tomorrow. We'll figure it out tomorrow."

Rosy fingers of light streaked the eastern sky. Max unlocked the front door to Confidential Commissions. *Somebody had to destroy something*. . . . He flicked on the lights, walked past his secretary's desk to the kitchenette. As he measured the coffee, he thought about the storage building that held Duff Heath's papers and childhood photos, Meg's discarded mementos from a varied and exciting life, odds and ends that had belonged to Meg's mother. He considered the dandy stranger who came to see Meg on Friday morning and was dead by Saturday night. They had, thanks to Max's efforts, a probable identification. He was Bob Smith from Atlanta. According to Emma, no one in Meg's family evinced any knowledge of Bob Smith. Someone Duff had known? But why would the stranger's arrival cause someone to push Pamela off the *Island Packet* excursion boat, shoot Smith, poison Meg, and set fire to the Heaths' storage facility? There was no refuting that the fire was arson. Was there something in Duff's or Meg's past that had to be kept secret?

Max waited until the coffee finished brewing, carried a mug to his desk. Lying there staring up at him was a copy of the altered print of the handsome ballplayer. Picture . . . pictures . . . mementos . . . fire. Max grabbed up the print, hurried to his scanner.

Annie's eyes opened slowly. She did not agree with Max that she awoke with all the grace and charm of a python having a bad hair day. Pythons didn't have hair. She thought sadly about pythons, creatures avoided by most, treasured by the odd few. Funny how quiet . . . She rolled over, sat up, looked at the clock, blinked. It couldn't be nine-fourteen. She grabbed the note atop Max's pillow: "Thought you should sleep in. I called Ingrid, said you'd be in midmorning. Missed Rachel, but she took a couple of raspberry Danish. Gone to the office. The fire means somebody's desperate about something!"

Annie took a quick shower, picked out a sky blue

sleeveless top and floral slacks with huge blue flowers. She might feel droopy, dark shadows beneath her eyes, her face slightly puffy from too much sleep after too little, but she looked like a summer bouquet, banishing the image of a surly python. Clattering downstairs, she found fresh papaya already cut in the refrigerator. She had the nicest husband on the planet as well as the sexiest.

But her breakfast—papaya, a warm cinnamon roll, milk, orange juice, and Colombian coffee—disappeared without conscious pleasure. Her eyes strayed occasionally to the telephone. She was tempted to call Emma and ask what she planned for the day. But that would give Emma a great opportunity to command action by Annie. Last night it had been easy enough—Annie refilled her coffee cup—for Emma to make grand pronouncements that they, unlike the chief law officer, would pursue the true suspects, those who could have poisoned the sherry decanter. But in the cold hard light of morning, Annie didn't see any graceful way to approach anyone connected to Meg Heath. Annie knew full well she was on Jenna Carmody's blacklist. Claudette Taylor would be under no compulsion to answer questions posed by Annie. Jason Brown . . . Annie took the last bite of papaya. She stacked the dishes, carried them to the sink. According to Ingrid, Jason Brown—or a male voice calling from his number—had tried several times yesterday afternoon to contact Annie. Annie rinsed the dishes, placed them in the dishwasher. She dried her hands, found the telephone directory, punched the numbers. She let it ring until voice mail picked up. She didn't leave a message.

"Did your dog die?" Amanda Parker slapped her backpack on the bench. Amanda was five feet two inches of bursting energy with frizzy blond hair and sharp blue eyes that kept track of everything in school.

Rachel lifted a startled gaze. "I don't have a dog."

"Dog, boyfriend, favorite aunt." Amanda popped the tab on a Pepsi, sank onto a shady portion of the wooden slatted bench. She gestured with the can, and soda fizzed from the opening. "Can you believe we have to go to school in August? Look at the water. It's brutal to make us sit on the terrace and watch the dolphins when we ought to be out there with them. Anyway, why so sad?"

Rachel's eyes jerked toward the pier that stretched out into the Sound. She'd followed Cole Crandall outside, then lost her nerve. Study hall students had the option in nice weather of taking their books to the terrace that overlooked the water. A half dozen benches were scattered in the shade of live oaks. The humid August heat made the air thick and heavy, but there was an illusion of coolness near the water. The brisk onshore breeze stirred Rachel's hair, fluttered the dangling straps of Amanda's backpack, flapped Cole's baggy trousers as he leaned against the railing, staring seaward.

With an effort, Rachel met Amanda's probing gaze. "You said it. School in August. Ugh." No way would she let Amanda know she was even aware Cole Crandall existed. Everybody thought he was a nerd. "And I think we're having a pop quiz next hour." She picked up her American Lit book, flipped it open to Hawthorne.

"Ms. Cooley? Yeah, she's mean that way. Listen, did you hear that"—Amanda scooted nearer to Rachel, dropped her voice—"Teddy Cosgrove got drunk and took his parents' car out and . . ."

Rachel half listened, as, her face screened by the book, she watched Cole Crandall walking toward them. He was slightly built, not much taller than she, with tangled brown hair and a nice-looking face— high cheekbones and a pointed chin and kind of an interesting mouth—if you didn't know he was a creep. Every step was heavy as if his feet were mired in muck. His face had a bruised look. Not real bruises but the kind of hurts Rachel had known when her mother died, the sagging muscles that tell of thoughts too dreadful to bear. Cole passed them, not looking their way, head down.

"Rachel, don't you think that's the worst thing you ever heard?" Amanda's voice rose in malicious pleasure.

Rachel slammed her book shut. "I forgot," she mumbled. "I've got to go by my locker. . . ." She was up on her feet, hurrying toward the wide glass windows framing the back entrance. But by the time she skidded inside, the bell was ringing and the hall filled. She didn't see Cole anywhere. She had to go to class. Maybe he was tired. That was all. Anybody could be tired. She hurried into Ms. Cooley's class, took her seat, third desk from the front in the second row. She got out her notebook, opened the text. But no matter how hard she tried, she couldn't forget Cole's face.

Max lined up the orange golf ball, held his new putter steady. He bent his knees. There was a hump in the indoor green, very similar to the contours of the green on the fifth hole. Have to adjust . . . He began his swing.

The phone rang.

Max jerked the putter and the ball sped across the putting surface, disappeared over the side, banged into a wastebasket, and caromed out of his office.

His secretary called out, "Hole in one—if you were aiming for that sculpture of justice blindfolded that your mother gave you for your birthday. Oh wait, the ball's quivering on the scales, nope, it's settling in place. Adds a bright note if I may say so."

Max didn't take time to check Caller ID. If this was the call he was hoping to receive . . . He yanked up the phone. "Hello?"

"Maxwell, I sense stress. Your voice . . . Perhaps you might brew a cup of chamomile. Of course"—his mother gave a trill of laughter—"if you were one of those private eyes of fiction fame you'd open your desk drawer and belt bourbon. One wonders how the poor boys kept their heads. But they often didn't. In any event—"

Max poked his putter into the umbrella stand, strolled toward his red leather desk chair, settled himself comfortably. He was hoping for a call in response to his e-mail with the attached picture. He checked his watch. Surely within the hour he would hear. He'd requested a return call, ASAP. Would Rodney St. Clair oblige? Would Rodney be able to help? Max knew the possibility that had occurred to him might be absolutely wrong. But if he was right . . .

"—I'm glad I caught you. I took a casserole out to the Heath house and had the nicest visit with Imogene Riley, the cook. I offered to help and we were soon quite chummy—"

Max's lips curved in a smile. He'd rarely met anyone his mother could not charm, from harried salesclerks to reluctant debutantes to taciturn sea captains.

"—and it turns out Imogene came back to the house Saturday afternoon. She wanted to get started on the Black Bottom Parfait for Monday evening. She said it takes a steady hand to add the gelatin to the hot custard and whip until it's smooth. She wanted the dessert to be just right because Meg was looking forward to that dinner so much. And then she muttered, 'Not like some I could mention.' It took a little doing, but in between cutting slices of cake and setting out Emma Clyde's famous rhubarb dessert, the one with tapioca, Imogene told me all about it. Saturday afternoon there was a heated argument between Jenna and her mother. Oh, I suppose it was Jenna who raised her voice. Apparently Meg always remained quite above that sort of interchange. Jason was there and he stormed down the stairs shouting that his mother was a damn fool and she better come to her senses and he slammed out the front door. Jenna came right behind him. Imogene said she didn't know what the fuss was about, but she put the cooling parfait glasses in the refrigerator and slipped out the back door. She didn't want Meg to know she'd overheard their quarrel."

Max reached for his pad, made notes. "Good work, Ma. We'll have to find out what the trouble was."

Call Waiting beeped.

"Got to go, Ma."

∾ *Eleven* ∾

A BLACK PAW FLASHED through dangling fronds of fern, swiping within a millimeter of Annie's wrist. Annie yanked her arm back and the spouted watering can in her hand sprayed droplets on the floor and a portion of the classic mystery section.

"Agatha, drat!" Annie glared at the big green jardiniere, which contained a huge whitmani fern and a ball of irritated fur. "How was I supposed to know you were asleep in there?" Annie plunked down the orange plastic container, hurried to the sink, grabbed a roll of paper towels, and rushed to the bookcase. She carefully dried the Josephine Tey titles, wishing she were as perceptive as Tey. The acclaimed British novelist had an uncanny ability to reveal the depth of evil so often hidden beneath the commonplace.

Annie took her time removing the traces of water. She knew she was dawdling. The phone rang. Annie froze, looked toward the front.

Ingrid's pleasant voice was courteous, helpful. "Yes, we have all the reprints of the Constance and Gwenyth Little titles and . . ."

Annie relaxed. She fervently did not want to talk to Emma Clyde. Annie imagined the likely conversation.

Querulous inquiry: "What progress have you made?"

Defensive, apologetic response: "I haven't had a chance—"

Stony demand: "Why not?"

"All right." Annie spoke aloud. She pushed up from the floor. "I'm not your lackey."

Agatha landed on the floor perilously near Annie's foot, cast a venomous golden glance, and hissed.

Footsteps clattered. Ingrid, carrying a note card, paused in the central aisle. "You girls having fun?"

Agatha stalked toward the coffee bar, outrage clear in every mincing step.

Annie followed. She shook out fresh dry food. "You must learn," she told her cat, "not to take everything personally."

A snort from the comedy mystery section indicated Ingrid's opinion.

Annie slid onto a coffee stool. Maybe she should heed her own advice. Maybe she was taking offense when none was intended. Moreover, even if Emma suggested that Annie lacked the skills of Marigold Rembrandt, Annie should take it in stride.

The phone rang.

Annie continued to sit up straight. She was as cool as Selwyn Jepson's Eve Gill sitting atop a chest of contraband whisky while revenue agents clambered aboard the *Peacock*.

Ingrid thrust the telephone into her hand. "Emma." She moved behind the coffee bar, began to measure coffee and milk.

Annie forced a smile. "Emma." She could handle this. After all, Emma prided herself on being the great detective—she and Marigold—but Annie knew about the fire, and Emma didn't. Annie was casual. "I'm going out to look over the burned storage building near the Heath house"—the plan came to her suddenly and it sounded vigorous—"as soon as I've talked to Jason Brown." The intent to question Meg's son indicated an on-top-of-the-crime investigator. "What's up with you?" Match that, pal.

Match and raise. "What's to see?" Emma's voice was dismissive. "A charred ruin. The firefighters stomped around and obliterated anything that might have been a clue to the arsonist. However, Lou found an empty gasoline tin stuck in the branches of a live oak. He removed it very carefully. I'd say they'll find prints, all right, but they won't belong to the person who set the fire. Anyway, glad to hear you've been thinking."

Annie's brows drew down. Not only did Emma know about the fire, she'd already checked out the site. Moreover, didn't her accolade actually imply that Annie should have been out doing something instead of sitting in her bookstore pondering?

The cappuccino machine made jolly noises.

Emma swept grandly on. "It's a good idea to talk to Jason. Lou Pirelli said Jason was camped out on the front step of the station this morning and insisted on talking to Billy. In a few minutes Jason slammed out the front door, looking as mad as the guy who lost out in the tussle for one of Barry Bonds's home run balls. Be interesting to know what ticked Jason off. I thought the family was relieved that Billy believes her death to be suicide. Yes, you definitely should include Jason on your list of interviewees. I've reserved a quart of fruit salad for you to pick up at Hasty's." Hasty's Fine Foods was the island's most popular purveyor of gourmet foods.

If there was a party in the offing, no one had told Annie. "Fruit salad?"

"You can say you're bringing it to the house on behalf of Pamela. After all, Pamela saw more of Meg the last few months than anyone but Claudette." Emma gave a bark of laughter. "There's nothing like a death in the family to open the door to all comers. Including you. While you're there, see if you can find out where Claudette was when Pamela went overboard. Ditto Jason and Jenna. I've got a phone brigade at work. We're gridding the entire excursion boat. We may come up with something interesting. Keep your cell phone on. Cheerio."

Ingrid brought Annie a steaming mug of cappuccino, topped with whipped cream and chocolate shavings. She pointed at the mug's inscription, "The Under Dog" by Agatha Christie.

Annie managed a wry smile. "Actually, the old"— she made a determined effort to be civil—"dear has a good idea. Several good ideas." Give credit where credit was due. Happily, pinpointing the location of everyone aboard the excursion boat at the moment Pamela went overboard would keep Emma occupied for a good long while. But first Annie was determined to relax and enjoy her cappuccino, although she did take a moment to open her purse and switch on the cell. Who knew? Maybe she'd get a call that she'd won the lottery. Better yet, maybe she'd have occasion to call Emma and announce the resolution of the investigation. Mmmm. The cappuccino was orange-flavored this morning.

The bell jangled at the front door. A customer?

Annie took another sip of the hot sweet drink, put it on the counter. "I'll go see, Ingrid." There was no hurry about the fruit salad. She banished a picture of Emma swooping into Death on Demand on a broomstick. As she headed for the front of the store, enjoying the sound of her shoes on the heart pine floor, she took pleasure in the rows of bookcases and the brilliant book covers face out on the end caps. The new Harlan Coben cover was so vivid it glowed. It would be nice to have customers, but on a sunny August day she had to admit the beach was better. She'd check the updated forecast. Was that tropical storm still building steam near the Virgin Islands? In a few days, she might have customers aplenty.

"Anybody here?" The call was brusque.

She came face-to-face with Jason Brown. She had last seen him pushing his mother's wheelchair aboard the *Island Packet*. Despite his scowl on that bright hot evening, he'd had the pampered, arrogant expression of a man who expects everyone to admire him and do for him. Not now. His handsome face—dark eyes, dramatic chiseled features so like his mother's—sagged with fatigue and misery, a preview of how he might appear as an old man. His eyes were reddened, his curly black hair uncombed. He stopped in front of her, hunched his shoulders, jammed his hands into the pockets of worn jeans. "You called the cops, said there should be an autopsy on my mother." Each word was distinct and harsh.

Annie thought that battle was over and done. She stood straight and defiant. "Yes. I did."

His gaze was unwavering. "I guess since you were there that morning, you and my mom must have been pretty good friends. Listen—"

Annie would have explained, made it clear she was at the Heath house because of Pamela Potts, but Jason

Brown had come to talk and the words blew faster than beach sand in a March wind.

"—maybe you can help me. I've been to the police station. They told me—the guy who's in charge—that it looks like my mom committed suicide because there was only stuff in her glass, not in the decanter. I told him he was nuts. Mom"—he stopped, swallowed, wavered on his feet—"never did that. She never would. I thought maybe you could talk to him, make him see. Somebody who really knew her might be able to make him understand what she was like. He thinks I don't want to believe it because she was my mom. But that's not true." He freed a hand, massaged his face. "She was flying high this weekend. I saw her Saturday and Sunday." He swallowed hard. "She was as happy as I ever saw her in my whole life." There was no joy in his voice.

"Because of Bob Smith?" It was a stab in the dark.

"Who's Bob Smith?" Jason looked bewildered.

"I'm sure everything that happened is linked to Bob Smith." Annie spoke with confidence. "He came to see your mother Friday morning." She saw sudden knowledge in Jason's eyes and intense attention. "He was shot Saturday night—" Jason's shocked expression stopped her.

She stared at him. "Didn't you know? Wait a minute. Come with me." She led the way to the coffee bar, hurried behind it and reached for her purse. She pulled out one of the pictures created by Marian and Max, handed it to Jason.

Jason took the sheet, held it tightly with both hands, but there was no emotion in his face as he gazed down at the handsome man.

"He came to see your mother Friday morning."

Annie watched Jason, tried to read the blank look that molded his face into a mask of emptiness. "He was murdered Saturday night. Pamela Potts took his card to your mom. Pamela was pushed overboard Sunday night. The sherry was poisoned Sunday night. And last night somebody set fire to the storage building out at your mom's house. It all has to be connected to him."

"No." Jason's denial was vehement. "That can't be right. No way. I didn't know about him. I mean, I didn't know he was dead. And I don't know about this Bob Smith stuff." He shook his head. "Anyway, that's crazy. Besides, Mother didn't know he was dead. She had no idea. Why, Sunday she was happy as a lark. She wouldn't have killed herself Sunday night."

Annie held out her hand for the picture. "If you know anything about him, you need to talk to the police."

"Talk to the police . . ." He took one step back, another. "Oh God, I can't. You say he's dead?" His eyes were wide with shock.

"Somebody shot him, left the body at Ghost Crab Pond without any identification, then used his room key to check him out of the inn early Sunday morning." As far as Annie could tell, all of this information was news to Jason. "If you know why he came to see her—"

Jason's hands clenched into fists. He swung around, ran up the central aisle, banged through the door.

Annie stared after him. Jason Brown knew about Smith, but didn't know he'd been killed. Or maybe— and the thought came quick and cold—he was making an excellent pretense of ignorance. Whatever, Billy had to talk to Jason, find out what he knew about Bob Smith and Meg. There was an air of panic about Jason's sudden flight.

Annie headed for the front door. According to Emma, Jason and Jenna had both been at the Heath house Saturday afternoon. Had Meg, a happy, excited Meg, told Jason about her handsome visitor? She might also have told Jenna.

It was time to deliver that fruit salad.

Max knocked on the partially open office door. A metal plate announced: Acting Chief Billy Cameron. Billy had finally moved from his smaller quarters to the chief's corner office with its sweeping view of the Sound.

"Come in." Billy's deep voice was firm.

Max stepped inside, held up a green folder. "Billy, I've got the goods on Bob Smith."

Billy sat with his back to the windows, but he could swivel in his chair to look out at the bustling harbor. Bright sails patched the Sound with color. Sleek speedboats thrummed, leaving wide wakes. Whistle shrilling, the *Miss Jolene* thumped into the dock. The ferry was packed with SUVs, pickups, and cars. Passengers with bikes clumped near the rails, waiting impatiently for the ramp to lower. August sunlight flooded through the panes, burnishing Billy's hair a bright gold.

Max admired the harbor scene. He hated to miss out on a perfect summer day. Was that a dark hint of building cumulus clouds to the south? But he and Annie, their duty done, could take a spin on *Fancy That*, his new speedboat, as soon as he told Billy. Max's grin was expansive.

He pulled a straight chair close to Billy's yellow pine desk. The desk was so new there was a definite smell of varnish, and truth to tell, the finish was a little sticky. Moreover one leg, the left front, was a trace shorter than the others, so the desk had a decided list, but Billy was extraordinarily proud of the piece. His stepson, Kevin, with help from Mavis, had made the desk this summer for Billy's birthday, working long hours in the woodworking shop at The Haven, the island rec center for teenagers.

Max slapped the folder on the desktop, loosened the edge of his hand from the varnish. "I have definite identification. Apparently the dead man had used the name Bob Smith ever since he returned to the United States in 1982. I haven't been able to trace him between 1976 and 1982, but for certain he was actually Tony Sherman, Meg Heath's second"—he paused for dramatic emphasis—"and presumably deceased husband. According to what I've found out, Sherman was given up for dead when his boat went down in a storm. Everybody thought Meg was a widow, including Meg." Max flipped open the folder, retrieved Meg's biographical sketch, handed it to Billy.

As Billy read, Max flapped the altered photo. "That fire last night at the Heath house got me thinking. Why would somebody destroy a storage building? Unless it was a pyromaniac impulse—and you know nothing like that's been happening on the island—it had to be part of a rational plan. Marian Kenyon said the building held papers and mementos that belonged to Duff and Meg. Maybe there was something in those papers that would give us a hint why Meg was killed. Like old scrapbooks. Like a picture that would be a clear match to this one." Max rattled the sheet again. "I know, officially you're considering Meg Heath's death a suicide. But it could have been murder. Annie figured it out." His tone was admiring. "Annie thinks someone dissolved the Valium tablets in the decanter. Sunday night Meg poured her evening sherry, carried the glass out on the verandah, drank her sherry as she always did. The killer knew she'd die. Late that night the murderer went to her room and poured out the sherry in the decanter, washed out the decanter, and substituted fresh sherry. That way the only Valium residue was found in her glass, and, reasonably enough, her death appeared to be suicide."

"That would work," Billy said slowly.

Max laid it out. "Meg's kids have keys. Claudette lives there. Anybody could climb up one of those wrought-iron decorated pillars and get to the balcony. The door from Meg's balcony to her room was unlocked that morning." He recalled Annie's words, repeated them. "Easy as pie, Billy."

The idiom resonated with Billy. Slowly he nodded. "Yeah." His voice was flat but thoughtful. "It could have happened." He yanked a legal pad close, held a pen poised. "Okay. If you can prove the corpse out at Ghost Crab Pond was her second husband—" He broke off, stared. "Presumably deceased?" His eyes raced through the data. "Wait a minute. God, no wonder somebody killed her. And him. If this guy was Tony Sherman, that means her marriage to Duff Heath wasn't valid. That means none of that money belongs to her. If anybody ever found out, she'd have to return it. My God, talk about a motive for murder. . . ." He trailed off as Max slowly shook his head. "Isn't that what you're saying?"

Max tugged at one ear. "You got it right on one count, Billy. Her marriage to Heath was definitely bigamous. But then it gets murkier. I did a little checking, talked to a wills and probate lawyer in Charleston. Whatever the legality of the marriage initially, she and Heath lived as man and wife for twenty years, so she was definitely his common-law wife, which would assure her a portion of the estate. However, I got a copy of the will that was put up for probate, and Heath left everything to her by name, so it doesn't matter what her marital status was."

Billy slammed down the pen. "So she—or her heirs, because that's who we're talking about—don't have any motive to kill Sherman. Or her. Right?"

Max had tussled with these facts all the way to Billy's office. "Not unless they just assumed she had no right to the money. None of them are lawyers."

Billy reached for another legal pad, flipped through it, face intent. Finally he stopped. "Let me see what I got. . . ." He skimmed the page. "That's what I thought." His tone was satisfied. "Mrs. Heath saw Sherman"—a pause and the careful addendum—"if that's who he turns out to be—Friday morning. But"—he held up a cautionary finger—"she had dinner with her lawyer Friday night." Billy clicked on the speakerphone, punched numbers. "Let's see what he's got to say."

Max frowned. If Wayne Reed and Meg Heath discussed legal matters, that conversation was privileged, but it wouldn't hurt for Billy to ask.

"Wayne Reed, Attorney-at-Law." The receptionist's voice was pleasant.

"Chief Cameron. Broward's Rock Police. Connect me with Mr. Reed." Billy's no-nonsense tone demanded a response.

There was an instant of hesitation before she spoke. "One moment, please." The call was put on hold.

Max had played tennis with Wayne Reed the week before. Singles. Max won, 6–4, 7–5. It was a match for the men's A ladder. Wayne played with good-humored intensity and had seemed surprised to lose to Max. As

Max had later told Annie, "Wayne didn't seem to take me seriously." She'd grinned. "Perhaps your image is a bit laid-back." Max didn't take umbrage. He'd grinned in return. "Being underestimated has its advantages." Right now, he wasn't grinning. There had been a couple of questionable line calls made by Wayne. Mischance? Deliberate? Max's mistake? Whatever, Max knew he'd watch the lines carefully if he ever played Reed again. And listen to whatever he said with close attention.

Billy was growing restive. He tapped the pen on the desktop.

Abruptly the speakerphone came to life. "Chief Cameron? What can I do for you?" The deep voice sounded forthcoming with no hint of reservation or concern.

Billy was somber. "Mr. Reed, I would appreciate some help from you in the investigation into Meg Heath's death. I understand—"

Max folded his arms, bent his head to listen to the speakerphone.

"—you had dinner with Mrs. Heath Friday evening."

"Yes." A single word, weighted by sadness.

"What was the reason for the dinner?" Billy wrote swiftly on his pad.

The answer came smoothly. "We are—were—old friends, Chief Cameron."

"You were also her lawyer." It wasn't a question. "Did you discuss her estate?"

Now the words came more slowly. "Yes. There was some discussion about the disposition of the estate. However, her death moots any points that were raised."

Billy slapped out the words like a dealer snapping cards. "Did you discuss the reappearance of her second husband, to whom she was still wed when she married Duff Heath, and its effect upon her inheritance from Mr. Heath?"

"Oh." There was silence. And an odd popping sound. Max wondered if the phone lines were picking up static from a storm at sea. He scooted his chair closer. He didn't want to miss a word. He wished they were in Wayne Reed's office. Billy would have been better served if he were face-to-face with the lawyer. Of course Max wasn't a temporary deputy as he'd once been, so he wouldn't have accompanied Billy. Billy hadn't noticed that Max had moved his chair. Max breathed lightly, the better to remain unnoticed. At any moment Billy might decide to wave Max out of the office. But Billy was focused on the speakerphone. Reed cleared his throat. "Communication with a client is privileged, Chief."

Max nodded. That was the answer he had expected.

"Mr. Reed." Billy was all cop, his voice heavy as a truncheon. "I understand about privileged communications, but your client is deceased."

"Meg's death does not abrogate my responsibility to her." He spoke with quiet determination. "If that privilege were to be waived, it would have to be done by her heirs. However"—Reed's silence was thoughtful—"I am confident they would grant me permission to reveal some of our discussion. In fact, this will be a service to my clients. You mentioned Meg's second husband. Meg sought counsel about her status as Duff's heir. I wish to be clear that her family was well aware of this discussion. Meg spoke with me about her marriage to Duff and whether the fact that her marriage was bigamous invalidated Duff's will. I reassured her that such was not the case. Duff bequeathed all of his holdings to her by name, so the status of her marriage"—Billy nodded toward Max—"was not determinative."

Max returned his nod, wished he were more pleased that his findings were correct. Money, money, who got the money still seemed to be irrelevant.

Billy loosened the legal pad from the sticky varnish, propped it on one knee. "Did Mrs. Heath discuss anything else with you that might be relevant to her death?"

"All of our discussion was confined to matters of the estate, Captain. I can assure you of that." There was no doubting his sincerity. "I know that when we finished dinner, she was quite pleased." Again there was a silence. "I wish I could be more helpful. I took her home, walked her to the door. She looked radiant. She thanked me for making everything easy for her. That was the last time I saw her."

"I appreciate your help, Mr. Reed. This eliminates"—Billy's expression was relaxed—"a troubling question."

Reed sounded weary. "If I can be of any further service . . ."

Max was frowning as the speakerphone clicked off. It seemed very quiet in Billy's office.

Billy tossed the legal pad onto the desktop. "You had me going there for a minute, Max. And it is helpful to be certain of the dead man's identity. But I still think we're dealing with one murder. All that washing out of a decanter is too fancy. What you see is what you get. The lady committed suicide. Maybe she was waiting for him to give her a ring on the phone Sunday night and when he didn't call, she got upset. Anyway, I'd lay odds that Sherman got killed because he was a stranger and he hooked up with the wrong folks. Sure, the fact that he knew Mrs. Heath is what brought him to the island. That's not in question. But once she found out she still had the moneybags, there was no reason for anybody to care that he'd come. And if she told her family about Sherman, she probably told them what Reed said to her. I'll talk to them. But it doesn't look like her heirs had any reason to worry."

Max slapped one hand on his knee. "Billy, listen, I found out Meg and her kids had a fight Saturday afternoon. There was apparently a shouting match. The cook doesn't work on the weekends, but she went back to get something ready for this special dinner Monday night and overheard them. Annie thinks the dinner was going to be in honor of Sherman."

Billy spread out his hands, his face magnanimous. "You just explained it yourself. She told them about Sherman on Saturday. Sure they were upset. Here she was, planning a big celebration for a guy who ran out on her. I expect they were furious. I'll check it out. But why murder her? Somebody washed out that decanter in the middle of the night, refilled it with sherry? I don't think so. She dumped the stuff in her glass. As for him, her family had no reason to kill the guy."

Max's face folded into a frown. Billy had the facts on his side, but Max recalled Emma's dour pronouncement. He, too, didn't give a rat's ass about the facts. His instinct—shades of Annie—told him that Meg was murdered because of her long-ago love. But why?

The cell phone's ring, which sounded like a creaking door reminiscent of cellars visited by gothic heroines, forced Annie to prop the fruit salad on the fender. She muttered an *ouch!* as she touched the hot metal, scrabbled for the phone.

"Hello." She opened the door, retrieved the salad and slid gingerly behind the wheel. She really needed to spread a beach towel over the leather. Oh, the joys of August.

"Annie, can you meet me for lunch at Parotti's?" Max spoke fast. "I've got a lot to tell you. . . ."

Rachel carried her Pepsi and a sack with a hamburger and fries past the table where she always lunched with her friends. "Got a story to do. See you all later." She was the only one in her crowd who worked on the school newspaper. She walked toward the exit to the main hall as if going to the *Blade* office. Cole Crandall, carrying a lunch sack, had pushed through the door just a moment before. Once in the hall, she looked left and right. The outside door was just closing. She ran down the deserted hallway—everybody was either in class or at first lunch hour—and eased open the door. This was a side exit, not the harbor exit from the lunchroom to the terrace. The midday heat was overwhelming. She felt as if someone had covered her with steaming wet paper towels. Rivulets of sweat trickled down her face, her back, and her legs. During study hall, the terrace was hot but bearable. By lunchtime, the heat kept everyone inside. The terrace was empty except for one disconsolate figure. Cole Crandall moved slowly, shoulders slumped, steps heavy, toward the harbor.

Rachel lost sight of him as he walked behind a weeping willow near the harbor wall. Willow fronds shaded two benches with a great view of the Sound. The willows also screened the benches from the main terrace, giving a delicious sense of privacy. It was a favorite haunt of couples when the weather cooled in

October. Rachel and her friends, none of whom had steady boyfriends at the moment, considered Those Benches—everyone knew precisely which benches were meant when mentioned in a special voice—quintessentially romantic. To be asked to walk there with a special guy was a thrill beyond measure.

She frowned. Why was Cole going out there now? There wasn't a soul around. She moved quietly, glad for her soft-soled shoes, to the end of the building, peered toward the doors into the lunchroom. They were closed, of course. She looked in all directions and saw only the swooping gulls, raucous crows, and diving terns. No one would know Cole was behind the willows.

Cole was a wimpy nerd, trailing after Stuart Reed like he was some kind of hero. But she couldn't forget Cole's face. She knew how it was to feel the way he looked. Scared, desperate, alone, weighted down. That was it, weighted down so that it was an effort to speak, to think, to breathe.

Almost without volition, Rachel slipped quietly across the terrace, edged up to the dangling green strands that hung in a thick curtain, blocking out the benches and the Sound.

"Hello." The word could scarcely be heard, a whisper of sound.

She stiffened. If he'd seen her, she'd die. How humiliating! How awful if he thought she'd followed him out here to be alone with him. Rachel's face flamed.

"Sorry." His voice was thin and strained. "Hello. I'm calling to see if—"

Enormous relief swept Rachel. He was on the phone. Of course, he was calling somebody on his cell. She bent forward, head tilted to listen.

"—I can speak to Mrs. Darling."

Rachel's eyes popped wide. He wanted to talk to Annie!

"Oh. Uh. Oh, I don't know." A pause. "Yeah. Please tell her Cole Crandall needs to talk to her. I was on that boat Sunday night. And she asked me—asked all of us—the guys who were keeping a lookout—"

Rachel swung around, tears burning her eyes, ran blindly toward the end of the building. Oh yes. Chief Cameron had asked Cole and that creep Stuart and those guys who did nothing but cause trouble to patrol the decks. Pudge probably thought Cole was a big deal and he was just a big nothing.

She reached the door, slammed inside, stood for a moment in the cool dimness, then resolutely headed for the *Blade* office. She wanted to be alone. She couldn't go back to the lunchroom with her face all splotchy. She'd eat lunch, forget about Cole Crandall and his hideous mother and Pudge. After all, Cole was calling Annie. Annie could invite him over to dinner when she talked to him. They could have a wonderful time. But she wouldn't be there. Not for anything. They probably wouldn't even miss her. Once again tears welled and she rubbed furiously at her eyes, streaking the back of her hand.

Annie stared at the container of fruit salad sitting on the table. "Do you think I should ask Ben if he'll put my fruit salad in the refrigerator?" If she carried it around much longer, it might rival the amazing peregrinations of the Lady Baltimore cake in Phoebe Atwood Taylor's *File for Record*.

Max was checking the catch of the day on the sheet attached to the printed menu. "Mmm, poached grouper with clams." He looked up. "Fruit salad? It'll be fine."

Ben plunked down a huge glass of freshly brewed, unsweetened, perfect iced tea for Annie, and a Bud Light for Max. "I hear you two claim somebody bumped off Meg Heath. And they say that dude found out by Ghost Crab Pond had been to see her."

Broward's Rock was a small town and Annie never doubted that Ben knew everybody and heard everything.

"That's right." Annie was crisp. Ben would also know that Billy Cameron didn't agree with their theory.

"Yeah. Well"—Ben's eyes gleamed beneath his grizzled brows—"I saw that dude. He had lunch here Saturday." Even now on a weekday the grill was packed and a line waited in the foyer. The rattle of crockery, the thump of boogie-woogie on the jukebox, and the dull roar of conversation signaled summer as clearly as bumper-to-bumper traffic and scantily covered sunburned bodies daubed with zinc oxide. Parotti's, however, required shirts and shoes. Shorts were okay. No wet swimsuits. "He told me the bait shop was the best he'd ever seen outside of the Keys."

So far as Annie knew, this was the first definite placement of Tony Sherman by anyone other than the maid at the hotel. She clapped her hands together. "What did he look like? What did he say? Was anyone with him?"

"By himself." Ben squinted. "Fried shrimp, fries, coleslaw, Dos Equis."

Annie gave Max an amazed glance. Ben's memory was always excellent, but this was phenomenal. "Weren't you jammed at lunch on Saturday?" The locals knew to come early or late, and sometimes even that didn't help because of the influx of tourists. Oh the tourists, the tourists, the noisy but necessary tourists.

"Yep. But he was one dandy guy. Blue-and-white-striped sport coat. I had Jolene take a peek from the kitchen. Told her I'd like one for my birthday." His face turned a dull red. "Not that I pay much attention to that sort of thing."

Annie lifted her glass to hide a smile. Ben was decked out in a sport coat, white trousers, and white shoes, the epitome of southern manliness.

Ben talked fast to hide his embarrassment. "I remembered what he had on when I saw that story in the *Gazette*. Had to be the same guy. And everybody's been talking about Pamela—hey"—his face lighted with relief and good humor—"that's great news that Pamela's okay. Anyway, everybody says she saw him at Mrs. Heath's Friday morning and how Billy thinks Pamela fell and Mrs. Heath took an overdose and somebody carjacked the dude. Anyway, when I heard you two was looking around, I thought you might like to know that he was bright as a new penny Saturday. He was grinning, and every so often his face lit up with a million-dollar smile. I noticed as I went past to other tables. He wasn't looking at anybody else. No, he was sitting there eating and thinking and looked to me like he had a stack of travel brochures, and man, was he happy."

Annie liked air-conditioning, but she didn't like the coldness that washed over her like a gray winter rain. Tony Sherman on Saturday was a happy man who had only a few more hours to live. That happiness mattered. Her eyes met Max's. Whatever had ensued during Sherman's visit with Meg Heath, there had been a cheerful outcome. Jason Brown insisted Meg Heath was happy both Saturday and Sunday, although Jason hadn't mentioned the fact that he and his sister quarreled with Meg.

"Anyway"—Ben pulled out his order pad—"thought you'd want to know. What'll you have today?"

Annie put down her glass. She didn't need to say a word. Max knew.

"Annie"—there was only a hint of a sigh in Max's voice—"will have the usual—"

Annie always ordered a fried fish sandwich, except on sodden winter days when she opted for chili covered with corn kernels, Vidalia onions, and cheddar cheese. And of course she always wanted a basket of jalapeño corn muffins. She assumed a pious air. Everything in God's world had its place, including dee-licious food. Max should get over it.

"—and I'll take the grouper with clams and coleslaw."

Annie squeezed the slices of lemon and lime in her iced tea, crushed the mint sprigs. "Tony Sherman was happy. Meg Heath was happy. Surely Billy will see that she didn't commit suicide."

Max drank his beer, shrugged. "Billy's got an answer. He says she was probably waiting to hear from Sherman, and when he didn't call her on Sunday, she thought he'd dumped her again. She didn't know he was dead."

The problem, Annie knew, was that Billy's analysis was eminently reasonable. "Billy doesn't think anybody would kill three people just to keep everyone from finding out that Tony Sherman came to the island."

Max kneaded his cheek with his knuckles. "That can't be the reason. The lawyer made it crystal clear. Tony and Meg's marriage had no effect on her inheritance from Duff and therefore didn't endanger the prospects of her children or Claudette. So nobody has a motive."

Ben served their food, tartar sauce squeezing from Annie's sandwich, the broth on Max's plate steaming.

Annie took a big bite of her sandwich, sighed with pleasure. She glanced at the fruit salad. It would gain entree to a house of mourning, but what then? Abruptly she slapped her free hand on the table.

Max looked at her inquiringly.

"Okay, Reed says Sherman's arrival didn't affect the disposition of Duff's estate. He should know. But Sherman's appearance on the island had to be the catalyst." Annie took another big bite, chewed. Her words were indistinct but determined. "And right now, nobody knows we know about Sherman—"

Max's face brightened. "Jenna and Jason and Claudette. Right?"

"—so we can take them by surprise."

∽ *Twelve* ∾

CARS LINED THE CIRCULAR drive to the Heath house. Annie turned into the lot hidden behind the palms. She recognized several cars belonging to women from the church. The ritual of food and caring was well under way. She parked at the far end and reached for the fruit salad. Her cell phone rang.

Annie punched on the phone, picked up the carton, tucked her purse under her arm. Once out of the car she hurried to the dappled shade beneath the spreading arms of a massive live oak. A cloud of no-see-ums swirled around her. She waved her hand, determined this should be one short call. Her nose crinkled at the acrid smell of burned wood doused in water. An oyster shell path curved around a stand of cane. A wisp of smoke curled above the cane.

"Hello." Damn the no-see-ums. She moved in a re-strained jog, knowing the tiny biting insects would not be the least dissuaded from attack. She wished she'd doused herself with repellent this morning, but she'd not planned on communing with nature. She preferred nature well tamed by insecticides.

"Annie, Henny here." The cell phone crackled.

Annie felt a moment of breathlessness. "Is Pamela—"

"She's fine." Henny's voice was calm and reassuring. "She drifts in and out of sleep. She's feeling better, though obviously her head hurts. A few minutes ago she was thrashing about, almost awake, not quite, and she kept muttering, 'Ladyfingers. There were ladyfingers.' But when she woke up, she was confused and didn't seem to know what it meant, and now she's fallen back asleep."

"Ladyfingers?" Annie was especially fond of the little sponge cakes when topped by pineapple, papaya, and honeydew flavored with tequila, triple sec, and lime juice. It was one of Max's specialities. "Do you think she's hungry?"

There was an instant of irritated silence. "Annie, I would not have called—"

The no-see-ums whirred around Annie. She flailed her arm and moved in a quick trot toward the path. They didn't like smoke. She came around the cane, stopped, and stared.

"—to talk about Pamela's appetite." Henny was crisp. "I can't imagine how cakes could figure in, but something about ladyfingers terrifies her. She must associate them with the attack. I've tried to catch Emma—"

Annie was listening as she watched Claudette Taylor. The secretary stood with her back to the path, head bent forward, body slumped. She was a figure of dejection and misery, brooding at a desolate scene, charred beams thrust askew, fallen walls, an occasional trail of smoke rising to disappear in the hot bright sunlight.

Annie retreated until hidden by the cane. "That's

good. See if you can find Emma." She whispered, hoping Claudette wouldn't hear. She wanted to catch the secretary unawares. "If anybody can figure out ladyfingers, it will be Emma, although right now she's busy trying to place all the passengers when Pamela went overboard."

"Just wanted you to know. There was something about Pamela's voice." Henny's pause was dramatic, portentous.

Annie's hand tightened on the cell phone.

"Ladyfingers." Always the actress, Henny used a high, thin, faint voice to capture in the single word a frightful sense of horror and shock. Her voice once again clear, precise, and charming, she concluded, "I'll ask her again when she wakes up." A pause. "Oh, Annie." Again her tone made clear her intent, clothing the sentence in quote marks. 'No one, however clever, should expect to get away with more than one murder.' "

Annie smiled. Henny was obviously relaxed and enjoying herself again. But Annie knew this one. "*Murder at School*. James Hilton. And I agree absolutely."

"So do I. Bye."

Annie turned off the cell phone. She didn't want any interruption when she spoke with Claudette. Ladyfingers . . . Annie shook her head and moved stealthily around the cane, taking care where she stepped.

When the storage building was intact, it would not have been possible to see beyond it to the graveled road that disappeared into the pines. Most likely the road curved around to join the Heath drive. Now, with the walls collapsed into blackened masses, the road was clearly visible. Even from this distance, Annie could see the ruts made by the fire engines in the muddy gray dirt. A yellow warning banner fluttered from a stake, declaring the area an arson scene and prohibiting entry.

The secluded yet convenient storage building was ingeniously placed, on a par with the hidden parking lot opposite the main stairway to the house. Obviously Duff Heath had spared no expense when the house was built, this airy, cheerful, elegant mansion-on-the-sea. He must have been very rich. So Meg had been very rich. Now Jason and Jenna were very rich.

Annie picked her way across the sandy ground, her shoes sinking into the moist ground. She stepped on a pinecone. The snap wasn't loud, but Claudette whirled to face her.

Annie was appalled. Yesterday Claudette had been upset, her blue eyes dazed, but her porcelain white skin had been lovely, her faded ginger hair loose on her shoulders yet shiny. She had appeared shocked by her employer's death, but not stricken. Today her face was pasty gray, her features locked in a scowl, her eyes reddened by weeping. Ash smudged her light blue, very summery shirtwaist dress, clumped on her canvas gardening gloves. Ash and mud discolored her espadrilles, a fashionable match for her dress and meant for sunny days and happy times.

"Claudette"—Annie walked slowly forward, spoke gently—"I'm sorry." Annie felt compelled to give comfort where comfort obviously was needed.

"All gone." Claudette's voice was deep with bitterness and anger. The words were a condemnation.

Annie cast a puzzled look at the destruction. Yes, it was ugly, but no life had been lost. "It's a mess." But that was all, wasn't it? It was an ugly scene, but surely not dreadful enough to account for Claudette's distress. She stopped beside Claudette, stared at the charred remnants.

Claudette's hands clenched into fists. "Nothing left. All his work, his papers, the scrapbooks, everything's gone. I put together most of the scrapbooks. I went with them on holidays. I took care of everything, the hotels and rentals for umbrellas and bicycles at the beach or skis and lift tickets in the mountains. They were such happy days. June"—the secretary's thin lips curved in a smile that looked odd on her ravaged face—"June was always kind and sweet. Gentle. She was lovely to me. I think she knew how I felt about Duff. We never talked about it. She understood he had no idea I cared for him. Happy days. Duff was doing so well. Everything he touched turned to gold. That was before Duff and Peter quarreled. That was such a heartbreak, and all because they were so much alike, both of them determined to have their own way, go their own way. I kept hoping they'd be reconciled, but it never happened. And then June died." She pulled her fingers through her tangled hair. "Now there's nothing left of Duff, nothing at all."

Annie began to understand something of the complex web of emotions that linked Meg and Duff and Claudette. Despite the sauna-hot afternoon, Annie felt cold. Duff, Duff, everything was Duff for Claudette. She didn't seem to care that all Meg's memorabilia had been lost, too.

Out of a sense of fairness to Meg, Annie spoke sharply. "Meg's papers are gone, too. That's why the fire was set, of course."

Claudette reached out, gripped Annie's arm. "Why did it happen? Who did it?"

The feel of the damp, dirty canvas glove was uncomfortable. Annie wanted to jerk away, but forced herself to remain still. "Meg's murderer wanted to keep the police from finding out the identity of the dead man at Ghost Crab Pond. You knew who he was, didn't you?" Annie wasn't certain of her accusation, but her instinct told her that Meg wasn't one to keep good news to herself. Meg would have told everyone about Tony Sherman's return. "Why did you keep it a secret? You and Jenna."

Claudette didn't respond. Her silence was an answer of a sort. She didn't pretend she hadn't known about Tony's return or the discovery of his body. Her grip on Annie suddenly loosened. She brushed back a strand of hair, leaving yet another swipe of ash on her pallid face.

Annie felt sorry for Claudette but dismayed by her, sorry for her evident anguish, dismayed by her selfish preoccupation. Claudette hated the burning of Duff's belongings, but murder twice accomplished and once attempted left her unmoved. "You knew who he was when you read the description in the *Gazette*." There was an edge of disdain in Annie's voice. "You didn't call the police. You didn't do a thing."

"About Tony Sherman?" Claudette's bleak face twisted in furious anger. "I don't owe him anything." She turned and headed across the clearing, walking fast.

Annie called after her. "How about Meg? Don't you owe Meg justice? You and Jason and Jenna?"

Claudette ignored Annie. She disappeared around the cane.

Annie didn't hurry after her. It would do no good to try to confront her now. Claudette had made her position clear. She cared only for the memory of the man she'd loved. Claudette had loved Duff. Had she hated

Meg? But however she felt about Meg, it could not have been Claudette who set fire to the storage building. She was obviously distraught at the loss of Duff's papers and mementos. If Claudette did not set the fire, she had to be innocent of Meg's murder. Moreover, Claudette had agreed that there should be an autopsy when Annie suggested Meg's death might be deliberate. Yet if Claudette was guilty, what better way to demonstrate innocence than to acquiesce when an autopsy was suggested and to destroy material obviously dear to her. Wasn't her demeanor too distraught to be over a fire?

Annie strode swiftly toward the house. No, she couldn't dismiss Claudette as a suspect. There were still three suspects, Claudette, Jenna, and Jason.

The two-story pink stucco condominiums reminded Max of Bermuda, but palmettos lined the walkways instead of masses of flowering bougainvillea. Max glanced at the slip in his hand with Jason Brown's address, then checked the numbers at the front. Even numbers on the shore side, so 107 faced the water. Max walked around the end of the building. Everything was in excellent repair. The lawn was as well kept as a golf green. On the ocean side, he shaded his eyes, admired the Olympic-size pool and, beyond, the sand dunes with their fringe of sea oats and the sweep of the Atlantic dotted with shrimp boats and pleasure craft. A faraway freighter looked small against the horizon. A Coast Guard helicopter whopped overhead.

The shutters of Jason's condo were closed. Several *Gazette*s lay near the front steps. Letters and magazines bunched out of the mailbox. Max frowned and ran lightly up the steps. He lifted the bronze knocker, pounded. According to Annie, Jason's abrupt departure from the bookstore bordered on flight. Had he truly not known that his mother's second husband was dead? If he didn't know, why was that news such a shock? Obviously he had never met the man. Why should he care? Max knocked again.

The door swung in. "Yeah?" A frowning young man peered out, his long thin face tight with irritation. "What do you want?"

Max recognized him from Annie's description, coal-dark hair, his mother's elegant features, but he had an air of distress, the look of a man shocked and shaken. Max held out his hand. "Max Darling. You came to my wife's bookstore. Annie said you think your mother was murdered. We do, too, and we hope you will help us convince the police that she didn't commit suicide."

Max's assertion was true as far as it went. That it didn't reveal the true nature of his quest was fair enough in the circumstances. Yes, it was important to change the focus of Billy's investigation, but Max wanted above all to find out why Jason and Jenna quarreled with their mother Saturday afternoon. Since Sherman's arrival had no effect on the disposition of Duff's estate, why should it have mattered one way or the other to Meg's children? And if they didn't quarrel with her about Sherman, what was the cause of their anger?

"She never did." Jason's anguish was evident, but just as apparent was the flicker of fear in his eyes. "I don't know." It was a mumble of uncertainty. "God, I can't believe . . ." Pleading eyes looked at Max. "I know what it looks like. But it can't be true." He raked his knuckles across his jaw, his eyes desperate. "Not Jenna." The disclaimer was scarcely spoken, his voice a hoarse whisper.

Max stiffened. The implication was obvious and explained Jason's distress. Jason was panicked at the thought that his sister was responsible for Meg's death. But if he believed Jenna to be guilty—or, a cautious amendment, was himself guilty and intended to use his sister as a decoy—there had to be a powerful motive, a motive both powerful and urgent. Urgent . . .

Max's gaze was accusing, his voice cold. "You and Jenna quarreled with your mother Saturday afternoon. I suppose that's when she told you. It must have been a shock."

Jason took a step back, his eyes wide with alarm. Clearly he had no idea anyone knew.

"You were overheard." Max folded his arms, waited.

"Oh God." Jason turned away, blundered down the hallway.

Max stepped inside. A suitcase sat at the foot of the stairs. Annie had said that Jason's departure had the air of flight. Was he actually planning to leave the island? Max followed Jason into a cheerless living room, the sun blocked by shutters, papers and magazines strewn haphazardly, the bright cushions on the wicker furniture dulled by the dimness. Soiled plates and glasses were stacked by the wet bar. There was a fusty smell of yesterday's whisky and pizza.

Jason walked blindly to an oversize leather chair, flung himself down. He sagged into the chair, his face a study in misery and fear, his posture stricken, defenseless.

Max felt a pang of sympathy. But two people were

dead and Jason might know why. Max moved across the room, stood by the chair, staring down. "You yelled at your mother that she shouldn't be a damn fool."

"You can't blame us for getting mad." Jason shoved a hand through his hair. "I mean, for God's sake, it was so crazy. I thought maybe we could talk her out of it, but once Mother made up her mind . . ."

Max stepped back, sat down on the sofa opposite Jason, and listened.

Rachel slid an impatient glance toward the clock. Ten more minutes until the last bell. It had been the most interminable day she'd ever spent. Well, no, not the longest day. When her mother was buried . . . She wrenched her mind away from that cold and aching memory. The subsequent thought—that Cole looked the way she'd felt on that gray afternoon—cut through her mind with the sharpness of a polar wind. She gripped her pen, stared down at the open textbook, but she wasn't seeing the questions to be translated into Spanish. She was seeing Cole out on the terrace, and overlying that image, she was seeing Annie, a disappointed yet kind Annie, at her bedroom door last night. Rachel didn't like combining the images but they lodged hard and fast in her mind, tenacious as the bite of a snapping turtle and just about as painful.

A sharp poke in her back brought her head flying up. She realized abruptly that there was uncomfortable silence in the classroom. She raised her eyes and met Miss Peabody's sardonic gaze. Margo Peabody was a superb teacher, but her lack of patience was legendary. She combined uncompromising devotion to her students with a scathing tongue when convinced of inattention.

The whisper behind Rachel was the faintest of sounds. "Paseo de Carlota."

Rachel was a good student and she loved Spanish, and she had indeed done her homework last night. She took a deep breath. "Paseo de la Reforma was originally called Paseo de Carlota after the French empress who ordered the creation of the avenue from the Zócalo to Chapultepec Castle. Official histories, however, say the avenue was patterned after the Champs Élysées and ordered built by her husband, the Archduke Maximilian."

There was a flicker of surprise on Miss Peabody's face. "Yes, Rachel. And now if you'll translate beginning at *Vimos a muchos. . . .*"

Rachel's eyes fell to the page. She translated, concluding as the bell rang. She took a moment as she gathered up her backpack to whisper a thank-you to prim Edith Callahan who sat behind her, then she turned and hurried toward the door. She moved fast, determined to be one of the first to the bike racks. She'd get her bike and look for Cole. All the way down the hall toward the door, impulses warred. He needed help. He wasn't her problem. Why did he look so scared? She couldn't go up and ask him, she just couldn't!

Annie carried a stack of plates to the dining room, nodding to friends, keeping a lookout for Jenna. So far she hadn't glimpsed either Jenna or Claudette. What if Claudette had found Jenna, warned her that Annie knew about Tony Sherman? Surely there hadn't been time between Claudette's hurried departure from the ruins and Annie's entry to the house. Besides, Claudette's exploration of the charred site had smudged her dress, stained her shoes. She'd probably gone to her room to change.

Annie hurried back to the kitchen. Imogene, her face flushed from exertion, lifted a cheese grits casserole from the oven.

Annie cleared a space on the counter, moving aside a platter with cut ham and several dishes of relishes.

Imogene set down the casserole, gazed at it with satisfaction. "No garlic. Meg said garlic in grits was an abomination. She'd be pleased." Her expression soured. "Jenna won't like it. She hates grits. Probably because her mama liked them."

Annie glanced toward the dining room. "I was looking for Jenna. I didn't know if she and Claudette were busy."

Imogene bustled to the sink, began to rinse cups and saucers. "Those two." There was no fondness in her voice. "They've been glaring at each other. It's indecent. They're fighting over where Meg should be laid to rest. Jenna says she should be by Duff, but Claudette was downright ugly this morning, said she should be put by her mama. See, her mama is on one side of Duff. Claudette wants Meg put past her mama, not next to Duff. I don't know what Claudette's thinking. A married woman belongs next to her husband. So I doubt Claudette's talking to Jenna. Claudette came through here a few minutes ago, said she'd be in her room. It's down the stairs by the front door." Imogene waved a wet hand. "You go through the dining room to the foyer. If you'd put that platter with the angel food on the table, I'd appreciate it."

Annie grabbed the platter and carried it to the dining room. She placed the heavy glass platter at the end of the dining room table. She poured a cup of coffee, took a small plate, and filled it with a ham sandwich, chips, cut cold vegetables, a dash of dip, and a chocolate cream candy. In the entryway, she didn't look down the stairs, she looked up.

Christine Harmon, her sweet face molded into the gravity induced by solemn circumstances, fluttered toward Annie, a bound notebook in hand. "Annie, will you take over the phone? Why, there have been calls from everywhere! There was one from Singapore."

"I'm sorry, Christine, I can't do the phone right now." Annie held up the plate and cup and saucer. "I'm taking these to Jenna."

"Oh, of course." Christine's sharp blue eyes flitted past Annie, seeking another volunteer. "She's in the sea room. That's what they call it. I don't know why. Somewhere up there." She gestured vaguely toward the stairs. "She said she had a headache. I don't think she's had lunch. Some food will be good for her."

Annie walked quickly up the stairs. She was getting accustomed to the unusual vistas in the house. Anyone on the stairs was visible in all directions, but drapes, shutters, or bamboo blinds effectively masked the interior of several rooms. She looked up yet another flight. The shutters in Meg's suite were closed. She looked down at a cluster of women in the dining room and a preoccupied Imogene in the kitchen. She was confident that Jenna was in one of the rooms hidden from view. Annie glanced again at Meg's suite. No. Not likely. Instead she moved toward the north end of the house, where a bamboo shade hung down, closing off a room. Her shoes clicked on the metal grid work that served as flooring. She stopped at a closed door, knocked, then, balancing the plate atop the cup, turned the knob.

She poked her head inside. "Jenna, I've brought you lunch." Annie blinked against brightness as she stepped inside, closing the door behind her. The corner room was a sweepingly empty, glorious tribute to the serenity of space. A single long, low, white leather bench and a huge square glass coffee table were the only pieces of furniture. The flooring was white, the frames for the windows white. Sun splashed through all the windows. Even the bamboo shades behind Annie were a brilliant white. The room hung suspended in a pool of sunlight, remote from the rest of the house, its focus the immensity of the sea.

Jenna Carmody sat at the far end of the white bench, looking out at the placid green water with scarcely a curl of surf. The sunlight turned her dark hair a gleaming ebony. She was all in black, a thin cotton top, knit slacks, raffia shoes. She didn't turn. She gestured toward the coffee table. "Thank you. If you'll leave it there . . ."

Jenna was, in effect, telling her to deposit the snack and depart. In the ordinary course of dealing with a bereaved family, Annie would have put down the plate and cup and saucer and slipped away with a murmur of condolence.

Not today. Annie put down the dishes, steeled herself, walked around the bench, turned to face Jenna.

Frowning, Jenna looked up. Slowly her pale face hardened, sharpening the jut of her cheekbones, thinning her mouth to a pinched line. "Why are you here? Haven't you done enough harm?"

"Harm?" Annie's reluctance to intrude upon grief disappeared in a surge of quick anger. "Do you want someone to get away with murdering your mother?"

Spots of color flamed in Jenna's pale face. "They're

calling it suicide." But her voice wavered and her eyes slid away.

Annie's tone was solemn. "Jason says that can't be true."

"Jason?" Jenna's thin hands tightened into fists. She surged to her feet. "Have you badgered him? Leave him alone. He's such a fool. We told him—" She broke off.

"To keep quiet?" Annie challenged her. "It won't do any good. You quarreled with your mother Saturday. The police know all about it." Annie didn't go on to say that the police in the person of Billy Cameron knew and dismissed the importance of that quarrel.

"But there wasn't anyone here. . . . Oh. Claudette." Jenna's face twisted with fury. "So she told the police. Well, I'll bet she didn't tell them everything. I'll bet she didn't tell them how she came to pieces when Mother told us what she was going to do. If it hadn't been so crazy, it might have been funny. Meg burbling on and on about Tony coming back and how it made her realize his love had always been the touchstone of her life. Oh"—Jenna began to pace, her hands flinging out in anger, her voice rising—"It was vintage Meg, so absorbed in herself she never even thought about how it affected all the rest of us, simply thrilled that she and Tony were going to be together again"—there was an echo of Meg's voice, light but impassioned—"and that she wouldn't take a thing with her, it wouldn't be right, and she was going to give all of Duff's estate to his son, and she and Tony would slip away to an island and spend their dwindling days together, the two of them. She laughed and said she and Tony had never had a penny between them. That's how they'd started and that's how they'd end. Oh God, it would have been funny"—there was a sob in Jenna's throat—"except that's how it was when she dumped us on Gram, Meg being true to herself. Well, why couldn't she be true to us?" Jenna lifted a trembling hand to press against her cheek. "How about Jason and me? Duff loved us. He was our father. He wanted us to have what he'd worked so hard for. Meg was going to take everything away from us, run away with Tony. She had it all planned. She'd already talked to the lawyer and he was coming for dinner Monday night along with Tony and we were all supposed to admire her, think she was wonderful. Well, I didn't think she was wonderful. I thought she was selfish and irresponsible. And I can tell you"—the words dropped like stones into water—"that Claudette didn't think she was wonderful."

Annie could well imagine that Claudette had been appalled.

"Meg was so self-centered." Jenna's judgment was harsh. "She never saw anyone or anything but herself. She was the sun and the rest of us distant stars, invisible when she was present. I don't think she ever saw Claudette, not until that moment. You know how Claudette's always the perfect secretary, respectful, self-possessed, amenable. Well, not that day. She screamed at Meg, told her she'd never deserved Duff, that she'd never truly loved him, and tossing away what he'd given her was an unforgivable insult. For once Meg didn't have anything to say. She just looked at Claudette like she was a piece of furniture that had started talking. I think Mother finally understood that Claudette adored Duff. As far as Claudette was concerned, Meg was discarding everything that Duff had earned as if it were nothing. Claudette couldn't forgive that." Jenna wrapped her arms tight across her front, tried to ease her ragged breathing, but her face was still flushed. "If Claudette's throwing us all into the fire, she's going to get burned, too. Let her explain to the police how she told Meg she wished Meg was dead."

Annie believed every word of it. Yes, Claudette had motive and to spare, as did Jenna and Jason. But one truth mattered most. "Your mother died before she could do anything about Duff's estate."

Jenna stiffened at the bald declaration. She stared at Annie, her eyes huge with misery and uncertainty.

Annie was relentless. "Tony Sherman came back, he and your mother made plans to go away together, she decided to renounce Duff's estate, but they were both dead before it could happen."

Jenna looked stricken. "Oh God, I don't know what to believe. I was so mad at her." She swung toward the windows, walked away from Annie. "Even though we were all upset, she didn't care. She was so damn happy." She jerked around. Her eyes implored Annie. "Maybe she found out he was dead. Maybe someone called and told her. . . . Oh, I don't know what happened. But I didn't hurt her. I wouldn't. And Jason never would."

Annie heard uncertainty in her voice.

"Not Jason." It was a cry from a big sister. "If anyone killed her, it had to be Claudette."

Max punched in the number as he drove. "Billy Cameron, please. Max Darling calling."

Mavis's voice was excited. "Billy's over at the country club, Max. Some kids playing golf bounced some balls into the lagoon on the fourth hole and the balls bounced back!"

Max raised an eyebrow, wished the SUV in front of him could decide whether it wanted to turn right or left. Bounced back? The broad lagoon on the fourth hole was at least twelve feet deep. He remembered a greens committee meeting and the greenskeeper's reluctance to ask his staff to dredge for golf balls, thereby irritating King Tut, the ten-foot alligator in residence. Had King Tut whopped the balls with his tail? "Came back?"

"Yes! Of course, they knew that was crazy. One of them rode his bike home and came back with a boogie board. The lightest one paddled out to where the balls had popped up. He poked with a stick and he found a car. Boys"—she gave a mother's sigh—"have no sense. They knew King Tut was there, but fortunately he was sunbathing on the far bank and ignored them. Anyway, there's a wrecker out there, and the last I heard they'd just pulled out this car and it belongs to the man killed at Ghost Crab Pond. So Billy's pretty busy."

Billy, Max thought grimly, was going to get a lot busier. But it was terrific that the car had been found. Max was convinced the trunk would yield Tony Sherman's suitcase. Very likely Sherman's billfold was somewhere in the muck at the bottom of the lagoon. If Max was right on both counts, Billy would see that his theory of a carjacking or holdup was all wet, about as wet as Sherman's car.

Mavis broke in on his thoughts. "Max? I've got another call. . . ."

"Sure. Listen, buzz Billy I'm on my way out there. I talked to Meg Heath's son and I've got important information and a hell of a motive for the murders of Tony Sherman and Meg Heath." He talked fast.

"Wayne Reed told Billy the truth as far as it went, but it didn't go nearly far enough. Reed said Meg Heath's conversation Friday evening had to do with the disposition of her estate, but Reed knew a lot more than he told Billy. And yeah, he can claim privilege. But the upshot is that Meg was about to screw her heirs big time. I'll explain when I see Billy. Thanks, Mavis."

Max drove slowly up the street. Wayne Reed had held his cards close to his vest. If Jason had a stronger character, no one might ever have realized there was a motive as big as a Mack truck. And if no one ever knew, Meg's death most likely would have been officially adjudged suicide.

Max braked for the stop sign, clicked on the right turn signal. Billy was going to be irritated by Reed's lack of communication. Max frowned. Did the killer know that Reed had it in his power to reveal a sterling silver motive for murder?

Max felt suddenly cold. Of course the murderer knew. Lord, had Reed given any thought to the kind of danger he might be in? Max scrambled in his memory for Reed's address. He'd called his office to set up the tennis game. Yeah. Sure. That business complex on Sandspur Lane . . .

Max wrenched the wheel, turned left. Chafing at the slow progress of an old Ford in front of him, he drove with one hand, grabbed his cell phone with the other, punched Annie's code. The Ford turned off. Max picked up speed. He drove as fast as he could and talked even faster. "Annie, I got the lowdown from Jason. . . ."

Rachel dumped her backpack into the basket of her bike, watched Cole Crandall out of the corner of her eye. Funny, she could tell he was hunkering down, trying to stay out of sight, bending over to adjust one of his brake pads. Oh, hey, here came Stuart Reed, swaggering along. He was too cool to wear his backpack. He dangled it so that the straps dragged on the ground. He unlocked his bike, a superexpensive Italian racing bike, then paused to pull a ringing cell phone out of his pack. Cell phones were going off all over the place. Everybody's mom and dad knew what time their kids got out of school. Sometimes guys gave girls a call from the locker room as they got ready for football practice. Judy Perry stood right in the middle of the sidewalk, so everybody had to walk around her and nobody could miss her squeals of laughter and piercing cries of "Timmy, I can't believe you said that!" Everybody knew Tim Larson, captain of the Cougars.

"Hey, Rachel," Gina Schwartz poked her head out of a green Beetle. "Meet us at Crescent Beach. At the old rowboat." A wooden bateau half buried in the sand was a familiar island landmark. "The usual suspects." Gina loved *Casablanca*.

"I'll come if I can. I've got some stuff to do at home first." Rachel rolled her bike down the path. She passed Stuart Reed and heard him grumble, "I was going to go over to Cole's house. Yeah, he's going home. . . . Okay, okay, I'll take care of it."

Stuart was frowning as he strode past her. He saw Cole despite Cole's best effort to disappear behind the trunk of a palmetto. Stuart called out, "Hey, Cole, I got to take the ferry. There's some package my dad needs for me to pick up on the dock. I'll come over to your house later."

Cole let out a breath. He took a moment, then said uncomfortably, "Give me a call when you get back. But I got some stuff to do this afternoon."

It seemed obvious to Rachel that Cole was in no big hurry to see Stuart anytime soon. But if there was any nuance to glean, it rolled right past Stuart. Guys. They were so dumb. Any girl would have picked up on Cole's relief. So maybe Cole was brighter than she'd thought if he was avoiding Stuart. Not that Cole looked too excited about anything right now. His face still had that achy look. Maybe he was just unhappy because he was going home to an empty house. If he wasn't mad at his mom, he could go where she worked, maybe give her a hand with something. Sometimes Rachel went to the store and unpacked books for Annie. Of course, she had plenty of friends and sometimes they came over to her house or she went to theirs. She always let Annie know where she would be. She snagged her cell out of her backpack, dropped it in the pocket of her slacks. She liked calling and talking to Annie after school. She hesitated. She'd give her a ring when she made up her mind where she was going.

Cole swung onto his bike, wove his way around the end of the parking lot to a bike path. Rachel wished she didn't feel an almost physical pain at the sight of his hunched shoulders. Darn it, he'd been rude to Pudge. Why should she care if he was miserable?

She climbed onto her bike. Their route home took both of them on the same path for about a quarter mile. When Cole kept straight on, she made a sharp left, plunging into the forest for a two-mile ride on a bike trail through a green tunnel. Today she slowed as she neared the turnoff. Cole continued straight ahead. His bike curved out of sight around a bank of azaleas.

Rachel set her lips in a determined line and pedaled after him.

∴ *Thirteen* ∾

MAX STRODE INTO a luxurious anteroom, gray walls the color of old silver, gleaming cherrywood desk, crimson Persian rug, rose velvet drapes accented by mauve swags. No expense had been spared, but it might have been a lawyer's reception area in Atlanta or Tuscaloosa or Dallas. The very luxuriousness of the surroundings reassured him. He felt foolish. He'd rushed to warn Reed he might be in danger. The idea of danger seemed absurd here.

The secretary, facing her word processor, turned toward the door with a professionally pleasant expression that changed into a welcoming grin. "Hi, Max. How's everything?"

Max began to relax. "Hi, Nellie. I'm fine, thanks. I didn't know you worked here. I thought you were at Island Realty."

Nellie fluttered crimson-tipped nails. "I did the paralegal training in Beaufort and started working for Mr. Reed in May. Did Barb tell you we're going to Colorado over Labor Day?"

"Oh yeah. She's excited." Nellie Bassett and his secretary were fast friends. They often went antique hunting in Savannah and never missed Friday night bingo. Nellie was as thin as Barb was curvaceous, as dark as Barb was blond, as soft-voiced as Barb was loud. They were good foils for each other. "She said she's pretty sure it's open season on park rangers." His tone was dry.

Nellie clapped her hands together and bracelets jangled. "That's our Barb."

Max had a little difficulty picturing bouffant Barb with her penchant for hot pink in the Colorado mountains, but hey, a park ranger? Of course.

Max stopped in front of Nellie's desk. His smile slid away as he looked past her at closed double doors. Cherrywood, also, with oversize ornate bronze knobs. "Nellie"—Max nodded toward the private office—"I need to talk to Wayne." Reed had to be warned that a merciless killer might want to be certain Reed never told what he knew.

Bracelets tinkled as she reached for a pen. "I'll take a message, Max. He's in conference."

Despite his law degree, Max had never practiced law, but he knew the lingo. *In conference* covered everything from intense work to afternoon delight to postprandial naps. "This can't wait. Tell him I'm here about Meg Heath's murder." Max was determined to see the lawyer. "Tell him his clients are under suspicion." That should get Reed's attention.

Her eyes widened. "Murder? Mr. Reed said it was an accident."

Max pointed at the intercom. "Give him a buzz, Nellie, please." Max rehearsed his message: Two people were dead, probably by the same hand, and another murder had been attempted. Reed could rest on privilege if he wished, but he would be well advised . . . Abruptly Max realized that Reed's secretary had made no move to speak to the lawyer. Max jerked his gaze from the doors to the desk.

Nellie's thin face puckered with worry. "I can't buzz him. Mr. Reed's a bear about not being bothered when he says he's in conference. He most specifically told me"—her voice was anxious—"that he wasn't to be disturbed under any circumstances this afternoon."

Max was not prone to presentiments. In fact, he wouldn't have known a presentiment if he fell over it except for explication by Annie in regard to the conventions of the gothic novel. Ill-defined apprehension, according to Annie, was an art form when practiced by Mary Roberts Rinehart, one of America's earliest crime novelists and at one time the most highly paid author in the country. Annie would have insisted that the sudden uneasiness in his intestines was exactly what a beleaguered heroine might experience when creeping down the cellar steps to explore that loud bang. Max dismissed the feeling. He was simply irritated, and he had no intention of being thwarted by Wayne Reed.

"I understand. I'll take care of it." He strode around her desk.

Nellie's chair squeaked as she pushed it back, clattered to her feet, calling out, "Max, wait, no. He'll be furious!"

Max was already banging at the huge double doors. "Wayne, Max Darling here." His hand dropped to the knob, tried to turn it. He jolted to a stop. The knob was unyielding, the door immovable.

Frowning, he swung toward Nellie, who stretched out a hand in appeal. One part of his mind registered that Reed certainly had his secretary cowed, but that didn't matter now. "Do you have a key?"

She blinked in surprise. "It's locked?"

Max tried the knobs, rattling them hard, then banged again with both fists. "Hey, Wayne, open up." Finally he stepped back, glared at the door. If Reed was there, surely he would have responded, quite likely in a tearing rage if Nellie's reaction was any barometer. If he wasn't there . . . Once again uneasiness swept Max. Okay, okay. If he wasn't there, he was out and about. No big deal. There had to be another exit. He'd simply not bothered to tell his secretary he was leaving.

But Max moved fast, propelled by that insidious, indefinable sense of wrongness. He hurried to the office door, flung it open, stepped into the hall. Yes, there was another door halfway down the hall. Max strode down the hall, tried the knob. Locked. How about . . . He reached the end of the hall and the back exit. He pushed outside into the afternoon heat. Stairs led down to a dusty alleyway. Max thudded down the steps, moved to a back window of the lawyer's office. He hesitated for only a moment, then pushed at the window. To his surprise, it moved up easily. He stood very still, listening to the matter-of-fact sound of Wayne's voice: ". . . and in the first instance, the court has made it clear that . . ."

The bike path crossed Painted Lady Lane. Rachel stopped in the shade of a huge magnolia, looked to her right. There was no sign of Cole. Painted Lady Lane curved in a lazy S to meander to a dusty dead end, a desolate, down-at-heel street with a modest past and little future. Rachel remembered her disdain the day she'd ridden her bike to see the place where That Woman lived. She couldn't believe Pudge would consider living on an ugly street like Painted Lady instead of staying in Annie's nifty tree house where owls and cardinals and ruby-throated hummingbirds hung out, so close you could see the shine of their feathers. Her judgment had been swift and merciless. That's why Sylvia was chasing Pudge. She wanted to live in a nicer house.

Rachel bit her lip. Her hands tightened on her handlebar grips. She could go home, change into her swimsuit, bike to the beach. Bobby Higgins was always funny. His freckled face would be splotched with zinc oxide, he'd have his baseball cap on backward with only an occasional wiry red curl escaping, his trunks would sag so far down they'd half cover his knobby knees, and somehow, without saying a word, eyes wild, arms akimbo, knees turned inward, he'd have them all rolling in the sand they'd be laughing so hard. Sun, sand, sea. Fun.

She wanted to turn her bike and fly away up the path, leave this shabby street, never see these trashy houses or Cole Crandall again. He would sneer at her. She knew he would. . . .

Abruptly she remembered the look on his face, the way he'd hunched his shoulders. Slowly she turned her front wheel a little to the right.

He'd laugh at her.

The idea of ridicule froze her in place. Then, not allowing herself to think, she grabbed her cell phone from her backpack. She punched the code for Annie's cell. She was disappointed when voice mail picked up. But it didn't matter. She'd leave a message. Once she committed herself, once she told Annie what she was going to do, well, she'd have to do it. She took a deep breath. "Annie . . ." The words spilled out fast before she could change her mind.

* * *

In the Heath drive, Annie cast a look back at the fairy-tale house shining in the sun, the expanse of glass bright as sunlit diamonds and just about as pricey. Emma had said she liked money as a motive. It looked as if Emma was going to be right, as usual. Or if not precisely on point, too close to quibble. Jenna Carmody and Jason Brown must have been shocked and appalled and furiously resentful when Meg informed them that there would be no great wealth for them, that, in fact, Meg intended to oversee the return of all Heath's estate to his estranged son, Peter. Jenna saw her mother's decision once again as an abandonment of her and Jason. Had Jason been as hurt as Jenna by Meg's turning away from them to a man who'd discarded her so many years ago? Or for Jason was the prospect of losing his comfortable status the primary offense? Claudette's anger might be twice as strong. She not only foresaw losing money that she had expected to receive and to which she surely felt entitled, but perhaps even worse, she saw Meg's willingness to jettison Duff's estate as the ultimate rejection of the man Claudette had loved for so long.

The late afternoon heat pushed against Annie as she hurried toward the parking lot. Earlier she'd walked to the house, uncertain whether her quarry was Jenna, Jason, or Claudette. She felt no nearer the solution. But of them all, perhaps Claudette was the strongest, most determined personality.

Annie reached the car, quailed at the thought of sitting on the equator-hot leather seat. She started the motor, turned on the air-conditioning, and escaped to the shade of the live oak to let the interior cool. Her thoughts tumbled: Jenna, Jason, or Claudette, Claudette, Jason, or Jenna. One of them, it had to be one of them.

She pulled out her cell phone, turned it on, began her jig to avoid the no-see-ums. Three beeps signaled messages. She ignored the beeps. Should she call Billy first or Max or Emma? Emma's grid of the excursion boat was looming large in Annie's mind. If anyone had spotted Jason, Jenna, or Claudette near the deck where Pamela went overboard, that would be important now, very important. Before she could make up her mind, the phone rang. A punch. "Hello?"

"Annie." Max's cell crackled, usually a signal he was in his car, something about radio waves on the island as she imperfectly understood it. "I talked to Jason and found out—"

She broke in. "I know. Meg was going to give the money away." Annie had a quick vision of Meg Heath, gay, imperious, hewing to her own vision of what was right, quite willing to let the devil take the hindmost. Annie could almost hear Meg's throaty laughter. But this time when Meg followed her own desires, this time had the price been steeper than she had ever imagined? Meg had lived her life blithely impervious to the anger or disagreement she engendered. But this time everybody was furious. And someone was mad enough to kill.

"Right. All of them kept their mouths shut about Meg's plans, as per instructions from Wayne Reed. Jason said Reed warned them that Billy would look more closely at Meg's death with that kind of motive on the table. Reed had every right to keep quiet about it, but I wondered if it had occurred to him that somebody might make sure he didn't tell the police. I went to his office. He'd told his secretary not to put any calls through. I banged on his door. No answer. I yelled."

Annie recognized the determination in his voice. When easygoing Max made up his mind, there was no stopping him.

"So I went around to the back."

Annie frowned, trying to visualize where Max was.

"Reed's suite is in the Black Skimmer office park. An alley runs behind the complex. I went outside and pushed up a back window in Reed's office. I heard him dictating a brief. I yelled again. He kept right on talking. No pause. I pushed aside the drapes and swung over the sill. I still heard him. But he wasn't in the office. Nobody was. His Dictaphone was on the desk and it was running."

Annie moved toward the car, slipped into the cooling front seat. "I don't get it."

"I don't either. Maybe he was listening to a tape, wanted to be sure of some citations, got a call on his cell, and left in a hurry. Or maybe"—now his voice was worried—"he heard me bang on his door and decided he better check with Jenna or Jason before he talked to me. I hope not." Max once again felt that nudge of uneasiness. But most likely Reed was fine. "Anyway, Billy needs to know about all this. Maybe he can have Pirelli look for Reed. Billy's out on the fourth hole . . ."

The connection faded.

Annie frowned. "Fourth hole?" Outrage lifted her voice. "How can he be playing golf?"

". . . found Sherman's car sunk in the lagoon. If his luggage is in the trunk, Billy will see that the murder doesn't figure to be the result of a holdup or carjacking. That will turn the investigation back to Meg Heath. Why don't you meet me at the fourth hole?" The connection ended.

Annie clicked End, saw the notice of three messages. She backed out of her parking spot and clicked the first message.

Rachel rode fast. She wanted to get to the Crandall house, talk to Cole, and leave. She was already regretting her message to Annie. If she hadn't promised that she would try to persuade Cole to come over with his mom Friday night, she would turn around right this minute and go faster than Lance Armstrong. Why had she been so stupid?

The memory of Cole's face again popped into her mind. She couldn't banish it. Okay, that's why she was going. She didn't want to ask him over with his mom. She didn't want to be around old witch-faced Sylvia. She wanted to hold on to Pudge and have everything be the way it used to be, Pudge and Annie and Max all together with her, the four of them laughing and having fun. But Annie's invitation to Cole gave her a reason to go up to his front door and ring the bell, and when he came to the door, she would see his face and know if he needed help. That's why she had to go. She had this bad feeling that Cole was in trouble and she was the only one who knew. Annie had helped her when things were so scary in her life that she'd not known what to do or who to trust.

If she was wrong, and Cole just had a headache or was in a bad mood, if he came to the door and treated her like dirt, well, she'd tell him what she thought about him and his mother. She could be snotty, too. Rachel hunched over the handlebars, legs pumping. Sweat streaked her back, puddled into her socks. Dust puffed under her wheels. What a crummy street to live on. She came around a curve. There was that creepy abandoned old farmhouse, the roof sagging, the windows broken out. Probably bats nested in the attic. On this far loop of Painted Lady Lane, the only structures were the wrecked farmhouse and, a hundred yards farther on, all by itself at the edge of overgrown woods, the blue rental house where Cole lived. Paint hung in tattered shreds from the faded walls. A front shutter dangled on one hinge. The second tread was missing from the front steps. Part of the latticework that screened the space beneath the house had fallen in, leaving a dark gaping hole. Lots of lizards and spiders under there. Cole's bike lay on its side not far from the steps.

Rachel rolled to a stop, frowned at the bike. Cole had a nice bike. Lots nicer in its way than his house. He kept it polished and clean. There was no trace of salt rust on the pedals or the kickstand or the frame. Funny that he'd bang it down, the handlebars twisted, the front wheel sharply angled, the good-quality blue leather seat stubbed against a rotten old tree stump. A skink poked his reddish head out of the broken center of the trunk. After a frozen instant, the lizard skittered over the tilted seat, disappeared into head-high grass.

Rachel waited a moment to be sure the skink wasn't coming back toward her, then balanced her bike on its kickstand. She skirted Cole's bike. She was halfway up the front steps when she heard a low, hoarse call from the side of the house.

The tour bus belched smoke. Annie poked out the nose of the Volvo, swung the wheel hard right to swerve back into her lane. The oncoming traffic whizzed past, making her progress behind the lumbering coach seem even slower. She listened to Ingrid's message: ". . . so I think I know who made the whispery call yesterday. You remember, there was a call for you that I could scarcely hear. Anyway, a few minutes ago"— Annie judged the time. Ingrid's call was logged in at 12:05 p.m. A few minutes prior to that would have been around noon—"you got a call. Young voice. Male. He was really disappointed when you weren't here, said he needed to talk to you, that you had asked any of the guys who had been on the lookout on the *Island Packet* Sunday night to get in touch with you if they had anything to report. I thought this might be important. He wasn't whispering today, so I guess he wasn't worried about anyone overhearing him, but he sounded stressed. I gave him your cell number and I wanted to alert you that he might call. He said his name was Cole Crandall. Hope Pamela's continuing to improve. We've had a lot of calls about her. I told everyone she was in Savannah at a private nursing facility. Everything's fine here. A book club from Beaufort came by and cleaned us out of all our Joan Coggin titles, said they'd seen your review of *Who Killed the Curate?* in our newsletter."

Annie turned off the air-conditioning to block the acrid fumes from the tour bus. She noted the Tomlin family's roadside produce stand with its mounds of squash and cucumbers and plump home-grown tomatoes and red onions and big green-and-white-striped watermelons. Their stand was less than a half mile from Sand Dollar Road. The bus then had to turn right or left. Hopefully not left, as that would be her turn to go to the Island Hills Country Club.

The second message began: 12:09 P.M. "Mrs. Darling, this is Cole Crandall. I was one of the guys on lookout Sunday night on the mystery cruise. The lady fell from the deck I was patrolling. You asked me if I saw anything. Well, I didn't see her. Like I told everybody, I'd gone in to get a Pepsi. Just before I went inside, I was walking toward the back of the boat and I heard a funny noise somewhere behind me, a kind of popping sound. I turned around and looked back. There was a lifeboat there. I didn't see a soul. Anyway, after a minute, I walked on down to the end. I looked over the stern, then came back along the deck to the doors. It was hot, and I decided since there wasn't anything going on outside I'd go in. Anyway, I was in line for a Pepsi—"

Annie wished she had a big fizzy Pepsi right this minute. She could almost feel the buzz on her tongue, the sweet trickle down her throat. Maybe she'd stop at the golf snack shop, get a couple for her and Max. Oh, one for Billy, too. Heck, she'd buy a half dozen. It would be a thirsty crew winching that car out of the lagoon. The bus slowed to a crawl. It took all Annie's willpower not to push the horn and hold it.

"—when all the commotion started. I ran out on the deck and people were pointing and yelling. I thought they were pointing at me, then I saw her falling. She'd gone over the side right by that lifeboat. By the time they got her out of the water and into the saloon, everybody wanted to know if I'd seen her go over and of course I hadn't. I didn't think even once about that noise. I mean, it was just a little popping sound. I never thought of it again until yesterday afternoon when I heard it again." His voice sounded thin. "The minute I heard it, I knew what it was. But it doesn't make any sense. Why would Stuart's dad have been up there on that deck? And if he was, why didn't he tell anybody? Maybe he saw something. He's a lawyer. I thought lawyers always helped out the cops unless they're on the other side. But I don't think Stuart's dad is that kind of lawyer. Like I said, I heard that sound just before I went inside. So he must have been on the other side of the lifeboat, cracking his knuckles. Yesterday afternoon—he and Stuart were fussing at each other cause Stuart wanted some money so we could go buy some CDs—"

Annie imagined Cole's discomfort, unwilling witness to bickering.

"—and I wished then that I could go home but I didn't want to see my mom, but that's about something else—"

About jealousy and resentment and grief for a faraway dad. Annie understood and realized, too, that Cole had no idea she had any connection to Pudge.

"—anyway I was stuck there at Stuart's at least for last night. Anyway Mr. Reed popped his knuckles and I guess I got a funny look on my face because he kept staring at me when he thought I wasn't looking. So he gave Stuart the money and we rode our bikes downtown. I tried to call you when Stuart was listening on the earphones but you weren't at the store then either. And last night when Stuart and I were out at the pool, his dad came out and he kept worming the conversation around to that Sunday night and what I'd seen on the boat. Stuart was making fun of me"—his voice was tight with embarrassment—"saying there I was right next to the big show and missed every bit of it. Mr. Reed said there probably wasn't much to see, and it was a shame when people got depressed and nobody helped them. I said I didn't know the lady, and Mr. Reed said she was one of those do-gooders—"

Annie's hand tightened on the cell. She heard the echo of Reed's dismissiveness.

"—and she'd almost been a pest to Mrs. Heath, but

Mrs. Heath was always nice to her because she felt sorry for her. Anyway, he finally went in the house and left us alone. Stuart said his dad was really sorry about Mrs. Heath. I didn't know who Mrs. Heath was, but Stuart said she'd just died and she'd been a big client of his dad's. Anyway, I thought I'd tell you because this morning at breakfast, Mr. Reed started to pop his knuckles again and then he stopped and stared at me and I felt creepy. I decided I'd go home after school even though my mom—anyway, I don't know anything about the lady who fell off the boat and I didn't see anything but I heard that noise and I think that's what it was." His voice was puzzled, but more than puzzlement, there was a thin edge of fear. "I know"— his voice dropped to a mumble—"that's what it was, but it's crazy. Nobody'll believe me. Maybe I shouldn't have called—"

Annie heard the faraway shrill of a bell.

"Anyway, I got to go to class." The connection ended.

The tour bus ground to a halt at the stop sign at Sand Dollar Road.

Annie felt cold and hot at the same time. Cold with apprehension, hot with panic.

Ladyfingers! Pamela had cried out in delirium, her voice frantic with fear. She'd heard those little pops just before she was struck and thought them to be tiny firecrackers. Annie had a quick memory of hot and dusty July Fourths, and taking strings of dainty fire-crackers out in the backyard and setting them off— pop, pop, pop—so similar to the crackle of popping knuckles. Pamela wouldn't have been surprised to hear vagrant firecrackers, not in the South on a summer night, but she would, of course, have disapproved, thinking them a hazard on the excursion boat. She heard the pop, pop, pop, and then there was the sudden searing flash of pain.

Pamela and Cole hadn't heard firecrackers Sunday night. They heard Wayne Reed, crouched in darkness behind the lifeboat, waiting his chance, desperate for Cole to go into the saloon and leave the deck clear for murder, waiting, every nerve taut, muscles tensed, one palm pushing against the knuckles of the opposite hand, an unconscious response to stress. A nervous habit. Probably he never heard the sound himself, was unaware of his action. Lots of people had nervous habits. A tic of a facial muscle. Repeated throat clearing. Cracking knuckles.

Wayne Reed . . . Where was he? Max had gone to demand an accounting. An accounting . . . That would surely be done now. What exactly had been in Duff's estate when he died? What had happened to those properties and those monies? Thoughts raced through Annie's mind. It would turn out to be something like that, money that had disappeared, a sale of property that was misrepresented to Meg, nothing that would matter or be discovered so long as Reed continued as the attorney for Meg and, especially, for her heirs. But if everything had to be listed and valued, theft or fraud would be revealed.

Where was Wayne Reed now? Why had he left specific instructions that he must not be disturbed? If the question ever arose as to his whereabouts this afternoon, his secretary would testify that he was in his office.

An alibi?

Annie swallowed, felt the thud of her heart as if she'd run all out. She stared at the car clock. School was over. Cole Crandall wasn't going back to the Reed house. He was too wary to return there, though still struggling to understand what he knew. Instead he'd chosen to go home, home to an empty house, his mother at work. Cole's house. Oh God, where was it? What had Pudge told her about Sylvia, that she'd rented a place that was pretty run-down and isolated but she said it had a great marsh view and every morning she saw a great blue heron she'd named Buddy, and he admired . . . Painted Lady Lane. That was it, Painted Lady Lane, a fancy name for one of those modest dirt roads that angled toward the Sound from Bay Street.

The bus, with a burst of oily black smoke, began a laborious turn to the left.

Messages. A third message. Had Cole called again? Annie punched, watched the unending procession of cars, snout to bumper, waiting for her chance to turn right. It was such a small island. She could be there in minutes, four or five at the most if the summer traffic didn't slow her. If she screeched up to Cole's house and everything was all right, well, it would be good for a laugh tonight with Max and Rachel. She could hear Rachel now, folding her hands to mimic a bugle call and shouting, "Annie Darling to the rescue!"

The third message began: 3:09 P.M. "Annie—"

There wasn't quite enough room, and a Mercedes jammed on its brakes and blew a horn that sounded like the steam whistle of the *Queen Mary* as Annie gunned her Volvo into the lane.

"—I'm going by Cole's house." Her voice was stiff, the words were hurried. "I decided to ask him to come over Friday night. I know he doesn't like Pudge and I'm going to tell him Pudge is *swell*." She put a militant emphasis on *swell*. "Then I'm going to go home and change and meet some kids at the beach. See ya."

I'm going by Cole's house, I'm going by—

"Rachel. Oh, Rachel, honey." Annie fumbled to end the call, swung out to pass a bread truck, swerved back just in time to avoid a collision. Tears burned her eyes. Her hand shook as she punched nine-one-one.

Rachel reached the edge of the shabby house. The hard yet cajoling voice grew more distinct. "Cole, where are you?" She eased close to the wood, felt a curl of peeling paint against one cheek, peered around the corner.

A man stood with his back to her. A soft slouch hat, brim turned down, hid his head. He had on a long-sleeved cotton work shirt, baggy khaki shorts, Adidas running shoes. He stood in a forward crouch, arms swinging loosely. He looked like somebody getting ready to jump, but there wasn't anything to jump at. The left side pocket of his shorts bunched and sagged. Dark gloves poked out of a back pocket.

Rachel's eyes fastened on the back pocket. Soft leather gloves. Annie had given Pudge some gloves like that for Christmas, but Pudge's were tan, not black. Nobody needed gloves in August. She couldn't take her eyes off the dark, empty glove fingers drooping out of that pocket.

The man took a step forward, his head moving in a slow survey of a dark thicket that bounded one side of the marsh, a stand of cane near a weathered old shed, and the dusty, hummocky stretch between the back porch and the reeds of the marsh. "I need to talk to you, straighten something out." The deep voice was pleasant, with an almost jocular tone. "I don't know why you dashed away like that. But it makes me think you're a little confused. Come on now, Cole. I told Stuart I'd pick you up and we'd go have pizza."

Rachel squinted, her eyes dazzled by the late afternoon sun off the bright green Sound. Pizza . . . He told Stuart . . . That meant he had to be Stuart's dad. But right after school Stuart got a call from his dad asking him to pick up something at the ferry dock. Did Mr. Reed mean they were going to meet later? And why did he wait, hunched and quiet, like Agatha watching a bird poised to flutter from a shrub?

The shrill peal of her cell phone started her heart hammering. She jerked back, turned, began to run. Over the pounding of blood in her ears, she heard the running thud behind her. She was almost to her bike when a rough hand caught her, pulled her around, held her fast. She opened her mouth to scream and was pulled against him in a vise-tight grip, his other hand clamping over her mouth.

A red-faced golfer in a sweat-stained pink polo shirt swiped at his neck with a wadded-up towel. "What the hell do you mean the hole's closed?" He teetered forward, his six-foot-four bulk looming over Lou Pirelli.

Unfazed, Lou gestured toward the fairway. "Detour, mister. This one's a crime scene. Closed until further notice." Lou moved a few feet away, drove a stake, looped crime scene yellow tape around the top.

A tall thin man followed him. "Crime scene?" The British accent was partially mellowed by a drawl. "What's up, old chap?" He craned to see beyond the wrecker that had backed until its rear wheels smashed into the reeds along the bank.

A foursome chugged toward them in a golf cart,

clubs rattling in the bags sticking out the back. The lean women, all blond, all beautifully dressed in fashionable golf attire, wearing identical white visors, rolled to a stop. One of them, her husky voice excited, announced, "I told you, Serena. They're pulling a car out of the hazard."

Lou's dark hair glistened like a crow's in the sunlight as he bent to attach the tape, moved briskly to pound another stake. He called over his shoulder. "Stolen property"—Lou pointed toward the lagoon and the backer winching up the front of a red Mustang convertible—"connected to a homicide."

Billy Cameron gestured toward the wrecker, directing the truck to keep going. He wore plastic gloves on his hands. When the car, festooned with reeds, draped with algae, water spewing over the sides and back, was free of the lagoon, Billy chopped downward with his right hand. The wrecker stopped.

Billy shouted, "Lower it."

The car eased to the ground.

Billy hurried forward, opened the driver's door. He jumped back as water gushed out, splashing his khaki uniform. He leaned inside the car, removed the keys. In two big strides he was at the trunk, unlocking it, lifting the lid. This time he moved faster, avoiding the wave of water.

Max stood on a rise near the green. "What did I tell you, Billy?" Max's tone was triumphant as he pointed at a nylon suitcase partially submerged in the residual water. "Sherman's killer went straight from the pond to the hotel, got Sherman's stuff."

Billy pulled the sodden suitcase forward, flipped open the leather identification tag. He unzipped the case.

Even from a distance Max could see that the contents were a jumbled, sodden mass. The clothing must have been gathered up and stuffed inside with no thought of order. Tony Sherman hadn't packed his case. Tony Sherman was dead when a hand grabbed his belongings.

Billy pushed the suitcase to one side, bent closer to the trunk. He ran his hand back and forth in the brownish water and in a moment lifted up a drenched leather billfold. He eased it open. "Money." His voice was gruff. "So it wasn't a robbery the way it looked at first."

Max didn't change expression. The fact that Billy hadn't linked Sherman's murder to Meg Heath's death and the attack on Pamela didn't matter. What mattered was that Billy now knew all about Meg's plan to divest herself of a fortune and the upheaval at the Heath home on Saturday.

Billy placed the limp billfold atop the waterlogged clothing, pulled down the lid. He walked around to the side of the wrecker. "Haul it to the station. We'll work on it there."

"Captain!" Lou's shout was sharp, urgent. He ran across the exquisitely groomed green, heedless of the gouges from his shoes. "Captain, nine-one-one . . ."

Rachel struggled against the painful grip. She was aware of overpowering strength, the feel of muscles rigid as steel, the smell of sweat, the scent of fear. A shirt button jabbed against her cheek. Pincer-tight fingers clamped on her shoulder. In a shocked portion of her mind, she understood she was captive and in danger. Yet the somnolent summer sounds continued without pause, the cackle of clapper rails, a strident mockingbird trill, the derisive caw of crows, the whine of mosquitos, the rustle of cordgrass in the onshore breeze. Despite the heat of the sun, her skin was clammy with fear.

His breath tickled her ear. "Don't yell."

"I won't." She spoke in a faint whisper against the bruising fingers pressed against her lips. Slowly he relaxed the pressure and she was able to stand apart from him, though one hand still fastened on her shoulder.

He was breathing fast, in spasmodic jerks that lifted and dropped his chest.

Rachel trembled, one long shudder after another. She looked into wild, staring eyes, jerked her gaze away. "I just wanted to talk to Cole." She knew her voice was high and thin.

He glanced toward the house. "You were coming over to see him? Nobody here but the two of you . . ."

Red stained her cheeks at the tone in his voice. "No, it's not—"

He wasn't listening. Without warning, he jerked her around until she was facing the house and one arm was pulled up behind her. "Let's walk that way." He pushed her toward the side yard.

Rachel's gaze darted toward the cane. Even if she got away, there wasn't anyplace to run. The cane was thick and wild, she couldn't force her way through. A path angled off toward the water. She felt a spark of hope. At the end of the point there was a dilapidated cabin on posts and a pier that stuck out into the reed-thick water. If someone was there . . . But the cabin drowsed in the afternoon sun.

Straight ahead was the marsh, the mudflats steaming, fiddler crabs swarming in search of food. A white ibis, red bill gleaming, stalked the crabs. The tide was coming in. Soon the water would reach the banks.

No place to run . . .

"Cole." Reed's shout was hoarse. "I know you're here." His eyes scanned the house in its dusty clearing, the marsh, the woods. "You couldn't have got past me. Well, you've got company. Your girlfriend's here." His voice was pleased, confident. He inched Rachel's arm higher, brought a gasp of pain. The demand was harsh, swift. "What's your name?"

She bent forward, trying to ease the strain on her arm. "Rachel, but—"

"Rachel's here. Pretty girl. I'm sure you don't want her to get hurt. I'll tell you what, you come out and join us and we'll talk everything over, see if we can work things out." There was a hideous parody of reasonableness in his tone. "I'll count to five. If you don't come—"

Rachel stumbled forward, almost fell as he let go of her.

"—she'll die. Take a look, Cole. I've got a gun and—"

Rachel felt the hard prod of metal against the back of her neck.

"—I'm ready to squeeze the trigger. I'll count to five, Cole. If you don't come out by the time I get to five . . ."

Rachel tried to speak. "No . . ." The strangled sound was lost in the crackle of the spartina grass and the rustle of the cane. Cole mustn't come. He couldn't save her. No one could save her. If Cole could get away . . . What if she whirled and ran . . . But the gun hurt her neck. There wouldn't be time.

He shouted the words in a deep, harsh voice. "One . . . two . . . three . . ."

*　　*　　*

Annie drove with one hand, held her cell with the other. Only a few more blocks. It wasn't far. The next turning . . . "I called Rachel's cell phone and there wasn't any answer." Her voice quivered.

Max was reassuring. "Don't panic. She may have forgotten to—"

"No. I told you. She called me just a few minutes before I got the message. She'd just gotten out of school. She always keeps her cell on after school. So I can get in touch with her. It's a rule we have." Tears burned Annie's eyes. That was their rule, a rule in a safe and ordered world, a rule meant to keep Rachel safe. And she hadn't answered!

"We're coming as fast as we can, honey." Billy's siren wailed over Max's words.

"Oh God. Maybe Billy should turn off the siren. What if Reed's there? What if—"

"Steady," Max urged. "We don't know for sure that he's the one."

Annie knew. Ladyfingers. Pop, pop, pop. She leaned forward to glimpse the street sign, slowed. "Max, I'm here." She swung the wheel hard right, churned up the dusty gray road, wheeled around a curve, noted the modest houses. No cars. This was a working-class neighborhood. People weren't home in the daytime. The very last house, that's what Pudge had told her.

"Annie, wait for us." It was a direct order.

She loved him, but she had to keep on. "I've got to find Rachel." She turned off the cell, eased to a crawl. Around this curve . . .

*　　*　　*

"Let her go and I'll come out." Cole's echoing voice sounded far away, muffled.

The pressure of the gun against her neck eased.

"Okay, Cole. That's sensible of you." Relief buoyed Reed's voice. "We'll talk, work things out."

Rachel knew this was a lie. What could be worked out? Mr. Reed had a gun and he'd threatened her. As long as they were alive, they could tell what he'd done.

"Cole, don't. He'll shoot you, too." She shouted and tried to twist away.

Hard fingers caught her arm, pulled her back. The muzzle jabbed into her side.

Reed pulled breath deep into his lungs for another harsh shout. "She's not going anywhere until you come out. It's up to you, Cole, whether she lives or dies."

Rachel felt dizzy. She'd never realized how precious the feel of the hot sun on her skin could be. She wanted to lift her face to the light. But death and darkness pressed against her.

"Four . . ."

A hinge squeaked. Part of the latticework at the back of the house swung out. Dusty, dirty, trailing spiderwebs, Cole edged out from beneath the house, eyes squinting against the brightness of the sun. He held up one hand to shade his face.

"Mr. Reed, listen, I got an idea." Cole talked fast. He moved stiffly toward Rachel and her captor. "Rachel and I can go out in a boat. C'mere, Rachel." His face was white as paste. His eyes looked huge. A spiderweb hung down over one ear. He would have looked silly, like a Halloween joke, except for the dreadful understanding in his glance. He knew that Death was there, waiting for them. He gestured toward Rachel, urging her to come toward him.

Rachel took one step, then another away from Reed.

"See, I've got a rowboat"—Cole pointed toward the distant dock that poked out into the Sound—"and we can go for a row while you—" Cole was even with her now. He stepped past her, moved closer to Reed. He was close enough that Rachel could see the spatter of freckles standing out against his dead white face. Cole pointed again toward the Sound. His face suddenly lightened. "Oh, hey, wait a minute. There's Mr. Durrell. See, he's coming—"

Reed jerked to his right, looked toward the marsh. He was a figure of danger and desperation, his face wolflike, his shoulders hunched to do battle. The hand with the gun swerved, too.

Cole's right foot flew up. The kick caught Reed's wrist. The gun went off, the sound enormous in the silence of the summer afternoon. Cole lunged forward, his face desperate and afraid. With the rigid side of one hand, Cole chopped at Reed's neck. The lawyer grunted in pain, wavered on his feet. The gun clattered onto the ground.

Cole yelled, "Run, Rachel."

Reed clawed at his throat. He took a halting step, then another, toward the gun, which lay near the base of a ragged saw palmetto.

His breathing ragged, air whistling through half-open lips, Cole started after him, his hand lifted to strike again.

Reed twisted and caught Cole's arm, flung him heavily to the ground, then reached down, pulled him to his feet, and heaved him through the air. Cole smacked against the ground, lay still, panting for breath.

Rachel wanted to run. She wanted to escape the dreadful struggle, the harshly drawn breaths, but Cole had come out to save her and she couldn't leave him alone to face this terrible danger. Her eyes fixed on the shiny blue-black metal of the gun, she stumbled forward, grabbed it, and turned to aim at the shambling figure coming toward her, face twisted in anger, hands outstretched.

Car brakes squealed. A door slammed. "Rachel!" Annie's agonized cry rose in the bright afternoon.

Rachel backed away as Reed came nearer and nearer. She held the gun straight, the barrel pointed at Reed's chest. She had to shoot. She must. He was close now, only a few feet away. If he got the gun . . . Rachel whirled, using every ounce of strength, and threw the gun in a high arc toward the marsh.

Reed's scream of anger was as vicious as a blow, harsher than the sirens shrilling nearer and nearer. Dust plumed beneath their wheels as two police cars roared down the street and bucked across the dusty yard. Doors opened and officers jumped out, service revolvers in hand.

Reed broke into a heavy-footed run.

The shout blared over a bullhorn. "Police. Halt. You're under arrest."

Reed was almost to the marsh when a swift Lou Pirelli came up from behind and slammed him to the ground. "Got him, Chief." The lawyer lay facedown in the gray dirt. Lou knelt, manacled his captive's hands behind him, jerked him to his feet.

Annie closed her arms around Rachel and Cole. Max gathered them all into a tight embrace.

Rachel twisted to watch as Lou escorted Reed to the police car. "He was going to kill us." Her voice wavered, high and thin and breathless. "But Cole came right up to him and karate-kicked the gun out of his hand and that's the only reason he didn't shoot us." She looked at Cole's pale face and dark eyes so near her own. "You saved my life."

Cole took a deep breath. "And you saved mine."

∻ *Fourteen* ∾

HENNY BRAWLEY BEAMED at the assembled guests. She was a regal figure atop the temporary wooden stage, a rhinestone tiara perched on her silvered chignon. A loop of her long red chiffon dress was draped over one arm. Matching rhinestone buckles glistened on white pumps. She might have been at the opera or a music hall. Annie was thrilled that Henny was playing her role so magnificently. Only Henny could carry off such a dramatic costume at a watermelon feast on a sweltering August afternoon. They'd sent invitations, of course, to everyone who had attended the mystery cruise.

The boardwalk by the marina was jammed. An accordion, tuba, and trombone oompahed the "Tic-Toc Polka." The summery crowd flowed in and out of Death on Demand. Many of the customers clutched newly purchased books. Children played hide-and-seek near a huge oak tree. Teenagers spit watermelon seeds in a distance contest. A cocker spaniel danced at the end of its leash, yapping at a schnauzer. The schnauzer's lips drew back in a ferocious growl.

Henny held up a garish costume jewelry necklace of shiny green stones. "Here are the fruits of the theft. As all of you on last Sunday's cruise will remember . . ."

Pamela Potts looked up happily at Annie. A bright orange tam hid most of the discreet white bandage on the back of her head. "I loved the little play!" Pamela was still pale, but her eyes sparkled from the warm reception she'd received. She was abashed to be the center of attention, but basking in her welcome from friends and well-wishers.

Annie patted Pamela's shoulder. "Thanks, Pamela. I didn't know you would remember."

"Oh yes." Pamela's eyes glowed. "I remember the play. Annie, it was so clever. And Henny's narration was wonderful. First she described the crime scene, an antebellum tabby house with double verandahs, Ionic columns on the first floor, Doric on the second—"

Annie didn't listen closely. After all, she knew the play. She'd written it! Her shopkeeper's eyes scanned the throng on the boardwalk. Whoopdedoo, the turnout had surpassed her most hopeful expectations. She grinned. A red-faced and beaming Duane Webb stood just outside Death on Demand, waving his straw boater in a pitch-perfect imitation of a carnival barker: "Step right in, ladies and gentlemen, books for every taste. Come right in and get your armchair passage to Zanzibar, St. Mary Mead, Istanbul, every destination guaranteed."

Pamela waved a hand at the live oaks on the terrace. ". . . a country house with live oaks and azaleas. It's springtime and the yucca and magnolias and daylilies are blooming. Wildlife abounds, otters and turtles and raccoons and possums. . . ."

Annie and Pamela applauded as Henny introduced the cast members one by one. ". . . Wanda Wintersmith, mistress of Mudhen Manor. Wanda is dressing for a dinner dance. When she emerges from her bath, she finds that the famous Green Fire necklace of matched emeralds has disappeared from the dresser in her bedroom. Present at the antebellum mansion that evening are her husband, Walter, niece, Periwinkle Patton, nephew, Augustus Abernathy, and two guests, Heather Hayworthy, an aspiring actress much admired by Walter Wintersmith, and Moose Mountebank, a handsome young man who has been attentive to Wanda." As each name was called, the player crossed the stage to thunderous applause.

Pamela clapped enthusiastically. "And such wonderful motives! Mrs. Wintersmith is mad at her husband because he's having an affair with Heather. Mr. Wintersmith needs money because Heather is a gold-digger. Heather's told everyone how great she would look in the emeralds. Periwinkle wants to escape to the isle of Capri and write the great American novel but her aunt won't give her any money. Augustus has embezzled from his bank and the auditors are coming next week. Moose told Heather maybe they should run away together, but neither one has a bean."

Annie's gaze moved on to a picnic table only a few feet from the stage. Her eyes misted. She swiped with an impatient hand. Now was no time to be emotional. Pamela Potts's arrival had brought forth cheers, and the watermelon feast to conclude the interrupted mystery cruise was a resounding success. But Annie was too near the trauma of Rachel and Cole's near rendezvous with death to be cavalier when she looked at those she loved. Once again thankfulness swept her. They had been a quiet and reflective but joyful group when they gathered for hamburgers Friday night. Cole had been recognized as their hero. But Rachel's rescuer had been somber, still shaken by Wayne Reed's arrest and the heartbreak for Stuart Reed. Cole had taken some comfort from knowing that

Stuart had left the island, gone to join his mother. But right now they were all here, everyone who mattered to Annie, gathered happily at the picnic table. They were here and they were safe—Max and Rachel and Laurel and Pudge, along with Sylvia Crandall and Cole. A grinning Cole, carrying two plates loaded with watermelon slices, held one just out of Rachel's reach. His mother, shoulder to shoulder with Pudge, called out, "Don't tease, Cole." Rachel whooped and grabbed Cole's baseball cap and backpedaled. "Catch me if you can."

Catch me if you can. . . . Annie took a deep breath. They had arrived in Painted Lady Lane with not a minute to spare. If they hadn't sped to the house, if Reed had found that gun in the marsh . . . But Lou Pirelli caught Reed in time. Now the lawyer was in jail and Annie felt sure he would be convicted. There was so much evidence once they started to look. The accountants had quickly discovered how he had plundered Meg's estate, a bogus sale of the great Mandarin Copper Mine through a dummy company. He'd tried to hide his tracks, setting fire to the storage building with all Duff Heath's business records. He'd told Meg the mine had been sold at a loss. Reed had pocketed almost two million dollars. There was no likelihood of discovery unless the worth of Meg's inheritance came into question.

". . . but of course the telling clue was about the raccoon who sat in the live oak tree to listen to Mozart." Pamela nodded decisively.

Annie jerked toward her, stared at her in amazement.

Pamela was emphatic. "Oh yes, I saw it at once. The emeralds left on the dresser, the late afternoon sun streaming in through the open windows to the verandah"—Pamela looked wise—"spring, you know. There was so much emphasis on the season, I knew it had to be important. Well, you only have open windows in the spring. And then Henny said how the raccoon—Harry, I think he's called—was known to climb up the live oak tree and listen when Mrs. Wintersmith played CDs. That made everything clear, especially since the door from her bedroom into the hall was locked and I doubted her husband had a key since they weren't on very good terms, and how could the others have gained access? Oh it was clear to me right from the start, and so clever of you, Annie, theft by a masked intruder, .Harry the raccoon. I wonder who's going to win?" She looked eagerly up at the stage.

Annie knew the answer. She took Pamela by the hand. "Let's go up close to the stage."

Henny moved to the edge of the stage, microphone in hand. "Despite the brilliant minds of our sleuth passengers, I am amazed to report that no one—"

Annie started up the platform steps. "We have a winner." She turned, tugged on Pamela's hand. "Right up here, Pamela."

Henny looked startled. "We didn't have an entry from Pamela."

Annie reached for the microphone. "Ladies and gentlemen, I am pleased to announce that the mystery of the jewel theft has been solved by Pamela Potts, who told me the correct answer just a moment ago. As most of you know, Pamela was the victim of an attack aboard the *Island Packet* Sunday night and so had no opportunity to submit a formal entry. However, I know all of you will be delighted that Pamela tonight revealed the identity of the jewel thief, and it is"—Annie paused for dramatic effect—"Harry the raccoon, the masked intruder who entered Mrs. Wintersmith's bedroom by way of the live oak tree and the verandah. Ladies and gentleman, our winner, Miss Pamela Potts."

Cheers mingled with a few boos. Annie was sure the boos were not directed at Pamela but at Harry as the miscreant. Annie nodded toward Henny.

Henny reached out, shook Pamela's hand. "Pamela, the prize is a hundred-dollar gift certificate to Death on Demand. Congratulations!"

Pamela's face flushed a bright pink. "Oh, Annie, I don't know what to say."

"Come on, let's go inside. You can start picking out books." They were stopped a half dozen times as they made their way across the street, and Annie was pushed to defend Harry as the culprit. She was a trifle defensive by the time they reached the coffee bar. "I think Harry was a fair choice."

Pamela's gaze was serious. "Of course it was fair. After all, no one else was wearing a mask."

Annie decided not to analyze Pamela's deductive reasoning. There had been quite a few clues to Harry, including the fact that there were no prints on the floor, and all the others would have left prints. Annie was recounting to herself the trail that would have been left by the others for one reason or another—wet feet, shoe polish, bath powder, mulch, sequins, mud—when she realized Pamela was pointing at the paintings.

"I love all these books—*Death at Wentwater Court* by Carola Dunn, *Masquerade* by Walter Satterthwaite, *Death by Misadventure* by Kerry Greenwood, *The Cincinnati Red Stalkings* by Troy Soos, and *Our Man in Washington* by Roy Hoopes."

"Pamela"—Annie's voice rose in awe—"you are definitely on a roll."

*Can't wait to see what's next for Annie
and Max?*

**Turn the page for a sneak peek at the next
Death on Demand Mystery,**

DEATH OF THE PARTY

**The Darlings are delighted when Max's new
case takes them to Golden Silk, a luxurious
private island and the scene of a high-profile
murder. The island's owner has invited
everyone who'd been present that fateful
weekend back for a return visit, and Annie and
Max join the party to catch the killer.
But fear is the unseen guest as each person
realizes a familiar face may mask a murderer!**

↭ *One* ↭

THE ROOM WASN'T MOVING. Britt Barlow held to that reality, no matter her dizziness. Yet the words in the letter blurred before her eyes.

Britt remembered a long-ago day in a small third floor apartment in Mexico City, the rumble of wrenched walls, the swaying floor, the sweep of gut-sickening terror. She'd survived that earthquake, just as she'd survived divorce and loss and sadness and, once, a fury that had threatened to capsize her world.

Britt waited for that first shock to pass. She would survive. No matter what happened, she had always been a survivor. Earthquake, fire, flood, pestilence . . . Damn the world. She would fight this new threat as she'd always fought, with steely determination, with craft and guile, with a devil-be-damned smile.

The words in the letter came back into focus. ". . . I saw you that morning . . . understand the estate is settled . . . perhaps we could have a little talk about financial matters. . . ."

Britt felt hot and sick. She glanced at the mirror above the fireplace. Other than the bright flush on her narrow cheeks, she looked much as she had when she finished dressing this morning, the vermilion sweater a vivid contrast to cream wool slacks. She stared at her image as if appraising a stranger: glossy black curls, clover green eyes, a restless look of expectancy. With a twisting pang of incipient loss, she remembered Loomis's words to her just before he left the island last week. "I love your face, Britt. You have—" He'd paused, searched for his thought, brought it out with a triumphant grin. "—the face of adventure. That's the kind of woman I've always written about. I made you up long before I met you. I didn't think you existed. Now I know you do. It has to be us, Britt. The two of us together." He'd kissed her, a kiss that held a promise of indescribable joy. "I'll be back. Count on it." Loomis was the late love of a life that had known so much loss. She'd never again expected to thrill when a man walked into her room. She loved the way he looked, the way he walked, the way he talked, his brilliance, his wry humor, his innate kindness.

She crumpled the letter, shoved it into the pocket of her slacks, folded her arms, began to pace. All right. The truth was going to come out. Jeremiah Addison had been murdered. Until now she'd pushed away all memory of that moment when she'd stood at the top of the staircase and looked down at the crumpled body lying at the base of the white marble steps, blood slowly pooling beneath his battered head. The downstairs hallway light had illumined death in a pool of brightness. She'd stared for a long moment, poised to hurry down if there was any sign of life. But death was obvious in the rag doll limpness of his limbs, the awkward crook of his neck. Jeremiah Addison had not survived his plunge down the steep stone steps. It would have been a miracle had he survived that headfirst fall.

He'd always considered himself a miracle man, but his luck had finally run out.

She'd pulled her gaze away, knowing that no one could help Jeremiah now. She'd looked instead at the taut shiny wire stretched ankle high from the wall to a baluster. Why hadn't he glimpsed the wire? The answer was easy and such a commentary on the man. Jeremiah expected the world and everything in it to give way before him. He always strode forward at top speed, his long legs moving fast. He was Jeremiah Addison and the world waited on him. He didn't look down. He always looked ahead, focused on the next encounter, the next objective, the next triumph. He'd plunged fast down the steps and the wire had snagged him, flung him headfirst to his death.

Britt felt the wad of the crumpled letter in her pocket. Jeremiah had been dead for a year and a half. Now she had to remember everything that had happened and accept the fact that she'd been observed that silent summer morning. She continued to pace, though her breath came quickly and her chest ached.

She could have made a different choice when she stood there at the top of the stairs. If she'd screamed, some of the staff downstairs would have come running. The truth would have been there to see, Jeremiah dead and the means of his death apparent.

Murder. The word was harsh but no harsher than the reality. An investigation would have been launched. Everyone on the island, the very private and isolated South Carolina sea island of Golden Silk, would have been caught up in a homicide investigation. Oh, there were plenty of suspects, each with a burning reason to do away with rich, powerful, arrogant Jeremiah Addison.

Including herself, of course. Everyone knew she hated Jeremiah. He'd barely tolerated her presence on the island even though she was a great help with Cissy.

She could have screamed when she found him dead. She had not. Instead, with scarcely a moment's pause, she'd drawn a deep, steadying breath and whirled to run down the hallway to a bathroom. She'd grabbed a washcloth, raced lightly back to the stairway, listening all the while for a door to open, footsteps, a cry of horror, but the hallway remained silent.

Silent as a grave.

She'd worked fast in the early morning stillness, pulling out the nail from the wall, unfastening the thin but formidable strand from the baluster, checking to see if the telltale hole was obvious, grateful when the speck in the wall was easily covered by a fleck of lint from the carpet. She'd mashed the wire into a lump, put the coil and the nail in the pocket of her robe, and fled down the hall to her room. She'd waited there until a maid's shout brought them all tumbling from their rooms.

Everyone said, "What a terrible accident."

She'd been glad to leave it at that. Because she had to take care of Cissy. It wasn't until after Jeremiah's funeral that she'd truly believed the chapter finished. In fact, she'd rarely thought about Jeremiah's death through the next harrowing months as Cissy weakened, the cancer ferocious and unrelenting. Finally, Cissy slipped away, leaving Britt numb and exhausted. Cissy had inherited Golden Silk as part of her portion of Jeremiah's estate. That had been included in the prenuptial agreement when Cissy became his second wife. With Cissy's death, the island belonged to Britt. Golden Silk became Britt's haven and joy.

She'd not spared an instant recalling Jeremiah and how he'd died.

Now she would have to remember every detail about Jeremiah and those who were there that fateful day. Thoughts fluttered through her mind. She walked more slowly, finally came to a stop, leaned her head against the cool white mantel.

Her fingers curled around the paper in her pocket.

Not much time passed, but time enough. Britt lifted her head. Her green eyes glinted. Her features molded into a mask of determination. It was always better to let sleeping dogs lie, but she had no choice. Oh, yes, she could make an arrangement with the letter writer— or to be clear about it, pay blackmail. If she paid off, that would be accepted as an admission of guilt and she would evermore be at the mercy of that silent observer. She had no intention of taking responsibility for Jeremiah's death. Behind her scheming and hoping and figuring, there was Loomis with his thin, kindly face, erudite, surprising, caring. He was worth fighting for. They could build a wonderful life together, but not if she had to look over her shoulder, worry and wonder what might happen.

Abruptly, she laughed. She loved to take chances. She always bet on the red. Maybe her penchant for gambling had prepared her for this moment. Now she would take the biggest gamble of her life. The only way to save herself was to trap a murderer, serve the accused up on a silver platter to the police.

But how?

Dana Addison kept putting off the moment. But finally, the twins were asleep. This was their time, hers and Jay's, the golden moment of peace at the end of the day. They usually relaxed against the softness of the tartan plaid sofa, his arm crooked comfortably around her shoulders, the chatter of the television a familiar accompaniment as they talked.

She stopped in the doorway of the family room. It was a haven of happiness against whatever happened in the world. She wanted to cling to the moment but she had no choice. She had to tell him.

Jay looked up, a smile lighting his sensitive face. She was swept by tenderness. She loved everything about him, his bigness, his gentleness, the way he impatiently brushed back the tangle of brown hair that stubbornly drooped into his face. He was doing so much better. It seemed to her that he was more confident every day, that he stood straighter, looked at the world more directly. He'd been so beaten down by his father. Jeremiah had been cruel and unrelenting in his disdain for his youngest son.

"Dana." Jay pushed up from the sofa, strode toward her, his face concerned. "What's wrong?"

She felt the hot burn of tears. He knew, of course. He always knew when she was upset.

"Teddy? Alice?" His eyes jerked toward the stairs.

"They're fine." She took a deep breath. "They're asleep. Oh, Jay, it's about your mother."

"Mama?" There was an echo of a little boy in his voice.

Dana reached out, gripped his hands. "I heard from Britt Barlow today."

He frowned, puzzled, uncertain. But not worried. Not defensive. Not yet.

Dana talked fast, wanting to get the words out, get past the pain she knew would come. "She's invited us to Heron House." His hands were suddenly rigid in hers. "She was doing some remodeling in the Meadowlark Room. You know she's turned the house into a bed-and-breakfast and named all the rooms. The Meadowlark Room—" She broke off at the terrible stillness of his face.

"Mother's room?" His voice was uneven.

Dana wanted to shout and cry, wrap her arms around him, push away the world and its awful weight. "Britt found some kind of note in that room. It has directions to a hidden spot. She doesn't know whether she should explore. She thinks the writing is your mother's. . . ."

The Honorable Millicent McRae did not have pleasant memories of Heron House, the exquisite South Carolina sea island plantation that had served as a showcase for Jeremiah Addison. Her last visit, hers and Nick's, had been in response to a summons from Jeremiah. There was no reason to sugarcoat the truth. She had received an invitation she could not refuse. Jeremiah had said only a few words in that telephone conversation, but enough for her to realize that she was in his power. So she and Nick had come. Now she had another invitation. But this one . . .

"Dear Representative McRae,

There have been hints in the newspapers in recent weeks that you are considering a run for governor. Since Heron House has often served as a backdrop in state history, I hope you will welcome an opportunity to meet with many who are excited about your future. Financial support can often make the difference between success and failure in politics.

As you may know, Heron House is now a resort

with elegant rooms available in the main house as well as the accommodations in the private cottages. You and your husband, of course, will be honored guests.

This special weekend is planned for the second weekend in January. I will be pleased if you can accept. I've enclosed an envelope for your convenience.

Very truly yours,
Britt Barlow

Heron House
Golden Silk Island, South Carolina

Financial support . . . Millicent relished the delicacy. So there were some people—she wondered who they might be—who saw her as a winner and wanted to establish rapport. Money talked. Of course, it always demanded an answer. That was the reality of politics. Give and take. If the well heeled took the most, who was she to fight the system? Because there was no other way to win. She was determined always to win.

Golden Silk. She'd hated the island. Jeremiah could have ruined her. But he couldn't hurt her now.

Millicent picked up her Mont Blanc pen, scrawled an acceptance, placed the card within the stamped envelope. She felt the same eagerness that suffuses a big-game hunter as the safari begins.